ONE LAST PRAYER

A DCI MICHAEL YORKE THRILLER BY

WES MARKIN

ABOUT THE AUTHOR

Wes Markin is the bestselling author of the DCI Yorke crime novels set in Salisbury. His latest series, The Yorkshire Murders, stars the compassionate and relentless DCI Emma Gardner. He is also the author of the Jake Pettman thrillers set in New England. Wes lives in Harrogate with his wife and two children, close to the crime scenes in The Yorkshire Murders.

You can find out more at:
www.wesmarkinauthor.com
facebook.com/wesmarkinauthor

PRAISE FOR ONE LAST PRAYER

"An explosive and visceral debut with the most terrifying of killers. Wes Markin is a new name to watch out for in crime fiction, and I can't wait to see more of DCI Yorke." – **Stephen Booth, Bestselling Crime Author**

"A pool of blood, an abduction, swirling blizzards, a haunting mystery, yes, Wes Markin's One Last Prayer has all the makings of an absorbing thriller. I recommend that you give it a go." – **Alan Gibbons, Bestselling Author**

BY WES MARKIN

DCI Yorke Thrillers

One Last Prayer

The Repenting Serpent

The Silence of Severance

Rise of the Rays

Dance with the Reaper

Christmas with the Conduit

Better the Devil

A Lesson in Crime

Jake Pettman Thrillers

The Killing Pit

Fire in Bone

Blue Falls

The Rotten Core

Rock and a Hard Place

The Yorkshire Murders

The Viaduct Killings

The Lonely Lake Killings

The Crying Cave Killings

Details of how to claim your **FREE** DCI Michael Yorke quick read, **A lesson in Crime**, can be found at the end of this book.

Text copyright © 2018 Wes Markin

First published 2019

ISBN: 9798412457079

Imprint: Dark Heart Publishing

Edited by Eve Seymour

Cover design by Cherie Foxley

For Jo

PROLOGUE

THOMAS RAY SCRAPED a chunk of sleep from the corner of his eye, uncurled and flattened his back against the arrow-shaped spindles of his rocking chair, yawned, and scooped his sawn-off shotgun from the floor.

Outside, it sounded like the thunder was going to split the sky in two. He smiled. It was time. The bastards were here.

He freed one hand from his shotgun to scratch at his beard. Dead skin rained down on his lap. He tugged at his sweat-stained shirt, ungluing it from his skin. A bath was long overdue.

Lightning licked the sky; his hand darted back to his shotgun.

The rain began; now just a slow tap-dance on his roof, it would quickly worsen. His father always told him nature would retaliate when they came again. He'd also told him what to expect. Horrible twisted faces coming at you like ghouls.

There was the creak of old wood from somewhere deep

inside his house. His eyes darted left. He waited for a repeat of the sound, but it didn't come.

With his finger solid against the trigger, he moved his eyes back to the front door. He smiled again. He'd waited his whole miserable life for this moment.

ALL IN ALL, local district nurse Danielle Butler's journey had been unpleasant. Not only had the dark clouds above her swelled to bursting point, but her old mini had whined since she'd set off from Salisbury.

There was no improvement in the weather when she reached The Downs. Around her, bony fingers of mist clawed at the sprawling fields.

Ignoring her vehicle's complaints over several sharp corners, she took a quick look at her watch. She still had plenty of time until she met her husband Harry for the IVF appointment, but this didn't stop her checking every five minutes. The mere thought of turning up late and losing that appointment after waiting for so long, caused her mouth to go dry.

The distance between each clap of thunder grew shorter, and as she reached Little Horton, the rain came. She cleared her window with her wipers and saw the yellowing sign for Pig Lane. She thought of Harry's words at their front door earlier this morning. 'I don't like it when you have to go there.'

'He's odd, but he's harmless,' she'd said. 'You coppers are always so paranoid.'

The gravelly road crunched under her wheels as she drove up the entry road into the pig farm. The sky continued to squeal like the condemned swine which had once lived here.

———

WHENEVER ANYONE HAD ASKED Thomas Ray about his reclusive life, he'd always told them he wasn't good with people. He'd never told them the truth. Never told them he was preparing for war.

He looked down at his small armoury. A handgun, a set of knives, pepper spray, a taser and a hand grenade from the Battle of the Bulge which his Uncle John had given him on his sixth birthday, four years after the actual battle; there had been a nail in it to stop him pulling the pin, but that was gone now. He smiled. If they got to him, he'd blow all of them, himself included, to kingdom come.

Rain battered his roof and the sky made a grotesque noise. It reminded Thomas of the bucket beside his chair that was a quarter full of his own crap. It must have been three days since he'd last emptied it onto the porch, but it would be dangerous to attempt to do it right now. The stench didn't bother him, he'd been a pig farmer most of his life. Next to the bucket were some bottles of mineral water and several cans of baked beans, most of which were empty. He felt hungry and wondered if he should eat to raise his energy levels. Best not. Again, too risky. They could be here at any moment.

He reached into the top pocket of his shirt and pulled out a dog-eared black and white photograph of his family around the pig-pen outside when he was only two years old. Nineteen forty-four. Hard to believe there had been eight of them back then. His two cousins held his excited younger self in the air by his feet. He ran his fingers over his father's face and remembered his warning. 'Beware the aliens, son. Their fiddly tests have given me cancer. Don't let this happen to you.'

He put the photo of his family back into his pocket.

February, nineteen fifty-two. The vermin had come for his father. Performed their tests.

Near the end, his father, in and out of delirious consciousness, had said, 'It's through this same door in fifty years, they will come back for you, they told me so. And remember, those creatures can come in human or animal form.'

Fifty years later, two weeks into February, Thomas was ready; he'd been waiting for them at his front door for the past two weeks.

Whatever happens, they will never be able to say they caught me by surprise.

WHAT IF THEY SAY NO? What if they tell us that we can never have children?

Concern pounded Danielle as incessantly as the rain thrashed the roof of her Mini. She stopped the car, and wiped some tears away; she checked her eyes in the rear view mirror and saw that they were still puffy from crying the night before.

You need to get control of yourself, Danielle, there will be no problem with having the IVF. And if it doesn't work, well you do what Sandra did, and you try again.

Taking a deep breath, she restarted the car and approached the farmhouse, which she struggled to see past her racing windscreen wipers.

Once she'd parked, she reached for her umbrella, and

stepped outside, surveying the rotten pens, dishevelled sheds and the decimated farmhouse with boarded over windows. After three generations, the legacy of the Ray family was crumbling.

After evading the threatening mud which spilled out from the cracks in the tiles, she walked the pathway to the farmhouse, noticing along the way a peculiar odour. When she reached the steps to the wooden porch, the smell worsened to a rancid stench, and she looked back at her car, wondering if she should turn back. In the rain, her vehicle was a blur. Knowing, deep down, that retreat wasn't an option, that she had a duty of care to Thomas Ray, she stared at the car a moment longer before covering her mouth and turning back to take the two steps up to the porch.

Splattered on Thomas' doorstep was a pile of excrement which seemed to be pulsating. She tightened the grip on her mouth. *I don't get paid enough for this.*

By leaning in, she saw that the pulsations were caused by a thin layer of flies. *Has the waste been left by some kind of animal?*

Doubtful ...

Thomas Ray? On his own doorstep? Or someone else perhaps – one of the many people he'd upset in his time?

She sighed. The last thing she wanted to do was manoeuvre around it to get to the front door, but what choice did she have?

After she drew down the umbrella, she climbed onto the porch. She skirted around most of the excrement, but the side of her right shoe made contact and the flies erupted into the air. Retching, she crossed the final metre to the door.

She knocked with venom. The old wood trembled on its frame.

There was no answer.

She tried again; fighting back the urge to look down at what she was standing in. 'Come on ...'

A third knock. Still nothing. Fighting repulsion, she squatted and the stench intensified. She pushed open a brass letter box and looked inside. It was dark, difficult to see anything, but when she squinted, she was certain that she caught a flicker of movement.

'Mr Ray?'

Silence. 'Mr Ray, it's Danielle Butler, local district nurse.'

She turned her ear to the open letter box, but struggled to hear anything over the rain. Raising her voice this time, she said, 'You haven't phoned in for over two weeks.'

Silly old man - are you alive in there?

'I will have to contact the police, Mr Ray.'

Still no reply. 'Okay, police it—'

Someone just behind the door coughed. She bolted back up and released the letter box with a bang. Her heartbeat quickened.Spinning around, she stared again at her car shimmering through the downpour. Something felt very wrong and the temptation to leave was great. But ethical obligations niggled at her again. *What if he's down on the floor after a fall; or, worse still, a heart attack?*

Her temples throbbed. Feeling as alone as the final pig in line for slaughter, she turned to face the door again. 'Shit.'

She pressed the chrome handle down and pushed. To her surprise it was unlocked and she gulped when it began to glide open.

THERE WAS a loud knock at the door.

Thomas flinched. *Jesus, they're coming in with a sledgehammer!* Sweat ran into his eyes.

Get control of yourself. His finger tightened over the trigger. *They'll die before they reach you.*

He took one hand off the shotgun to press his sleeve against his wet forehead, his eczema stung, but at least it stopped the sweat.

There was another knock, even louder this time.

A knot formed in his stomach. With trembling hands, he raised the shotgun.

Bastards! You think you can make a fool out of me? Like I'm just going to get up and let you in?

Following yet another deafening series of thumps, the letter box opened and Thomas held his breath. *They're looking right in! Can they see me? Surely not, it's too dark.*

With the gun pointed at the thing's eyes, he thought, *how easy it would be ...* Despite having the upper hand, he needed to control his excitement. *Steady your hands, Thomas, not yet. You need a good clean shot. If the door takes most of the buckshot, the thing might carry on living.*

'Mr Ray?'

The voice is female ... familiar.

'Mr Ray. It's Danielle Butler, local district nurse.'

The polite lady from Salisbury?

His father's voice squealed somewhere inside his brain. 'Those creatures can come in human or animal form.'

'You haven't called in for over two weeks.'

But it sounds just like her. Surely they can't mimic someone that precisely?

Lowering the weapon, he saw his father staring at him from his death bed, shaking his head; nerves in Thomas' left eyelid started to twitch.

Don't be weak.

He lifted the shotgun back up again.

'I will have to contact the police, Mr Ray ... okay, police it—'

His chest tightened and he coughed. The letterbox closed with a bang.

Now, they will know I'm here. Come on you bastards.

Nerves in his right eyelid had started to twitch too. Watching the door, he fought back another cough, despite the growing tightness in his chest. The handle went down and he felt his trigger finger go numb. He looked down at it. *Don't fail me now, not after all this time.*

The door opened.

God almighty ... it looks just like her!

Inside, a small part of him screamed out that he should stop, that nothing in existence could possibly mimic another being so perfectly. He almost said hello, almost apologised for his behaviour. Almost.

Somewhere in his memory, he heard his father tutting.

This is for you, father.

His trigger finger didn't fail him.

1

S IMON RUSHTON WIPED the sweat from his brow as he ran. *You idiot,* he thought. His face would now be streaked with blood.

He stopped at the library reception desk. The librarian, Paula Moorhouse, looked up.

'Get the police,' he said. 'Now!'

She started to edge the wheeled chair away from the desk, the colour draining from her face. Several fourteen-year olds stared at him from a table in the library. They disliked him at the best of times. Never usually gave him a second look, but now their stares were unflinching.

'Why?' Paula said, continuing the roll away. After stopping dead by the door of the storage room, her eyes darted left to right.

'In the boys' toilets ... it's disgusting. Phone the police,' he said, turning to continue his sprint back to the classroom, thinking, *Paul might have returned to my room, he could be safe, the blood just some peculiar hoax.*

He flew down the corridor, past framed maths formulae; his fifty-five year old legs had not been pushed this hard since his days as an army officer. He ran through the burn, avoiding the whitewashed concrete walls, not wanting to spread the blood. Students of all ages watched him through the large classroom windows; many of their mouths falling open.

He burst through his classroom door. The heads of thirty eleven-year olds turned simultaneously. There was a collective gasp, while outside the clouds moved and the room suddenly dimmed.

'Has Paul come back?' he said, stepping into the room.

The children rose to their feet, their eyes widening.

His eyes darted from face to face. No sign of Paul.

'Shit.'

He looked down and noticed he had smeared blood onto his shirt.

Raising his eyes, he saw Jessica Hart, his teaching assistant, take a step forward as the children scurried back.

'You've got blood all over you,' she said.

He stared down at his stained palms and clenched them into fists.

'Year Seven, stay where you are,' Jessica said.

But it was too late. The children were moving fast. A table was knocked over, exposing dried chewing gum which resembled grey matter.

'Paul's gone,' Rushton said. 'In the toilets ... there's blood everywhere.'

'What do you mean, everywhere?' Jessica said.

He could see her lips trembling.

'What do you think I mean? It's everywhere ... *fucking* everywhere!'

Most of the students were pinned against the windows shadowed by Salisbury Cathedral; its jagged, black finger stroking the ever-darkening sky. Other children were jammed underneath a range of posters explaining prime numbers, Pi and other mathematical enigmas.

He unclenched his hands; they looked like two poppies blooming. Jessica gasped and his students started to cry.

MICHAEL YORKE STEPPED in from the cold and pounded crusts of snow from each of his brogues. Then, he reached into his pocket for a tissue, spat out his gum and fed it to a large silver bin beside the door.

The missing boy is a Ray, he thought, surveying the Salisbury Cathedral School reception area, *expect the phone calls from Harry to begin at any moment.*

Tiny speakers hummed Christmas carols from the corners of the room. In front of him, a real six foot Christmas tree, ruined with shoddy decorations, shed needles onto a pile of presents. He thought of the mountain of gifts he had to wrap back home. He had a feeling that was about to move even further down his list of priorities.

Paul Ray, he thought, missing the gum already. *Danielle's killer Thomas Ray is a distant relative; is this more than just a coincidence?*

An elderly woman was sitting behind the reception desk. She still hadn't looked up at him.

'DCI Michael Yorke, I'm here to meet with PC Tyler,' he said, strolling forward. The woman lifted her head, revealing a flash of silver hair pinned back with a yellow flower. She nodded, dabbed at her bloodshot eyes with a handkerchief, picked up the phone and mumbled something into it from the side of her mouth.

Less than a minute later, a muscular woman burst through the door to the left of him. Her black suit was tailored. It reminded Yorke of how baggy his own suit was; two sizes too big after the weight had fallen off him during his last bout of marathon training. She thrust out her hand. 'Laura Baines, Head Teacher.'

He shook her hand; her grip was tight. 'DCI Yorke. I'd appreciate it if you can take me directly to my officer at the crime scene Ms Baines. Then, I will need you to take me to the man who found the blood.' He flicked through his notebook. 'Simon Rushton?'

'Yes, he's in his classroom with one of your officers and Jessica Hart, a support teacher.'

'No-one has left?'

'No-one. Teachers are in their rooms with their students. I have not heard of anyone having seen anything yet ...'

'We'll get to that soon; first, let's get to the bathroom and on the way, can you run me through everything?'

Yorke followed Baines out of the festive reception. She walked with a straight back, with her dagger-like nose raised high. Keeping up with her, he felt a painful twinge in his knees; a not-so gentle reminder that he should have replaced his running shoes after the Paris Marathon.

The school was an archaic stone structure, a perfect match for its attached cathedral and huge walled gates; inside, however, it was a complete contrast: white, modern and bursting at the seams with technology.

Baines led him down a long corridor with classrooms spilling off at either side. The rooms were full of children and staff, speaking in hushed voices. To see a school so quiet was eerie. He glanced at his scratched watch. Eleven fifty-five AM.

He had his pad ready to take down notes as they spoke.

'It was period three,' Baines said. 'Simon was teaching a Year Seven Maths class.'

'Year Seven?'

'Eleven and twelve-year-olds.'

Yorke nodded and Baines continued, 'One of the students, Paul Ray, asked to go to the toilet just after break at eleven. Usually, a teacher would refuse such an early request, but Paul said he was sick. He wasn't back after fifteen minutes, so Simon went to the toilet to find him. Inside, he discovered the huge pool of blood on the floor. When he knelt down to look under the cubicle doors for Paul, he slipped and got it all over his hands.'

Slipped in the blood? Yorke thought, making notes. *Really?*

'As you can imagine, when he got back to the classroom he looked a mess—'

'Back to the classroom?' Yorke said, stopping. She halted too.

'Yes. He ran all the way there to see if Paul had gone back by a different route.'

'I see.'

'Gave the students a horrible fright.'

'How would you describe Simon Rushton?'

'He's in a bad way, very shaken up.'

'No, sorry, how would you describe him *generally*?'

'Overly firm sometimes with the children, but he's a good teacher. He's an ex-army officer.'

An army officer, Yorke noted. *Wouldn't that mean a higher tolerance to blood than civilians?*

'How many children are in his class?'

'I would have to check, but we average a class size of twenty-five.'

They continued walking. There were no reminders of

13

his personal school life here. This was a posh private school, not the hospital-styled state one he'd gone to. He grimaced as he recalled the decay of his own school: the decade old posters and the shit work by disinterested children hanging off the walls.

He looked down at his notes. 'Paula Moorhouse phoned the police?'

'Yes. She's our librarian. Simon instructed her to, on the way back to the classroom.'

'Do you think Paul could be truanting?'

'I doubt it. We don't really have any problems with truanting here. Paul Ray is a good student with a comfortable home life.'

Yorke nodded, the cost of coming to this school was high. He doubted parents would suffer truanting, but it was an angle he'd have to consider, especially before this whole situation hit the news.

'Have you contacted the parents?' Yorke said.

'No. I didn't want to start a panic.'

'Sure, but we need to find out if he's gone home.'

They entered a corridor where one side was made completely of glass. Yorke felt like he was in a walk-in aquarium; it was murky outside and the snow resembled swirling plankton.

'Sir,' Jake Pettman said in his usual booming voice, emerging through another set of doors further down the corridor. Yorke approached the six-foot four Detective Sergeant, whose toned muscular frame made him look overweight in his baggy, disposable white suit. He turned to the head teacher. 'Could you give us a moment alone, please?'

She took a step back. Yorke turned to Jake. 'Are you okay?'

Jake had a face that could have been chiselled out of a slab of Stonehenge rock. He raised his eyebrows. 'Yes, still getting over the shock of your phone call. I've been wondering recently if you were still alive.'

Yorke smiled. They were good friends, despite the twelve year age difference. 'I know. Too long and all that. Poor excuse, I admit, but I've been very busy.'

'You're right, poor excuse.'

Out of earshot behind the next set of double doors were two PCs Yorke didn't recognise. Jake must have brought them along with him.

Jake said, 'I was nearer than I thought when you phoned me. Unbelievable, isn't it? A Ray. Not sure how this is going to be received at the station. Some of them still go green at the gills at the sound of the name.'

'Well, they're going to have to get over it, and fast. We're talking about a twelve year old boy here. Has Sean filled you in on what he found in the boys' toilets?'

'He says it's disgusting in there. Pints of blood all over the floor and it smells rank. He didn't tell me much else.'

'From what he told me on the phone that's all he found. I'm going to take a look before I talk to Simon Rushton.'

'Well, I brought you the oversuit; Hanna has it through there.' He gestured towards the officers behind the doors.

'Thanks. Could you get one of your officers to go and see if Paul Ray has returned home and, if not, collect his parents for interview? Also, we need some more officers outside for when word breaks and the other parents start arriving.' He turned back to the head teacher, Baines. 'How many children have you got on roll?'

'Over a thousand.'

He turned back to Jake. 'That's a lot of parents, we don't want them in the school until we've established some facts, processed the crime scene and found out which students have witnessed anything.'

'I'll send Hanna to pick up Paul Ray's parents, and I'll have Neil call more officers to establish a perimeter around the school, so we can keep parents outside and *calm*.'

Yorke looked back at the head teacher again. 'Could you wait here please, Ms Baines? I need you to take me to Mr Rushton shortly.'

'Yes, Detective Chief Inspector.'

Yorke approached the uniformed officers. Hanna's vest was riding too high; from her duty belt hung a baton, handcuffs and CS spray - a lively addition since the days he'd patrolled. Noticing his eyes, she nervously tugged her vest down with one hand, while handing him a sealed bag with the other. Neil, whose voice seemed high-pitched for someone with so much facial hair, said, 'Here you are, sir,' and gave him some bagged up overshoes.

Jake led him down the corridor to the taped line where Sean Tyler, a young and lanky PC, waited. Tyler scribbled Yorke's name into a logbook.

Yorke could see Tyler's uniform underneath his white oversuit.

'Thanks Sean, I'm going to take a quick look and then head over to see Simon Rushton. Anything I particularly need to know about what's in there?'

'I didn't want to disturb the scene too much, so I couldn't look in the cubicles properly, but I knelt down on the floor to check the boy wasn't in them.'

Yorke tore open the sealed bag that the officer had handed him and slipped the oversuit on. After ripping open the second bag, he buried his worn-out brogues into the overshoes.

'Here,' Jake said, lifting the police line, and ushering Yorke under. Tyler took a step back.

Beginning at the toilet door, a trail of gluey red footprints came ten metres or so down the corridor before eventually fading to red smudges. Tyler had allowed a further couple of metres before stringing up his line.

The footprints would have to be matched to Simon Rushton's shoes.

Yorke looked at his watch again. Five minutes past twelve. He slipped on some latex gloves and manoeuvred down the corridor, dodging the bloody footprints, until he was at the door to the boys' toilets.

He checked the oversuit was completely covering his neck. At scenes like this, it always felt cold.

He put his palm on the door. *You're just a child*, he thought, *and had nothing to do with what happened to Harry's wife.*

The door made no sound as it was opened. A movement sensor was triggered and the bathroom light flickered on. As he stepped in, he was assaulted by the smell of metal tinged with citrus – it was almost as bad as the mortuary.

The school toilets were impressive and a far cry from what his had been like. He recalled sinks yellowed by smoke and phlegm, and walls blistered by graffiti and urine.

He glanced down at the pool of blood. Like a sleeping red monster, it stretched its body far underneath the three cubicles alongside the left wall, while resting its long claws beneath most of the opposite sinks and the urinals at the far side.

'Pints of blood,' Tyler had said to Jake. *He'd not been wrong.*

A couple of crimson handprints glowed on the white sinks.

Supposing Rushton is not lying about slipping and accidentally putting his hands in the blood, could it be him that leaned over the sink? Maybe, he threw up, or thought he would do?

Or if Rushton is not our man, could we get lucky? Could the person who set up this whole scene have been stupid enough to have left their gloves at home?

Salisbury Cathedral's spire peered through the tiny window above the urinals.

Too small for someone to get through.

He pondered the three white cubicle doors lining the left side of the boys' toilets. The first door was slightly ajar, while the middle door was shut and the third was wide open. He looked into the mirror at the reflection of the third cubicle interior. Nothing of interest.

Yorke did what Tyler had done, and what Simon Rushton had claimed to have done prior to his accident, he knelt down to look under the cubicles; the blood had curled around the base of the three toilets and, as Tyler had said, there was no sign of the boy.

Yorke's mind wandered back to an old case file he'd read. One in which the victim was chopped up and stuffed down a toilet.

Yorke manoeuvred around the teacher's footprints and positioned himself at the beginning of the line of sinks. He then managed to wiggle himself into a tiny gap between the blood blister and the furthest basin. From there, he was able to stretch onto his toes, and crane his head to look into the cubicle. Despite his thirty-nine years, regular running and stretching kept him more agile than most of the fresh-faced twenty year olds he encountered at the station.

The toilet seat was up. He stretched a little further ...

No body parts. But a message in blood, hand-written in

big, sloping letters on the wall above the toilet.

In the Blood.

Back outside the toilets, Yorke strode back up the corridor, avoiding the footprints, until he reached Jake and Tyler. 'There's a message. Words are written in blood on the wall.'

'Really, sir?' Tyler said.

'The second cubicle, above the toilet. The words are "In the Blood."'

'How did you see into that cubicle without disturbing that mess on the floor?'

'A tiny space next to the sink, and a stretching regime that I won't bore you with.'

'Can't believe I missed it,' Tyler said, looking down at the floor.

'There's something else too,' Yorke said. 'There's mud all over the toilet seat; maybe from the person who stood on it to write the message.'

'We are surrounded by the cathedral grounds, it may just have been carried in from there,' Jake said.

'The ground here is frozen solid,' Yorke said.

Jake nodded. 'I would have known that if I'd taken you up on those running invitations.'

'The toilets here will be cleaned regularly. The mud is important.'

He went to the window, and lifted his phone to his ear to update HQ. Very soon, the empty car park before him would be thriving, and the major incident van would be sitting at its centre like a beating black heart.

He turned back to Tyler. 'Sean can you keep the scene secure, while I go and talk to Simon Rushton? The SOCOs are minutes away.'

'Yes, sir.'

'I can't stop thinking the worst,' Jake said.

'Be positive. He could be alive.'

'There's so much blood in there,' Tyler said.

'You're assuming it's his blood because he's missing. If he'd been killed here, wouldn't someone have noticed the murderer walking off with a dead boy under one arm? And you can forget about that small window above the urinals; there's no way anyone is going through that.'

'Chopped up?' Tyler said.

Yorke frowned. 'Come on Sean, too many late night movies. He was gone fifteen minutes. You'd need a big axe! And do you not think someone would have heard?'

'I've just eaten,' Jake said.

Yorke turned back to survey the footprints. He hoped he was right, but he couldn't help being niggled by doubt ... there'd been an awful lot of blood.

He turned back and said, 'Jake, while the SOCOs are here, could you get the camera footage from the school organised, and get another officer onto the local CCTV. You never know, the boy could have just walked out of here.'

'And we could just be running around after a practical joke?'

'It's happened before.'

'I'll handle the school camera footage after I phone in for some officers for the local CCTV.'

'Thanks, Jake.'

He found the head teacher, Laura Baines, back in the corridor. She was standing with her hands clasped behind her back, looking out over the snow.

'Could you take me to Simon Rushton now, please?' Yorke said as he approached.

'Of course - it's quicker to take the fire exit and go outside.'

Outside, in the bitter cold, he looked up at the iconic cathedral with awe, before surveying its grounds; despite the snow worsening, the place was still drawing visitors.

They entered another building and a burst of excessive central heating brought quick relief from the cold. Baines led him down a corridor lined with framed statistics about education. She then pointed through a window into a classroom at a round oak table, at which a robust-looking middle aged man with cropped hair was sitting wearing a white shirt streaked with blood. Beside him, was a fair, petit woman wearing a floral dress. She looked in her early thirties.

'Is that the support assistant with him?'

'Yes, Jessica Hart.'

DC Collette Willows was stationed at the door. She had recently cut her hair short, and it took Yorke a moment to recognise her.

'Hi, Collette, I like your hair.'

'Thanks, sir,' she said and smiled, exposing a new set of braces on her teeth.

He turned to Baines. 'It would be better if you headed back to reception, it's going to get very busy over the next half hour.' He then turned past Willows into the room. 'Mr Rushton?'

Rushton looked up.

'DCI Michael Yorke, I'm the Senior Investigating Officer in the disappearance of Paul Ray. I've been to the bathroom and I've seen the blood. I need to ask you a few questions.'

He nodded.

'Ms Hart, if you could head back to reception with Ms Baines please.'

Jessica Hart put her hand on Rushton's shoulder. She

21

let it linger there as he looked up at her and smiled; then, she exited the room.

Yorke dragged out a plastic chair and sat down beside Rushton. He noticed the smell of blood coming from his shirt. 'You've had a massive shock, Mr Rushton, but you're the first person who entered our crime scene. That makes you the most important person here right now. Try and understand that as you run me through everything that has happened.'

Rushton ran a hand over his head; it wasn't particularly warm in here but Yorke noticed yellow sweat marks under his arm. 'I'd only just got them all through the door and working on an activity when Paul asked to go to the toilet. I refused immediately. It's school policy that they are not allowed to go for thirty minutes after break. He started to well up, so I asked him what was wrong. He said his stomach was bad and he had diarrhoea. I believed him and I let him go.'

'What time was that?'

'A couple of minutes past eleven.'

Yorke made some notes. Rushton pulled a handkerchief from his pocket and dabbed at his wrinkled forehead.

'I've just walked from the toilets to your classroom, and it took me about half a minute. Would you agree?'

'Hmmm ... Depends on the student, some like to walk slowly, as you can imagine.'

Yorke could imagine; he'd not been the most enthusiastic student himself.

'Do you think Paul Ray is the type of student who would walk slowly?'

'He's a good boy, works hard. He has a tendency to daydream and not always listen, but I doubt he would waste too much time meandering outside the classroom.'

'What time did you leave your room to go and look for him?'

'About quarter past eleven, maybe a bit later.'

Yorke made a note. Everything would have to be checked and verified with witnesses. 'Did you see anyone on the way?'

'Paula Moorhouse, the librarian. We have an open-plan library. She asked where I was going, I told her I was looking for Paul Ray. I saw a few students I teach in the library.'

'I need the names of all the students.' He turned the notebook to Rushton who wrote them down. As he wrote, his forehead started to glisten with sweat.

'Anyone else?'

'Not that I can remember. I went into the bathroom ...' He stopped to dab his forehead. 'I saw some stuff in the army, but I never imagined I would see something like that in a school. There was blood everywhere.' The colour left his face.

'Are you okay?'

'I feel quite sick.'

Yorke reached into his pocket for his chewing gum. 'Will this help?'

'Maybe,' Rushton said, taking one. 'Thanks.'

'Please continue.'

'The smell was disgusting. I didn't want to get too close, so I knelt down to look underneath the cubicle doors. That was when my hand touched the blood and I slipped. I had to use my other hand too, otherwise I would have gone in face first.'

'Did you get cleaned up straight away?'

'No. A short time after. I panicked. I wanted to find Paul. It was all I could think of.'

'There were bloody handprints on one of the sinks, were they yours?'

'I'm not sure ...' he paused to think, chewing as he did so. 'Probably. I steadied myself against it, I felt dizzy for a moment.'

'Did you get it on your shoes too?'

'I must have done because I could feel my feet sticking as I ran.' He lifted his leg and stared at his soles, nodding when he saw the traces of blood.

'What happened next?'

'I sprinted back to the room to see if Paul had taken another route. Although, in retrospect, that clearly wouldn't have happened. The only other direction is quite a distance and he would almost certainly have been picked up by a teacher on patrol.'

'What happened on your journey back?'

'I stopped to tell Paula Moorhouse to phone the police.'

'Anyone else see you?'

'The students in the library again.'

'What time did you get back to your room?'

'I really can't remember. A couple of minutes after I'd left I guess.'

'Well, you said it takes about thirty seconds, and you ran on the way back, so that would put you back somewhere between eighteen and twenty minutes past eleven.'

'That sounds about right, although I didn't check the clock when I came back.'

'Of course, you were distressed. I'm going to need a class list. I'm assuming the other classes saw you as you ran past too?'

'They will have done, yes.'

'Tell me more about your relationship with Paul.'

Chewing, he leaned forward and ran his hand over his

cropped hair again. The smell of blood mingling with sweat intensified. 'I've been teaching him about three months. He's in a top set for English and Maths, and is on the gifted and talented register. He keeps himself to himself but, as I said before, he works hard. Every child has a performance target for the end of the year, and Paul has already surpassed it. Occasionally, I catch him daydreaming and not listening, but there have never been any incidences of poor behaviour. At least in my class. You'll have to speak to other teachers regarding his conduct in other lessons.'

'Apart from behaviour, how would you describe your relationship?'

Rushton creased his brow. 'What do you mean?'

'Well, did you get on? Or argue perhaps?'

'Neither really, I just taught him. I don't remember ever having a personal relationship with him. I've not even met his parents.'

'You said he keeps himself to himself, but surely he has some friends?'

'He sits next to a boy called Nathan White; another nice child. His parents run a successful veterinary surgery in Woodford. Whenever I see him around school, he is with that boy. Off the top of my head, I cannot think of any other child he is friends with. His form tutor, Abbey Lingard, might be able to give you further insight into that.'

Yorke wrote the name down. 'Can you think of anyone he had a problem with?'

Rushton shook his head.

'Could you think of any reason that he may have run away?'

'I really don't know him that well. Maybe, Nathan or Abbey would have a clearer idea. You think he's run away then?'

'I don't know, Mr Rushton, at the moment I just need all the facts.'

'I just assumed, when I saw that blood, that something really bad must have happened ...'

There was commotion from the corridor. Yorke looked at the classroom door; Willows was blocking somebody from entering the room. He jumped to his feet and went to assist her.

Yorke had never met Paul's parents, but he recognised them from the trial. Joe Ray, who was invading Willow's personal space, was a tall, slender man in a pinstripe suit with gelled-back blonde hair and a large black mole under one eye. He looked smarter than his wife Sarah, who stood a metre behind him; she was taller and had broader shoulders. Her shoulder-length jet black hair was badly parted in the middle and needed brushing. Even several metres away, Yorke could tell that her black frock was covered in bits of fluff.

'Where's our son?' Joe said, his eyes were wide and his lips were trembling.

'I'm DCI Michael Yorke, Mr Ray, and I'm here to find that out.'

'*Where's my son?*'

Yorke saw the flecks of spit hit Willows.

'At the moment, we don't know,' Yorke said, speaking as slowly and quietly as possible without being condescending, 'but I can *assure* you, that we will get to the bottom of it.'

Joe pointed a finger over Willow's shoulder at Simon Rushton. 'What have you done with him?'

Yorke noticed Sarah squeezing her hands together at her waist; her white knuckles sparkled like broken glass.

Willows said, 'Last warning, sir, or we will have to restrain you—'

Yorke glanced at Willows and raised his eyebrows. She received the message and bit her lip. The school had failed in its duties to their son; aggression was not the key here.

'I didn't do anything with your son,' Rushton said, standing up. 'I let him go to the toilet, and when he didn't come back, I went, but he wasn't there—'

'Liar,' Sarah said. It came as a hiss and seemed to propel Joe forward. He barged past Willows, and Yorke moved sideways to block him off.

'Mr Ray, we can help you if you stay calm.' Yorke managed the tone of his voice to try and pacify him. 'Talk to us, help us find your son.'

Joe turned his boiling eyes on Yorke. 'Get the fuck out of my way!' Spit bubbled at the corners of his mouth.

He started to advance again, trying to barge Yorke this time.

Shit, Yorke thought, gripping Joe's arm and turning it behind his back as gently as he could. 'I can only ask you so many times, Mr Ray. Listen to me. This isn't what anyone wants, or *needs*.'

Joe squirmed.

'We are slowing the search down. Help us find Paul.'

He saw Willows out the corner of his eye coming to assist him and tried one last time. 'Mr Ray, please.'

Joe took a deep breath. 'Okay.'

'Thank you,' Yorke said, nodding at Willows, who turned her attention to easing Sarah into the corridor.

He released Joe's arm. Joe turned round to face him, gasping for air. His eyes were wide, and a vein was throbbing next to the mole under his eye.

'How did you find out?' Yorke said.

'Jane, Nathan's mother rang us.'

Nathan White, Paul's best friend.

'How did you get through reception? Someone should have stopped you.'

'We came through the fire exit. We knew where his class was. What has *he* done with our son?'

'Mr Ray, I can understand how you feel, but I need you to join your wife and then I need to interview both of you. We have very limited knowledge of what has happened so far—'

'There's blood, apparently. A lot of it. Is our son dead?'

Yorke thought for a moment. 'We're not going to jump to any conclusions. Please, Mr Ray, I need you back out in the corridor with Detective Willows.'

Joe glared at Rushton one last time.

'I'm sorry,' Rushton said, 'I had nothing to do with this.'

Joe turned around and stomped out of the room. Seconds later, a white suited SOCO appeared at the door holding a plastic bag; beside him was Andrew Waites, the Exhibits Officer, also suited up.

'We are here to collect his clothes,' Andrew said, glancing at Rushton before writing onto his clipboard.

'That was quick,' Yorke said, 'I only phoned fifteen minutes ago.'

'We were working a case nearby. This took precedence.' Andrew did not look up from the clipboard.

'Have you got something to change into?' Yorke said, turning to Rushton.

'I have my sports gear, I was going to play squash after school.'

'Either myself, or one of my officers will be back shortly to continue the interview.'

'Okay.'

He said 'thanks' as he passed Andrew; he didn't respond.

Outside the classroom, Willows was talking to Joe and Sarah Ray by a window overlooking the snowy playground. He started to approach them when someone coughed behind him. He turned to see a man with a similar build to DS Jake Pettman leaning over him. Despite being smartly dressed in a designer suit, he was unshaven and he had shaggy shoulder-length black hair, which looked damp.

'Are you the police?' the man said.

'DCI Michael Yorke, and you?'

'Phil Holmes, IT technician here. I was wondering how long we have to wait?'

'At least until someone has spoken to you. Why? Where do you have to go?'

'Hospital appointment.'

Phil struggled with eye-contact. *Hiding something or just socially awkward?* Yorke thought. 'Do you not know what's happened here today?'

'A kid went missing. I was told to wait in my room.'

'Do you know the missing boy, Paul Ray?'

'No. There're a lot of children. I only speak to them when they forget their passwords to the VLE.'

'VLE?'

'Virtual Learning Environment.' Phil's eyes settled on Yorke's, momentarily, but then darted away. 'An online domain, where they can do their homework and chat.'

'Very twenty-first century.'

Phil stripped off a blood red tie and undid his top two buttons, freeing a tangle of chest hair. He looked hot and bothered, and far too concerned with rearranging a hospital visit.

'I'm sorry, you'll have to cancel your appointment. Someone should be along to interview you soon, okay?'

'Fine. As I said, I don't really know anything ... but

whatever you want.'

Yorke turned away, pulled his mobile out and contacted DI Emma Gardner. 'Are you near?'

'Five minutes,' she said. 'Iain and Mark are with me.'

'As soon as you get here, get someone to bring you down to the Maths department; I want you to assist with interviewing the parents. They're very emotional as you can imagine. Also have Iain speak to Nathan White, Paul's best friend and Mark to Abbey Lingard, Paul's form tutor.'

'Okay.'

He then phoned Jake. 'Paul's parents are already here, can you phone Hanna and bring her back to help with other parents as they arrive? What's the news on the school camera footage?'

'Not good. Some of their cameras were working, but not the one covering the exits nearest this toilet. They're getting the available footage together for me, and Neil has already started checking with local businesses around the cathedral for any CCTV.'

'I want you to come down to the Maths department and continue interviewing Rushton while I interview Paul's parents with Emma. I'll brief you before you go in.'

He hung up and went back over to Joe and Sarah. 'I would like to talk to you in one of these classrooms.'

'What about him?' Joe said, pointing at Simon Rushton, who was peeling off his shirt for the SOCOs. Yorke noticed a nicotine patch on his upper left arm.

'Don't worry, he's not going anywhere.'

YORKE WAITED for Gardner at the door to the classroom; he'd not seen her in a while due to her maternity leave. She greeted him with a large smile and Yorke was glad to see the perky DI back.

She threw a tic tac into her mouth.

Yorke grinned. 'Still addicted then?'

She smiled back. 'Always. Want one?'

'Thanks,' he said and then quickly briefed her. 'You ready?'

'Yes.'

They turned into the room. Paul's parents were sitting quite far apart. Joe was leaning forward, looking down, while Sarah was staring at her phone. There was no physical contact between them.

'This is DI Emma Gardner,' Yorke said as they approached.

'I'm so sorry for the shock you've had,' Gardner said. 'Everybody is being very helpful, and we're doing everything we can right now.'

'The blood,' Sarah said, fiddling with her phone. 'Is it his?'

Yorke pulled over a chair for Gardner. 'We don't know.' They both sat down opposite the parents. Sarah didn't look up and continued playing with her phone.

'Does Paul have a mobile?' Gardner said.

'Yes, we've tried it, it's switched off, I've left messages. He's always very good about phoning us. It's unusual.'

'Can we take the number?'

Joe gave him the number and Yorke wrote it down.

'What happened exactly?' Joe said, lifting his eyes from the floor to Yorke. He'd been crying.

'All we know is that Paul complained of feeling sick, asked to go to the toilet and didn't return ...' Yorke paused to consider how best to deliver the next part. 'Simon Rushton went to investigate. He discovered the blood and nothing else—'

'I saw the blood on his shirt,' Joe said, his raw eyes widening again.

'He says he got blood on his hands looking under the cubicle doors, and this was transferred to his shirt when running back to the classroom.'

'And you believe that?'

Yorke paused. 'We are still in the stages of establishing what happened.'

Joe crossed his arms. Sarah reached into her pocket and handed Gardner a passport sized photo; her hand was trembling. 'I had this in my purse.'

Gardner looked at the picture and then passed it to Yorke. A blonde twelve-year old boy with a side-parting, wearing a school blazer, smiled up at him.

'This will help, thank you,' Yorke said. 'I know it's tough, but we'll have to ask you a few questions.'

'That's fine,' Sarah said, slipping the phone into her pocket.

Joe uncrossed his arms.

'Has he been ill, reported feeling sick to either of you over the last few days?'

'No. He was out on his bike yesterday, and he made quick work of his dinner,' Sarah said. 'I asked him to be careful about indigestion, but gone are the days when he does what I ask.'

'Was he upset about anything?' Gardner said.

Sarah and Joe exchanged a glance before she spoke. 'He complained about having a lot of homework to do in the evening, but he always moans about that.'

'Anything else regarding his state of mind this week?' Yorke said.

Again, Joe caught Sarah's eyes. She looked down.

'No,' Joe said. 'He's a happy boy, always has been.'

'If there is anything else at all, no matter how insignificant, or private, it is important you tell us,' Yorke said.

'He was fine,' Joe said.

'Has he ever run away before?'

'My son has *not* run away,' Joe said.

'So, he's *never* run away before?'

'*Never.*'

'Ever threatened to?'

'He's a happy boy, I've told you,' Joe said as a vein next to his mole flickered. 'Nothing like that ever happens in our house. Besides, I'm taking him to Stamford Bridge to see Chelsea this weekend; he wouldn't miss that for the world.'

'So, he likes football?'

'Football and reading sci-fi,' Joe said. 'Can't get him away from either.'

'How does your son get to school?' Gardner said.

'He walks. He sets off at seven thirty when I leave to open the shop. He likes to read in the library until eight forty-five, when his tutor time begins with Ms Lingard.'

Yorke noticed that Joe had taken centre stage. *What was he worried about his wife saying?* 'Did he leave on time today?'

'Yes,' Sarah said, finally re-joining the conversation.

'And how did he seem?'

'Good spirits. As always. He's an early bird,' Sarah said.

'Does he walk alone?' Gardner said.

'Sometimes he meets his best friend Nathan on the way. I'm not sure if he did today.'

Yorke wondered if DS Iain Brookes had discovered anything useful from interviewing Nathan White.

'We are going to request his medical history,' Yorke said. 'Is there anything you can tell us about that in advance?'

'He's had his tonsils out, but other than that, he's had no other problems,' Sarah said.

Joe crossed his arms again. 'And *no* psychological problems.'

'Paul is very strong in that way,' Sarah said. 'And he's a very caring boy.'

'How much do you know about his school life?' Yorke said.

'He enjoys it,' Sarah said. 'He is gifted and talented in Maths and English. His levels are always high.'

'Socially?'

'He usually just spends time with Nathan; sometimes, with another boy called Bryan. He's never mentioned any bullying.'

'Girlfriends?' Gardner said.

'Not that I know of,' Sarah said.

Joe rolled his eyes. 'He's only twelve.'

'Are there any family members he's close to outside of school?' Yorke said.

'Our parents are dead,' Joe said. 'I have a sister, Lacey, but she stays in Southampton most of the time and we have little to do with her.'

Yorke made a note. 'We are going to have to contact her.'

Joe grunted. 'She won't be of any use.'

There was a knock at the classroom door; it was Jake, here to assist him with his next interview with Simon Rushton.

Yorke turned to Gardner. 'Could you continue here please?' He turned back to the parents. 'Please excuse me.'

'Is Paul dead?' Sarah said, leaning forward.

Yorke opened his mouth, but held back on his

immediate response. He was aware of Gardner's awkward shuffles on her chair next to him. 'Without a body, we remain hopeful.'

Sarah reached out and took Yorke's arm. 'I'm begging you, *find him.*'

Yorke looked down at her hand. 'We'll do everything we can.'

'Please, I'll do anything.'

Yorke had seen this many times before in people who suddenly lost someone; it quickly made them flounder, and it quickly made them desperate. As uncomfortable as he felt, Yorke resisted pulling his arm away from her hand.

'You don't have to do anything, Mrs Ray, it's my job. If I can find him, I will.'

A tear ran down her face. 'Promise me.'

'It wouldn't be appropriate to promise,' Yorke said, enveloping her hand with his and gently trying to move it away.

'Please ...'

'Mrs Ray–'

'I need you to, I really do.' The grip on his arm suddenly tightened.

'Okay,' Yorke said.

'Thank you.' She released his arm.

As he walked out of the classroom, Yorke looked out of the windows at the falling snow, and wondered how Harry would feel about him making a promise to the relatives of the bastard who'd murdered his wife.

Yorke said to Jake, 'Change of plan, you interview Rushton alone, I want to get back to the crime scene and check everything is okay.'

'It's best you do, it's swarming with forensics already. I also saw half of Wiltshire's police force in reception; I hope no-one decides to rob a bank in Salisbury today.'

'Get Rushton to run through what happened again, and then start gathering details of his private life, history in the school, relationships with students, staff and ... ' Yorke narrowed his eyes, spun and marched back down the corridor.

'The crime scene is the other way,' Jake said after him.

'Something was bothering me before and it just started bothering me again,' he called back to Jake.

He opened the door, nodded at Willows and approached Rushton who had changed into a pair of shorts and a tattered t-shirt. He took a seat opposite and Jake joined him.

'Feels good to be out of that shirt,' Rushton said.

'Why did you go and look for Paul Ray?' Yorke said. 'Why did you not send the support assistant?'

Rushton sat up. There was a pause. 'I was worried.'

Yorke looked at his notes. 'You said he was gone fifteen minutes. Was that really enough time to start worrying?'

'It was unusual.'

'But still, why suddenly worry? He could have gone to see the nurse. Why did you assume the worst?'

'We don't have real problems with truanting or wandering off from lessons here. Something must have been wrong.'

'How long have you worked here?'

'Over three years.'

'And in that entire time, no student has ever disappeared from your classroom for fifteen minutes?'

'I didn't say that.'

'So, they have?'

'Yes, once or twice.'

'And did you panic then?'

Rushton looked down. 'I can't remember. Look, he's a good student, like I said. He wouldn't just disappear, I think I had a reason to worry.'

'I still don't understand why you wouldn't send the support assistant.'

Rushton raised his eyebrows. 'Because she couldn't go into the boys' toilets.'

Yorke made a few notes. He reflected for a moment on Rushton's explanations, deciding that the best way to verify them was to speak to other witnesses. 'I'm going to leave you in DS Pettman's good hands. Run through everything you've told me and then he'll take some more details off you.'

He leaned over to Jake. 'Keep me updated.'

DESPITE THERE BEING MORE warm bodies, the crime scene felt colder than it had done before. Scientific Support Officer, Lance Reynolds, nicknamed 'the Elf' due to the spritely dance he conducted around crime scenes with his camera, was snapping the bloody footprints on the corridor. He was in charge of a small group of SOCOs who were dusting for prints and scouring the floor for evidence. He noticed Divisional Surgeon, Patricia Wileman, who Yorke had asked for in case a body materialised in the vicinity, talking to a SOCO. Despite her forty years, Patricia did not look a day over thirty. She had a keen sense of style and wore expensive well-cut skirts and blouses. Jake was always trying to get Yorke to ask her out on a date.

Yorke hung back behind the taped line with PC Sean Tyler, who was still managing the logbook.

'We can be sure of one thing,' a familiar voice said from behind. '*If* that is the boy's blood, he's dead.'

Yorke turned around and grinned at DI Mark Topham. 'Always positive, aren't you?'

'I did emphasise the *if*.'

'It's been a few months,' Yorke said, shaking his hand. He noticed Topham was tanned. 'Been on holiday?'

'If Sunseeker's Salon could be considered a holiday.'

'As long as it isn't sprayed on. Have you interviewed Abbey Lingard?'

'I just spoke to her. Nice eyes. I have to be honest, I struggled to stay focused—'

'Come on, Mark, not now; there's chaos all around you.'

For some reason, Mark Topham considered being in the police as glamorous, making his lifestyle rather hedonistic. Several failed marriages behind him and an overwhelming fascination with appearance over substance were testament to that. But he had an uncanny ability to keep witnesses and suspects at ease and, despite being excessively vain, was well-liked by his colleagues.

'You're right,' Topham said, unable to supress a grin. 'Abbey claimed to have had a good relationship with Paul. Said he turned up this morning on time and didn't seem under duress. She also pointed me in the direction of best mate Nathan White, who Iain is with right now. She didn't have much time for Simon Rushton though. Must have mentioned him in a rather negative way three or four times.'

'How so?'

'Said he was too strict with the children and let them have it when he wasn't in a good mood. She claimed his marriage is on the rocks, and he hasn't been in the best of spirits. Knew nothing about his actual relationship with Paul Ray though.'

Topham looked through his notes while playing with a professionally plucked eyebrow. 'Oh, and she didn't buy the fact that he went looking for the boy, rather than his support assistant. She thought that was very odd.'

'I did too.'

'What did you make of him?'

'Too early to tell. Jake is with him now.'

'As soon as this hits the press, you know who'll be calling, don't you?'

'I know. I've also been thinking about the message left on the wall.'

'"In the blood?"'

Yorke said, 'Yes ... do you remember, back when it all happened, I thought about quitting the force?'

'I remember.'

'And do you remember what you told me?'

'I told you quitting was nonsense, because you're a copper, and it's in your blood.'

'So, what's in Paul's blood?'

'Well, he's a Ray by blood, and that's never a good thing, considering their history...' Topham paused and a faraway look entered his eyes.

'Mark?'

'Do you remember how horrible that day was?'

'I remember it taking three of us to get Harry to the ground.'

'Yes, me, you and Emma. Then, I had to pry that camera he snatched off Reynolds from his fingers. That bit sticks with me the most. His grip was like a dead man's.'

'What are you two talking about?' Straight to the point — it had to be DS Iain Brookes.

39

'Look around, take a guess,' Topham said.

Despite his questionable social skills and emotional intelligence, Brookes' talents with computers was unrivalled; he should really have been a DI by now, but he had a poor, often disrespectful attitude toward senior officers.

Yorke said, 'Iain, good to see you.'

Brookes shrugged. 'Thanks.'

'What does the best friend, Nathan White, have to say?'

'Lots of tears and snot, so it was difficult to probe him for too long. He did say he wasn't spending that much time with Paul at the moment. They used to meet up in the mornings to walk in together; recently, Paul started to walk in earlier and *alone*.'

'Did Nathan give a reason?'

'Not really. He said they'd not fallen out or anything; it was just they were spending less time together. Nathan suggested it might be because Paul wanted to spend longer with his head in a book. He did mention that Paul had been upset recently regarding his mother and father not getting along. He'd called his father a bastard on more than one occasion.'

'That's interesting,' Yorke said.

Brookes shrugged again. 'Yes. I didn't think much of it at the time. Probably because my father's a complete bastard too. But I guess it's relevant. What are you thinking so far?'

'Difficult. If Jessica Hart confirms that Rushton was only gone a few minutes and he has done the unthinkable to Paul, then the body would have to be stashed somewhere in the school.'

'And if he is lying and he was gone longer? Could he have managed to get the body out to the grounds around the cathedral?' Brookes said.

'Possible, I suppose. PoLSA are on the way; they'll be tearing up the grounds with Alsatians within the hour. If it's not Rushton, then it's plausible someone else could have snatched him from the toilets or elsewhere in the school.'

'But if the blood is Paul's—'

'I know,' Yorke said. 'But I'm struggling to see it. Could someone really have enough time to kill him, wrap him up, change his own clothes, and carry him out without anybody seeing anything?'

Topham swept his hand through his hair, giving it the messy look he admired in the teenage indie musicians he listened to regularly. 'What do we know about Joe and Sarah Ray? Do they own much? Is it worth kidnapping their son?'

'When was the last time we had a kidnapping?' Brookes said, screwing up his face. 'It's too difficult for them to get away with it. What if the boy is just truanting?'

'Maybe,' Topham said, nodding. 'Could be as a result of the issues that he has with his father at the moment?'

Yorke said, 'Still, it seems rather elaborate for a twelve year old boy. All that blood and the writing.'

Topham continued his nod.

'Well, there are hundreds of people in this school, someone must have seen something,' Brookes said.

Yorke took a deep breath. 'Mark, get officers to circulate the classrooms and brief everyone on the fact that Paul Ray has gone missing from the toilets. Provide them with the time frame, but keep the details of the actual crime scene out of it. Hopefully, a teacher or a student will then come forward to give us more information on what is going on around here.'

Topham nodded.

'And me?' Brookes said.

'I would like you to interview Paula Moorhouse, the librarian who phoned us, and saw Rushton running back and forth from the toilet. I'll interview Jessica Hart. Let's see just how tight Rushton's version of events really is.'

JESSICA HART WAS AN ATTRACTIVE WOMAN, and her blonde, lively hair, coupled with her well-fitted dress, made her glow. Yorke wondered if he would have enjoyed school more if she had been teaching him.

'Can you describe your relationship to Simon Rushton?'

Her eyes widened. Yorke knew that it was a peculiar question to open with. That had been his intention.

'I've been supporting him in that class since September, looking after a boy with Asperger's.'

'So, would you describe your relationship as good?'

'Yes, of course,' Jessica said, fiddling with her engagement ring. 'He's a fantastic teacher, who always tells me what he wants me to do before the lesson begins. Not many teachers go to that much trouble.'

'I've heard reports that he's quite strict.'

'Yes, but that's important,' Jessica said. 'It brings a calmness to his lessons that I see missing in other classrooms. The children are more productive.'

'Even if they don't like him?'

'It's not about liking him.'

'Did Paul Ray like him?'

'I don't know. Their relationship didn't seem any different to Simon's relationships with other students.'

'Do you think Simon Rushton could have anything to do with what happened?'

'Not a chance,' Jessica said and crossed her arms.

Yorke made some notes. 'Can you take me through your version of events this morning?'

She brushed a strand of hair away from her eyes. 'A minute after break, Paul asked to go to the toilet. Of course, Simon said no at first, but then he started to get upset because he had diarrhoea. At quarter past eleven, Simon told me to watch the class while he went to check whether Paul was alright.'

'Sorry to interrupt, Ms Hart, but did you not think that was strange?'

She looked confused. 'Not really—'

'Why didn't he send you?'

'I don't know, I haven't really thought about it. Maybe he was worried about him. He does care, you know, despite what other teachers might say.'

'Still, wouldn't he just assume that he was still in the school toilets, or with the nurse? Surely, it would make sense to send you.'

'I don't know. You'll have to ask him.'

'I have. Continue please.'

'At twenty-five past eleven, Simon appeared back at the door—'

Yorke's heartbeat quickened. '*Sorry*, what time?'

'Twenty-five past eleven.'

'You sound so sure?'

'Yes, I looked at the clock just before he got back because I noticed he'd been gone a really long time.'

'And he definitely left at quarter past eleven?'

'Yes. We'd looked at the clock to see how long Paul had gone—'

Yorke stood up. 'Excuse me, Ms Hart.'

Outside the room, he phoned Brookes. 'Are you with the librarian?'

43

'Yes. I'm just running through her version of events.'

'Does she know the exact times she saw Rushton walking to the toilet and then running back?'

'I'll ask her now, give me a minute.'

Yorke kept his phone in his hand as he commenced the walk back outside to where Jake was interviewing Rushton. He stared at the heart of Salisbury, the cathedral. With no shops or chain stores in sight, it was easy to feel you'd been transported back to medieval times. Even the modernised city around it had attempted to keep outward appearances gracious to culture and history. Victorian villas, Georgian mansions and half-timbered Tudor houses welcomed the visitor to a living museum.

His phone rang. 'Iain?'

'She's not sure on the time when he first came past, but he asked her to call the police at twenty-four minutes past eleven — she remembers looking at the time on the phone display when she contacted them.'

'Thanks Iain, I'll speak to you soon.'

He moved quickly down the corridor, peering in at Gardner still interviewing Joe and Sarah Ray. He reached Willows again, who couldn't resist cracking a smile.

'I know, Collette, I'm in and out like a yo-yo.'

Yorke noticed his heart was still beating fast as he sat down next to Jake, opposite Rushton.

'Mr Rushton, I've already talked to you about how important your version of events is; important to us, and of course, important to yourself. There are discrepancies in what you told me. You told me you left the room at quarter past eleven and estimated that you arrived back at seventeen minutes past.'

'I estimated because I can't be sure of the exact time.'

'Yes, but two witnesses are sure. The librarian said that

you asked her to call the police at twenty-four minutes past, and Jessica Hart said you arrived back at twenty-five minutes past.'

Rushton grew paler. 'So, it was ten minutes?'

'You told me it only takes thirty seconds to walk to the toilet, and you ran back. What happened during those ten minutes Mr Rushton? And you must be completely honest with me now.'

'I called my wife before I went to the toilet. I'm sorry, it slipped my mind with everything that happened—'

'Do you often leave your classroom to phone your wife?'

'No, of course not.'

'So, why today then?'

'She'd phoned three times.' He paused to sigh. 'Something was wrong. I didn't really have a choice.'

'So you used Paul Ray's disappearance as an excuse?'

'Yes, but of course I didn't realise he'd actually disappeared.'

'Can I see your phone log?'

'Yes,' Rushton said, hoisting his phone out. He showed Yorke the three missed calls from his wife between eleven and eleven fourteen; he also showed his return call to her which began at eleven sixteen and finished at eleven twenty-one.

'What was the emergency?'

Rushton looked down at the table. 'It wasn't an emergency, she was angry.'

'Why?'

'It's personal, can I not keep it that way?'

'I'm afraid not.'

He sighed. 'My wife's friend saw me having a drink with Jessica Hart last night at a pub after work.'

'Was the drink innocent?'

'Not really,' Rushton said, and sighed again. 'We kissed.'

'You're having an affair?'

'Not as such, we've only kissed. Too much to drink I think.'

'Jessica's engaged to be married?'

'Yes. That's why she wanted me to keep this information out of the interview. Will her fiancé find out?'

'I don't know, but right now, that is not a concern. Will you come to the station and make a statement?'

'Am I a suspect?'

'As I said, you discovered the crime scene, you are important. I hope you can continue helping us.'

'Of course. I'll go.'

'DC Willows will take you.'

Yorke found a quiet spot to contact HQ and request background information on Simon Rushton and Paul's parents. Rushton was clean, but he suspected this would be the case – to work in this school, he'd have to have had a sparkling Criminal Records Bureau check. He'd had a very eventful career in the army, but was well decorated, and highly regarded.

Joe Ray had never wanted for anything. The pig farm run by his grandparents had made a fortune. He'd invested his inheritance on an expensive little shop in town which sold colonial styled furniture imported from China and lived in a cottage which was worth over half a million.

Yorke joined Gardner back in the room with Paul's parents. Sarah was still tearful; Joe still looked angry.

'I need to know if there's anyone that has a problem with you. Any annoyed customers? Neighbours perhaps?'

'No,' Joe said. 'We've always kept a low profile in that way. We prefer not to be as boisterous as some of my relatives were.'

'Still, it will be worth you compiling a list of recent customers.'

'You think Paul has been kidnapped?' Sarah said. She had an annoying habit of polishing the screen on her phone over and over again with her sleeve.

'It's a possibility. A customer, someone who knows you, may be aware of your wealth.'

Her eyes widened.

'So, the best thing is for you to consider all the people that may be capable of doing this. Mrs Ray can you think of anyone who has acted suspiciously around you lately, or might bear some kind of grudge?'

'She doesn't know anything,' Joe said. Yorke noticed the aggressive tone in his voice.

'Maybe, it's best if you let your wife answer?'

'She's upset, and this is going to make it—'

'Ask my husband about his girlfriends,' Sarah said.

Yorke heard Gardner's chair squeak as she shifted position.

Joe turned to his wife. 'Sarah ...'

'Don't you dare start pleading, you bastard! Our son is missing. Go on, ask him, Detective, ask him about his girlfriends.'

'Mr Ray?'

'Some minor indiscretions—'

'Minor!' Sarah said and then snorted.

'There're a couple of incidences I'm not too proud of—'

'A couple!'

'How many affairs have you had?' Gardner said.

'He won't even remember,' Sarah said, standing up. 'Excuse me for a moment.' She walked out of the room.

Gardner turned to call after her. 'Mrs Ray, it's better—'

Yorke touched Gardner's shoulder. 'Let her go.'

47

Joe said, 'She's exaggerating of course. Recently there have been two. Chloe Cox, a parent of one of Paul's friends, and Amie Yao, my Chinese interpreter at work. But I can tell you now, those women have nothing to do with this.'

'Are they married too?' Yorke said.

'Chloe is.'

Gardner said, 'You said you were keeping a low profile. Does her husband know?'

'No, of course not.'

'Well, we'll have to speak to him,' Yorke said. 'I need a list of all the women you've had relations with.'

They could hear Sarah Ray crying outside.

'She needs your support right now,' Gardner said. 'Not this.'

'You don't understand - she's been ill for such a long time, it's been difficult.'

'What's wrong with her?' Yorke said.

'OCD. She's disgusted by germs and cleans continually. It isn't good for Paul to see, it always upsets him. It upsets me.'

No wonder she has OCD with you having all these affairs, you dick, Yorke thought.

'Does your son know about these women?' Gardner said.

The vein next to Joe's mole began to throb again. He looked up at the ceiling, gritted his teeth for a moment and then looked Yorke straight in the eye. 'He caught me in the office, just last week, with Amie ... kissing.'

'And?'

He chewed his bottom lip for a moment and then said, 'He threatened to run away.'

OUTSIDE, Yorke said to Gardner, 'Rushton, and now Joe Ray! Does no one believe in the sanctity of marriage anymore?'

'I do,' Gardner said, popping another tic tac.

Yorke smiled. 'Good. So, what's your take on all this?'

'Like you, I think it's too elaborate a set-up for a twelve year old. But, we can't rule out the possibility that he's run away, especially after what he saw his father doing.'

'If he is on the Town Path, or sitting by the river, I want to know as soon as possible, before this investigation escalates any further.'

He phoned Jake, who had returned to the reception area to assist the officers with calming parents. He quickly brought him up to speed.

'I want you to escort the parents back to their house. Arrange for an FLO while you are there, but the priority is to look over Paul's room *thoroughly*. If he's run away, Jake, we need to know, *quickly*.'

'Okay, sir.'

His phone beeped. He looked at the message. *Hi DCI Yorke, Martin Price in reception, the press is already gathering like wolves. They know a child is missing. I need to talk to them, and quick.*

Martin Price was the senior Wiltshire County police public relations officer.

'Emma, Martin Price is in reception. I would like you to brief him. Have him tell the press that we suspect truanting and that the boy has run away. No doubt they will have heard about the blood, but tell Price to neither confirm nor deny it. It is likely the press will question the scale of an investigation for a boy who has only just run away, but we'll have to keep them in the dark at the moment regarding all the peculiarities. At least if the story hits the press, the boy will be found sharpish if he's just hiding out.'

'Okay, sir,' Gardner said.

YORKE LOOKED at his watch and saw that it'd gone two. Paul Ray had been missing for almost three hours. He stood by the taped line, waiting for Lance Reynolds, who was managing the SOCOS, to give him an update. Ahead, he saw the Exhibits Officer, Andrew Waites, recording all evidence onto his clip board, narrowing his eyes, occasionally tugging on his wispy white sideburns.

Reynolds came over. 'Okay, we've already matched the bloody footprints leading from the door to Rushton's shoes, but we're still working on the muddy ones on the toilet seat. They're not as clear. We have sampled the mud, but I wouldn't be too hopeful on this.'

'Why not?'

'Because we'd need a sample from the area of origin to work with for comparison. The comparison would be good evidence; it would consider animal waste, pollen and other factors. But the other option isn't great. It would take weeks, possibly months, to work backwards and identify the origin of the sample.'

'Are there fingerprints around the message?' Yorke said.

'There was nothing around the message, but we lifted the fingerprints from the bloody handprints.'

'Rushton claims he steadied himself against the sink, they're probably his.'

'We've also lifted some faecal matter from inside the toilet bowl, which has already been sent back to HQ along with a sample of blood and the mud.'

'Good, anything else?'

'Not yet, but we'll keep at it.'

'Thanks.'

Yorke caught up with Topham outside a classroom. 'Any witnesses yet?'

'Not yet,' Topham said. 'Officers are moving from classroom to classroom. A few students have come forward to say they saw Paul Ray walking quickly past their room toward the school toilets, and that they saw Rushton running back covered in blood, but no-one has given us anything we didn't already know.'

Yorke's phone rang. It was Jake.

'Talk me through the room, Jake,' Yorke said.

'Typical teenager's room. Cans of deodorant, creased magazine posters. He's obsessed with Chelsea football club; his walls are painted dark blue and his duvet is covered with caricatures of the players. There are a few Doctor Who pictures, but the most common posters are of Frank Lampard, Chelsea's midfielder.

'On his bookshelf, he has a lot of sci-fi books; he has all of Asimov's Foundation series – I loved those books myself as a kid. I've looked through his drawers and cupboards, clothes, board games. He has a laptop which is password protected, and his parents are not aware of the password, so I'll bag that up.'

'Anything else.'

'No ... hang on—'

'What?'

'A Chelsea calendar with today's date circled, he's made a note ... Frank Lampard interview, five PM.'

'TV or radio?'

'It doesn't say what show, just the time.'

'Hopefully, that interview will bring him home. Is the

FLO there yet?'

'Bryan Kelly has turned up.'

'Good, he can continue probing the parents. I need you back here to manage your officers searching out CCTV footage. I would also like you to contact the station for me and have Rushton put his statement on record.'

'Okay.'

He turned back to Topham. 'I want to start setting up an incident room and I want you to manage it, okay?'

'Of course, sir.'

'We'll grab Emma from reception, where she's briefing Price, and I'll get Iain to manage the officers moving from room to room hunting witnesses.'

CHALLENGING THE METEOROLOGISTS' predictions, the snow continued its heavy assault on Salisbury. Yorke, Gardner and Topham stayed close with arms folded as they marched through a crowd of parents being held off by ten uniformed officers. The parents paid them little attention, but the three members of the press recognised Yorke, and they started to advance on him.

He managed to get to his beige Volkswagen Beetle before they caught him, but he still swung around and said, 'Martin Price will brief you in a moment. Thank you.'

He climbed into his car, while Gardner and Topham got into the police issue Lexus beside him.

His phone rang, he looked at the screen.

Harry ... that was quick.

He sent him through to voicemail. There was too much going on right now without throwing Harry and emotion into the mix.

2

FORTUNATELY, YORKE'S BROODY Beetle was in one of its better moods today, and maintained its distinctive, contented hum as the air cooled its engine.

Shortly after three, Yorke finished the run up to Devizes. He went and sat in a large incident room and took an update by phone from Jake.

'PolSA still haven't turned up anything in the cathedral or the school, the SOCOs are still working the bathroom hard, my officers are looking over the CCTV footage from the local area, but have nothing yet.'

'Thanks Jake.'

Yorke looked around. The incident room was as white and sterile as a hospital operating theatre. Whiteboards, lining the far wall, had been polished by an overenthusiastic cleaner. Soon, the official name of the incident would be scrawled across the top of it in DI Mark Topham's handwriting, jagged like electricity.

Yorke noticed the table reeked of varnish. He longed for the older, grittier incident rooms with sharp-cornered tables, distributing their huge splinters.

He heard the rattling of a teacup against a saucer behind him and turned to smile at Wendy, a Management Support Assistant.

'Thanks,' he said, taking hold of the saucer.

Topham came into the room. Across the top of the central whiteboard, he scrawled the words, 'Operation Haystack,' a random incident name which the computer had churned out.

'Well, that doesn't inspire optimism,' Yorke said.

It took Topham a moment to get the joke. 'Well, we've found tough needles before.'

Yorke smiled. 'True.'

DI Emma Gardner came into the room next, followed by Jeremy Dawson from HOLMES, looking young enough to be on work experience from a local secondary school. He greeted everyone and then started setting up his laptop.

Yorke looked down at his notes and said, 'Everybody in the school will be given an opportunity to come forward with anything they've witnessed. I have Simon Rushton at Salisbury Station preparing a statement. Following the disappointment over the school's lack of camera footage, CCTV from the surrounding area currently remains our best shot at finding out where Paul went. DS Jake Pettman has DCs interviewing the two women Rushton claims to be having an affair with to see if this event can be connected to their husbands in any way. FLO Bryan Kelly is with the boy's parents and will be gathering a list of all the women Joe Ray has had an affair with. PolSA and the SOCOs are still working the area. We've thrown a lot at this, and if the boy does turn up at five PM to watch his favourite footballer on the TV, we are going to look very stupid.'

'But in this instance, looking stupid would be a good thing,' Gardner said.

Yorke nodded while waiting for Dawson to finish furiously tapping on the keyboard. 'Anything to add?'

Gardner shook her head.

Topham said, 'Do the Rays have a lot of money?'

'I'm not sure about disposable income, but they have a healthy business and a good property.'

'If the boy has been kidnapped though, couldn't the kidnapper have chosen a more lucrative target?' Topham said.

'I hear what you're saying, Mark, that's why I'm leaning towards the idea that someone is just pissed off at him.'

'The bloody message they left would then make some sense,' Gardner said.

Yorke and Topham nodded.

There was a knock at the door.

'Come in,' Topham said.

Divisional Surgeon Dr Patricia Wileman walked in, her eyes were wide. 'We've tested the blood, it's not human.'

Yorke leaned forward while Patricia screwed her face up in disgust. 'It's pig's blood.'

Jeremy Dawson stopped typing and the room went silent.

It took Yorke a few minutes to collect his thoughts. 'Having pig's blood all over the bathroom floor is more than a coincidence. Since the beginning of the twentieth century, the name Ray has been linked with pig farming. Whoever took Paul, if he has been taken, is leaving these messages on purpose,' he paused to let everyone draw the obvious conclusion, 'every person who has ever had a problem with the Rays needs to be identified ASAP.'

'That will be a long list,' Gardner said.

'And one that would include Harry,' Topham said.

The room went quiet again.

'You know Harry as well as I do,' Gardner said to Topham, narrowing her eyes. 'And you know he hasn't got a malicious bone in his body.'

'True,' Topham said. 'But we have to consider it.'

Yorke gritted his teeth as he thought of the phone call from Harry he had ignored earlier. This had the potential to get very messy. 'Mark's right, Emma. You know as well as I do, grief does horrible things to people, especially when it involves violent death.'

Yorke's phone rang, the number was unknown. He answered it.

'Sir, it's Lance Reynolds, we have another interesting result.'

'Go on.'

'The tests on the faecal matter splattered in the toilet bowl has revealed a very high dose of saline laxatives. At a normal dose, saline laxatives can take half an hour to three hours to work, but this kind of dose can go to work a lot quicker.'

'Is it possible that Paul could have taken this laxative during his break, between ten forty and eleven, causing the onset of diarrhoea at two minutes past eleven?'

'Possible – seems fast though. It's more likely that he had a very bad reaction.'

'Thanks. Anything else?'

'Yes. We've examined the footprint on the toilet seat. CATs - men's Silverton steel toe boots, size eleven.'

Yorke felt adrenaline whip through his body. He hung up and told Gardner and Topham about the boots.

'Size eleven?' Gardner said, looking down at the table. Yorke could sense the hope draining from her as quickly as sand through an egg-timer.

'Paul could have had abnormally big feet?' Topham said, trying to make light of the situation.

Yorke then told them about the laxative.

Gardner said, 'If it wasn't for the boots, I would still hope for the possibility that Paul administered the laxative himself.'

'Still, we should keep this option open,' Topham said.

Gardner nodded. 'But where is Paul going to get a saline laxative?'

'We will still check with his parents, and his medical records,' Yorke said. 'But, let's say he was spiked at break. The abductor would have expected him to go to the toilet either during his eleven to twelve lesson or his twelve to one lesson. They would not have expected it to happen so quickly. Reynolds suggested Paul might have had a bad reaction to the laxative which reduced the onset time.'

'Regardless of timing, the abductor managed to pull it off,' Gardner said.

'Well, whoever spiked him would have to be waiting somewhere near the toilets so they could follow him in. But his unexpected early arrival might have meant the abduction was not carried out as flawlessly as they would have liked. Maybe, they had to rush; maybe, they panicked and maybe that's why the abductor overlooked the muddy footprints left on the toilet seat.'

'Any ideas on how Paul could have been spiked?' Gardner said.

'We have to consider the possibility that it was someone in the school who Paul trusted,' Yorke said, looking down at the table. 'There has been a register taken of every person in the school. We need to examine which adults were absent today; preferably, someone who was present before the possible abduction, and then disappeared straight afterwards.'

He paused and glanced at Jeremy Dawson, ensuring everything was being recorded. The droplets of sweat on his forehead offered some evidence that it was.

Topham said, 'If the abductor was someone Paul trusted that could explain how they got him out with little fuss. The boy might have just complied and exited of his own volition.'

They all nodded.

'What about the mud from the footprint?' Gardner said. 'Can we trace it?'

Yorke said, 'I've been through this with Reynolds already. They'd need a sample from the area of origin to work with for comparison; it would take far too long to work the other way round. It's currently being checked to see whether or not it's from the immediate area surrounding the school and the cathedral, which will help us decide on the mud's importance. However, I don't think it will be. The ground is frozen solid.'

'If it's from a farm,' Gardner said, 'it could link to the blood and the Ray family's history.'

Yorke nodded. 'Then we need to start sending officers out to farms in the area to collect samples.'

'We're in Wiltshire,' Topham said, flashing laser-whitened teeth. 'It would take days, weeks even.'

'Hopefully, once the mud has been examined, we can narrow it down a bit. We may, for example, find out what animals are kept on this particular farm.'

The phone rang again; it was Jake, sounding breathless. 'We've got CCTV footage. Both Paul and the person who drove him away are on it. It's on VHS, so you might want to get straight down to Salisbury nick to watch it, rather than wait for us to make a digital copy and email it to you.'

Splodges of seaweed-coloured mould felt its way around the corners of the room. Cracks in the walls resembled the eager, raised tentacles of an octopus. This was a far cry from the incident room Yorke was sitting in less than an hour ago. He preferred it.

The CCTV camera used by Sapphire Restaurant was poor; the TV screen flickered and the sound crackled. *Bit cheap of them really,* thought Yorke, *considering the money that place makes - it's impossible to get a table in there most nights.*

A white transit van was sitting by the curb on Exeter Street outside the restaurant. Over the road, a group of pram-pushing young mothers strolled past. Next came a man in a tracksuit, who spat on the floor, and then stopped to look down on what he'd produced.

A young boy, wearing the school's uniform, emerged from the tall medieval gate which led to the cathedral and crossed the road.

'Paul Ray,' Yorke said, recognising him from the picture Sarah had given them.

He came alongside the transit van. The camera was facing the passenger side. A tangled mess of blonde hair was in focus. He unlocked the passenger door, climbed in and closed the door. The time on the display was eleven minutes past eleven.

'He had a set of keys,' Yorke said to Jake, who was sitting beside him. 'Roll it forward until we see the driver of the van.'

DC Collette Willows blocked most of the TV as she leaned over to operate the VHS player, but Yorke could still see some pedestrians shoot across the screen like bullets; he could also see the time in the top right corner racing forward.

As the time passed twelve, Yorke said, 'Whoever did this was still in the school when we were there.'

Willows played it from twenty-one minutes past twelve and then moved back out of the way.

'Paul's been in the van for an hour and ten minutes. No exhaust fumes either, so the engine's not on. How could he just sit there waiting? Wouldn't he be cold?' Jake said.

'Drugged again maybe?' Yorke said.

The windows were tinted, and the quality remained bad, so it was impossible to tell if Paul was asleep.

A large man crossed the road and came into focus.

Yorke's vision blurred. He suddenly felt like he was turning over and over in the sea, being squeezed by the waves. Clutching his mouth, he looked at Jake, who had clearly not recognised the man.

'Have you found out who owns this van?' Yorke said.

'It's a hire vehicle, we have someone contacting the company,' Willows said.

'I need some air,' Yorke said as he marched from the room, concerned that he might throw up.

YORKE STOOD OUTSIDE THE STATION, jacketless, the snow soaking through his clothes. He looked up at the snowflakes, sparkling like buckshot in the streetlamps, and closed his eyes; the past came back to him out of the darkness ...

He held Harry tight in his arms and his shoulder went damp from the tears.

'I told her not to go, we had an appointment with the hospital about IVF,' Harry said, stepping back, swiping tears away. 'I hated her going to the mad bastard's farm, she knew that.'

Yorke could smell perfume. Was it Danielle's? Had Harry been spraying it on himself? Was he worried about forgetting her, or did he do it just to feel close to her?

'She really wanted a family. I couldn't give her that,' Harry said.

The words were cold and flat; the blame game had begun—

A car backfired and Yorke's eyes burst open. A snow flake caught him in the eye. He rubbed at it.

A couple of teenagers, confident enough in these brash times to smoke marijuana outside a cop shop, were laughing over the road. He had better things to do than bust them; he had to wait for confirmation of what he already knew. He looked back at the door to the station, still no sign of Jake. Still no sign of the bad news that was surely coming.

On the wall, beside the boisterous teenagers, red graffiti read "welcome to the jungle." Salisbury was anything but a jungle. The graffiti dripped down the wall like pig's blood. He closed his eyes and journeyed into the past again ...

Yorke saw her. Lit up by blazing blue lights. On her side. Her head tilted back so she was staring right at him. Her arm fully extended and her hand open to him.

Was she asking for help?

No, of course not. The natural order of her body had been changed. Parts that should have been inside her body were outside of it. Like road kill.

From nowhere, Harry arrived, charged and grabbed the

camera from Reynolds. Yorke grabbed him from behind, but his good friend fought hard. Topham and Gardner helped, and together they took him to the ground. They all slipped about on the mud. Harry writhed and Yorke felt like he was betraying him.

Thomas Ray was led out of his farm house. They all looked up from the mud and stared. His shaggy hair and beard were as white as wilting lilies in an ossuary, he wore moth grey overalls and his eyes were hollow. He said, 'I have saved myself and I have saved you—'

'Sir!'

Yorke opened his eyes and saw Jake standing at the door to the station. His phone started ringing. He looked at the screen. *Harry*.

He looked up to see Jake approaching him. His friend didn't say anything; he didn't have to, his eyes did the talking.

Yorke leaned against the side of a parked police car and sent Harry to voicemail again.

The man on the CCTV footage had been Thomas Ray.

3

ALL THOSE WOMEN, *all those betrayals, it's my fault.*

Trembling in the rocking chair built by his great-grandfather, Joe Ray reached to the floor for his glass of bourbon. Two gulps did little to shift the shakes. He needed to tell FLO Bryan Kelly what he'd just seen on his computer screen upstairs moments ago, but he'd gone out to get them something to eat.

Besides, I've not even told my wife yet and she should take priority.

He lowered his head, closed his eyes and prayed that when he opened them, the horror of what he'd seen would fade like an old dream. But when he did eventually open them, he was startled by Sarah standing over him. He leaned forward and rubbed his head against her thigh like a neglected dog. Despite everything, she ran her hand through his hair.

'I was wrong,' he said.

'About what?'

'He's not run away.'

'You don't know that. The snow isn't too bad yet; he could still be hiding out there.'

'No. I've seen where he is.' Tears sprang from the corners of his eyes.

'What have you seen?'

It was horrible. Truly horrible.

'I have to take you upstairs.'

She had to see. It was her right as his mother.

As they went up the stairs, he reached out to her. He wanted her to close her hand around his with the same affection with which she'd just stroked his hair. But she didn't. Instead, he had to take hold of her hand. It felt cold, almost dead.

Now more than ever he needed her, and in a few moments, when she'd seen the e-mailed video, she would need him too.

At least he hoped she would.

'You've made a shambles of our marriage,' Sarah said.

'I know,' he said, glancing out of the little window at the top of the stairs. There were swirls of snow around the streetlights. Really heavy snow was due overnight. He couldn't imagine being snowed in, *trapped here*, knowing something dreadful was happening to his son.

'Nothing you can show me could be worse than what you've already done to our family.'

I wish that was true, Joe thought, *I really do.*

He led her into his office which still smelled of Fisherman's Friends and bourbon, his chosen cocktail.

Fortunately, she'd had her own cocktail already – forty mg of Valium and a large amount of sherry. Hopefully, it would help. *If anything really could.*

He sat her in his office chair. After kneeling before her,

he reached up to stroke her face. At first, she welcomed it, but then she flinched and pushed his hand away.

He gestured at the computer monitor. 'I want you to know that before you watch this, I'm sorry.'

'You should be ashamed.' There were tears in her eyes too now.

'I am.' He used the mouse to press play on the digital video.

He reached into the pocket of his trousers and checked the bottle of Valium was still there. Just in case.

He put his hand on her thigh.

She brushed it away. 'Not now.'

He turned away and sat on the floor. He didn't want to see. *Not again.* He covered his ears with the palms of his hands and cried as quietly as he could.

———

At first, nothing happened, and Sarah let her eyes close. The Valium and the sherry were cooling her tortured mind. She was desperate for peace. For emptiness. Her head fell forwards ...

There was a sudden tortured wail. She snapped her head back, opened her eyes and gulped back a huge mouthful of air. Then, she snatched the mouse and shifted the volume slider down.

She saw a whiteboard; on which the words "Pig Productions" were written in blood. The board trembled and the blood streaked until the words were no longer legible. She put her hand to her mouth. Then, there was a loud thrashing sound which caused the small speakers on the table to hiss.

The board dropped away and Sarah stared into darkness. 'I can't see any—'

Light exploded from a bulb hanging from the ceiling, revealing the inside of a dilapidated barn. In the distance, something was twisting in the air. The camera started to zoom in, losing focus slightly, giving the writhing things the appearance of two pink, pulsating organs.

'Oh God,' Sarah said. 'What's happening?'

The camera completed its zoom and she held her breath as it auto-focused.

Three pigs hung upside down with meat hooks skewering their trotters. Two of them screeched and thrashed while the third quivered as it bled out through its neck.

The sherry in her stomach rose up and burned the back of her throat. She turned to her side and retched. Joe stopped the video.

It took her over a minute to regain control. She could taste the sherry in her mouth, but had managed to stop herself throwing up. 'Is our son ... okay?'

'He's okay,' Joe said, rubbing her back.

You're lying, Sarah thought, *but that's fine. Right now, that's fine.*

'I think we should stop it, now,' Joe said. 'There isn't much left anyway—'

'No. This is my son. Whoever sent this has him. I want to see it.'

'It gets worse,' Joe said, taking hold of her thigh. She didn't brush him away this time; she was too busy rubbing her throbbing temples.

She took a deep breath, reached over and restarted the video.

A large man, with his back to the camera, strode out. He

wore bulky grey overalls and long hair crawled down his back. A jagged strap was wound around his head clamping something to his face. A mask perhaps.

'God,' she said, tears blurring her vision. 'What's he wearing?'

With his left hand, the slaughterer shone a torch into the eyes of one of the pigs. Wide-eyed, the creature thrashed even harder, flogging itself against the wall.

The man took two long, slow steps toward the animal. The pig's scream cut into Sarah's skull. With her shaking hand, she halved the volume.

The bastard's right hand fell to his side, revealing a gutting knife. The blade flashed across the pig's neck and blood jetted across the barn, speckling the camera lens like dead flies on a car windscreen. She resisted the impulse to stop the video. Her eyes darted to the information bar. One minute remained.

Hold on ... otherwise, you'll have to come back and switch it on again ...

The large man watched the squirming pig until it steadied to a quiver; beside it, the first pig, wounded prior to filming, had gone completely still.

Then, in a final bid for freedom, the third pig almost tore its trotters to pieces.

Forty-five seconds remained.

The slaughterer, who lumbered like he was either intoxicated or half-asleep, placed the tip of the knife against the poor animal's flesh and then eased the five or so inches of steel into its gut. There, the killer kept the blade rooted as the pig jolted and mangled its insides; then, he jerked it out.

He stood there for a moment, watching his victim, seemingly enjoying its suffering. Then, as if someone had just speeded up the footage, the man burst into life, thrusting the knife into it over and over again until it was dead.

He stood back to watch the blood gout from the pig's chest and stomach.

Twenty-one seconds left. Please let this end.

The slaughterer flicked his wrist and the poor animal's guts hit the barn floor with a splash. Turning around to face the camera, he pointed the torch up at his face like children so often do in the dark to scare one another.

At first, she thought the slaughterer was in fact a monster, but then she recognised the large flapping ears and protruding snout of a pig. Tiny pupils stared out through the holes where the beast's eyes used to be. She put her hand on top of Joe's hand and clutched hard.

If it wasn't for the jagged, bloody sides where the animal's face had been sawn from its skull, she may have been fooled into thinking she was looking at some kind of genetic cross between human and pig.

The slaughterer switched the torch off. She winced at the sight of the bastard's blood smattered apron and then the light bulb went off too. It was pitch black again.

Nine seconds left.

'That can't be it, where's Paul? *Where's our son?'*

'I'm sorry,' Joe said.

Light exploded from the bulb again. The pig-faced slaughterer stared at Sarah, cradling her only son in his bloody arms. The screen went black.

Realising it was too late to run for the toilet, she instead slipped, almost lifelessly, from the chair into her cheating husband's arms and vomited down his front.

4

YORKE TORE ALONG Salisbury Road in a police issue Lexus GS. Fog lights sliced darkness into chunks of snow white emptiness. Frozen bushes and branches chewed into the side of the car. The speedometer flipped past one hundred.

Yorke had a bad case of déjà vu. Eight years ago, he'd journeyed to the same disused pig farm with the same break-neck intensity. And what he'd found there would haunt him until his final day.

Following a fatal high-speed pursuit last year, these sporty sedans had been fitted with specialised winter tyres. It showed. Over the steep frozen hills, the car rose and sank with no fuss; around sharp corners, the wheels squealed, but never slipped. But, with so much of his conscious thought dedicated to Harry's wife's murderer, the car's handling alone was not enough to keep him alive. He also needed the wailing siren.

He looked into his rear-view mirror, but the road was empty; Jake, who had followed in his car with Willows, must have fallen behind.

Blazing through Tilshead – virtually the geographical centre of Salisbury plain – he ignored the slowdown signs and caught sight of the Rose and Crown public house where he'd once been for Sunday lunch with Harry and Danielle almost ten years ago. Into his mind crept the final day of Thomas Ray's trial ...

Yorke held Harry's shoulder gently outside the court, making it seem like a gesture of support, rather than what it really was. Concern that Harry might just go for his wife's killer.

Sucking hard on the cigarette in his hand, Yorke watched Thomas Ray, hiding behind that wild mane of white shaggy hair, being led away. Diminished responsibility. Murder to manslaughter in two simple words. As if blowing someone to pieces couldn't really be your fault.

The press rounded in on the killer.

'I have saved myself and I have saved you,' Thomas said, and not for the first time.

'What have you saved us from, Mr Ray?' A young journalist from a local newspaper said.

With a huge paw he split his mane and revealed his eyes. *'Them.'*

Harry threw his burning cigarette in Ray's direction and then turned his back—

A shrieking horn drew Yorke from his trance. He had started to stray into the wrong lane and two oncoming headlights swelled at an alarming speed. Swerving, he felt his chest freeze.

After managing to steady the car, he looked at his eyes in the rear-view mirror. 'Pull yourself together!'

His phone rang. Seeing it was Gardner, he answered with the handsfree. 'Yes Emma?'

'Thomas Ray was released from the secure hospital in Bristol three months ago—'

'You're joking? *After eight years?*'

'If you remember, he was detained at Her Majesty's pleasure due to a successful insanity defence, the trial judge set a minimum of eight years, and when he was reviewed, three months ago, they deemed him sane.'

'But still, eight years, for what he did. It's bollocks.'

'I agree. But I think they made their decision based on the fact that he had terminal cancer, less than four months to live, they sent him home to die.'

He thought about the Sapphire CCTV footage. Crap VHS, but that slight hunch in Ray's back had been a giveaway, as had the eyes. Eyes as hollow as the Grim Reaper's.

'If that's him on the footage, then they made a bad decision. Have you checked into his current state of health?'

'I contacted the hospital and they confirmed they have been making visits to the farmhouse to treat him for the pain—'

'Have they told the nurses *what* happened there? I bloody well hope so.'

'I don't know, sir, but I've spoken to a doctor, who claims he's near the end and is in no fit state to drive, never mind conduct that abduction. You're not going there alone are you?'

'Of course not, I have Jake and Collette in the car behind.'

'You might be best waiting for more back-up.'

'You just said he was incapable of doing anything. Besides, I don't want to go in all guns blazing, in case he does have the boy, and he *is* capable of doing harm. I'll be in touch shortly.'

West Lavington, a small village and civil parish, suddenly hovered into view like a curious but careless moth investigating a lit candle. The village disappeared as quickly as the immolated insect.

Something moved in the road ahead of him. It was too late to stop, so Yorke braced. There was a thump and the car hopped. He glanced in his rear-view mirror, but it was too dark to see what he'd left for the early morning drivers.

The phone went again.

Yorke answered on hands free. 'Jake, you've fallen behind.'

'I just heard from the station. Sean has contacted the hire company. Thomas Ray received the van yesterday.'

'Funny that, because I just heard he was at death's door.'

'What?'

'I'll explain when you get here. Hurry up.'

He slowed down slightly as he passed through Potterne, one of the most swollen villages in Wiltshire. There was traffic coming the other way, so he turned off his full beam.

'I can't drive as fast as you. Not only do I value my life, but I've not been lucky enough to get on that high speed pursuit course you did.'

'I've seen you drive, you don't need a course; speed up, and I'll buy you a pint of *Summer Lightning* later.'

'Okay, and that's because it's rare that you offer to buy.'

He hung up and tore over a roundabout, his tyres screeching; he came off at the second exit, which bore right to Little Horton, his destination.

If it was Ray, why would he give his name when hiring the van? Did he want to get caught? Maybe, he doesn't care if he's dying anyway?

But it doesn't add up. Where would this dying man have

been hiding while we were in the school? There are plenty of coppers there who would recognise him through any disguise after what he did to Harry ...

He shut off his siren before entering a quiet, dark farming community. He drove down Pig Lane, heading south into Little Horton and cruised along several winding roads until he arrived at the Ray's eighty-eight acre farm yard.

Long grass poked out of the snow like nerve endings. Broken fences lay scattered as if there'd been an animal stampede.

There was no moon, and no streetlights, so he relied on his full beam, and second gear to negotiate the Ray farm entry road. Along the way, he noticed a decrepit barn on his right.

He reached the end of the road. The lights were on in the farmhouse, so he switched off his full beam. Reaching for the door handle, he stared at the house in the middle of the field.

It glowed like a burning corner of hell.

THE GROWL of a car engine shook Paul Ray from his sleep.

Is it too late to run to the window and wave Dad off on his way to work?

He rolled onto his back and the memory of what he'd seen his dad doing the other day oozed into his thoughts like an infected cut. *I'm never going to wave him off again, not in a million years—*

The wind squealed, the cold raced over him and he stared deep into two pebble-sized black eyes. He felt a scream rushing up his throat.

The eyes neared. His heart pounded the inside of his chest. The beast stroked his cheek with its twitching snout.

Where am I? Lewis, where are you? Help me ...

The scream burst free, partly made up of Lewis' name, partly made up of a sound he'd never heard himself produce before. The animal reeled in the air and backed away.

Despite feeling as if his blood had frozen solid in his veins, Paul scurried backward, moving like a crab until he banged his head on the wall. Using his sleeve, he rubbed at the warm, gluey residue on his cheek; his eyes darted from side to side, unable to settle.

Am I in the barn on Nathan's parent's farm? No, it's bigger, dirtier, emptier ...

Paul shook, tears began to build. 'Lewis, where are you?'

In a small pool of light given off by a tiny lamp, the pig that had licked him grunted and shook its large head side to side, flapping sail-like ears, baring black and white teeth, beating its trotters on the floor and raising small clouds of dust and hay.

'Lewis, help me!'

Paul rose, sliding his back against the wooden slats behind him, staring at the beast. 'Don't come near me ... please.'

This is horrible, how did I get here? He eased himself along the slats, determined to carry on going until he found a door.

Lewis said he was going to take me to the doctors and that'd he'd just let my school and parents know. Then, I got into his van.

Why can't I remember anything else?

Around him the slats clattered as the screeching wind attacked them. He tasted sick in his mouth, but carried on pushing himself further along. He could feel splinters of wood poking and scraping his shirt, but they weren't getting through, weren't cutting him. *Yet.*

The beast stopped pounding and moved back into the darkness.

I hope it's scared of me.

'I don't understand any of this.' He wiped at his tear filled eyes and then the corners of his mouth where the sick oozed.

Lewis gave me something for the runs. Was it that tablet which made me sleep? Did Lewis bring me here? Why? Why would he do that?

When he reached the barn door, he shook it with trembling hands, noticing his palms were sweating despite the ice cold wind.

But the door was locked. He shook it for a long time and his arms started to burn; eventually he let them fall to his side, and turned back to look into the dark barn.

The wind relaxed and Paul could hear more pounding coming from the darkness.

More of them ...

Crying even harder, he turned back and continued to shake the barn door.

WITH THE SHRIEKING wind at his back, Yorke and Jake hurried through the pelting snow to the farm house. Willows stayed back to observe the area in case the dying man tried to make a run for it.

Yorke's bad case of déjà vu continued. He looked down at the floor at the exact spot on the path where Danielle's body had been thrown by the shotgun blast. A layer of snow covered the area, but Yorke could feel the broken concrete and frozen weeds under foot, a result of eight years of neglect.

The curtains in the front room were drawn, but the lights were bright enough that Yorke and Jake could find their way to the door without a torch.

His phone buzzed. The message told him he had three voicemail messages. He sighed. *Harry, for sure.*

He slipped the phone back in his pocket and knocked on the door; they both took a step back.

No answer. Yorke tried again, glancing at Jake, who suddenly looked paler than usual. 'You okay?'

'After what happened on this particular doorstep, not really.'

'He wasn't riddled with cancer when he did that.'

'I'm sure he could still pull a trigger.'

True, Yorke thought, kneeling down, *but what if Paul Ray is here now?* He shouted through the letter box. 'Thomas Ray, Police. You need to open up immediately.'

They waited. Yorke tapped his foot on the ground; he could hear Jake pacing side to side.

Then, Yorke pressed down the chrome door handle.

Jake darted back. 'You're mad!'

The door was locked.

'Three of us here is not enough,' Jake said. 'The man is a murderer.'

'Okay, phone for more back-up. I'll try the back door.'

'Maybe, you should wait, we can have some officers here in ten minutes.'

'A child is in danger. We have enough evidence for entering and arresting. I'm trying the back door.'

'Stubborn bastard, Mike,' Jake said, sighing.

'Stubborn bastard, *what?*' Yorke said with a grin.

'Stubborn bastard, *sir.*' Jake said, grinning back.

Yorke slipped around the back of the farmhouse, leaving Jake to his mobile phone call. At the back door, he tried knocking, but again got no answer.

He tried the handle. Unlocked.

He slipped in and paused to listen for someone in the house, but could pick up nothing over the wind.

The kitchen was dark, so he used his Maglite to look around. Cupboard doors were either open or hanging off; drawers had been pulled out and emptied. Cooking instruments were piled high on the surfaces. Someone had been through this place like a Tasmanian devil.

Suddenly feeling shaky, he contemplated stepping back outside and waiting the ten minutes for the extra officers. He turned and looked at the open back door, and then the image of the twelve-year-old boy with the blonde hair flashed through his mind, and he could feel Sarah Ray's hand gripping his arm as he made the promise. He turned back.

An inch at a time, he opened the kitchen door, peering through the widening gap as he did so. The hallway was lit by a shaded bulb from the right hand side room.

He turned off his torch and slid along the wall; a rancid smell of old dogs intensified. At the edge of the doorframe to the lit room, he paused and listened, but he still couldn't hear anything except the wind outside.

He slipped his small torch into his pocket and turned into the room.

Inside was a white rug on which slept a Dachshund. Next to that was a fireplace piled with logs and a couple of old wooden chairs facing a giant, old style TV showing nothing but static.

He stared at the Dachshund until he was sure it wasn't

breathing. He stepped forward, kneeled down and put his hand on its cold, hard back. Stuffed.

Fascinated, he picked the animal up and was surprised by how light it was. Something glittered in its mouth, so Yorke shook it and a padlock key fell out. He picked it up and slipped it into his pocket.

The TV was old and it reminded Yorke of one that he had grown up with. He fondly recalled his mum and older sister having to lift it together while he opened the doors for them.

Beneath the TV was an equally old-fashioned VCR. Yorke pressed the large square play button and listened to the mechanism start playing the tape with a clunk.

On the screen was the barn he'd seen on the way into the farm. It had been filmed on a lighter evening when the moon was completely full. Twenty seconds passed without the shot changing, so Yorke stopped the tape and hit fast forward. The VCR screeched. He pressed play again and the image of the barn returned.

He tried again, and again. The image didn't change. The barn was all he was getting.

Jake came up alongside him. 'We have several officers from a local station less than ten minutes away.'

After looking through the entire house and confirming that nobody was home, Jake and Yorke headed outside and drove back to the old barn. Two police cars pulled up beside them. Jake exited the car and ran over to them, while Yorke turned the vehicle to face the barn and stopped in the same spot that the camera would have been set up. The moon wasn't bright, so he used his full beam to light the exterior of the barn. It looked unchanged from the video footage.

He exited the car and, through the whipping wind, sprinted towards the barn door, brushing snow from his face along the way. He grabbed hold of the rusted padlock and, from his pocket, plucked the key that fell out of the stuffed Daschund's mouth. He slipped it in the padlock. A perfect fit.

AT THE OPPOSITE side of the barn to the pigs, Paul was sitting with his back against wooden slats. He'd grabbed the small lamp and now kept it between his legs. It didn't give off much warmth, but he felt slightly safer in the light. With his cold hands, he rubbed his cheeks and was surprised to see that he was still crying. He'd never thought it possible to cry as much as he'd done in such a short space of time.

Lewis, he thought, *where are you? Who's doing this to me?*

The wind relented for a moment allowing him to hear the pigs wrestling. He gulped and his throat tingled from all the attempts earlier to shout for Lewis' help.

Will Mum and Dad know I'm gone yet? Dad, I'm sorry for saying I'd run away.

He drew his knees up to his chest, taking care not to knock the lamp over. Then, he rested his head on his knees, recalling the advice his father often gave his obsessive mother about "mind over matter".

I'm warm, he thought, shivering, *and I'm safe, I'm warm and I'm safe—*

One of the pigs grunted loudly from the darkness. It sounded nearer than all the others. Bolting upright, he thrust out the lamp so he could see the outline of the beast skulking in the shadows.

Not the one that woke me up, it looks different. Angrier—

He rose to his feet.

Don't show it you're afraid.

'Get away!'

It spun and vanished into the shadows. Paul breathed a sigh of relief—

There was a loud clunk. *The door...* He scurried backwards. The pigs were squealing louder.

Help? Lewis?

But if he really believed that, why was he retreating further into the barn, clutching the lamp with a trembling hand? Along the way, he scoured the floor for a weapon. There were several farmyard implements, but they were all too bulky to wield. What he really needed was a spade or a rake.

The door started to open as Paul reached the far corner of the barn. *Please be help ... please.*

He switched off the lamp, held his breath and slipped down into the corner.

SEVERAL STEPS into the old barn, Yorke took a deep, cloying breath of air, scented with death. Around him, barn slats juddered as they sliced the wind into burning cold slithers. He heard loud beating noises above him and he turned the Maglite up at them. Shadows darted and hidden creatures hissed down at him.

He continued ahead, piercing the dark, mote-filled air with his torch. He revealed an old cobweb filled trough; a smashed up lawnmower; a pile of rusted spades and rakes; a wheel-less small tractor on its back and ... his breath caught in his throat ... a naked body hanging from a rail.

'Sir, are you alright?' Jake called from behind him.

'Contact HQ immediately, we have a body,' Yorke said,

bypassing the smashed up lawnmower, and drawing close enough to identify the corpse as male. The hook on the rail had been worked into his back, so his shoulders and head slumped forward like a forgotten wooden puppet's. He hung a good metre off the ground and his toes pointed down. Gases generated by decomposition had emptied his stomach and intestines on the floor.

He'd been tortured. Enthusiastically so. With his torch, Yorke traced deep cuts. He looked like an old chopping board. Gluey gulfs glimmered where his nipples used to be. The end of his penis had been attacked with some kind of rudimentary saw and it looked like a floret of cauliflower.

He ran his torch over the pulpy gash in his neck; the flaps of skin looked like the lips of a smiling fish. He shone the light into those familiar, hollow eyes.

Thomas Ray.

Death had surely come before today which meant Thomas Ray had not rented a van or been spotted by Sapphire's CCTV.

Something on Ray's leg caught his eye. He homed in with the torch and saw a black and white photo attached to his leg with a drawing pin. He leaned closer. It showed several generations of Rays assembled in front of a pig pen on this very farm.

A GIRL, wearing a head torch, stepped into the barn. 'Hello?'

From his position at the far side, Paul could tell she was young.

She turned the head torch on him. He shielded his eyes with his quivering hand.

'There you are,' she said.

'Who are you? Why am I here?' His throat still stung, and his voice crackled. 'I'm locked in here with pigs.'

'Turn on the light.'

'Why am I here?'

'I don't know.'

'Why are *you* here then?'

'I'm here to feed you.'

He switched on the lamp as she came nearer. She wore a long jacket and grey wellingtons. Drab, brown hair covered most of her pale face. In one hand, she held a dog bowl; in the other, a long yellow cattle prod. She must have been about the same age as him, but something about the expression on her face and the look in her eyes made her seem younger somehow.

Paul rose to his feet. The young girl stopped, took a step back and pointed at him with the crackling end of the prod. 'Mother says I have to be careful.' Her voice was really slow; she had a strong Wiltshire accent. 'She said, if he gets up, hurt him.'

Paul stared at the blue spark trembling between the two ends of the fork and knelt back down with his hands in front of him as a gesture of surrender.

'I don't want to hurt you, I've never hurt anyone before.' She knelt down and placed the dog bowl on the floor. 'Look at this!' She suddenly smiled. 'You're going to love it! Roast potatoes. Hmmmm. I've even brought some of Mother's yummy apple sauce. She only ever gives me this when I've been a good girl.' She stretched her words out for an agonising length of time, and the vacant expression on her face was unchanged. He could only imagine some of the abuse she would get at school; students had been alienated as "retards" for much less.

'I don't understand what's happening.' He could feel himself welling up again. 'Where's Lewis? What have you done with him?'

'Lewis has gone out.'

'I don't believe you, he's my friend, he wouldn't just leave me here with all these pigs everywhere.'

'They won't hurt you,' she said, looking over in the direction where the grunting animals were.

'Where's he gone?' He wiped away tears with the back of his hand.

'I don't know.'

'He told me he didn't have a daughter. Are you his daughter?'

'No, I'm Martha. Lewis is Mother's friend.'

'Who's your mother?'

She put a finger to her lips. 'Shush! She'll kill me if I tell you.'

Martha brushed knotted hair out of her eyes and tucked it behind her ears; Paul noticed that she was pretty.

'All I can do is feed you and I never fed a person before. Only thing I ever fed was my hamster. Lewis said not to give you any of the good food, he said you were only allowed the pig food, but I got you some good food here anyway. You know, he can be so mean sometimes. But he did say you've done bad things.'

'He wouldn't say that. This is all a mistake.'

'No mistake. He can be a really mean man if you've done bad things.'

'You should know that if I call him Lewis, then I *must* be his friend. He only lets those close to him call him by his middle name.'

Martha stared at him blankly.

'You've got to help me!' He was unable to to keep the frustration out of his voice.

'I can't—'

'But I've done nothing wrong.' He rose, holding his hands out in the air. 'Nothing at all, help me, please, I beg—'

The fear and panic he was feeling must have been contagious; her eyes narrowed, her knuckles glowed white and the cattle prod darted towards him. 'Sit back down!'

With the spark hovering an inch from his face, he stumbled back, banging his back against the wooden slats. When she flew in again, there was nowhere to run and the spark must have come to within a centimetre. He closed his eyes, lost control of his bladder and felt the top of his legs go warm.

Keeping his eyes squeezed shut, he waited for the pain. But when nothing happened, he opened them to see she'd backed off.

'Mother said this would happen. She said you'd want to do bad things to good girls. That's why I shouldn't have come here.'

'You've got to let me go home.' He clutched the back of his head, and slid down the wall. 'I've done nothing wrong.'

The girl turned and marched away.

'No, don't leave me. I don't want to be alone in here—'

The door slammed and the padlock clanked as it was reattached. Managing to crawl forward, he took up the dog bowl and threw it across the barn; then he listened to the pigs scurrying towards the spilled food, squealing in delight.

5

LACEY RAY STARED out over Southampton waterfront from her hotel window; the boats in the distance looked like dying stars. She glanced at her watch and saw that she didn't have much time left. So, she dimmed the lights, put her music player into its docking station, turned 'Sounds of the Forests Volume 4' up loud, sat on the floor in the lotus position, closed her eyes, took several slow, deep breaths, and transported herself into the Blue Room.

She wandered around, marvelling at how deep she'd taken herself tonight — the walls were the darkest shade of blue she'd ever seen and the coldness was almost unbearable.

Apart from the colour and the temperature, the Blue Room took on the same shape and organisation of the place in which she currently meditated. She ran a hand over one of the oak posts on the grand bed, caught a glimpse of her naked body in the television screen and paused. It was a shame she had things to do, she could happily stare at her perfect figure for hours.

There was a knock at the Blue Room door.

Ah, Brian, come in and bring your fat, swollen hands this way.

She was always glad that time did not work in the same way in the Blue Room as it did in reality. That she could skip the sex with a man that disgusted her. In her reality, she would have to suffer it, but she had established coping mechanisms for that already.

She fast-forwarded until afterwards, where she lay tangled in sweaty sheets on the four-poster bed. Beside her, Brian snored.

Always wanting to do it without a condom. No matter what I say to you ... no matter how many times I tell you no.

She touched the bruise on her shoulder; in the Blue Room, the pain felt just as real, if not worse.

She looked over at the sleeping obese brute.

I can feel your rabid discharge bubbling inside me.

She bared her teeth.

Lacey took herself outside of the Blue Room and her meditation. She switched the mood music off and, from the minibar, whipped up a vodka tonic, which she drank in three mouthfuls.

She double-checked her handbag; everything was there, ready.

Right on schedule, there was a knock at the door.

She opened it and saw Brian Lawrence in a large blue suit; sweat patches crept out from his armpits.

'I like your suit.'

Brian grinned; sweat shone on his brow. 'Thanks.'

'I've always had a thing for blue.'

Brian stepped in and Lacey closed the door behind him, smiling.

FOLLOWING THE SEX, she touched the bruise on her shoulder – it was the other shoulder from the one he'd hit her on in the Blue Room. It didn't matter. It meant the same thing.

She let him sleep for a short while before rummaging in her handbag at the foot of the bed for the handcuffs, gag and rope. Then, she convinced him to get into a wooden chair by the dressing table. *They always look so excited at this point*, she thought, as she cuffed his hands behind the back of the chair, slipped the gag over his head and wedged it into his mouth.

With a sharp tug, she tightened the gag; he moaned, pleasurably. Using the rope, she secured his ankles to the legs of the chair.

From her handbag, she withdrew her secateurs, and watched his expression morph into one of confusion. Then, she stationed herself behind the chair. He forced his head back to look up at her; his wide, jaundiced eyes full of confusion.

'Many people think that blue is an emotional colour. A sad colour. What do you think, Brian?'

She ran her long fingernails down his bulbous cheeks; his fat mouth quivered.

'Don't try and speak, Brian, the gag won't let you; I know it's my fault because I asked a question, but let's keep it to a nod or a shake, okay?'

He nodded. Fear crept into his eyes.

'Do you feel sad for what you've done?'

He nodded.

'You're not just telling me what I want to hear now Brian, are you?'

His face went pale and he shook his head, frantically. She stroked his cheeks with the tip of the secateurs, and his eyes filled with tears.

'Stop it, Brian. It's too late to cry. Too late to plead like those who pleaded with you.'

He started to writhe in the chair; she tucked the secateurs under one arm, put her hands on his shoulders and pressed down to steady him.

'Look at it like this, Brian, the Chinese use blue light to soothe illnesses and treat pain, so maybe you should do the same. Use it to heal your disease. Your hatred for women. Don't deny it. I saw it in your eyes. I'm very good at spotting it in people's eyes.'

As he twisted, straining his ankles against the chair legs, scraping his wrists against the cuffs, the chair squeaked and threatened to collapse under his massive weight.

'Brian, relax. It's no good, blue means forever. Yes, like the sky, like me, I am forever.'

She knelt down and snipped a finger off. The gag swallowed a deep, long moan. The chair trembled.

'Welcome to the Blue Room Brian. It's a humble place, but a place of judgement nonetheless ...'

With each snip he writhed harder until, eventually, he slumped forward in the chair.

She returned to the handbag. 'The heat and redness of blood brings disharmony, but it is a fleeting change.

Necessary change. When the constancy of the blue and cold returns, the world will be better for it.'

She leaned over his back. Unable to hear her heartbeat loud and clear like she could in the Blue Room, she was content to listen to steel clinking bone as she thrust the penknife in over and over again.

AFTERWARDS, having cleaned all traces of herself from the room and changed back into her disguise, she answered a call on her mobile phone from her sister-in-law, Sarah.

'We thought you should know,' Sarah said.

Lacey smiled. *I haven't spoken to my nephew in over five years, why would you think I want to know anything about him now?*

Nevertheless, it was important to keep up the pretence. 'Thanks, I'll be right there.'

She was on her way to her home city of Salisbury anyway to meet up with Jacques Louvre for a new passport and a new identity. Tonight, she'd reached victim number three and it was time to move on. To Nice in France. She'd overstayed her welcome in the UK.

After saying her farewells, she slipped the mobile phone back into her bag.

She looked at the bathroom in which Brian Lawrence, or what remained of him, waited to be discovered. With her family suddenly on the radar, it had not been the best time to commit a murder. Still, she felt no regret. She was incapable of doing so.

An oval shaped British Rail guard eyed Lacey Ray up and down; he had the hungriest eyes she'd ever seen.

A gust of cold wind raced across the platform as the train tunnelled through the snow toward them. She fastened the top button of her cream, knee-length coat, an expensive gift from one of her richer clients and patted the pocket, checking that her souvenirs from this evening's exploits were still inside.

The train thundered up to the platform, and screeched to a halt. She stood back for a moment, making eye-contact with the guard. She raised a suggestive eyebrow at him. *Why not? Give him a thrill he's never had before!*

When the train door opened, she strolled on board; her black high-heeled alligator boots, an eight thousand pound gift to herself after a solid month of work, clicked on the floor.

She glanced back and saw that her admirer had found a new target for his obsessive stare.

Men are so shallow, she thought as the doors closed behind her. She looked down at her bulging coat pocket. *Isn't that right, Brian?*

She found a seat by an old man doused in vinegary cologne. As she took off her coat and scarf, she noticed him stroking the creases out of an antique suit which he'd probably got married in over fifty years ago. She sat down and laid the coat and scarf across her lap.

'Evening miss,' the old man said. His smile was crowded with gleaming false teeth.

'Je ne parle pas anglais,' Lacey said, shrugging.

He creased his brow. 'Bonjour! If you need help with anything, you tell me.' He was speaking slowly and making ridiculous hand gestures.

'Je ne parle pas anglais,' she said again, and turned away from him. He'd get the message.

As the train rumbled toward Salisbury, she ran her hand over the bulge in the coat pocket, admiring her blue painted nails as she did so — not a mark on them, despite this evening's hard work.

Chewing her bottom lip, she relived the pinging noise the penknife made when it had clipped Brian Lawrence's spinal column over and over again. She stopped when she caught the old man looking at her with lust in his expression.

She closed her eyes for a moment as the motion of the train soothed her, but was careful not to fall asleep. Salisbury was only about half an hour away.

Someone tapped her on the shoulder. She opened her eyes and saw the old man leaning towards her, pointing at her lap. 'Excuse me there, miss, but I think you're bleeding.'

She opened her eyes and looked down. A large red stain was opening up on the pocket of her expensive coat. *Shit*.

With the ruined garment gathered up in her arms, she stood up, dropped the scarf onto the seat, and marched down the aisle.

She bypassed a deodorant spraying teenage girl, who could offer herself to Clearasil as a human guinea pig and receive a blank cheque. She caught a lungful of the aerosol and coughed in the girl's face; then, she went into the vacant cylinder-shaped bathroom.

She pressed the close button, and the curved door slid shut with a whoosh. She hit the lock button which flared green. There was loud clunk.

The train company must have burned its entire budget on the impressive toilet doors, because inside it was grim. A blob of phlegm floated in a half-filled tiny stainless steel sink; the dryer was hanging off the wall and the toilet seat had a huge crack in it.

She emptied the sink and then plucked the sandwich bag out of the coat and held it in front of her. The bag had split because there was too much in it. Gluttony had ruined her beautiful coat. She scooped out the souvenir she wanted to keep and dropped it into the sink. With a sigh, she shook out the rest of the bag's contents into the toilet bowl. Then, she turned on the tap and rinsed the blood from his wedding ring. She dried it on her coat, pocketed it in her dark jeans and then flushed the toilet.

As she waited for the toilet to clear, she opened the window and dropped the split plastic bag out onto the tracks. When she looked back at the toilet, she saw three persistent fingers still bobbing up and down in the water. She smiled and tried again. Two more fingers disappeared. To a septic tank? She wasn't sure, she'd read somewhere that some trains still flushed out onto the track.

Frustrated with the final bobbing finger, and not wanting to wait for the tank to fill again, she scooped it out, wrapped it in a piece of toilet paper, opened the small window and threw it out.

She closed the window and wiped her fingerprints from it with a handful of toilet paper; she then ran it over everything she'd touched, including the door buttons.

Shielding her fingertips with another piece of tissue, she punched the open button. The girl with zits was waiting to go in. Lacey stared at her; the girl looked away.

Back at her seat, the old man said, 'Are you okay, miss?'

She turned to him. 'Je ne comprends pas.' She pointed at her nose and mimed blood coming out.

'Ahhh.'

A few minutes later, the old man dozed off, and Lacey

unfolded her coat. She would be able to position her scarf over the stain when she was back out in the cold.

A good thing really, because her erect nipples, pointing through her blouse, would have sent the next British Rail guard wild.

———

FOR THE SECOND time in less than ten years, Thomas Ray's farm was a major crime scene.

Yorke stood at the blue and white taped line where Willows had been given the essential, if not onerous, task of recording names in the scene log. Lights had already been set up inside, and a violent violet glow sprayed from the slats, as if some kind of secret scientific experiment was going on inside.

Divisional Surgeon Patricia Wileman emerged from the barn and headed toward Yorke with a disgusted look on her face.

He heard DI Mark Topham behind him and turned to see a heavy clustering of police vehicles; the orange on their bodywork was the only colour in a gloomy mix of black sky and snowy white fields. Topham, who'd just emerged from the hulking black Major Incident Vehicle, was approaching Yorke in a grey suit, which fit so well, it could almost be an extension of his skin. Yorke had never really felt too much concern over his own appearance; his suit today was too baggy, and the heavy overcoat he wore blinded the observer to the fact that he was in reasonably good shape. He smiled when he realised that Topham was so proud of the way he looked, he'd not worn a coat despite the extreme cold; as per usual, he suffered in the name of looking good.

Topham addressed Patricia first, who was now alongside Yorke. 'At least there's a body for you this time.'

'What's left of it,' Patricia said, scrunching up her face again. 'Too early to say how long he's been dead, but we're talking days if not longer. A pathologist is on the way.'

'With no official ID, are you sure it's Thomas Ray?' Topham said.

Yorke said, 'I'm sure, and you will be too, once you've been in and had a look.'

Topham didn't look too happy about Yorke's request; probably didn't want to get his suit close to that ripe body. 'Ray's not our man then.'

'No, but I'm wondering if Paul's abductor is responsible for this. He wanted us to look here; he left a video of the barn at the farmhouse and a key that he knew we'd find. He also left a photograph showing several generations of the Ray family. *In the Blood*. Seems like a continuation of the game which began back at the school.'

Topham and Patricia nodded. They turned around to continue surveying the scene. Scientific Support Officer Lance Reynolds was conducting his usual dance as he led a team of white suited SOCOs into the glowing wooden husk. He noticed another SOCO behind the taped line videoing Gardner and Brookes returning from the farm house.

'The house is a mess, SOCOs are working on it now,' Gardner said when she drew close enough. Yorke could smell the spearmint tic tacs on her breath. It was a welcome relief from the fetid smell of decomposition which had lingered in his nostrils since he'd left the barn.

'There'd been a struggle in the bedroom,' Brookes said, not making eye-contact with anybody. 'But no blood; at least none yet. Looks like the bastard was grabbed in there and then executed in here.' He gestured over his shoulder with a thumb at the barn, as if pointing out a car parking spot for someone.

Yorke thought for a moment and then said, 'Iain, could you take some officers around the local farms? Neighbours *must* have known Ray had returned, and they may have noticed any visitors. I bet most of these farms have CCTV too.'

'Aye, aye, sir,' Brookes said, disappearing towards the cluster of vehicles.

'Emma, we need to ensure soil samples are taken, as well as have the entry road scoured for footprints and tyre tracks. You may not find anything due to all the heavy snowfall — but it's worth a shot. Also, could you please get all these vehicles moved back thirty yards or so? They're too close.'

'Yes, boss.'

'Mark, time for your look at the body, and get Andrew to bag up that photograph stuck to Ray's leg and bring it out, I want to take another look.'

He looked around for Jake. No sign. He must still have been contacting PolSA in the car.

Topham stepped nearer and started to speak quietly, Yorke knew what was coming even before he'd finished his first word.

'You must be thinking what I'm thinking?'

Yorke nodded, but looked dead ahead, avoiding Topham's eyes.

'It's too much of a coincidence. They're both Rays; one's missing, one's dead. The message said, "In the blood." It all stands to reason, who would hate them this much—'

'I already agree, Mark.'

'So?"

95

'Listen, the Rays have history, right back since Reginald bought this farm at the beginning of the last century, they've pissed people off. See that tree?' He pointed at an old oak in the distance.

'Yes,' Topham said, 'Reginald was hung from it by angry neighbours after he killed six local kids.'

'Precisely. They've never been popular, with *anyone*, let's not lose sight of that—'

'You sound like you're defending Harry, after what he did—'

'What he did can have nothing to do with this, and you know that.'

'His phoning you – the SIO on the case – is really striking me as a smart piece of subterfuge.'

Yorke sighed. 'Okay, stop with the hassling. I'll arrange to meet him, but I'm not dragging him into the station. Not only will it look like I'm getting personal but, despite everything he did, he was still one of us, and is owed more than that.'

'Okay,' Topham said. 'Time to face the barn.'

Yorke watched him change into a white oversuit. He looked at his watch. Eight twenty-seven. Paul Ray had not been seen for nine and a half hours.

'Sir,' Jake said, coming alongside him. 'I've just been on the phone to Sean back at the station. Joe and Sarah Ray have received a video by e-mail. Their son is on the video.'

Yorke turned and lifted his eyes to meet Jake's. 'A ransom demand?'

'No. Violent scenes of someone butchering animals.'

'Pigs?'

'Yep. The butcher was also wearing a real pig's face as a mask like some kind of freak in a horror film. At the end of the video, the man reveals Paul to the camera.'

'Jesus. How must his parents feel after seeing that?' He sighed. 'Could you go personally to their house and watch the footage, then decide whether to take the laptop as evidence? I will join you there shortly.'

Jake nodded and left. Topham approached him, hurriedly peeling off his white oversuit. Yorke could see the plastic bag containing the photo in his gloved hand.

'Thanks for that,' Topham said. 'I've only ever seen one death more gruesome, and that was an accident on a railway track.'

'It's all experience.'

'If experience is the death of my belief in the goodness of the human condition, then you're right. By the way, we will have two bodies in there, if we don't get it back to Andrew soon; the vein throbbing on his head looked particularly unhealthy.'

Topham came alongside Yorke and held the photo up. Yorke used his Maglite. White snow scratched lines into the narrow tunnel of light.

There was a hole at the top of the black and white photo where it had been pinned to Thomas Ray's thigh. Reginald's descendants were sitting under a sky painted red by their own blood.

Yorke had seen the photo before. Almost ten years ago when Thomas Ray had killed Danielle Butler. In fact, a copy of this was currently sitting at HQ in an old brown file.

The photo had been taken in Nineteen forty-four. Sitting on the pig pen fence were Thomas' aunties and uncles.

'Thomas Ray,' Yorke said, pointing the light at a small child being dangled in the air by a young girl and a young boy. Thomas Ray looked over the moon. *And a far cry from the tortured individual he would later become.*

'The boy is Richie Ray, Joe's dad.'

'The young girl?'

Yorke moved the torch across the photo to her. 'His sister, Beatrix Ray.'

'She was killed, wasn't she?'

'Yep, by Richie.' He flicked the torch back to her brother. 'A childhood scrap that resulted in a fatal fall. The authorities weren't totally convinced it was an accident; he spent a lot of his youth institutionalised. When he was released, he married Joe's mother.'

'Where are Paul's grandparents now?'

'They died in a car accident in the late nineties.'

Yorke moved his torch over to one of the men sitting on the fence. He had a boxer's nose and a beard like tangled straw. 'That's Andrew Ray, Thomas' father. Obsessed with aliens, he managed to recruit people to his cause and set up a small cult. Couple of local churches suffered during their riotous marches. This was around the time that the phrase, "Pray for the Rays" became commonplace.'

'I know all this. You're still trying to argue that the Rays have generated a lot of enemies over the last century. But, we can't get away from the fact that Andrew Ray, on his deathbed, blamed the aliens for his lung cancer, and managed to convince his son to commit murder fifty years later. The murder of an innocent woman. *Harry's wife.* The more I think about it, the more I become convinced that Harry should be brought in immediately.'

'As I said before, I'm on it. Meanwhile, you'll be organising a team to consider everyone else that has a reason to hate the Rays – living and dead. You can start by grabbing an update into the investigation of Joe Ray's lovers and there's also Lacey Ray to consider.'

'Lacey Ray has been gone almost five years.'

'True, but she is one of only four Rays left alive. Last I heard she was prostituting herself in Southampton. It could be connected. Get someone to contact Southampton and have her questioned.'

After Topham had headed off to return the photo to Andrew Waites, Yorke scrolled down to Harry's number. As the phone rang, he stared at the glowing barn, thinking about those that used to pray for the Rays.

They obviously didn't pray hard enough, he thought.

6

IT TOOK ALMOST ten minutes for Lacey to reach her apartment at Spire View from the train station. Pushed back in an industrial part of Salisbury, the modern apartment blocks dazzled like a new car in the middle of a scrapyard. She could afford a property in the better end of town, but there'd never seemed much point; she was hardly ever back. Neither did she ever consider getting rid of it, thinking it important that she had a permanent residence.

At her apartment, which was regularly cleaned by a local agency, she bundled her ruined coat and clothes into a bin liner, and slipped Brian's platinum wedding ring underneath the fridge. After re-dressing, extracting a quilted coat from her wardrobe, and an umbrella to fend off the snow, she set off on foot to her brother and sister-in-law's cottage, dropping the bin liner in a skip beside a row of Indian restaurants.

She passed under a grubby arched bridge, which suffered under the fast modern trains in much the same way that some parts of historic Salisbury suffered under the brash, contemporary chain shops. As she walked beside the run-down pub, *Deacons,* in the toilets of which she'd lost her virginity at the age of fifteen, she heard Slade's "Merry Christmas everybody" and caught the scent of real ale. She smiled over the memory of drinking pints in there with her first serious boyfriend.

Beside the turn off to Salisbury Theatre, she switched on her mobile phone and listened to a message from the police, who desperately wanted to talk to her regarding her missing nephew.

It took her about twenty minutes to reach the whitewashed cottage. Once she was under the porch, she lowered her umbrella and knocked on the door. A squat man with cheeks like a bulldog opened it. A blast of hot air rushed out over her.

'Hi, I'm here to see Joe and Sarah,' she said.

'Sorry, who are you?'

'I'm Lacey, Joe's sister.'

'Ahhh ... I'm the family support officer, Bryan Kelly. My colleagues are eager to talk to you at the station.'

'I would prefer to speak to my family first, if that's okay?'

'That's fine, but I have to notify the station immediately, so they can send someone to collect you.'

Lacey nodded, and Bryan opened the door wider. Her brother approached and stood beside him. He used to be a very thin man, but he'd put on weight since she'd last seen him, and he was starting to swell around his chest, making his choice of an almost skin-tight white polo neck questionable. 'Lacey - what are you doing here?' He took a step back as he spoke and his face turned paler, as it always did when she paid a visit.

'Sarah phoned me.'

Sarah appeared behind the two men, looking uncharacteristically dowdy in a shapeless dressing gown.

Lacey's eyes darted between the couple's repugnant clothing. *Is this what grief and sadness did to you?* If so, she was glad she would never have to experience such feelings.

Sarah wriggled between the two men; her eyes were glassy and her breath smelled of sherry. 'We need family here with us.'

'Yes, of course,' Joe said. 'I was just surprised, it's been...'

'So long?' Lacey said.

'Yes,' Joe said and swallowed.

'You always did know how to make me feel welcome! If it's not a good time—'

Sarah took Lacey's hand and gently pulled her through the door into the hot hallway. The two men parted to allow them past. 'Please take off your boots and come into the lounge.'

Lacey propped the umbrella by the wall, peeled off her boots and followed Sarah. She noticed a tilted picture of her brother show jumping on the wall. She straightened the picture as she passed. *Wouldn't want you to fall now ...*

Lacey sat down on a black, leather sofa on the side furthest from the burning fire and closest to the Christmas tree. She stroked the tree's real needles, while surveying the clean and organised lounge. There was an open medicine bottle on the sparkling glass coffee table, with a half-filled crystal tumbler of sherry beside it. Further along the table was Joe's glass of bourbon.

Joe and Sarah sat down on the sofa opposite her while Bryan left the room to call the station.

'Can I get you a drink, Lacey?' Sarah said.

'No thanks.' Lacey leaned forward and offered the most sympathetic look she could manage. 'Any developments?'

'We received a video,' Sarah said. The colour drained from her face and she pressed a tissue to her mouth.

Joe explained what was on the video. 'The police are on their way now to watch it and collect the laptop.'

Bryan came back into the room. 'There'll be here shortly.'

Ah, I really must be on my best behaviour then.

'What do you think the kidnapper wants?' Lacey said.

'We don't know. Money, presumably,' Joe said.

'Well, if you need any help with that.'

Joe's hand trembled as he took a mouthful of bourbon. *Do I still scare you Joe, after all this time?*

'We have enough,' Joe said.

'Okay, but the offer is there.'

But you'll never take my money, will you Joe? Not when you know where it comes from.

Someone's phone beeped. Joe identified it as his and took it out of his pocket. He fiddled with the keypad and his eyes opened wide. While reading, he leaned forward. Bryan came over to him.

'What does it say?' Sarah said, clutching her husband's leg.

'Tomorrow. The entrance to Tesco on Southampton Road.' He clasped the back of Sarah's hand. 'Have your wife drop fifty thousand pounds in the bin adjacent to the RBS cashpoint at two PM and then return to her car.'

'Is that it?' Sarah said.

'Not exactly.'

'What else does it say?'

'I don't—'

'What else?'

Joe took a deep breath. 'If she's late or is with you or the police, your child will be slaughtered in exactly the same

103

way as the pigs were. Your son will be left outside Tesco only after the money is received.'

Before taking a breath, Joe grabbed his glass from the table and filled his mouth with the remaining bourbon. Lacey watched Sarah's hands whiten as she tightened her grip on Joe's leg. 'But this is good, Joe. It means we're going to get him back.'

'Can I take your phone please?' Bryan said. 'I need to contact the station.'

Joe handed him the phone and Bryan left the room again.

'Yes, dear, we just need to get the money together.' The tone of Joe's voice did not reflect the certainty of his answer.

'Remember,' Lacey said, 'I can help with the money.'

'Who could be doing this to us?' Joe said.

Sarah said, 'Who do you think? All those people you hurt, is it any wonder—'

'*Not now.*'

'One of those women, one of their husbands. Why do you think the police were so desperate for that list?'

Lacey wanted to smile, but forced it back. *So, Joe, you've still not gotten control of yourself? You're still indulging.*

Sarah reached into her dressing gown pocket and pulled out a dust cloth. She stared at the table for a moment and then scrunched the cloth up into a ball and hid it in her fist. 'I should have left you, years ago. Look what you've done to us.'

The doorbell went. Bryan called in. 'I'll get it.'

Joe put his glass down on the table with a clunk. He looked up at Lacey. 'Maybe, you should leave us to talk.'

'I want her here,' Sarah said, opening her fist and looking at the cloth again. 'Just because you struggle with the idea of family.'

'That's nonsense.'

In fairness, he always cared more than I did, Lacey thought.

Sarah leaned over and using the cloth, started to polish the gleaming coffee table.

Lacey straightened her razor-sharp fringe. 'Sarah needs your support, Joe.'

He looked at his wife, who was now on her knees cleaning the table. 'Stop cleaning, Sarah.'

As she polished harder, the table surface squeaked.

'Would you like me to leave, Sarah?' Lacey said.

Sarah didn't answer; she was polishing so hard she was out of breath. They both watched her begin to sweat.

Joe said, 'For God's sake, Sarah, stop it!'

Lacey stood up and crossed the Persian rug. Joe straightened up as she neared. With narrowed eyes, she stared down at him. 'Your wife has had a shock. Be respectful.'

Joe lowered his head.

Lacey offered Sarah a smile, but she didn't notice; she was now polishing the underneath of the table.

'Hello,' someone said from the lounge door.

Lacey looked and, for the first time in a long while, she was genuinely surprised. It was her first boyfriend; the one she'd been thinking of earlier as she passed *Deacons*.

'Hello,' Lacey said.

'Hi Lacey,' DS Jake Pettman said, nodding. 'It's been a long time.'

As JAKE INDICATED LEFT at the traffic lights, Lacey said, 'So, if I hadn't have come willingly, would you have arrested me?'

'Why? You've done nothing wrong, have you?'

'And what do you define as wrong? We used to get up to all sorts of things which could be considered wrong.'

She watched his Adam's apple flicker up and down as he gulped. The light went green and he made his turn.

'This is precisely why I won't be the one interviewing you. *History*.'

'Too much or not enough? We could make some more.'

Jake laughed as he slowed for another traffic light. She laughed too, but not because it was a joke, but rather because he thought it was.

He looked at his watch and sighed. 'I have to make it back to your brother's before my boss does or he won't be happy. I should just have got someone to pick you up.'

'You could run me back to my flat, it's nearer. There's no need to bother with an interview, I won't be able to help you.'

'You'll be surprised. Help comes from unlikely sources in situations like this,' Jake said, moving through the traffic lights and heading towards a roundabout.

'I haven't seen Paul in five years.'

'Still ...' Jake peeled left off the roundabout.

Lacey noticed a card in the car door pocket. She picked it up.

Jake Pettman, personal trainer. Below that was his e-mail and mobile number.

'Personal trainer now?'

'Tried to get something set up, but it's so slow at the moment and I'm too busy.'

106

She pretended to put it back, and then slipped it into her pocket instead. He didn't seem to notice.

'We could meet up for a drink to catch up,' she said, only realising the stupidity of her suggestion on the last word. *He's a policeman – what are you doing?*

'I'm married, Lacey.'

'Most of the men I meet see marriage as a rather challenging institution.'

'It's probably best not to stereotype men from those you meet in your line of work.'

She flinched. *So you know about my profession?* 'I don't know what you mean.'

He looked at her with the ghost of a smile on his face.

Judgement? Quit while you're ahead if I were you.

'How could you degrade yourself like that?' he said, taking the turning into the station.

Lacey clutched the handle on the car door hard. She was surprised. She only usually felt sudden surges of irritation when manhandled.

'So, that's a "no" to the drink?'

Jake rolled his eyes, parked the car and led her round to the reception entrance.

'You know, it's been ten years, you could have been more polite,' she said.

He opened the door for her. 'I was being polite. What you do is illegal — whatever you say to me, I will have to follow up on. It's best you save it for your interviewer.'

As she passed him, she said, 'What's happened to you, Jake, when did you get so serious?'

'When I got married. You should try it.'

After checking her in, he pointed to a chair among a group of people from the school. 'Wait over there. It'll be about five minutes before someone comes to collect you.'

'I'll be in touch,' she said, waving over her shoulder.

Sitting down, she noticed him lingering by the reception desk, probably concerned she might make a run for it. When she smiled over at him, he pretended not to notice. She slipped her hand in her pocket and thumbed the corner of his business card.

THE PROMISED five minutes quickly passed; during which time, a large, suited man sat down beside her. Fearful of awakening the need for the Blue Room, she tried to stave off the irritation that her judgemental ex-boyfriend had aroused in her by flirting with the large man.

'I've always hated waiting,' she said and smiled. 'Unless I have someone to talk to, of course.'

He glanced at her without turning his head. An anticlimactic reply was a long time coming. 'I've never seen you at school before.'

'And why do you assume I'm from the school?'

'Everyone else is.'

'Really? Why are you all here?'

'A young boy has gone missing. This is our second interview of the day.'

'A young boy? *A child?* Who would do such a thing?' She paused. 'What's your name?'

He tucked his long black hair behind his ears to reveal a wide, strong jaw; she noticed he was struggling to hold eye contact with her. No worries. She was used to men being shy around her.

'My name's Phil Holmes, I'm the IT specialist at the school.'

Nodding at a cluster of people chatting opposite them, she said, 'How come you're not over there with them?'

'They don't like me.'

'Why not?'

'Don't know. Maybe it's because the school pay me more.'

'Does it now?' She said and smiled at him.

He managed to hold eye-contact with her for a longer moment than last time. *Good, now we're making progress ...*

'My name's Lacey Ray.'

His eyes widened.

She said, 'Sorry — I should have been honest with you. Paul is my nephew.'

Phil started to fiddle with his watch. 'I'm sorry for what you and your family are going through.'

'Thanks.'

'Lacey Ray?' A tall, thin policeman said. 'I'm PC Sean Tyler. I'm here to take you to an interview room.'

'Could I have a second?'

'Of course,' Tyler said. 'I'll wait over there.' He pointed to a door out of the waiting room and walked over to it.

She turned back to Phil. 'Do you have a pen?'

'Yes.' Phil's hand delved into his suit pocket and re-emerged with a biro. She pried it from his fingers, drew his large hand toward her, and inked her mobile number onto the back of it. 'As you earn more than everyone else in this room, pick somewhere nice for dinner.'

He nodded and she left him to follow Tyler through the door.

WHILE PARKING, Yorke saw Jake locking his car. As he jogged over to him, he fastened the silver brass buttons on his muddy brown jacket, but didn't bother with the strap and buckle; it banged awkwardly against his thigh. 'I thought you were in there already.'

'I was. Joe Ray's sister made an appearance. I drove her to the station to be interviewed.'

'Lacey Ray?'

Jake looked at him for the first time since Yorke had caught up with him. He nodded.

'Your ex?'

'Uh-huh, which is why I gave the honour of interviewing her to someone else. Update?'

'Joe Ray's phone has been collected. I've tried contacting Harry, but there's no answer, so I eventually succumbed to Mark's demands and sent some uniforms to pick him up.'

They approached a large whitewashed cottage on Crane Bridge Road, opposite the Town Path — a popular, gritty walkway he ran on regularly. After bridging the river, it sliced through a large park and offered spectacular views of the cathedral, before climaxing at a riverside medieval pub, The Old Mill. Yorke often joined some of the locals for a game of backgammon there.

'Imagine owning a place worth half a million?' Jake said, eyeing the cottage up and down as they crossed the road.

'The Rays have never wanted for anything since that grotty pig farm made a fortune. Joe put some of his money to use on an expensive little shop in town that sells old colonial style furniture imported from China.'

'I know all about it. Sheila has spent a small fortune in that shop.'

Yorke knocked and within seconds, Family Liaison

Officer, Bryan Kelly, opened the cottage door and shouting spilled out onto the porch. Bryan shrugged; big cheeks which old women liked to pinch, wobbled.

'They've been drinking hard to calm down, but it seems to have had the opposite effect,' Bryan said, reducing his voice to a hiss. 'I told them it wasn't a good idea. But since when can you tell someone, with a crystal decanter costing more than you earn in a month, what to do?'

He led them into the piping hot cottage. Yorke and Jake peeled off their jackets as they walked down a corridor lined with framed pictures of Joe Ray as a teenage show jumper. Bryan went ahead and when Yorke and Jake entered the sitting room, they saw him kneeling before the Rays. 'It's important that we all stay calm.'

Sarah turned her head away. 'Easier said than done. You don't know what this man is like.'

The room had too much black furniture for Yorke's liking. The Christmas tree, the off-white rug and the glow of the dying fire embers brought some variation to the room, but there were no bright colours; he wondered if the Rays had been through the house and stripped them away following the kidnapping of their son.

Bryan stood up and turned to Yorke and Jake. 'I've got a few calls to make.'

'That's okay,' Yorke said.

Yorke looked down at the troubled couple. Sarah stared into space as she lifted the crystal glass to her lips. Joe was fidgety; his eyes were darting around the room and he seemed unable to focus on anything. 'Mr and Mrs Ray, this is DS Pettman, I believe you met briefly just before he took your sister to the station.'

Joe's wandering eyes settled on Yorke's face. 'Yes. Take a seat.'

'Thank you,' Yorke said, taking a step forward.

'Your shoes first,' Sarah said without looking at them. 'Please.'

Yorke looked down at the rug which was soaking up the snow crumbling from his boots. 'Yes, of course.'

They both slipped back out of the room to deposit them at the front door.

Back in the room, Yorke reached down and picked up a dog-eared Isaac Asimov book from the sofa before he sat. He remembered Jake telling him about the Asimov books which he'd seen in Paul's room earlier.

'Paul's?' Yorke said, reaching over and putting it on the table.

'Yes,' Sarah said. 'Didn't bother to put it away. It's the first thing he'll look for when he gets back.'

Yorke nodded. 'You mentioned he was a book worm.'

Sarah forced a smile.

Jake sat down to the right-hand side of Yorke, nudging against him as he tried to get comfortable. Jake was such a big man that he made everything and everyone around him seem small and in the way.

'Before we get to the logistics of tomorrow's ransom drop,' Yorke said, 'I need you to answer an important question.'

'Go on,' Joe said.

'When was the last time you saw your uncle, Thomas Ray?'

'I wondered how long it would take you to get onto that one.'

Sarah said, 'We haven't seen him in years. Not since the trial.'

'Is that the same for both of you?' Yorke said, staring directly at Joe.

'Yes, of course. We also had very little to do with him before all that happened with the nurse. We've spent most of our lives distancing ourselves from the farm and that part of my family.'

'Why?'

'Why do you think? They've never been anything but trouble.'

'Current events in mind, Mr Ray, that trouble does seem to have followed you.'

Joe sighed. 'Yes, it has. I thought all that *history* was over and done with.'

'So, do you think the kidnapping has any connection to your uncle or the farm?'

'I can't see how it could be connected.'

Yorke looked through his notes. 'I haven't seen the video. Your laptop is at the station, but I have a thorough breakdown. The kidnapper wears a pig's face; slaughters three pigs; introduces the video with "Pig productions"; there's pig's blood at the school and someone wrote us the message "In the Blood". Are you *really* telling me you haven't thought about the connection to your family?'

'I haven't,' Joe said. 'The last I heard my uncle was dying. A social worker contacted us, asking for our help. I refused. A man like that does not deserve any compassion.'

'Well, he hasn't been shown any. He's been murdered.'

Yorke carefully watched Joe's face; his mouth hung open and he took two sharp inhalations through his nose, causing his mole to tremble. The shock looked genuine. Beside him, Sarah had her hand to her mouth.

'*What?*' Joe said.

'It's not on the news yet but I just came from his farm, it's definitely him—'

'Who did it?' Sarah said.

'It may be the same person who abducted your son. I can't really see it being a coincidence. We really need to know of anyone who has a grudge against your family.'

'We've told you absolutely everything we know, I've been through every customer on my database, and I've given you all those names you asked for.' He glanced at Sarah as he said this and she looked away. 'There really isn't anybody else I can think of.'

'The man we caught on the CCTV footage coming out of the school was disguised as your uncle. We know this because Thomas Ray has been dead for days. Is there anyone on that list you gave us who has a similar appearance to your uncle, a similar build perhaps?'

'No, I don't think so,' Joe said and finished his glass of bourbon in one quick mouthful. 'What about that detective whose wife was killed? Wouldn't he have reason to kill my uncle?'

Sarah opened her medicine bottle with shaking hands and swallowed a white tablet with her sherry. Yorke could feel Jake move in the chair beside him and heard his trousers squeak on the leather.

'That is being considered, and if anything comes of it, you will be the first to know,' Jake said.

Yorke looked at Jake and with a swift nod of his head offered him a thank you for delivering the brush off so calmly and concisely.

Yorke saw something in the corner of the room which made his eyes widen. 'That chair.' He nodded at a rocking chair with a back like a birdcage. 'Was it your uncle's?'

'Of course not.'

'That's funny, because it's a dead ringer for the one that Thomas Ray shot Danielle Butler from. Where did you get it?'

'There are several in the family. Our great-grandfather used to make them.'

'Good with his hands, was he?' Yorke said.

'Yes, when he wasn't farming, he was a real craftsman.'

And a child-killer, thought Yorke.

Bryan Kelly looked into the room from the door. 'Sir?'

'Excuse me,' Yorke said and joined Bryan in the hallway.

'I just got a call from the station, they said they tried you, but you weren't picking up.'

Yorke took his phone out of his pocket and saw that he'd accidently knocked it onto silent. Two missed calls. 'Shit. Go on.'

'They've located Harry. He clocked off twenty minutes ago from a taxi firm he's working for; the manager there knocked back an offer to join him at the Haunch of Venison for a drink. Shall I have him picked up from the Haunch?'

Very public, Yorke thought, *and exactly what I wanted to avoid.* 'No, Bryan. I'll go as soon as I've finished here.'

When Yorke came back into the room, he saw that Sarah had wandered over to the patio door and was staring outside. He looked at Jake, who shrugged.

'Okay, we need to discuss the ransom drop.'

Joe said, 'It didn't seem like a lot of money to me – why go to so much effort for fifty grand?'

'To some it's a lot of money and a massive motivation. It's also an amount that can be accessed overnight.'

'Yes, the money is already confirmed, I'm to collect it from the bank in the morning.'

Sarah, who was staring out of the patio doors on the other side of the room, said, 'And then I have to deliver it.'

The pills, the alcohol, the OCD, we'll have to give that serious consideration, thought Yorke.

Yorke said, 'We have to have the money marked.'

'It can be washed anyway, can't it?' Joe said.

'It's hard, but there are ways. But rest assured that we will have the area under surveillance and a tracker with the money. It's very difficult for them to succeed these days, hence the reason we haven't had a case like this in a while.'

Sarah, who was cleaning the patio door with the sleeve of her dressing gown, said, 'Am I going to get my son back tomorrow?'

She focused her polishing on an area which was already sparkling. *Was she imagining dirt there, a smudge perhaps?*

Yorke said, 'The Tesco he's chosen is quite closed in – a peculiar choice. We'll have an excellent chance of retrieving your son and catching the kidnapper.'

If he comes.

Sarah abandoned her cleaning and turned to look at him. 'Remember what you promised us?'

'I remember.'

Jake looked at him with a confused look on his face. Yorke shrugged.

After sweeping the Asimov book up from the table, Sarah stormed out of the room.

AFTER FINISHING HER INTERVIEW, Lacey walked outside and phoned Jake. When he answered the phone, she smiled. *Pass judgement over me, will you? You'll rue that decision.*

'So, have you thought any more about that drink?'

'Lacey? How did you get this number?'

'Maybe I need a personal trainer.'

He didn't reply.

'You sound like you're driving.'

'I am, I'm heading to HQ ... *shit,* I'm hanging up now, this is totally inappropriate, and I'm very busy.'

'Hanging up is no way to treat someone who has missed you for ten years.'

'*What?* Bye, Lacey—'

'Hang up and I'll contact Sheila.'

'You threatening me?'

She smirked. 'Look, why can't we just be friends?'

'Because I'm a police officer, and I know what you do for a living!'

The smirk fell from her face. 'Before you were rude, now you're just being plain nasty. How long have you been struggling with Sheila?'

'What makes you think we're struggling?'

'A sexless life like that must be a challenge for you.'

'What the—?'

'I know what sex does to a man. The fact that you're going without was written all over your face earlier.'

'Goodbye, Lacey.'

She waited. The phone didn't go dead. She'd got to him. The smirk returned.

'Even if that were true, which it isn't, do you really believe everything is about sex? You're emotionally stunted. Heard of love?'

Ah, you're angry.

'Does a man need love?' Lacey said.

'Well I do.'

'You never seemed too bothered about those things when you were shagging me in the pub toilets. You know I walked past Deacons this evening. Those are good memories.'

'I don't remember. Besides, we were young. I've obviously changed.'

She snorted and said, 'Men don't change; they're not the same as women.'

'That's a very sexist view.'

'Or realistic. Men are like chameleons, adapting to their surroundings, but actually changing is beyond them.'

'I'd love to chat about gender roles all night, Lacey, but you're keeping me from very important matters.'

'Like trying to find my nephew?'

'Precisely, something you don't seem to care about.'

'I think I've just fallen in love with you.'

She paused to listen to him snort.

'I'll be at my flat in Spire View if you want to talk some more. I can be good company, you know.'

'I am sure there're a lot of men who could testify to that.'

'Bye Jake.'

She hung up and thought about the conversation.

Did she feel victorious? Not really. He gave as good as he got. And his rejection niggled her. It was something she really wasn't used to.

She sighed. She wanted to carry on playing, but she was leaving the country in two days, and winding up a police officer was not a good idea.

She was going to have to resist.

And that was something she always struggled to do.

7

YORKE BYPASSED THE bar at the Haunch of Venison, resisting the smell of hops, and the urge for a pint of *Summer Lightning* to cool his boiling brain.

He walked up the uneven stone steps, weaved around the enormous oak beams taken from fourteenth century sailing vessels, into the snuggest and warmest part of the pub, where he found Harry Butler reading a newspaper.

Harry looked very different from last time Yorke had seen him. He'd started to go bald, but he had the kind of weathered, chiselled features that allowed him to shave his head without looking aggressive. He'd put on weight, but looked healthier for it, and his dress sense had improved; he wore a smart shirt which fitted him perfectly – much more perfectly than any of Yorke's clothes fitted him.

'Harry?'

'Mike,' he said, rising to his feet. 'I've been calling.'

'I know.' Yorke sat down.

Harry retook his seat and drank a mouthful of ale. 'I thought I'd have been called in for an interview by now.'

'You have. That's why I'm here.' He nodded down at Harry's pint. 'But you can finish that first.'

'You always were a gentleman, Mike. Even after everything that happened between us, you still wouldn't want to see me hauled in.'

'Why did you phone me first, Harry?'

'I knew I'd be a suspect after I saw the news. Thought I'd try to pre-empt that.'

Yorke remembered Mark's view that this could be a smart piece of subterfuge.

'Well, if that's the case, why didn't you just come into the station? Why wait until we found you?'

Harry shrugged. 'Needed to work. I get paid hourly now. My days of earning a regular salary are long gone.'

Less than a year after the death of his wife, Harry had planted evidence on an innocent man, believing him guilty of murder. It allowed the real perpetrator to run, and disappear into hiding. Not only had this cost Harry his job, but also his friendship with Yorke, because the victim of this particular murder had been Yorke's older sister.

'Are you anything to do with this Harry?'

Harry took another mouthful of beer. 'What do you think, Mike? Do you really think I have that in me?'

'There was a time when I would have answered that question without a moment's hesitation.'

Harry fixed his eyes on Yorke's. 'I had nothing to do with it.'

'You'd have motive. More than anyone else seems to have.'

'That man killed Danielle, yes. I have to wake up to the fact every morning, but this child had nothing to do with that. Additionally, there would be nothing to gain by it – this boy does not have any contact with Thomas Ray.'

'And how would you know that?'

Harry narrowed his eyes. 'I spoke to his parents after the trial. They tried to apologise on his behalf, said they would be having nothing to do with him anymore. They were convincing.'

Yorke nodded.

Harry gazed up at the black rafters for a moment. Yorke looked too, wondering how on earth they had managed to last so long.

'Every day I wonder what things would have been like if she'd not gone to that bastard's farm that day. We were having IVF – trying for a baby, you know?'

'I know.'

He took another gulp of his pint. 'Is this case connected to Thomas Ray?'

Thomas Ray's death was yet to be released to the news. 'I can't discuss the case with you Harry, you know that. I need to know where you were this morning.'

'I was working. Check with the cab company, they'll give you all the details of my fares.' He sighed. 'You know he's out, don't you? Eight years - that's all he got!'

'I know.'

'Eight years for ruining our lives. It's not enough.'

'It's not enough.'

After another sigh, Harry looked around the pub. 'You know seven hundred years ago this place would have been rowdy as hell. Cathedral craftsmen, fighting and gambling. In the fourteenth century, it was a brothel with a secret tunnel for clergymen to move between St. Thomas's church and the tavern. Uncivilised, but it's no different now really, we still haven't moved on.'

'I disagree. What happened to Danielle was unthinkable. But I still disagree. We have to make these occurrences less commonplace, and more often than not, we succeed, and we have to succeed in the *right way*.'

'The right way,' Harry said. 'Guess I know where you're going with this one.'

Yorke didn't reply.

Harry slid a card across the table. 'My company. Phone them to check. I worked all day from eight AM.'

Yorke pushed it back. 'Keep it for the station. I'm going to have you officially interviewed by someone else rather than me.'

Even if Harry's alibi ruled him out of the kidnapping, there was still the hideous murder of Thomas Ray to consider.

'Have you been in touch with Thomas Ray since his release?'

Harry stared at him. 'No.'

There'd been a pause as Harry thought. Yorke felt his body stiffen. 'Or while he was inside?'

'*No.*'

'So, you've not reacted in any way to his early release? No phone call, angry letter, nothing?'

'It was a compassionate release. He's dying, what revenge could I possibly have?'

'Still, if I put myself in your shoes, I would struggle to stay so calm. Go to work, drink a pint. As we said before, eight years is *not enough*.'

Harry reached behind himself and tapped the lit glass container. Inside was a mummified hand. It had belonged to a whist player who'd paid a high price for cheating. 'You know already Mike that this pub is haunted; disappearances and reappearances of that hand have bothered the bar staff for hundreds of years. Back after it happened, I used to sit here most nights wondering, *hoping,* that I might suddenly disappear like this hand. The idea didn't bother me, and I remember thinking that it wouldn't bother anyone else either. Now, I can honestly say, I don't want that to happen. I've met someone else and I'm happy. Why would I put everything in jeopardy by getting involved with the Rays again?'

'It'll be in the press tomorrow morning so I'll tell you anyway, Thomas Ray has been murdered.'

Harry's eyes widened. 'Shit.' He looked at the table, deep in thought, shaking his head from side to side. Then, with a trembling hand, he finished his pint in two gulps. 'It wasn't me.'

'We need to go—'

'How was he killed?'

'I can't tell you that.'

'I've been nowhere near him, Mike, believe me. When was he killed?'

'Days ago. Come on Harry. It's time to go.'

IN THE CAR, Yorke took a call on his mobile phone from Topham. He didn't run it through the handsfree because Harry was in the passenger's seat.

'SOCOs have discovered more evidence at the farmhouse.'

'Go on.'

'Are you sitting down?'

'Driving.' He looked across at Harry who was looking back at him curiously and wondered whether to tell Topham he was in the car with him. He didn't.

'They found a letter to Thomas Ray, dated over a month ago. It's from Harry.'

Yorke felt the blood rush to his head. 'Shit — what does it say?'

'It's not long. He goes into detail about how Ray ruined his life and finishes up with a few cold comments about how he's glad he's dying, and he hopes he experiences as much pain as he inflicted on him.'

'Okay, could you e-mail me a copy?'

'Yes.'

He hung up and dropped his phone onto his lap. 'You sent him a letter, Harry.'

Harry looked down.

'Lying to me ... again,' Yorke said, tightening his grip on the steering wheel.

'I didn't think it was relevant.'

'Bollocks. I should have had you hauled straight in.'

'Ah, crap, Mike, I wrote that fucking letter years ago, but they'd never have let me send it to him while he was inside. So, I sent it when he was released.'

'There's the motive. Signed, sealed and delivered.'

'I know it doesn't look good, but it was a parting shot, that was all. He was dying anyway; why risk my own freedom by killing him?'

'A good lawyer could argue that you probably felt it was your right to take his life, rather than the cancer.'

Harry sighed as they pulled into the station. Yorke turned and stared. 'Are there any more surprises?'

'No.'

Yorke continued to stare.

'No, Mike, *honestly*.'

PAUL RAY OPENED his eyes and saw that he was lying on his side by a camping lamp. Remembering where he was, he bolted up into a seating position, and gasped for air.

Someone was here ...

His eyes focused. It was Martha. Sitting cross-legged with the cattle-prod on her lap.

'You don't snore like Mother, she makes a racket.' She flashed Paul a huge smile; her white teeth glowed in the lamplight like angel's wings.

'You have to let me out of here.' His voice was weak, so he cleared his throat and repeated the plea. 'It makes me sad that you didn't eat the food earlier,' she said, pointing into the darkness where he'd thrown the dog bowl.

He looked in the direction she was pointing. The pig, which had woken him earlier, stood barely two metres away in the shadows, staring at him with eyes like burnt wood.

'Don't worry,' Martha said. 'It's just interested, we don't get many visitors.'

'I want to go home, it's so cold in here and I'm starving.'

'Well, Mother would have said you were cutting your nose off to spite your face by throwing that food away. I know that Mother and Lewis want you to stay. If you stop doing all those bad things, I'll try and get you more food. Mother still doesn't know about the last food I took, I went into the kitchen, all quiet.' She smiled, and started to whisper. 'If she knew, I wouldn't be allowed back in ... are you crying?'

'Why are you doing this?'

The girl lifted the cattle prod. 'Mother is always sad. It's been worse since she got sick. The best thing to do when she's sad is to leave her alone. Would you like me to leave you alone?'

He raised his voice and clenched his fists. 'I just want to go home!'

'If you shout, Mother will come in and you won't want that. Can you stop being mad? If you can, I'll stay and we can be friends.'

There was an unbearable burning itch on his thighs. He tugged at his trousers, which had been glued to his skin by dried piss, and groaned. Tightening her grip on the prod, Martha said, 'You want to touchy feel yourself!' Her eyes widened and she ignited the spark at the end of the cattle prod.

'I wet myself earlier. It itches—'

'You dirty boy!'

She thrust the prod toward him.

'Please,' Paul said, leaning back and raising his hands to shield himself. 'I meant nothing by it.'

He could feel his heart about to burst from his chest, but he knew that he had to think. He was reasoning with someone very different to him. There were students at his school with severe special needs, some even went into different classrooms, but he'd never met anyone quite like this. Not only was she childlike, but she seemed like she'd come from a different world altogether.

He needed to understand her world, tell her what she wanted to hear. 'I don't want to do bad things anymore. I want to be your friend.'

Her eyes narrowed, there was a moment of silence and then she started to lower the prod. 'Really?'

'I was going to eat your mother's food, it looked so nice. But one of the pigs came too close, and I got scared, so I threw the bowl at it.'

The spark died; then, smiling, she placed the prod back on her lap. 'That's okay, there's plenty more. Mother always cooks and I help. She says I'm the best pair of legs she's ever had. She's in a wheelchair, you know. I'm Martha by the way. My Mother calls me Barfa Martha because I used to get sick loads when I was a baby.' She blushed. 'I can't wait to tell Cuddles about you.'

'Cuddles?'

'Cuddles is my hamster. Hopefully you can meet soon.'

Paul looked at the cattle prod in her hand. His dad had once told him that they packed about eight hundred volts, which would give you a nasty shock, but wouldn't actually kill you. Maybe, he should just tackle her. If he won, he'd be away. If he lost, he'd probably just wet himself again. However, there was the risk it could also draw Martha's mother and Lewis in to hurt him.

Lewis ...

Would he really hurt me? He couldn't believe it, but ... *how else did I get here?* It must have been him.

He didn't know what to do, but he did know he needed to focus and think. *God, I've never wanted Mum and Dad so much in my whole life.*

'Do you have any pets?'

'No.'

'I should try and sneak Cuddles in here so you can meet him.'

Was he dreaming? The whole situation seemed to be getting crazier.

'Mother has an illness called MS, she can't walk so well anymore. I push her everywhere. Sometimes I sing to her. Round and round the garden like a teddy bear, one step, two steps, tickle you...' She blushed again. 'Mother used to sing that to me all the time. She can also make yummy scrummy food.'

Paul tried to think what Doctor Who would do in this

situation. He wouldn't succumb to fear and despair that was for sure. Knowing him, he would probably enjoy it. He would definitely be trying to work things out – find out what and who he was up against. 'How did you meet Lewis?'

She put her hand over her mouth and shook her head.

'I don't understand.'

She pulled her hand away. 'I'm not allowed to talk about Lewis.'

'My father will find me you know, and when he does, you'll all get into trouble—'

The barn door burst open and an ice cold wind surged in.

'*Shush,*' Martha said. 'It might be Lewis. We're not supposed to be talking.'

The barn door slammed shut. Paul took a deep breath and held it. His heart thumped painfully in his chest.

'Martha, come out, you've been in here with this little runt long enough.' The voice rasped and gurgled like a very old woman's.

'It's Mother, I have to go.'

Paul heard a squeaking noise like an old shopping trolley being pushed.

'Don't go, you can't leave me alone again.'

The squeaking grew louder.

'I have to, sorry.' She rose to her feet, still holding the prod.

A wheelchair rolled out of the dark. A tiny old woman, covered in a blanket, stared at him from the chair. Her shrivelled face reminded Paul of the old apples that rotted beneath the tree at the bottom of their garden. His first thought was that this must really be Martha's grandmother.

Unless, and he shuddered at the thought, Martha had been stolen from her real parents?

'You've been told already, not to make friends with the pigs,' Martha's mother said.

'Sorry, Mother.'

'Do you remember why?'

'Yes.'

'Tell me.'

'Because it's sad when they die and you have to eat them,' Martha said more quickly than she'd said anything up until this point.

The old woman smiled; most of her teeth were gone. 'Go Martha.'

Martha mouthed 'bye' to Paul, before turning and scurrying out of the barn.

Paul, sweating all over, watched the old woman turn slowly in her wheelchair to follow her daughter. The ancient contraption crawled back toward the door.

Be brave, thought Paul, *this may be your only chance to get out of here. The Doctor wouldn't just sit here, he'd push her from the chair. She must weigh next to nothing.*

He surprised himself by rising to his feet and moving forward. *You have to, you have no choice, just remember to be ready for Martha and that prod when you reach the door...*

The chair spun back. Paul froze. The old woman stared at him again. There was a darkness in her eyes he'd never seen before. He took several steps backward, feeling the energy drain from his body.

'That's it, little Ray. Be still.'

She turned her chair back and followed her daughter out of the barn door. Paul wanted to follow, but slumped to his knees instead.

In the incident room in Devizes, Yorke drank a cup of coffee in two mouthfuls; then, with a ruler, he pointed at the enlarged map of Tesco and its immediate area. DI Emma Gardner, DS Iain Brookes, DS Jake Pettman, DC Collette Willows, PC Sean Tyler, incident room manager DI Mark Topham and Jeremy Dawson from HOLMES all stared up at him.

'Let's go through this one last time. Then, Iain and Jake, you must return to Salisbury and check all tomorrow's officers are fully briefed.'

Jake nodded. Brookes doodled on a notepad in front of him.

'If he drives, he will come off the main roundabout here.' He traced the route with the end of the ruler. 'Then immediately right at the small roundabout, past the petrol station and into the car park, where he will be hemmed in. The only way out is the same way by the petrol station or here.' He ran the ruler over the bollards and bushes lining the side of the car park. 'Dukes of Hazard style.'

They all looked down at the copies of the maps on their tables and then looked back up.

'And, if he does opt for the bollards and bushes, we will have him covered with unmarked cars here and here.' He tapped two roads opposite the car park. 'I will be in one car with Jake. Mark and Hanna Miles will be in the other.'

'If he should come in by foot here.' He tapped the Park and Ride stop to the left of the store. 'We will have foot patrol waiting for him, led by Emma.'

He paused for Gardner's acknowledgement. She crunched a tic tac before nodding.

'Tyler and several other officers will be hovering, plain-clothed, around the store, in case he makes a run for it. Iain will be parked alone by the cashpoint and the bin where the kidnapper wants the money dropped.'

'I have decided that Collette will be driving Sarah Ray's car and leaving the money. It is my opinion that Sarah is not psychologically fit enough for the task. She has not been made aware of this yet. FLO Bryan Kelly will be breaking the news to her later. We will endeavour to make Collette look as much like Sarah Ray as possible.'

Brookes stopped doodling and looked up. 'Do you really think he will show up? He knows we'll block the exit if he drives in by the petrol station. He also knows that we'll be all over the Park and Ride.'

'He might trust Joe and Sarah not to get the police involved,' Gardner said, but her expression suggested she didn't believe this.

'Why would he have kidnapped the boy in the most public place imaginable and left all that blood if he didn't want us involved?' Topham said.

Gardner nodded and sighed. 'Why is nothing ever simple?'

Yorke said, 'Would there be any point being a copper if it was?'

THE COLD, dark night was laced with possibility and it was the only blanket Lacey needed, preferring to leave the stifling, claustrophobic duvet to the snoring meat sack beside her.

Earlier, she'd found sexual satisfaction in Phil Holmes. She'd handcuffed, hit, choked and finally, fucked him. It'd been all about her.

Lights from a parking car broke through the windows of her Spire View apartment, and swept over her body. Her nipples were sharp, and her diamond encrusted belly-button ring sparkled.

You're a lucky man, Phil. She smiled. *I just don't have time right now and I'll be gone in a few days.*

There was a buzzing sound. A fly hovered next to her face.

You're defying the usual. It's far too cold for you to survive.

The world was made up of patterns, and she'd always prided herself on her ability to manipulate these to her will; however, she did enjoy the occasional surprise. *Everyone needs challenge.*

She looked at the huge man beside her. *If I had longer, and the police weren't hunting my nephew, there would have been no surprises with you. Everything would have run smoothly.*

There was a lot to be said about everything running smoothly.

Phil would have been a perfect fit for the Blue Room. She'd not seen it before at the station, or even on their date, but she'd spotted it in her bedroom. Yes, their first romp had been all about her, but during the second romp his aggression had reared its beautiful head, and although it wasn't satisfying sexually, *could never be so for her,* it meant that he would have settled well into the Blue Room, and that would have been satisfying in so many other ways.

Jake, on the other hand, was not a perfect fit — there wasn't enough aggression in him. Yet, if she'd possessed both the time and anonymity to pursue the man who'd irritated her right through to her bones, she would have embraced the challenge, and succeeded.

I could have stoked your feeble fire, Jake, until it raged like an inferno!

The night passed, but she didn't sleep; content to bathe in visualisations. When the sun eventually came up and her blanket of darkness was replaced by a bloody glow, unusual for this time of year, she leaned over her new lover and stared at him until he woke up. 'You're pathetic, do you know that?'

'Why?'

'Because you've spent all night in bed with me and you've only screwed me twice.'

She spat in his face. With wide eyes and gritted teeth, he bolted up and wiped his cheek with the back of his hand.

'What you waiting for?' she said. 'Stop being pathetic.'

He pounced.

She heard the fly land on the pillow next to her ear; the buzzing sound grew quieter and quieter until it stopped. She suspected it died. Patterns always won out in the end.

Phil's movements were quick, his touch rough. She smiled.

8

EVERYONE HAD BEEN careful getting into position and had arrived one by one over the past two hours, just in case the kidnapper had the area under surveillance.

Yorke and Jake were sitting in an unmarked car on Dairy Meadow Lane, the first road off Bourne Way, and opposite the entrance to Tesco's petrol station and car park. When, and if, the kidnapper went into the car park, Yorke would be able to block off his main escape route.

Further along Bourne Way, Topham and DC Hanna Miles waited on Hatches Lane, exactly opposite the Tesco store, in case the kidnapper ploughed his vehicle through the bushes lining the car park.

On the opposite side of the Tesco car park was the Park and Ride stop. There was the possibility that the kidnapper could use that route and approach on foot, so Gardner and several other officers were stationed there.

DS Iain Brookes had parked in a disabled spot near the RBS cashpoint and the bin targeted for the drop. Tyler and several other plain clothed officers were hovering around the area on foot ready for the kidnapper, should he try to run.

Contrary to the weather forecast, it hadn't snowed all night and during a cloudless morning the sun had seized a rare opportunity to blaze through the bleak surroundings; consequently, the roads were much safer, and therefore, busier, than Yorke had anticipated.

Jake's eyes were closed with his head against the glass.

'I've told you already,' Yorke said. 'You need to buy a decent bed for your spare room, no human being can sleep on a sofa bed for this long.'

'And I've told you already, it's only temporary.'

'I remember, but this temporary situation is starting to feel a lot more like a permanent one, and I need you more alert than this. Get bed shopping.'

'So sympathetic, sir, thanks for your help. You know, most people aim to solve the cause of the marital dispute, rather than focusing on making the problem more manageable by buying a comfier bed.'

'Why are you having so many problems anyway?' Yorke said, taking a mouthful of cold coffee.

'Hormones.'

Yorke smiled. 'She's your wife, not your teenage daughter. Besides you're the one who guzzles growth cocktails, are you sure it's not your hormones?'

'Very funny. She worries about me while I'm working. She listens to the news too much.'

Yorke looked at the clock on the dashboard and saw that it was five to two. He spoke into his handsfree. 'Five minutes till the drop, are we all ready?'

He received a series of affirmations through his earpiece.

When the clock on the dash changed to one fifty-eight,

Yorke caught the glint of silver and saw the BMW Coupe negotiating the roundabout. He spoke into his handsfree, 'Collette's here'.

The BMW slid down Bourne Way, passed right in front of Yorke and Jake. Yorke saw that Willows was wearing a jet black wig, and the dark frock Sarah had been wearing in the school yesterday. They were both broad women and Willows had pulled it off remarkably well.

'Dead ringer,' Jake said.

'You know, that's just what I was thinking.'

She indicated right and turned into the car park entrance, she passed the petrol station and a line of traffic queuing both to get into the petrol station and to get back out onto Bourne Way. If the kidnapper did show up and try to get out this way, he'd have to get around that long queue.

It was an absolutely ridiculous place to choose a drop and not worthy of someone who'd pulled off the feat of staging a bloody crime scene and then smuggling a twelve-year old boy out of the school unnoticed.

Yorke watched her crawl into the Tesco car park and disappear into the swell of metal-housed consumers. Jake was wide-eyed – any indication that he had missed a night's sleep long gone. Yorke chewed his bottom lip as he waited for one of the other officers to report a sighting. He felt like he was observing the beginnings of a dangerous storm from a safe enclosure, wanting desperately to rescue those out there, but knowing there was nothing that could be done.

Brookes said, 'Our Sarah Ray clone is parking three spaces from me. Badly, I might add.'

Willows could hear the conversation through her earpiece but was not wearing a handsfree to communicate. Jake came to her defence with humour. 'Part of her cover.'

Yorke said, 'Everyone focus. Sean, keep as close as you can without being spotted.'

There was no reply; communication with Tyler was also one-way.

Brookes said, 'Okay, she's parked.'

Yorke chewed on a fingernail. Jake opened his window to let some air in.

Brookes said, 'She's getting out of the car with the paper bag ... she's dropped it into the bin. A couple of kids on skateboards are watching her.'

'Why?' Topham said.

'Dunno. Sean keep an eye on them.'

Yorke had moved onto another nail. There was the sound of interference over the airwaves, followed by Gardner, 'A group of people just got off the Park and Ride, I'll keep an eye on them.'

'Nothing here yet,' Yorke said.

'She's already on her way back to her car,' Brookes said.

'Anyone moving for the bag?' Yorke said.

'No, not yet ... wait ... no, no, *no* ... one of the kids is going for the bin. Maybe, Sean should move now.'

Yorke's mind was racing, and his heart, desperate not to be left behind, began to speed up. 'No. If it's not the actual kidnapper, we have to use the tracker to follow the money back—'

'Don't worry, false alarm,' Brookes said. 'He's just throwing his gum into the bin.'

Yorke sighed. Jake looked at him and said, 'I always assumed the youth of today just chucked it on the floor.'

'You're always stereotyping. Maybe we have a skater here with a Blue Peter badge.'

Someone bashed their horn and Yorke's eyes darted to a dirty white transit van tearing around the roundabout to their right. He read the license plate as it thundered onto Bourne Way, it was the one on the Sapphire restaurant's CCTV footage. 'The van signed out to Thomas Ray is here.'

The van screamed past them. A bearded man wearing a beanie hat took a sharp right into the car park entrance.

'I can't believe it,' Jake said. 'He came.'

'Driving like that, I'm surprised he survived the journey.'

The van rallied past the queue, spraying snow from the gutter. After vanishing into the car park, Yorke started the Lexus.

Seconds later, Brookes' voice surged through the ear-piece. 'The nutcase is not even bothering to park, he's pulled up right alongside the bin and the cashpoints.'

'If it's him, make the grab.'

'He's out of the van now. Guy looks like shit. Long dirty jacket and boots, beanie, unshaven. He's way too thin to be the man on the CCTV footage.'

'Shit,' Yorke said.

'Is he definitely alone?' Topham said.

'Someone could be in the back of the van. He's in the bin already ... he's got the paper bag. He's looking in the bag, now he's ... oh shit, one of the skater kids is coming back over—'

Yorke heard Jake swallow.

'The kid is asking the man something. He doesn't want to answer and is turning away and now ... shit the bed! The kid is making a grab for the bag.'

Yorke felt his blood run cold.

'What was that you were saying about stereotyping?' Jake said.

Brookes said, 'The bag's torn ... the money is on the floor.'

Yorke put his hands on his head.

JOE RAY's pulse danced like the wild sparks springing from the logs on the fire.

He glanced at his watch. It would be about now that the kidnapper would be wrapping his pig blood stinking fingers around his money. Not that the money mattered too much right now; he'd have given this idiot everything to have his son back.

FLO Bryan Kelly had taken Sarah to visit her mother to try and keep her calm during the drop. At the time, he welcomed the opportunity of a break from Sarah; now, he realised, he felt lonely. He stood up and paced the living room until he stood at the foot of the spindly rocking chair by the patio doors.

A family heirloom, Sarah would say whenever Paul would rock in it too hard, *treat it well, might be worth something one day*.

Pig farm used to be full of them, Joe would say in defence of his son, *they'd burn them on the fire once they'd worn out and winter had turned their farm into an ice-rink.*

He never said: *my grandparents had rocked in them eating local children off plates on their laps and my Uncle Thomas had been rocking in his when he blew that pretty nurse to bits.*

He shoved the chair as hard as he could. It was unbelievably heavy, but he managed to topple it. Despite landing on the parquet floor with a thud, it didn't crack. He felt like kicking it, but thought better of it, he had no shoes on. Maybe, he should just take it outside and burn it.

I've worked my whole bloody life to bury my family's reputation, and then some bastard has the audacity to walk into my life, grab my kid, steal the fruits of my hard labour and no doubt turn my family name to mud again.

'I hope they've got the bastard already,' he said.

Tap-tap.

He froze. The patio doors ...

Tap-tap.

He turned slowly to look and his blood ran cold; someone was standing there.

His hand flew to his mouth and he took a step back. A scream rose in his throat; yet, he suppressed it just in time. He'd been fooled! Drizzle had taken the layer of snow from the convex top of his barbecue, making it look like a snowman wearing a black helmet.

He made straight for the drinks cabinet beside the sofa, and poured himself a glass of bourbon with trembling hands. After two gulps, he waited for the sudden anxiety to dissipate, then topped it back up and sat down on the sofa.

He thought about all the lies he'd told Sarah over the years and how often she'd forgiven him. He took another mouthful. If anything happened to Paul today that well of forgiveness would run dry and then he truly would be alone.

Tap-tap.

Instinctively, his eyes were drawn outside again. Nothing but a snowman shaped barbecue, frozen grass and a frosty swing.

What was it? Hail?

He scanned the room as if the answer for the strange tapping somehow lay within it. His eyes drifted over the

Persian rug on the floor, lingered on the Christmas tree for a moment, wandered over a pile of Sarah's knitting on the sofa, before again, finding the glass in his hands. He finished his drink.

His thoughts turned to his sister. She'd always been this way. Insulting him, hurting him, *abusing* him.

When he was ten, she'd made him undress in front of her teenage friends, so they could laugh at him. The memory was more vivid than his own wedding day, even more so than the birth of his own child.

They'd all teased him, made him hard, and when he'd tried to touch them, they'd slapped him in the face, laughed and pointed.

He thought about the two women he'd been sleeping with this last year. He felt himself growing excited and felt ashamed —his son's life was in danger for fuck's sake—

Tap-tap.

This time something really was there. The glass slipped from his fingertips, smashing on the parquet floor beside the rug.

The huge man from the video, still wearing his pig's face and bloody apron, was staring in at him from the garden, tapping his finger on one of the patio doors. Rooted to the sofa, Joe's eyes widened as the twisted bastard ran his fingers down over the glass, leaving long, red smears. Then, he rubbed at his nose and part of the rotten snout broke away. His stomach churned.

While springing to his feet to make for the lounge door, he turned awkwardly; he crashed down and his head bounced off the edge of the coffee table.

Rolling onto his back, clutching his forehead, he turned to look outside. Pig-man was gone, yet the smears remained – he'd not imagined it. Time to get out of here. After sitting up on the rug, he managed to ease himself back to his feet using the sofa for support.

Outside of the lounge, he stumbled down the hall-way. For over twenty-four hours, he'd been anxious, and last night, he hadn't slept a wink, add to that the fact that he was half-pissed. It could be possible that his eyes were playing tricks on him, that he was having flashbacks to the horrendous e-mail. Colliding with the wall as he fled, he dislodged the framed picture of his show-jumping exploits; it smashed on the floor behind him.

He jerked open the front door. The sun had retreated behind the clouds and his automatic lights threw an orange pool onto the snow-covered porch. Pig-man moved into the light, hunching slightly, almost submissively, like a begging animal. He hung his head forward, revealing the torn jagged skin where the pig's face had been sawn away and had been threaded with straps. Part of the bastard's greasy black hair glimmered in the lights.

'Who are you?' Joe said.

Pig-man looked up. 'Nice house, Joe.'

White eyes, intense as if they'd been chipped from bone, darted back and forth from behind the mask.

'Where's my son? I want him back.'

'You've always had what you've wanted, Joe, haven't you?'

'I don't know what you're talking about—'

'You're greedy.' He lifted a meat hook, turning it lengthways, so it looked like a menacing grin. The hook flashed.

'Greedy as a pig.'

For a while, Brookes' voice had been coming like surges of high voltage electricity; now, it was like the constant buzz of a faulty plug.

'The skater kid is grabbing the bag of money ... his friends are walking over ... our man realises he's in danger and is starting to retreat back to his van, *without* the bag of money and the tracker.'

Yorke said, 'Grab him now Sean, and get some of the officers to stop those kids before they get off with the money.'

Brooke took a moment to reply. 'Christ, this is sick. The guy's dragged a blood soaked potato sack out of the van and slung it on the ground. Someone please tell me it's not the kid in there.'

Yorke looked at Jake, who stared back, wide-eyed. 'So, does Sean have him?' he said into his handsfree.

'Almost ... shit ... this wiry bastard is quick ... he's in the van ... Sean has hold of the door ...'

Gardner joined in the dialogue from the Park and Ride. 'We're coming to assist.'

Yorke listened to Gardner wheezing as she ran.

'Tell me Sean's got the door open,' Topham said.

No answer.

'Iain, what's *happening?*' Yorke said.

'Sorry, the doors locked, Sean can't get in. Shit, he's fallen. Christ, Mark, he's driving right for you—'

'Fuck me,' Topham said.

There was an explosion of green, and Yorke watched open mouthed as the white transit burst from the bushes lining the car park. Amplified through his ear-piece, the ambush sounded like it came from a large primordial creature. The van turned sharply left, before it could demolish Topham's unmarked car on the narrow road directly opposite the bush.

'You okay?' Yorke said.

'Yes, he's coming your way,' Topham said.

Yorke considered moving out and blocking, but the van was accelerating quickly, and it could be a suicide mission. Instead, he paused for the van to pass and then shot out onto Bourne Way in pursuit.

'We'll block him off at the main roundabout,' Topham said.

Yorke jammed his foot down, tearing over the roundabout the van had already cleared. Irate drivers bashed horns, but remained composed enough not to get in the way.

'Not sure I'm going to enjoy this,' Jake said.

With no snow falling, visibility was good, but there was only one lane at this part of the A36, and it had been narrowed significantly by the build-up of snow at the sides of it. It was imperative that Yorke kept the Lexus as straight as an arrow; one false swerve and they would be spinning to a possible death.

Ahead, the van clattered into the bumper of the car in front of it leaving the terrorised driver little choice but to swerve off the road into a car park on the left. Three stores received a sudden influx of customers at terrifying velocities. One Mini took out a trolley of alcohol beside an off-licence; split cans sprayed beer in the air like tiny geysers.

'Not long until the roundabout at the end of the A36, Mark. Update?'

'We have a couple of cars and a bike. ETA, 35 seconds,' Topham said. 'Do you think there is more than one kidnapper?'

'Either that, or he could have sent this man to divert us.'

'Divert us from what?'

The words "In the Blood" suddenly shot through Yorke's head. 'Get someone to Joe and Sarah Ray immediately.'

'Okay, you don't think—'

'I'm not sure what to think right now, Mark, *just do it!*'

He tensed both hands on the wheel as he dinked the van's bumper.

'Brace yourself,' he said to Jake, and thrust even harder this time, jolting both of them forward.

'Easy tiger,' Jake said. 'That's not going to make him stop.'

The A36 divided, and the van driver flipped lanes, weaving around the other vehicles like a race car in a computer game.

Brookes' voice came through his ear-piece. 'Good news on the skaters, we retrieved the money.'

'What about the sack?' Yorke said.

'Emma and I are going to take a look now.'

Yorke fired up the flashing blue lights on the front grille. The accompanying two-toned siren always charged him with adrenaline: he streaked around a Toyota, an Audi and then rammed into the back of the van again, bringing another mutter of disapproval from Jake. Then, the van's brake lights glowed; a car in front of it must have slowed. The van zipped to the other lane, leaving Yorke to pound his own brakes to avoid hitting a braking Ford. He screeched into the other lane without checking his mirrors, praying that the traffic behind them had slowed to a crawl to avoid the battle.

Realising he was seconds from the roundabout that led onto the major ring road, he said, 'Mark have you got both directions completely covered if we fail to stop him at the roundabout?"

'Yes, sir,' Topham said. 'We have vehicles at New Bridge Road roundabout, and then others at the Churchill Way one.'

'Good.'

'Which way do you think he'll go?' Jake said.

'Left, I hope,' Yorke said. 'Because then there's nowhere for him to turn off before we get him at the next roundabout. Right, he could swerve off into town. We'll still get him, but there's bound to be damage that way and the last thing I want to deal with right now is a dead pedestrian.'

At the roundabout, the van driver opted for the right turn and was half-way round, when Yorke saw the police-bike burst onto the roundabout. The biker tried to align himself alongside the van.

'He's confident,' Jake said.

The biker thumped the van driver's door several times. Inevitably, the driver swerved and there was a shower of sparks as both the bike and the man danced along the concrete. Then, the van exited.

Yorke careered over the roundabout. 'Stay on the ring road, you dickhead.'

Despite the two tone, Yorke could hear the throbbing of a helicopter descending from the clouds.

On the ring road, the van continued to weave around traffic, sideswiping cars, clipping wing mirrors, and Yorke's Lexus crunched through the debris left in its wake. A hefty bill would be finding its way to the Wiltshire police force. Houses loomed over the ring road, everyone was crammed in together like an upmarket version of a Brazilian slum.

Yorke's speedometer danced around eighty. He showed the back of the van his bumper again;

unfortunately, the van also showed its brake lights again and swerved, leaving Yorke hurtling toward a Saxo. He stabbed the pedal. A cry came from Jake as the front wheels locked, and they skidded almost ninety degrees toward a snowy covered barrier. Yorke gagged on the impact of sudden fear.

From the corner of his eye, Yorke saw the van taking a hard left as, unbelievably, the barrier ended, sparing their lives and, with a stroke of good fortune, leaving them facing the right direction to continue chasing the van. Back in control, he accelerated, caught the transit up and breathed in his quarry's diesel fumes.

He could hear sirens raging all around. The idiot was heading into a multi-story car park. *What the hell was he doing?*

'We're following the suspect into the multi-story car park, first left off the ring road.'

'Okay, back-up will follow you in,' Topham said. 'I'm with Iain now; he's throwing up. We've opened the sack. It's disgusting—'

The white van hit the barrier head on like a homing missile and wood rained down on Yorke's windscreen.

IT'D BEEN a long time since anyone had asked Lacey Ray what her brother Joe was like, but when she was younger, she'd always described him in the same way:

Weak.

She probably should have used more than one word, but there'd never seemed much point, not when the man was only worth one.

Yesterday, she'd detected an aggressive tone in his voice;

so, today, she considered it essential that she cast an eye over Joe's treatment of Sarah.

Despite it still being quite early, it was very cloudy overhead, and the porch was bathed in an artificial orange light. She walked up the drive towards it and saw that the door was ajar. When she reached it, she pushed the door open slightly and said, 'Hello? Joe? Sarah?'

She waited. No answer. She caught a familiar citrusy tang in the air.

Blood?

She pushed the door open fully. One of the show-jumping pictures was smashed on the floor.

A struggle?

She knelt down at the doorstep and stared at some droplets of blood. She then stood up and moved down the corridor, stepping over the smashed picture along the way. The smell intensified.

Are you in trouble Joe?

He always was such a needy little mummy's boy. A weakling who'd still been suckling on her at six.

'Joe? Sarah?'

She entered the sitting room and noticed the crystal glass smashed on the parquet floor.

Have you collapsed somewhere drunk, perhaps? Split your head open?

The drink had always been a weakness of Joe's – as had the shagging.

She'd learned all about men's flaws from Joe; she'd watched them chew him up.

The smell was less pungent here, so she backtracked to the kitchen door. She held her breath when she pushed it open.

On the floor was a pool of blood; ruby red, peaceful and

still. The joins between the tiles glowed dark, like thick veins, and made the pool look like an organism.

Bled dry?

She read what was scrawled on the window above the sink: *In the Blood.*

She looked back down. *Something in this blood?*

She couldn't see anything floating in the pool.

Unless, was it metaphoric? A reference to our blood, our family?

She reached into her pocket for her phone and phoned Jake.

As soon as the phone was answered, she said, 'Jake?'

'Sorry, he accidently left his personal mobile at home. Can I help you?' Sheila said.

'Hello Sheila, it's Lacey, I need to speak to Jake urgently.'

A moment of silence. 'What do you want? How do you have Jake's personal number?'

'Someone's dead.'

'What are you talking about?'

'My brother has been murdered.'

'Well, you need to phone the police, Jake is *not* here.'

'You're still feisty then?'

'What? I'm hanging up now—'

'Does he still mention me?'

'No, of course not? Why would he?'

'We have history you see. There's lots to tell.'

She hung up, phoned the police station, gave her name to the woman who answered and asked to be put through to Jake's work mobile. 'It's an emergency, I have important information regarding the case—'

'What information?' the woman said.

'I'll only talk to Jake.'

It was over a minute before she heard Jake's voice. 'Hello,' Jake said; he sounded breathless. 'It's a bad time, this better be important.'

'It is. I'm at my brother's house; there's blood everywhere.'

She listened to him tell his partner.

'Okay, Lacey, wait outside for response to get there.'

Lacey could hear the sounds of screeching tyres. 'I also have a confession to make.'

'What?'

'I just phoned your personal mobile and Sheila answered.'

'Shit, Lacey! What did she say?'

'Not much, but it does concern me that she has such anger issues.'

'APPARENTLY, there is blood everywhere, Lacey Ray just called it in from the cottage,' Yorke said into his handsfree.

'Response is seconds away,' Topham said.

With sweat running into his eyes, Yorke tore up the multi-story levels, while Jake shouted into his mobile phone. 'You need to stay away from me and stay away from my wife.'

As Yorke curved the Lexus up to the third level, the smell of burning rubber filled the air.

'I'm not threatening you,' Jake said.

The parked cars alongside him melded into a psychedelic blur. He went into the next turn, stabbing the brake pedal. The car squealed.

'I can't meet with you; I *don't* want to meet with you!'

On the fourth floor, Yorke saw people pressed against

the sides of their cars, wide eyed. He could only imagine their fear; roaring diesel engines, echoing in a confined space, must have sounded like a tsunami rushing in. Yorke struck out left to get a deeper turn to reach the fifth level.

'Lacey? You there? ... stupid woman!' He slipped his phone back into his pocket.

Setting himself a new personal best, Yorke took the corner at over twenty miles per hour. Concrete gnawed into the side of the car and sparks spiralled like fireflies.

'Christ!' Jake said.

'Iain,' Yorke said. 'You still haven't updated me on the sack, tell me the kid wasn't in it.'

'He wasn't. It was a pig's carcass,' Brookes said.

'Nice,' Jake said.

'There's too many games going on here,' Yorke said.

Snow piles covered the top level like mole hills and some idiot had built a snowman right at the top of the ramp. Unable to avoid hitting and dismembering it, Yorke slowed as the windscreen wipers dealt with the snowy body parts. After restoring visibility, he realised, with a sudden tightening in his stomach, that the van was no longer ahead of him. Only four snow covered parked cars, and beyond that, an aging barrier.

'What the ... ?' He said, slowing down to a halt, ten metres from the edge, parallel with the parked cars. From behind them, up the ramp, came the deep rumble of a diesel engine. 'The bastard tricked us.' His mouth fell open at the sight of the oncoming van in the rear-view mirror.

The impact was massive. The coffee cup flew from its holder, bounced off the dashboard and fell at Jake's feet. Yorke stared at the beanie-wearing junkie through the rear-view mirror as the Lexus was thrust toward the edge.

'Sir, do something!'

Yorke did all he could – he yanked the handbrake, and stamped on the foot brake. It slowed them, but the van was too strong and the Lexus clunked as it was shunted forward. If he turned, the van would just drill into the side of them.

Topham's voice crackled in the ear-piece. 'Joe Ray's gone, same MO as last time ...'

'We need to get out of here now,' Jake said, fumbling for his seatbelt clasp. Yorke did the same.

'Blood on the floor, the same words on the wall ...'

There was less than two metres to go, Yorke reached for the handle. 'Get out!'

With the metal barrier so close he could see the smatterings of dead flies, Yorke jerked the handle on the door and hurtled himself sideways. He hit the concrete. The air was bashed out of him. Pain took root in his shoulder, and flowered down his arm.

As he rolled clear, he could still hear Topham. 'The sister, Lacey Ray, was waiting outside.'

The bumper of the Lexus chewed through the old metal barrier like liquorice and disappeared over the edge. The sound of it being crushed by a six-story drop vibrated through the air.

Yorke sat up and stared left, desperate to see Jake, but instead saw only the side of the transit van, which had failed to stop in time, and had left its front wheels dangling over the edge.

Yorke rose to his feet as the transit van door clunked open. The gangly driver peered over the edge at the drop that was about to end his life and then glanced up at Yorke. The back end of the van started to lift.

Yorke held out the palm of his hand. 'Don't move.'

'Help me,' the driver said, showing yellowed teeth and miserable eyes.

Yorke sprinted to the back of the van with his arm stretched out. His fingertips brushed the rising back door handle ...

But then the rear of the van was high in the air and, for a brief moment, time seemed to freeze, leaving the van vertical, waiting to fall, while Yorke listened to his rasping breaths and thumping heart...

... Then it was gone. The man screamed the entire six levels until the smashing and crunching silenced him.

Yorke saw Jake lying on the floor. He ran for the edge and peered over. He could hear Jake behind him shuffling towards him on all fours.

Both vehicles lay side by side, upside down, showing underbellies like overturned woodlice. Steam streamed out of a smashed radiator. Wailing sirens grew louder.

'It's going to take me a long time to get that out of my head,' Jake said.

The thrumming of helicopter blades seemed to synchronise with the beating of Yorke's heart. The first police car arrived on the multi-story roof, burning the white wilderness with flashing blue lights.

'We need to have a talk about Lacey Ray, right now,' Jake said.

'You want to talk about being stalked by your ex seconds after I've just seen my life flash before my eyes?'

'Yes, there's more to this than just stalking me; I think she could be involved with everything going on.'

'And how have you reached that conclusion?' Yorke stared at Jake, suddenly interested.

'The reason that she's my ex. She's just like some of her infamous ancestors. Cold, calculating ...'

'And mad?'

Jake rose to his feet and dusted off the snow. 'Yeah, although I'm afraid this one could be the maddest yet.'

Yorke stared out at Salisbury. It was early afternoon, the sun, having acknowledged it was somewhat out of practice and lacking its usual bite, was retiring, and Salisbury was returning to its white, ghostly self. 'I'll interview her.'

9

AFTER VISITING THE crime scene, submitting a preliminary report on the chase, and grabbing a large Cornish pasty from the bakers, Yorke drove to the local station to interview Lacey Ray.

He took a call from DI Gardner as he parked up. 'Hello Emma.'

'Hi sir, just ringing to let you know we are checking DNA on the driver of the van now.'

He recalled Brookes' gruesome discovery. 'How's Iain?'

'Still throwing up. He actually grabbed hold of the carcasses' bloodied trotter, it left him a little worse for wear.'

'Strange really, you'd have thought the relief that Paul Ray wasn't inside the potato sack would have neutralised any disgust. Do SOCO have anything from the crime scene yet?'

'A bloodied fingerprint on the outside of the patio door.'

'Good, keep me updated. Have you spoken to Bryan?'

'Yes, he took Sarah to her mother's during the drop which is why Joe was alone.'

'What a cock-up. Is he with Sarah now?'

'Yes, at the safe house.'

'Well, he better not move an inch from her side. Did the skaters have any connection?'

'No, it was purely opportunistic. They saw our driver acting suspicious, taking the bag out of the bin and examining it. They wanted to know what was in it.'

'Is all the money accounted for?'

'Yes, how do you think the kidnapper is going to react to the failed drop?'

'I don't know, but I don't think it was ever about the money. He wanted Joe Ray. There's some kind of vendetta going on here.'

'Do you think Sarah is in danger too?'

'Not sure. She's not a Ray by blood so, hopefully, no. I'm at the station, heading in to interview Lacey.'

'Okay, good luck,' Gardner said.

On the way into the station by foot, Yorke wolfed down his Cornish pasty.

SHEILA, wearing the skimpy laser-blue nightslip Jake had bought her last Christmas, gave him the worst look she'd ever given him in their three years of marriage.

'But there's nothing going on!' Jake said.

'Bullshit.' She yanked out a menthol cigarette. Realising she'd broken it; she threw it down on the table and reached for a second.

'Before yesterday, I hadn't seen the crazy woman in years.'

She lit the cigarette. 'Bullshit.' She sucked hard and the end of her cigarette flared.

'It's ten years since we dated! I gave her a lift to the

station from her parents' yesterday and she picked up my fitness card from one of the car pockets – that's how she got my number.'

'Bullshit.' She grunted out a plume of smoke.

Jake scratched at the underneath of the wooden table as if he was trying to claw his way out of a box. It was Sheila's turn to cook, but no food had emerged this evening. He stared over at the fridge.

Sheila launched her burning cigarette at him. He swooped to the left and it sailed over his shoulder. Glancing back, he saw smoke rising from the carpet outside the kitchen door. Seconds later, he was on it, pounding out the threat with his bare foot. 'You're crazier than she is!'

He turned around to see Sheila taking off her wedding ring. 'Here take this as well.' Too many hours with a personal trainer had given her good upper body strength; the ring came like a bullet and clipped his top lip.

He rubbed, but it did nothing to stop the stinging. He almost said, "I nearly died today," but held back – it would have inflamed the situation further. Instead, he said, 'I had an awful day and then this is what I have to put up with?'

'Try telling someone who gives a shit,' she said, flying out of the kitchen and bounding up the stairs. He was sure he felt the foundations of the house tremble.

He shook his head. 'Back to the sofa bed for you Jakey.'

A shame really – she'd looked good in that blue slip.

He jerked open the fridge door, pulled out some wafer thin ham and shoved a handful into his mouth like a Neanderthal. Then, he eyed up the rest of the packet of processed meat. *Where was the harm? It was only wafer-thin.* He finished it off.

His phone rang. 'Sir.'

'How's it going?'

'Just arriving at the station, you?'

'Great. After you almost killed me today, I came home to find my wife on the verge of divorcing me. She's just tried to burn the house down and guess what?'

'What?'

'I'm still on that sofa bed.'

Yorke sighed on behalf of Jake. 'It'll blow over – I'm sure.'

'I'm not.'

'Anyway, Louise Tenor just phoned me. Nothing on the mud samples so far.'

Louise Tenor was a Crime Scene Investigator at head office that many senior officers went to for assistance; diligent, conscientious and above all, brutally honest. If she thought the angle wasn't worth pursuing, she'd let you know.

'Louise was also concerned that some of the samples were either too small, or had been contaminated by other elements; one had been corrupted by oil.'

'I'll speak to my officers, ensure they're more thorough.'

'I want you to go one better than that.'

'Go on.'

'Louise has managed to narrow it down to a smaller area. She's going to e-mail you over a list of farms and I want you to check them out tomorrow.'

'Great, you're putting me to good use then! I thought that when I got promoted to sergeant, these menial tasks were for others.'

'I am putting you to the best possible use. If you stumble on the right farmyard, I need someone with keen senses. You've got the keenest senses I know.'

'Well, thanks, it's been a while since someone said something that nice to me!'

'Right, I've got to interview Lacey now.'

'Well, don't exchange any pleasantries with her whatsoever; she's likely to ruin your life!'

Yorke laughed. 'See you tomorrow, Jake.'

He hung up, opened up a second packet of ham and consumed it in two mouthfuls. After picking up his wife's wedding ring, he headed upstairs to the sofa bed, rubbing his sore lip.

AFTER FORCING ON A WOOLLEN JUMPER, which had endured too many tumble dries and was almost child-size, Yorke led Lacey into an interview room nicknamed the 'icebox'.

As she took a seat, he looked through the cracked single-paned window, which split the outside world in two, and he saw the flash of new snow in the streetlights. A cold draft clawed at his face, so he hoisted down the blind to stop it dead. Out of curiosity, he ran a hand over the radiator, but quickly hauled it back — it felt like it was full of coolant rather than hot water.

'It's like a morgue in here, Inspector Yorke.'

'Sorry Ms Ray, the heating's bust in here and it's the only room available right now,' Yorke said, turning around.

'I'll be okay,' Lacey said, buttoning up her quilted jacket.

I never asked you if you were okay, thought Yorke, *and after what you've been putting Jake through – I have to say I really don't care.*

'I just have to let you know that we're filming this interview,' Yorke said, pointing at a camera mounted in the corner of the room behind her.

'Why?'

'You were first at the crime scene – that makes your statement very important.'

'As I told the officer who brought me here, I don't really know anything. I just went to see Joe and Sarah and ...' She paused and looked down at the table; a tear sparkled in the corner of her left eye.

Convincing, Yorke thought, laying a cardboard folder on the table in front of him.

'It must have been a shock.' A plume of white air billowed from his mouth.

'It's hard to get the sight of all that blood out of my head.' She continued staring at the table, while dabbing at the corners of her eyes with a tissue, smearing her mascara.

'In your own time, could you talk me through exactly what happened?'

'Do I need a solicitor?'

'Not unless you've done something wrong – we just need your help really. Afterwards, I'm going to have to get a signed statement.'

She took a deep breath. 'It was about quarter past two when I arrived. I was there to see if Joe and Sarah needed any support while Paul was being returned ... ' She dabbed her eyes again.

Yorke opened a pad, made some notes and waited for her to continue.

'I immediately noticed there'd been a struggle – there was a picture shattered on the floor, and a glass smashed in the sitting room. I called out for them before I went into the kitchen, but no-one answered. Then, I saw it ...' She looked over Yorke's shoulder at the broken window. 'Sorry.'

'I know it's hard, but could you describe it?'

'Blood everywhere ... all over the floor. It stank too,

almost like rotting meat. There was writing on the wall. *"In the Blood"* it said.'

'What do you think that means?'

'I have no idea. Something left in the blood on the floor perhaps? I wasn't about to check though ... it was disgusting.'

'Okay, what did you do next?'

'Phoned the police.'

Actually, you phoned Sheila, but we'll come back to that, Yorke thought.

'Where were you before you arrived at the house?'

'My flat at Spire View. With everything going on, I struggled to sleep last night, so I slept in rather late. I watched TV until close to two before walking around to my brother's house.'

'Could you describe your relationship with your brother?'

'We're not close. We speak every now again, but I haven't seen him in years, before today that is.'

'Why did you come back then?'

'There's a big difference between 'not close' and cold. They're going through a horrendous ordeal.'

'Of course. Can you think of anyone who would kidnap Joe or your nephew?'

'I live in Southampton, I rarely see or speak to them. I have no idea who would be this angry with them.'

'How would you describe Joe and Sarah's relationship?'

'Strained. He's always had problems resisting the opposite sex. She also has huge problems with OCD. I think they stayed together more for Paul, rather than for each other.'

Tyler tapped on the window.

'Excuse me, Ms Ray,' Yorke said.

'Of course.'

Outside the room, Tyler handed him another cardboard folder. 'Fifteen years ago, one of Lacey's teachers contacted social services regarding her peculiar behaviour; against her parents' wishes, Lacey was forced to see a child psychologist. The report and recommendations for treatment are in there. I've also included information from Southampton HQ regarding her 'job.'' He mimed quotation marks with his fingers.

'Okay, could you go in there and have Lacey prepare and sign her statement regarding the discovery of the crime scene while I have a quick look over this.'

'Of course, boss.'

After going over the contents of the cardboard folder, Yorke returned to the icebox. Lacey was just signing the statement.

'Thanks Ms Ray,' Tyler said, leaving the room. He nodded farewell to Yorke.

Yorke turned to Lacey, who was again dabbing her eyes with a tissue. He put the new folder down on top of the old one.

'Is there really any need for me to stay longer? I think I should go and see if my sister-in-law is okay.'

'There are a few more things I would like to discuss with you. Is that alright?'

'Of course, but I'm feeling very tired, and emotional, and I'm sure I have been as much help as I can be—'

'I cannot stress enough the importance of your statement, Ms Ray. Your nephew and brother could be in serious danger.'

'I know, but I've told you everything.'

'Do you know of anyone connected to your brother, or your family that would be capable of doing this?'

'You've asked me that already and I told you no. I share none of Joe's relationships, so I can't help. Our family has never been popular, as you probably know, but I do not spend enough time in Salisbury these days to identify anyone that harbours a grudge.'

'Is there anyone you have encountered in your line of work whom you've divulged your brother's financial situation to?'

Lacey sat up straight in her chair. 'Define 'line of work' detective?'

'I am led to believe you work as a model for a company called "Nightlight."'

'That's correct, but why would you assume that people I work with are unsavoury and may be drawn to my brother's wealth?'

'Southampton officers have evidence that this company moonlights as an escort company.'

'What evidence?'

'Are you a prostitute, Ms Ray?'

She narrowed her eyes. 'Do I need that solicitor now?'

'Entirely up to you. I have time to wait, but every minute you leave it will count against your missing family.'

She looked down at the table, deep in thought. *Come on,* thought Yorke, *you're going to have to at least pretend you care.* Yorke chewed his bottom lip as the wait became unbearable.

She lifted her head. 'Just because I make a good living modelling, people always assume you're selling your body.'

'So, that's a 'no' then?'

'Yes, it's a *'no'.*'

He made some notes and without looking at her said, 'When you were younger, your parents took you to a child psychologist.'

She started to tut.

'You remember then?'

She leaned forward. 'Sounds like you suspect me for my missing family?'

Yorke looked up. 'Please answer the question, Ms Ray, it is my duty to cover everything. And, if you think about it, you will realise it is your duty too.'

She reached up and adjusted her fringe; it looked as if it'd been cut with the aid of a ruler. 'Yes, I saw a child psychologist.'

'Can you remember why?'

'Because I was an angst ridden teenager?'

'Your parents were concerned about you bullying others, and your incessant need to dominate every situation.'

'Yes, as I said, angst ridden teenager.'

'The psychologist identified narcissistic tendencies; an incredible thirst for attention and a feeling of supremacy.'

'Did they? News to me! I never read that report.'

'Can I point out something else in the report, Ms Ray?'

'Be my guest.'

'The psychologist claimed these tendencies were 'malignant' and included a disregard for human life which needed to be addressed urgently by a psychiatrist. Unfortunately, according to your file, they never were. How do you feel about that?'

Lacey smiled. 'Hopefully, I've grown out of it.'

I hope so too, thought Yorke, *because sadism and joyful cruelty are common behaviours with malignant narcissism.*

Yorke tapped the folder. 'It says in here, your father killed your auntie when they were children.'

Lacey shrugged. 'By accident.'

'Still, it must be upsetting.'

164

'It was before I was born, and I never found out until after he died!'

'Did you like your father?'

'No, and neither did Joe. He was an animal.'

'How so?'

'He used to hit us, and mother. *Hard.*'

'I'm sorry to hear that, Ms Ray.'

'No you're not. There must be thousands of people around here with a similar story.'

'It must have been hard for you being in a house with a man like that. You must have had a torrid time.'

'Yes, we did, where is this going exactly?'

'How did your parents die?'

'Car accident. Is that not in there?' She nodded down at the file.

'I've not had chance to read it thoroughly yet.'

'I can assure you, detective, that I have nothing to do with Paul or Joe's disappearance. Your attempts to profile me are distracting you from better lines of inquiry.'

'One thing really bothers me, Ms Ray. Why did you phone DS Jake Pettman from the house?'

'We go way back. I knew he was a policeman and so when I panicked, I phoned him.'

'Except you didn't, you phoned his wife first.'

Lacey leaned back in her chair. 'It was his phone I called. When his wife answered, I apologised and then phoned the station to be put through to him.'

'Sheila Pettman reported that you were quite rude to her on the phone.'

'Really?'

'Yes. She said that you accused her of being feisty and then you started to insinuate that Jake still had feelings for you.'

'Well - she was rude to me first, and I was very emotional, considering what was currently happening.'

'What did she say to wind you up so much?'

'She was very abrupt with me over the fact that I had Jake's number.'

'And how did you get DS Pettman's number?'

'Jake gave me a lift to the station, yesterday. I saw his card advertising his personal trainer services. I took it and he didn't seem to object at the time.'

'DS Pettman claims he knows you saw the card, but didn't know you actually took it.'

'I must have misunderstood him; I thought he wanted me to take it.'

'He claims that he has already told you to stop contacting him, so why would you? Especially at a moment when you should have been phoning us in the conventional manner.'

'I don't know. As I said, the situation shocked me. Maybe I wasn't thinking straight?'

'Well, Ms Ray, you need to think carefully about this. If you approach DS Pettman or his wife again, either by phone or in person, you will be back in here. Only this time, you will be under arrest.'

'I understand,' she said. 'And I wouldn't want that. I'm already feeling rather *blue* as it is.'

AFTER ANOTHER OFFICER had interviewed her, and she'd signed a second statement, Lacey walked home, quickly.

She'd been a fool responding to Jake's criticisms and rejection. Now, this obnoxious detective Yorke was all over her like a rash, raking through her private life and dragging up her past.

She was confident that the ingenious tampering of Mummy and Daddy's car, which had been undetectable following their deaths in a fireball, would remain undiscovered; but her role as an escort was something she really didn't want probed, especially following Brian Lawrence's demise two days previous. She'd be in Nice with a new identity two days from now, but after that grilling back at the station, that was starting to feel like a long time away.

But even now, knowing that her anger over Jake's arrogance had caused her problems already, she could feel her frustration toward him grow further.

She pulled her phone out and stared at it.

He was content to pass his snide little judgements over me; yet, when I respond, he runs crying to this boss.

Her finger lingered over the call button.

You deserve the Blue Room, Jake, you really do. What have I got to lose now anyway? It is only a matter of time before they find out anyway and in a day and a half, I will be long gone. Could I squeeze you in at the last minute, just before I run?

Stupid, she knew, but she couldn't deny the tingle of excitement that ran down her spine ...

She scrolled through her contacts and hit call.

Phil Holmes answered the phone. 'Yes.'

'It's Lacey Ray.'

'Hello, Lacey, I—'

'What are you doing now?'

'Nothing, why?'

'I've had a strange afternoon. Could you come round and fuck me please?'

10

'THE DEAD VAN driver has been identified as John Lockley. It was actually the coroner, local to Salisbury, who identified him.' Gardner spoke quickly, punctuating her sentences by crunching tic tacs. 'Lockley was a homeless man, sleeping and begging on Salisbury's streets. He used to live with the STFH — Salisbury Trust For Homeless – until two months ago when his heavy drinking got too much for them. I've already had someone talk to the STFH, but they have no idea who he has been associating with in the interim. Most people who know of him, say he only talks to the people he begs from.'

'Yet the kidnapper knows him, or at least got to know him,' Yorke said. 'Emma, if you could keep some officers on the back of STFH, someone there must know of Lockley's favourite begging locales, maybe we can pick him up on CCTV somewhere talking with the kidnapper.'

Ambushed by the fumes of cheap polish in the incident room at Devizes HQ, Yorke breathed through his mouth rather than his nose. It was one assault too many on the senses, after a day which had left him completely jaded.

'Any money on him?' Topham asked, continually clasping and unclasping the strap of his expensive watch.

'Fifty pounds, in ten pound notes, screwed into a tight, little ball.' Gardner finished the sentence with another crunch.

'Not good pay for a mission that cost him his life,' Yorke said.

Topham abandoned his watch strap to look down at his notes. 'SOCO did not come up with any more dirt at the Ray house.'

'Could we trace the farm from the dead pig in the sack?' Yorke said.

DS Iain Brookes spoke for the first time, 'Thought of that, but parts of the skin had been sliced off to hide the branding.' The colour drained from his face as he was forced to relive the experience that had seen him side-lined for the last few hours.

'What do any of you know about Lacey Ray?' Yorke said.

'Promiscuous,' Gardner said. 'She was a couple of years below me at school. A very clever girl, always in the highest classes, but she was very popular too and was often behind the bike sheds, she seemed to enjoy having boys fighting over her.'

'Lacey is giving DS Jake Pettman a hard time because they used to be an item ten years ago. She's been phoning him and his wife. She even phoned him from the crime scene rather than contacting us directly. I just interviewed her.'

'And?' Gardner said.

'Well, when she was younger, a child psychologist diagnosed her as a malignant narcissist.'

'What's that?' Topham said.

'In a nutshell, she thrives on power, cruelty and a sense of superiority.'

'I knew they had a word for what Mark suffers from,' Gardner said.

'Ha, ha, very funny.' Topham screwed his face up at Gardner.

'I just interviewed her and at first, she seemed very skilled at keeping her personality disorder under wraps, but there were moments in the conversation when a colder and more calculating side emerged. Information from Southampton suggests she is working as an expensive escort. She's definitely trouble, and the way she's lingering around this drama like a dog in heat makes me worry. I'm sending Jake out collecting mud samples tomorrow to keep him out of her way until I know more. The investigating officer should be in touch with me tomorrow regarding this prostitution racket. Then, we can get some more information up on the wall about her.' He pointed at the whiteboard, which covered the entire length of the right side of the room. On it, Operation Haystack was growing at an incredible rate. Apart from the pictures, information was tattooed on the board in permanent ink; it prevented anything from being accidentally wiped off, and could easily be removed with a solvent once the case was finished.

At the top of the collage was a school photo of Paul Ray. To one side of him were his parents, looking uncharacteristically happy in a press release photo taken years ago at the opening of Joe's shop; beneath it, Yorke had scribbled the word 'Joe Ray: missing' and today's date. Beside the photo of the parents was a picture of Thomas Ray being led out of the courtroom on the day of the trial; someone else had written an estimated date of death, which had been confirmed by the coroner as over a week ago.

Other familiar faces joined the cast list of Operation Haystack. Simon Rushton and Jessica Hart were up there. As well as other teachers and staff at the school who had piqued the interest of interviewing officers. It was a testament to just how many hours of police time had already gone into the case. Underneath each picture were many captions including: 'claimed Paul Ray could be arrogant when challenged', 'sent him out of the classroom for arguing', 'parents were unsupportive'. Normal events in the lives of a teacher, but in the lives of a kidnapper or murderer, they were possible motives.

At Yorke's request, further along the board, was a section completely dedicated to the Ray family tree. It dated back over a hundred years. It began with a faded black and white picture from an old newspaper of child-killer Reggie and his wife. Beneath them was a picture of their three children; the youngest child, Thomas Ray's father, Andrew, was looking up at the sky - *was he looking for the aliens he would one day educate his son about?* Then, there was a picture of a young Thomas Ray and his cousins Richie and Louise. Beneath this, was a photo of Richie's young child, butter-wouldn't-melt-in-her-mouth Lacey, and beside that, a wedding photo of Joe and Sarah. Underneath them, was a second copy of the school photo of prepubescent Paul.

It was shocking to think that there were only two people alive in that whole family tree that he knew the whereabouts of.

'We have Sarah safe,' Yorke said. 'We need to put Lacey under surveillance too.'

'In case, she's connected or she's targeted?' Gardner said.

'Both I guess,' Yorke said.

'I'll arrange it,' Topham said.

'Does anyone have an update on that list of Joe's lovers?' Yorke said.

'He listed five,' Brookes said. 'They were all interviewed. Four were married. All of these claimed that their husbands never found out, and we confirmed this by surprising these men with their wives' dirty little secret.'

'There's that compassionate side getting the better of you again Iain,' Gardner said, rolling her eyes.

'So out of the four husbands, not one knew?' Yorke said.

Brookes shrugged. 'Yep.'

'I think it's worth a second look,' Gardner said.

'I really don't,' Brookes said.

Yorke thought for a moment. 'There's no harm in checking again. Let's re-interview the wives and husbands. Surely, at least one of them could be itching for revenge?'

Brookes sighed. 'Okay, we also still have officers looking into Joe Ray's run-ins over the past ten years, but nothing there yet either.'

'Speaking of motive,' Topham said. 'Has there been any further news on Harry, following the discovery of the letter?'

Gardner said, 'Taxi passengers are providing an alibi for the time that the Paul Ray kidnapping took place, and we were keeping tabs on him today during Joe's abduction.'

'That doesn't mean he isn't working with anyone, and it also doesn't mean he didn't kill Thomas Ray.'

Yorke said, 'Of course, Mark, I agree. But my instinct still says no. After all, Ray was dying anyway – so why take the risk? And as for taking Paul Ray - why? Paul and Thomas weren't close, not even in contact as far as I'm aware.'

'He could think the family owes him something?' Topham said.

'He used to be one of us,' Gardner said. 'He knows about poor kidnapping success rates; again, why would he take the risk?'

'That could have been the reason he asked for a small amount because it would be easier to acquire in a short space of time—' Topham continued.

'But he still knows the money would have been marked. And then why go to the trouble of having an accomplice grab Joe too? It doesn't add up,' Yorke said. 'But we'll bring him in for another interview just to be sure.'

There was a knock at the door. Topham stood up, adjusted his suit and went outside. A moment later, he came back in, sat down and sighed. 'No match so far on the fingerprint on the patio door. Looks like whoever left it is clean.'

There was a second, much more forceful, knock at the door. Topham shot up again, but there was no need, Dr Patricia Wileman burst in of her own accord.

'I wish you'd stop doing that,' Topham said and smiled.

'I wish I was on holiday in the Caribbean drinking piña colada – you help me out with that one, I'll see what I can do for you.'

Yorke swivelled in his chair. She wore scrubs, but she'd opted for a small size, so her impressive figure drew lines in the material. 'Hello Dr Wileman.'

'DCI Yorke,' she said in a softer tone to the one she'd greeted Topham with. She then flashed him a grin.

Topham coughed. 'Dr Wileman?'

'Ah, yes.' She broke eye-contact with Yorke. 'The blood in the fingerprint is pig blood. However, the guy has changed his MO. Considerably.'

Everyone sat up in their chairs. Jeremy Dawson from HOLMES typed hard and fast.

'The blood in the kitchen was human this time. Type O.'

'Joe Ray was Type O,' Brookes said.

'It's also the most common blood type in the UK,' Yorke said.

Patricia met Yorke's eyes again. She let her stare linger. 'And both Thomas Ray and Paul Ray have type O blood. But it's in for DNA testing, so hopefully, we should know whose it is shortly. Now, I'll head off to dream about those piña coladas, while I wait for my taxi – my car's in for repair.'

'Thanks, Dr Wileman,' Topham said.

She glanced at Yorke, smiled and then left the room. Yorke could feel his heart beating in his chest.

'We had no luck tracing the source of the e-mail ...'

Yorke jumped up out of his seat. He ran out the door and chased Patricia down the corridor. 'Dr Wileman?'

'Pat, please,' she said, turning and coming back his way. The purpose in her stride suggested that she wasn't surprised. She swept her hair back and smiled.

'I'll give you a lift back,' he said as his adrenaline almost reached the same level as it had done earlier during the car chase.

'Are you sure? You must be busy in there—'

'Fifteen minutes. I'll meet you out front.'

'Okay.'

Yorke watched her walking away, noticing that his heart was beating faster. There was a moment of guilt as there always was when he flirted with someone, but Charlotte was long gone. Twenty years gone to be precise. It was time to put an end to it.

He jogged back into the room and looked from one inquisitive face to the other.

'And?' Topham said.

'Just had a hunch about something. I'd like to see if it comes to anything before I let you all know about it.'

ON THE BEDSIDE TABLE, the lava in the lamp stirred.

Lacey had taken her mind to the Blue Room. Here she played 'Who am I?' It used to be her favourite game, and as she played it, she realised that it had lost none of its appeal.

Who am I? Intelligent, good-looking, yet arrogant enough to think I can pass judgement on others?

Unfortunately, her safety demanded she keep some of her senses partially tuned to reality, so she watched Phil's face grow sweatier as he thrust. From the Blue Room, she commanded her eyes to meet his, to deceive him into feeling as if she was there, in bed with him, *wholeheartedly.*

Who am I? She continued to ask herself in that cold and blue place. *In a loveless, sexless marriage, but still pompous enough to reject Lacey Ray?*

Her partially tuned senses made her aware of Phil's short, sharp breathing and his rolling eyes. She ordered her hand to stroke his back, coax an orgasm from him, and trick him into believing that she cared.

Who am I? She asked herself as she turned naked, and free, in a place with no disorder. *Cruel enough to turn the police against Lacey Ray when all she offered was comfort?*

The tremor and then the quiver of Phil's release came like a burst of electricity, conducting its way through her body and finally her mind, shocking her back to reality and back to her bed . . .

'Jake Pettman!'

She watched Phil's expression morph from pleasure to confusion and then to anger. She let her head slump to one side, so she could watch clumps of lava break away and ascend like rising devils.

'What did you call me?' he said.

'I didn't call you anything—'

'You just called me Jake Pettman.' He climbed off her and onto his feet.

Behind him, the curtains were open; the light from several flats around the block illuminated the overly-furnished room. He paced the room, naked.

'Ah, you're angry,' Lacey said.

'That would be the normal reaction when you call someone by another man's name.'

She looked at his massive, hairy body; he was feral and repulsive.

A bloated red bubble burst free in the lava lamp. She could hear the horns of the motorists from the main road near the flat.

'Have you met him?' Lacey said.

'No.'

'He's a DS investigating my nephew's disappearance. He was on my mind.'

'While we were having sex?'

'Seems that way.'

He still paced, back and forth.

'Maybe, you should close the curtains?'

He obliged, exposing his nakedness to the neighbourhood momentarily as he snapped the curtains closed. 'A different name slipped out. So what? You don't owe me anything.'

Funny, you never struck me as the forgiving type.

'You're right, and in a way you should be grateful.' She turned to watch lava being spat like bullets from the bottom of the lamp. She swung her legs off the side of the bed and sat up.

'Grateful?' he said, taking a step towards her.

'Because I was with you in body, if not in mind.'

'Why would I be grateful for that?' He took another step and stood directly in front of her.

'Because you're getting all the pleasure he should be getting, but does not want.' She reached out to stroke his manhood. 'And, you know, you're not all that bad. A little dim-witted perhaps, but that just makes you easier to control.'

'What? Nobody controls me—'

'Really? The point of the weak-willed, *the point of you,* is to be controlled.'

She smiled at him and he struck her across the face. She slumped back and heard the lava lamp crash to the floor as he leaned over her ...

It would have been easy to retreat back to that cold, blue, organised room, but she preferred instead to stay and be mindful of the pain — it would make her more competent later.

———

'I have a confession to make,' Patricia said.

'Go on,' Yorke said, watching the spire of the great cathedral growing as they thundered towards Salisbury in the Lexus.

'I knew your sister.'

Not the confession I was hoping for ... or expecting, he thought.

'Ah.'

'Very well in fact. We met up quite regularly during that period you weren't talking.'

'She told you about us then?'

'Yes.'

'*Everything?*'

'I didn't pass judgement, I just listened.'

'And if you had to pass judgement?' he said, realising, with sadness, that the laughs they'd had during the previous twenty minutes were now a distant memory.

'I don't know the ins and outs of the situation.'

'There isn't much to know. My father was dying of cancer and I refused to go and say goodbye. He'd spent his entire life a drunk, with his back turned on his family. He left my mum a drug addict, yet my sister deemed my actions inappropriate. It's never easy to see eye-to-eye when family are concerned I guess.'

'You really don't have to talk about it. I just wanted you to know that I was friends with your sister, before you found out from someone else.'

Yorke looked at her. She had a contrite expression. 'I probably didn't know that already because I wasn't allowed on the case.'

'I know, it's a shame, you'd not have sent Tom Davies to jail while William Proud got away.'

'I don't know about that. There was a lot of evidence that pointed towards Davies at the time from what I hear, and Proud was slippery, hence his disappearing act.' He stopped the car on Park Street and looked at Patricia. 'Is this okay?'

'Yes ... I didn't accept your lift because I knew your

sister, *honestly*. I just wanted you to know in case ...' She looked away.

'In case of what?' he said, immediately thinking, *shit, I'm just making this awkward.*

'Thanks for the lift, Mike. I enjoyed it. I really did.'

Yorke smiled. 'Me too. I'll call you.'

'That'll be good.' She returned his smile and exited the car.

As he watched her disappear up her driveway, he felt his phone buzz in his pocket. He looked at the screen and sighed. Harry.

HAVING BEEN moments away from sleep, Jake cursed as he reached out from the sofa bed for his mobile phone. 'Yes?'

'Jake, is that you?' Lacey said.

'You have got to be kidding.'

'No, please listen.' She was whispering. 'Don't hang up, please. I'm in trouble—'

'You can say that again. This is harassment.'

'I've been attacked, Jake, I'm hurt, badly and in danger—'

'Why?'

'Phil Holmes.'

'The IT technician at the school?'

'Yes.' She was still whispering.

'What happened?'

'He hit me. Several times.'

Jake sat up. 'Where are you?'

'I'm in my bedroom, the door is closed. I'm not sure if he's gone.'

'Lock your door if you can, I'll call response.'

'Can't you just come?'

'No.'

'Wait, I heard someone—'

'Don't move.'

'Jake—'

The phone went dead. Jake climbed off the sofa bed.

11

S TARVING, BUT DIZZY from having been knocked out, Joe Ray struggled to break the stale bread. His handcuffs rattled as he eventually pried loose a piece and forced it into his mouth. As he chewed, blood ran from his throbbing temple where the large man wearing the grotesque mask had hit him; he rubbed it away before it reached his eye.

At all times, he kept his eyes on the wheelchair bound woman, and the girl who stared into space; the line of drool hanging from her mouth looked like a silvery strand spun by a spider. They were sitting to the right of a large, misshapen table which he headed. One other place was set with an empty bowl and a rustic plate holding a chunk of brown bread. Plumes of sweet-smelling steam rose from a large broth-filled pot in the centre of the table; some of the liquid had spilled out and crystallised down the sides.

He'd not long woken in this large, sparsely furnished cold room. Despite the occupants, the place felt empty and lonely. Around him, grey wallpaper peeled and sagged, and even though there was a window, there was no light outside to show him where he'd been brought.

The old woman said, 'You can start now, Martha.'

Martha smiled and the line of drool snapped and glued itself to her bread like a slug trail. She tore off a piece of bread and threw it into her mouth. Joe felt another sudden throb in his temple and rubbed more blood away with the back of his hand.

While Martha chewed, the old woman regarded him.

He'd asked several times already, but he tried again. 'Where am I?'

She smiled, revealing a mouth with few teeth.

'Where's my son?'

'All in good time.' Her voice was hoarse and difficult to understand.

'Please tell me.'

Ignoring him, she turned away. He let his fists fall down onto the table. Martha flinched. Then, he tried to move his feet; the heavy chain looping around his ankles and the chair legs clanked against the floor. A rising surge of adrenaline helped ward off the disorientation and he raised his voice. 'Tell me now, or I won't be responsible—'

'Shush,' Martha said with a finger to her mouth. 'If Lewis hears you getting angry, he won't be happy.'

He could see that she looked genuinely concerned.

'And we're expecting him any minute now,' the old woman said. 'Martha, can you serve our guest?' Her mouth was as empty as a black hole, and with every croaked word, Joe felt as if he was being pulled further and further into it.

Martha jumped to her feet and, ladle in hand, skipped around the table to him. She had her jacket zipped up tight. Her long hair was knotted and her hands were caked in dirt. After leaning over and dragging the pot towards them, she plunged the ladle into the broth and scooped some into Joe's bowl. It splashed over the table and down his front. 'It's yummy,' she said.

Ravenous, he clutched the bowl with cuffed hands, tilted his head back and drank, just like he'd seen Japanese men do in a small Ramen restaurant he frequented in Southampton. The lukewarm broth was sweet and gristly.

When he'd finished, he put the bowl down and took a deep breath.

'Teach him about manners,' the old woman said. 'The same way I taught you.'

Martha slapped the back of his hand.

'How do you expect me to eat properly with these on?' Joe said, raising his cuffed hands and then curling up his top lip.

'It's for your own good,' Martha said. 'Lewis doesn't like bad manners.'

'Who is this Lewis anyway? Is he the freak wearing the pig's head? The one that assaulted me? Does he have my son?'

'Again Martha, the way I taught you,' the old woman said.

Joe pinched his eyes shut to await the blow. When nothing happened, he opened his eyes to see Martha hesitating.

'Now!'

Martha cracked the back of his hand with the ladle.

'Argh! You brat —'

'And again, even harder!'

'Please Mother,' Martha said. 'I don't like it.'

'I shall tell Lewis you disobeyed me.'

Martha hit him even harder.

'You little cow,' he said, lunging at the girl, but the

restraints around his legs took control, and he plunged face-first, crushing his cuffed hands beneath him. His chair, which had been chained to his legs, crashed down onto his back.

Gasping, he opened his eyes, and stared at the withered, duck-like feet of the old woman poking out of the bottom of a woollen shawl.

'Someone's going to pay for this.' He tried to turn over, but the weight of the chair pinned him down. The hag cackled.

'Stop laughing!'

She stopped immediately, not because of Joe's demands but rather because of the sudden roar of a car engine.

Martha darted back to her seat.

Was it the man wearing the pig's face?

A hot stone of fear burned in his stomach. He writhed on the floor, trying to untangle himself from the restraints.

'Shush,' Martha said. '*Please*. He'll hurt you.'

The car engine stopped.

'Be quiet, Martha,' the old woman said.

There was a loud yawning sound as cold wind rushed into the house through the opened front door.

'Help me.' Spit ran from the corners of his mouth as he struggled. The handle on the dining room squeaked and he gave every last ounce of energy he had to try and wriggle himself free. It was useless and just seemed to make the chair on his back press down even harder, causing him more pain.

When the dining room door opened, the hot stone of fear skimmed over his insides.

He lifted his head as far as he could. He could see a baggy pair of jeans tucked into giant brown CAT work boots, but most of his view was obscured by the table. The man crossed the threshold into the room with a heavy step and closed the door shut behind him.

'Hello Lewis,' Martha said.

'Hi Lewis,' said the old woman.

Lewis didn't reply; neither did his wet, glistening boots move. Joe heard the wind whistle as it explored the cavernous parts of the old house.

'It's not too late to think about what you're all doing, you won't get away with this, you can't get away with this.'

Still no reply and no movement.

'Are you listening? I want to see my son!'

Lewis began to take heavy slow steps towards the table. Each thud seemed to vibrate through Joe's already tiring neck. When it started to burn and he couldn't hold it up any longer, he let his injured forehead return to the floor.

'Starting without me – you could have waited,' Lewis said in a deep, but clear voice. It was definitely the man who'd come to his house. The sound of his words, "you're greedy, Joe," remained clear in his memory.

'It was going cold,' the old woman said.

Lewis snorted.

'Lewis, today I went to the barn,' Martha said. 'Paul was so cold. I would like to take him a blanket.'

Lewis said, 'You shouldn't have let her go to the barn, Stella. You were told to take him the food.'

'Can I take him a blanket?' Martha said.

'Not now,' Lewis said. 'I would like you to go and get me some coffee from the kitchen.'

'Okay,' she said, and left the room.

'She's not to go again, Stella.'

'I couldn't see the—'

'Not again, *okay?*'

'Okay.'

'What's in the broth tonight?'

'Pig,' she said. 'What else?'

Lewis moved again. Joe managed to crane his neck again and saw him coming around the side of the table towards him. This time with no mask. Despite a large body, his face was gaunt. Long, black hair streamed down around his shoulders.

He looks familiar ...

His abductor lumbered past him. Then, he felt large hands slip under his armpits. He was scooped up; it felt like it was being done by a mechanical crane.

'Hello Joe,' Lewis said into his ear.

'He's not been the best company,' Stella said.

'How's the food?' Lewis said.

'It would be better without these on,' Joe said, lifting his cuffed hands. He was trying to maintain an air of dignity, but he struggled to keep the quaking out of his voice.

'I see.' Lewis leaned over him and used a key to unclasp the cuffs. 'Better?'

'Yes, where's my son?' he said, flexing his wrists.

'I will take you to him after you've eaten.'

'No, I want to see him now.'

'Okay.'

Joe felt an energetic tingle of hope run through his body, before realising for the first time that he was shaking quite hard.

Lewis went to the back of the room. Joe couldn't see him, but it sounded as if he was rifling through a drawer. Eventually, he came back over. 'Are you ready to go?'

'Yes.'

Lewis removed the chains from his legs. 'Stand up and turn around.'

Joe obliged and saw Lewis aiming a sawn-off shotgun at him.

'I've killed before and I will kill again, do you believe me?'

'Yes, I do,' Joe said. *I really do.*

'You walk a metre in front of me. If you walk too fast, too slow, turn or attempt to run, I will kill you. Do you understand?'

PC KELLY STAMP stared up at the modern flats towering over the medieval city. She'd never really liked Spire View; it was sterile, and the old world hunching desperately beneath these claws of modernisation made her feel sad.

After parking, and exiting, she adjusted her duty belt; the handcuffs hung on her left side, her baton on the right. Her partner PC Neil Chappell didn't check his duty belt as per usual.

'You need to take more care.'

'I've checked it once already today.'

'You know procedure, check it again. I can tell your handcuffs aren't set from here. He could still be up there.'

Neil ensured his handcuffs were in the preloaded position as they approached Lacey's flat.

They buzzed Lacey's number. Over a minute later, they heard, 'Yes?'

'Ms Ray.'

'How can I help you?'

'PCs Kelly Stamp and Neil Chappell, we're following up on the report you made to DS Jake Pettman. Are you safe?'

'I'm fine.'

'We have reports of assault and a possible threat to your safety. Can we come up please?'

'I would rather you didn't. I said already, I'm fine.'

Kelly looked at Neil. He shrugged. This callout was so common around Salisbury, especially on the council estates, that it wasn't even worth discussing. They'd have to check she was safe; it was their duty.

Kelly blew on her numbing hands and pressed the buzzer again.

'Ms Ray, we are obligated to check on your safety.'

There was a buzzing sound and the door was released.

Bypassing two chained-up muddy mountain bikes, they climbed white stairs. An elderly man stood at the top, squinting at them through spectacles, fiddling with a long hair poking from his eyebrow.

'Evening sir,' Neil said.

The old man stood to one side to allow them past.

'She's trouble,' he croaked from behind them. 'Always has been, always will be.'

Kelly heard his cane tapping the stairs as he descended.

They knocked on the door. When it opened, Lacey stood there in a velvet dressing gown. Her left eye was black and her bottom lip was split. Her chin was covered in blood, making her look like some kind of gorging vampire. Kelly heard Neil take a deep breath behind her.

HARRY BUTLER OPENED the door for Yorke; he was unshaven and his eyes were puffy.

'Thanks for coming, Mike.'

Yorke winced at the whisky fumes. 'Are you okay? You sounded desperate on the phone.'

'Anna's left me.'

Yorke sighed. 'I'm sorry to hear that, I really am.'

'Can you come in?'

'It's not a good idea. Someone is coming to pick you up for a second interview. I think it's best to leave it to them.'

'Please, five minutes?'

Yorke sighed and entered the house. With widening eyes, he observed the chaos around him: takeaway boxes, piles of letters and unwashed mugs.

'When did Anna really leave?' Yorke said, wincing at the musty smell of clothes that hadn't been aired properly.

'Last month.'

Yorke stepped into the lounge, raising a cloud of dust from the carpet; the place was an asthmatic's worst nightmare.

Resting on a shag rug on the floor were photo albums and an open jewellery box. He looked down at the photos and saw Danielle's beautiful face staring back up at him.

'I still miss her, Mike,' Harry said, taking a gulp of whisky.

Yorke didn't say anything.

'That's why Anna left.'

Yorke nodded and drew his hand back. He paced around Harry's dirty living room and stopped next to the mantelpiece, where he took a deep breath and sighed; a small cloud of dust billowed up from an ornate clock which had frozen at two fifteen PM.

Harry said, 'I couldn't cope when that bastard got out. I really couldn't. He should have died in jail.'

'I agree,' Yorke said, turning to face him.

'I spent so long rebuilding my life and then it just ... well, fell apart again.'

Yorke took a deep breath. 'Why did you call me here?'

'I know you hate me. After I let Proud get away, who can blame you? But I was doing it for you, I really was. I was convinced it was Davies.'

Yorke forced back a wave of anger, he'd already buried his resentment over Harry's poor judgement and he didn't want to unearth it again right now.

'I've tried to find Proud for you, I really have, for years ... but the man's gone.'

Yorke nodded, biting his lip, wanting to say: *Stop telling me you did these things for me. You did these things for yourself. Because you couldn't handle the game anymore. Couldn't handle having to prove the truth when murder was involved.*

'I don't blame you for not wanting to know me.'

'Is that the only reason you called me here, Harry?'

'No. I called you because I've not been completely honest with you.'

Yorke's phone rang, he looked at the screen; it was Topham.

'Excuse me,' Yorke said, disappearing out of the lounge. He answered the call.

'Sir.'

'Hi Mark.'

'The blood at Joe Ray's house has been identified as Thomas Ray's blood.'

'Meaning Paul could still be alive, good news—'

'Mike, listen, Harry's DNA has been found on Thomas Ray's body.'

Yorke took a deep breath and ran his hand through his hair. 'Christ, I'm with him now.'

'Jesus ...'

'Send someone to pick him up.' He hung up and turned

around. Harry was moving towards him. He felt his blood freeze.

'What was that about?' Harry said.

ON THE FLOOR, Lacey saw that the lava from her smashed lamp had solidified; it reminded her of the pool of blood in her brother's kitchen. Next, her eyes moved over the tangled bed sheets, soaked with the sweat of sex and sadism.

The two officers were looking around the flat. She was allowing this; it was the only way she would be able to get rid of them. There was nothing to see, or find anyway; she'd purposely kept the place sterile and innocent of her true nature.

Her plan had backfired on her. She had wanted to draw Jake to her, arouse sympathy in him, make him realise he still cared, before seducing him and informing Sheila of his betrayal. This revenge might have satisfied her growing need, *desire rather*, for the Blue Room and his death. But he wasn't that dim, wasn't that unprofessional. She'd underestimated him.

As for Phil Holmes, he was a gorilla. There was no danger of underestimating him! *And*, she thought, stroking her split lip, *nothing can satisfy me now, apart from the Blue Room*. It was a risk she'd have to take; she couldn't leave her incarnation as Lacey Ray the day after tomorrow and let the bastard get away with that. She'd be careful; she'd leave it right to the last minute. By the time they discovered him, she'd be gone and her identity changed.

'It was just a bit of fun that got out of hand,' Lacey said to the officer who'd introduced herself as PC Kelly Stamp.

'Ms Ray. You're not thinking straight. We deal with this

all the time; you press charges and he won't be allowed near you again,' Kelly said.

'There's no need to press charges.'

'You can't let him get away with what he's done to you.'

I won't. Don't worry.

'You're bleeding. Quite badly. We need to get you to the hospital,' the male officer, Neil Chappell, said.

'Nonsense, I'm fine.'

'You need an x-ray, possibly stitches.'

'Did anything else happen?' Kelly said.

'You mean, did he rape me?'

Kelly nodded.

'No, we had sex; it was consensual.'

Lacey stared at the inquisitive officers, who looked at each other, several times, realising, no doubt, that their time in this apartment was coming to an end.

After they left, Lacey phoned Jake's mobile. It reported that he'd blocked her number. She smiled.

She still had plan B. She reached into her top drawer for her laptop. After logging on, she located and double-clicked the appropriate folder.

Once upon a time, she'd wanted to be an actress. Now, with fondness, she recalled standing in front of her bathroom mirror collecting those Academy Awards, her acceptance speech becoming more flowery and enigmatic each time she delivered it.

She stared at the extensive list of video files on the laptop screen. The acting in these movies wouldn't win her any awards, but they still made her feel good, and in no small way.

She scrolled through the list until she found the file called "Jake P".

A far streetlamp, little more than a dot of light at this

distance, poked through the tiny gap in the curtains. Lacey likened the image to the half-opened eye of a gigantic creature.

JOE GLANCED over his shoulder at the large man, whose shotgun was slicing through the moonlight like a shark fin, and said, 'It's not too late to stop this.'

'I told you if you turned, I'd kill you. You will not get another chance.'

Joe continued through the snow, dabbing his bleeding forehead with a napkin he'd taken from the dining table. Looming ever closer was a giant wooden barn.

'Please tell me why you're doing this.' He spoke as loud as he could. The wind was playing havoc over the empty fields.

'That list of rules now includes not talking. It would be a shame if you died before you got to see your son again.'

The shotgun touched the back of his head; every nerve in his body tingled. Tears began to well up in his eyes – no doubt this was how a prisoner of war felt. Expecting to be thrown a shovel at any moment and told to dig their own grave.

At the barn door, a key was pushed into his hand. 'Open it.'

He fumbled with the padlock and the barn door creaked open. Inside, the tears that had welled in his eyes from fear began to fall with joy. Paul rose to his feet and met Joe in the centre of the barn. After embracing, he held his son at arm's length to examine him.

His hair was dishevelled and greasy; his face pale. *He looks like he's been to hell and back.* Paul's body trembled in his arms and he was crying so hard, it was difficult to understand everything he was saying. 'Dad, I'm scared, it's been awful.'

'I'm here now.'

'Throw back the padlock and key,' Lewis said.

Paul tightened his grip on his father. 'That man ...'

'I know, just let me do what he says.'

Joe prised himself from his son's grip, turned and threw the padlock and attached key to the shotgun-wielding bastard in the doorway.

When he turned back, his son looked up. 'What happened to your head Dad?'

'Don't worry about that right now.'

'Did he hurt you?'

'Not now, please,' Joe said, stunned by a strength in his son he'd never seen before. A strength that must have grown from this harrowing experience.

'Do you really care, Paul?' Lewis said. 'You told me you hated him.'

Paul looked up at his father. 'I didn't mean it.'

'It's okay,' Joe said. 'I deserved it.'

'You told me you were my friend, Lewis,' Paul said.

'I said a lot of things to make this work.'

Fresh tears ran down Paul's face. 'I told you ... everything.'

'And I listened to everything you said, but none of that is important. Not anymore.'

The barn door slammed shut.

'Not again, please,' Paul said, wrapping his arms around Joe's waist as tight as he could.

Joe heard the pigs grunting and moving in the darkness. They knelt together in the centre of the barn, hugging.

Eventually, when they'd both taken control of themselves, Paul said, 'How did you get here Dad?'

'I'll explain it all to you.' He stroked his son's hair. 'And you need to explain to me how you got here too.'

'What do you think is going to happen to us?'

'The police will come.'

'Are we going to be okay?'

'Yes. I promise.'

He continued to embrace his son, and tried to think of more promises he wouldn't be able to keep.

———

IN THE INTERVIEW ROOM, Yorke stared across the table at his old friend.

'Are you sure you don't want a solicitor?' Yorke said again. This was the first ever time he'd repeated this question with a suspect. Despite everything he'd done, Harry was still ex-police and had suffered horrendously; he wanted to give him the best possible chance to exonerate himself.

'No.'

'Okay, we have two signed statements from you. The first claims you did not go anywhere near the school the day of the kidnapping. Do you stand by that?'

'Yes.'

Yorke looked up at Harry's wide eyes. He looked almost enthusiastic – maybe, he believed Yorke would get him off the hook.

'The second signed statement says that you sent a letter to Thomas Ray. A letter we have in evidence. The statement also says that you didn't approach Thomas after his release.'

'Yes, that is the statement I'd like to retract.'

Yorke exchanged glances with Gardner. 'I'm going to be blunt now, Harry, and ask you a direct question.'

'Okay.'

'Did you kill Thomas Ray?'

'No, I did not.'

Yorke was relieved at the answer, but still felt a surge of frustration. He'd yet to hear the reason Harry had called him this evening. After Topham's phone call, he told Harry it was better to keep it for the station when it could be recorded and heard by another officer.

The frustration came from the fact that Harry should never have let it get to this stage; he should have been open and honest with Yorke last night in the pub.

Whatever this reason was. It'd better be a good one.

Gardner said, 'A Phadebas test revealed saliva on Thomas Ray's face and this is the DNA profile.' She opened the brown folder and pushed it over to Harry.

'I don't need to look,' Harry said, pushing it back. 'It's mine. I admit it. I spat in his face.'

Yorke clenched and unclenched his fists. 'Harry, you don't need me to tell you how this is looking.'

'I spat in his face after he died. I found him how you found him, dead ... and mutilated.'

'What were you even doing there?' Gardner said.

'This is what I wanted to tell you about tonight, Mike.' He pulled out a handful of photographs from his jacket pocket and threw them onto the table. 'When he was released, it drove me crazy. I mean, eight years? How was I supposed to cope with that?'

Yorke forced the image of his sister's murderer from his mind – a man who had served no time; ironically, because of the man whinging about injustice in front of him.

Harry continued, 'I followed him, took those photos. I wanted to see if he lied about the cancer, wanted to see if he was still enjoying his life.'

'And?' Gardner said.

'He wasn't lying, he was sick.' He pushed the photos over to Yorke. 'There are photos here of nurses arriving. They were coming about once a week. I even went right into his house one day and saw him in his bed. He saw me, but he was that out of it on medication he thought I was a doctor. I had chances to hurt him, if I'd wanted to; not that there was any need to, he was suffering enough.'

'Why didn't you tell me all of this last night?' Yorke said.

'Because the next thing I tell you is going to get me into trouble.'

'Go on.'

'Six nights ago, a large man,' he said, reaching over and tapping a photo, 'stopped by. It was dark, and I was some way away, so the photos aren't clear.'

Yorke looked at the photos of a heavyset man with long black hair. Harry was right, the picture had been taken at some distance and the face wasn't clear.

'He took Thomas Ray into his barn.'

'Did you get a photo of him leading Thomas Ray inside?'

'Yes, but it didn't come out. I only got this one of the man arriving at the farmhouse.'

Yorke rubbed the sides of his head with his thumb and forefinger. 'You were there when Thomas Ray was being murdered?'

'Yes, but obviously, I didn't know he being murdered.'

'But you discovered the body, afterwards, and didn't phone it in,' Yorke said, widening his eyes.

'Well, I couldn't, could I? You'd have thought it was me.'

'And you still didn't think of telling me last night in the pub? With a young boy missing?'

Harry looked down. 'Sorry.'

'Everyone is going to think it is you now anyway,' Yorke said, slamming the palm of his hand down on the table. He stood up and leaned over so his face was an inch from Harry's. 'You spat in his face! You were a policeman for Christ's sake. How stupid are you?'

'I was angry ... disgusted ... I didn't think.' Tears appeared in the corners of his eyes. 'That bastard killed my wife.'

'You saw what this psycho did to him – why couldn't you have left it at that? Putting your DNA on the body. Jesus, Harry, you were never that dumb when I worked with you.'

'I was all shaken up. Listen, Mike, I'd rather he'd not have died at all.' He looked away. 'I wanted him to rot in jail. The way he died gives me no satisfaction - he was probably so out of it on medication he didn't even realise what was happening to him.'

'You should have contacted us,' Yorke said.

'I know. But I just assumed the nurses would realise he was missing and report it.'

'We checked that out,' Gardner said. 'There was a mistake. An agency nurse phoned in sick, twice, and both times they failed to cover the shift.'

Yorke said, 'We are going to need all the details. In a statement. The time you were there, everything you saw, the reasons you didn't call us immediately. *Everything.*'

'Don't worry,' Harry said, dabbing at the corners of his

eyes. 'I've been through it in my head a million times since. You'll get everything. And, Mike, I was going to tell you tonight. That's why I phoned. You have to make that count for something.'

Yorke sat back down and took another deep breath. 'Let's just worry about the possible charge of murder first, before we think about the fact you didn't report the crime.'

12

FOLLOWING A FITFUL night's sleep, Yorke was woken early by a call from Salisbury station. There was a CCTV camera over the road from Joe Ray's cottage and part of his abduction had been caught on film.

After viewing the footage, Yorke managed to fill a small room with officers important to the case; Gardner, Brookes and Topham were all present. Several other officers including DC Collette Willows and PC Sean Tyler were also in attendance.

Yorke said, 'Joe's abductor drove another white transit. This one had been stolen the previous night from outside the Grey Friar's council flats. This morning, it's been found abandoned near the gas works. Forensics are working on it now.'

'The footage shows a larger man wearing a pig's head. He does have the same build as the man on the ransom demand e-mail and the man disguised as Thomas Ray on the Sapphire restaurant CCTV footage. We know that this man is not Harry Butler, not so much because of the size, but rather because Harry was being watched by us during the time of Joe's abduction.'

Topham raised his hand.

'I know what you're going to say, Mark—'

'Can I say it anyway?'

'If you must.'

'We still do not have any evidence that the kidnapping and the murder are linked, so the saliva and DNA makes him our prime suspect for the latter.'

'We are all aware of this – this is why Harry remains in custody.'

'If the cases are linked, Harry could be working with the abductor—'

'Again, noted Mark. We can pick up this discussion following the meeting. Now, returning to the CCTV footage. The kidnapper wore a backpack, presumably with Thomas Ray's blood bagged up inside. First, he went around to the back of the cottage and several minutes later, after he'd left that print on the patio door, he returned to the front of the house to ambush Joe. He whacked him over the head with a piece of metal that looks like a large hook; then took a syringe from his jacket pocket and injected something into his neck, which either killed him or knocked him out.'

'Let's hope for the latter,' Gardner said.

'The man then disappeared into the house for approximately four minutes, presumably to deposit the blood and leave the message, before carrying Joe up his driveway to the back of his van. The man does this with remarkable ease. Not only is he very big, but he's strong.'

'And no one saw him hoisting an unconscious man into the van?' Brookes said.

'Several cars drove past, but no one stopped to do or say anything. Collette, could you run the plates on all the vehicles on the CCTV and send some officers to interview the car owners – see if anyone saw anything?'

Collette made a note in her pad.

'Something else of interest happened last night,' Yorke said, 'involving both Joe's sister Lacey and an IT specialist employed by the school, Phil Holmes. DS Jake Pettman received a call from Lacey reporting an assault by Holmes. Jake sent two officers to investigate. She'd been badly beaten, but denied rape, and said she didn't want to press charges.'

Gardner said, 'How did she meet this Phil Holmes?'

'At the station while they were both awaiting interview.'

Brookes said, 'And how did he fare in his interview?'

'I played the video back earlier. He denied having any contact with the boy. He does have a rather awkward manner, and his answers are often monosyllabic, but other than that his interview seemed to have no consequence.'

'Still, it's strange,' Topham said. 'Following the strange vibes you picked up off Lacey Ray yesterday, she suddenly makes our headlines again today with this man from the school.'

'I agree,' Yorke said. 'That's why Emma and me are going to the school later to question Holmes again. Not only do we need to know more about his relationship with Lacey and this alleged assault, but we need to check he's not connected to this kidnapping.'

FOLLOWING HER ARGUMENT WITH JAKE, Sheila Pettman had not slept a wink and now, to make matters worse, the morning sickness was ruthless. She'd taken the day off and sought distraction in a reality TV show focused on cooking. She turned it off after realising that the show, like all other reality game programmes, was based around conflict rather than the quality of someone's cooking.

Something clattered through the letterbox.

Expecting a new book, she was intrigued to receive a shabby brown envelope with 'Sheila' scrawled across the front in blue biro. She ripped open the envelope and shook a purple memory stick out into her hand; she continued to shake, but it contained nothing else.

She opened the front door, hoping to see whoever had posted it, but was too late. The only person in sight was a woman sitting at a bus stop opposite, wearing a fur coat; it was snowing hard, and it was impossible to see her face clearly.

After closing the front door and sitting back down on the couch, she switched off the reality show, opened her laptop and looked at the picture of Jake on her screen. She stroked his face. *I want to tell you, but there never seems to be a good time at the moment.*

She inserted the memory stick. There was only one file available to view: a video file entitled "Jake".

LACEY RAY YAWNED and her injuries stung. *A good thing.* It reminded her of Phil Holmes' continued existence and so enthused her.

She reached out from underneath the bus shelter into the fuzzy world; the cold sensation of snow on her hand reminded her that she was still here, in reality. Next, she slipped her other hand into her pocket and thumbed the passport she'd collected over an hour before from Jacques Louvre.

She shouldn't be here having fun with Jake Pettman's life, but he had her riled, and if she could only take a slight bit of revenge between now and her trip to Nice tomorrow morning, she'd take it.

Her phone buzzed and she saw that it was the misogynistic bully, Phil Holmes. *How excellent.*

She answered. 'Don't call me—'

'I want to see you.'

'After last night?'

'Yes.'

'Do you think I'm mad?'

'No. Of course not. I promise I want to make amends.'

'It's not a good idea. I still haven't made up my mind whether or not to go to the police yet.'

'I understand if that's what you want to do,' Phil said. 'Just see me and hear what I have to say first.'

'It takes more than an apology.'

'I know.'

Lacey paused ten seconds to let him believe she was deep in thought. 'Mercure Hotel at eight. I'll be checking in under a friend's name: Laura Bryce. She is a member of the hotel chain and gets me a good discount.'

'Okay, Laura Bryce.'

'Don't be late.'

'I won't.'

She hung up and held out her hand again, but the snow had stopped. It was risky she knew, but worth it. This time tomorrow, they would be looking for Laura Bryce, just like they'd be looking for a Sylvia Seddon in Southampton for the murder of Brian Lawrence.

The Blue Room wouldn't let her down. It never did.

WITH HER HAND trembling so hard, Sheila doubted she'd be able to use the remote control, but she managed. The reality TV show restarted; she watched a girl talking about the best way to put together a cottage pie with a grating Birmingham accent.

Lacey and Jake had been much younger in the video file – definitely before Sheila had started dating him, but it had been hideous just the same.

Here I am, pregnant, watching a sex tape made by my husband.

She turned the TV back off and flung the remote control as hard as she could against the wall. It spat its batteries back at her. Then, she jumped up and slammed the laptop on the floor. It announced its refusal to ever work again with a crunch.

What is this woman's agenda?

She hoisted her mobile phone out of her pocket and attempted to scroll through to Jake—

The woman outside ...

She turned slowly and looked through the lounge window. The woman in the fur coat had crossed the road and was now standing on her driveway, smiling.

Sheila's hand flew to her mouth.

AFTER THE MEETING, it was Gardner rather than Topham that approached him for a chat.

'I hope you're not going to moan at me too,' Yorke said.

'No, I agree with you. Harry's innocent.'

'And are you sure that's what I think?'

'Reasonably sure. I wanted to talk to you about something else. It'll be quick.'

'Fire away, Emma.'

When Gardner wasn't munching on tic tacs, the corner of her mouth twitched; it usually flared up when she was nervous about something. It was flaring up right now.

He pulled out some gum and held some out to her.

'You noticed then.'

'We've been friends for a long time.'

She smiled and took a piece. 'Anyway, the thing is, me and Barry were wondering if you wanted to be Anabelle's godfather?'

'I'm not Catholic.'

'That doesn't matter.'

Yorke looked away, but quickly looked back – he didn't want to give Gardner the impression that he was uncomfortable with the request. This had been the reason she was nervous – she knew he'd try and wriggle out. 'I'm not sure I'd be the best godfather.'

'I disagree.'

'Aren't you best asking a friend who's a father already? I mean, I'm not sure I have any paternal attributes whatsoever.'

'Never mind, just thought I'd ask anyway.'

As she turned to leave, Yorke said, 'Okay.'

'Really?'

'Yes, you took me by surprise that's all. Sounds good. Who knows? I might even take to the whole fatherhood idea.'

She smiled. 'Thanks, sir.'

'No, thank you for thinking of me.'

After she left him, he sighed; it'd been too long since he'd used those words.

———

Yorke was sitting in a pokey little room that could have doubled up as a broom cupboard, but it was big enough for a desk and a filing cabinet stuffed full of old cases - most were solved, but some remained unsolved and grew colder by the day.

He squeaked back into a leather swivel chair and watched the CCTV footage of Joe's abduction again. Watching that large man prance around wearing a pig's mask was like watching a poorly made eighties' video nasty; he could only imagine how bad it must have smelled inside that scooped-out hog's head. Was the psycho wearing nose plugs?

He re-watched an interview with Francis Weller, an English teacher with straggly tufts of hair which seemed to have grown around the arms of his spectacles like vines around a drainpipe.

'Last year, he was in here every morning before most of the other kids had arrived, talking about books with me. It was verging on obsessive. Sometimes, I'd have to pretend to be listening so I could get on with my work while he sat there. I'd be doing duty breaks and lunches, and he'd be following like a shadow.'

'So, you'd say he was needy then?' the interviewing officer said.

'Very. But then it just stopped. Really peculiar. Six or seven months ago. He lost all interest in talking to me.'

'How did you feel about that?'

'Honestly? The first few weeks, relieved. After that, it kind of hurt my feelings a little bit.' Weller paused to smile. 'Wondered what I'd done to upset him, but he still worked hard and was polite to me in lessons, so I guess he just became bored of spending his mornings with an old man.'

Yorke picked up a paper folder full of photos and emptied them on the floor. It formed a rather gruesome collage.

His eyes scanned the images: pools of blood, a smashed up transit van, peculiar words written in blood, an old man hanging from a hook, an aerial shot of the school, the Ray family's cottage, Thomas Ray's barn. He spent almost ten minutes looking for a pattern.

From the door, Topham greeted Yorke.

Yorke didn't speak, just lifted his hand in the air to signal a greeting.

'You pissed off, boss?' Topham said.

'Not really.'

'I would be.'

'Why? Your suspicions are credible. I know we may have to arrest him. But I cannot ignore my gut. And in this instance, both of our guts are saying two different things.'

Topham sighed. 'Your judgement is clouded.'

Yorke swivelled in his chair. 'If that was the case, wouldn't I be more likely to have him arrested? Some would argue that getting his face on the papers might give me some sense of personal satisfaction.'

'His DNA is on the body!'

'He spat on the man who murdered his wife! And as much as I dislike the man, putting the press on his doorstep, again, is not going to help anyone, especially not Paul and Joe Ray. This conversation is over, Mark. If you really believe Harry is behind all of this, go and check up with the uniforms watching him. Right now, I've got things to do.'

'Shit, you're stubborn, sir!'

'I'm hearing that a lot at the moment.'

'Well, I guess you're the boss.'

'That I am.'

'So, what now?'

'Come over here and look at these with me.' Yorke pointed at the bloody collage on the floor.

From another folder Yorke pulled out another photo. The malignant narcissist, Lacey Ray. She was much younger and dressed in her tartan sixth form uniform. 'Around the time Jake was getting to know her better.' He dropped the picture and it floated for a second or two before landing on the collage. It sat beside a close-up picture of the words, "In the Blood" scrawled across the toilet wall. 'Lacey Ray has no children. She's the last Ray by blood we know the whereabouts of.'

'And?'

'Get rid of her and the line ends.'

'You make it sound like a vampire movie.'

'With all this blood everywhere, it might as well be. Let's see what she's up to.'

He contacted the officer sitting on her place. 'Can I get an update, please?'

There was a pause. Yorke didn't like it one bit. 'Shit - don't tell me.'

'Sorry, sir. She must have seen me in the car park. She disappeared out the back door.'

He hung up without saying goodbye, and flicked through his notebook until he found her mobile number.

'She's slipped out,' he said to Topham as he phoned her. She answered straight away. 'Yes?'

'It's DCI Yorke here. I would really appreciate it if you could come in and help us further with our enquiries.'

'I'm busy, right now.'

'Where are you?'

'Visiting the wife of an old friend.'

'Who?'

'Do I have to answer that question?'

Yorke was already on his feet, pacing around the tiny office, suddenly aware of how a large zoo animal in a small cage must feel. 'Listen, Ms Ray, we've no time for this. People in your family are missing. When are you free?'

'I've told you absolutely everything I know.'

'You've not really told us anything about last night.'

'What do you want to know?'

'What happened would be a good start.'

'I fell in with the wrong man. It's happened before and, knowing me, it will probably happen again. He was a bully and he hit me hard, several times.'

'Phil Holmes works at the school your nephew was taken from.'

'Yeah, so?'

'Do you think he could be connected to the kidnapping in any way?'

She snorted. 'Phil? No, he's a gorilla. He doesn't have the intellect to pull off anything like that.'

Yorke sighed. 'We really need to speak to you properly, Lacey.'

'Later.'

He choked back his anger and tried a different approach. 'New evidence has come to light suggesting you could be in danger; it would be safer for you to come to the station.'

'Danger, how so?'

'Well, whoever has your nephew and brother may not stop there. You saw the message yourself. It is possible there is a vendetta against the Ray family.'

There was a pause. 'Ah, so you want to use me as bait?'

'Police don't do that, Ms Ray.'

'That's good to hear. I'd hate to be a pawn in some kind of game.'

'Ms Ray. Forgive me if I'm wrong, but it sounds like you don't care enough about your brother and nephew.'

'Is that what you think, Detective?'

He detected anger in her voice.

'I think you *should* be expressing more concern.'

'*Should?* We are all individuals, Detective, and we are all capable of defining our own sense of morality.'

'If you don't come into the station now, Ms Ray, I will have to send someone to find you.'

'Be patient, Detective, right now, my sense of morality has brought me to someone else.'

'Who?'

'A woman, a very broken woman. My battery is about to die, detective—'

'Her name?'

'Every now and again we meet someone special, Detective. And when they throw it back in your face, it becomes even more painful to deal with.'

The blood drained from Yorke's face. 'Are you with Sheila?'

But the phone was already dead.

'What's happening?' Topham said.

'I don't know exactly,' Yorke said. 'Something bad. Get a search out for Lacey Ray immediately.'

Topham nodded and disappeared out of the door while Yorke located Sheila's phone number in the directory in his phone. When he hit call, he was sent straight to voicemail. He left a brief message saying that he was trying to contact her. Then, he called Willows. 'Get to Jake's house now. Take help. And don't, *whatever you do*, call Jake until after you've spoken to me again.'

13

THE SPRAWLING FIELDS, caked in ice, closed down around Jake. He turned off onto a gravel track, which made the three dirt samples installed in the plastic box rattle like old chains in a derelict factory. He phoned Yorke.

With a mouth dry from the previous three interviews, he said, 'The case will be over before I've visited all these farms.'

'Hopefully,' Yorke said.

'You sure there's still no match on the samples from yesterday?'

'Louise Tenor hasn't been in touch again, so it doesn't look that way. Sorry, Jake, I've not got time now.'

'Desperate to get rid of me?'

Yorke laughed. Jake noticed the laugh sounded forced.

'Something's wrong,' Jake said.

'Nothing's wrong, it's just the press need another statement and I've got that on my mind. I'll speak to you later. Just take care, okay?'

'Now, I know *there's* something wrong, you rarely even say goodbye, never mind tell me to take care.'

The phone went dead as Jake neared his next farmhouse. *The case is driving you off your rocker, Mike.*

On his right was a wooden-slatted barn; the sun angled shafts of light through the slits between the slats, making it look as if it was burning.

JOE HEARD car tyres chewing gravel outside and held his son's head tighter to his chest.

God, don't let it be that twisted bastard again. The next person I see opening that door has to be a policeman. It just has to be.

He kissed his sleeping son's face. *I won't let him hurt you.*

At the sides of the barn, the pigs shuffled and grunted, but he was becoming less and less concerned about them. Over the course of the long cold night, in which he'd laid awake trembling and crying, it had been the ravenous insects which prowled the hay that had bothered him most.

It was the gaping, bloody wound on his head that had drawn them in. He'd heard too many stories about insect eggs getting into open wounds, so had fought the pull of sleep and instead swatted flies, ticks, fleas and other creepy crawlies through the many hours.

Why was that man, Lewis, doing this?

Before he slept, Paul had told him all about the friendship he'd struck up with Lewis at the school. *How long had this bastard been planning?*

He hoped that the worst was over; he hoped that Lewis

would pay for what he'd done to them; but above all, he hoped that he could get his son back to his mother.

———————

JAKE PARKED and approached an old veranda with a string of lights hung across the old timber frame. Despite the daylight, they were switched on, making each bulb look like a sparkling snowflake.

After trudging through the deepening snow, he stopped at a short staircase to look up at an old lady scrunched up in a wheelchair. One hand was buried under a blanket, while the other skeletal hand stroked the knotted hair of a young, pale and dishevelled girl sitting on the slats in front of her.

'Stella Morris?'

'Yes, how can I help you?'

Jake was surprised, he'd not expected to hear the reply of such a withered creature over the shrill wind. Her voice crackled like burning wood.

He took the creaky steps one at a time until he stood a metre from the odd pair.

He held his ID up in front of Stella. 'I'm Detective Sergeant Jake Pettman; I'm here regarding the disappearance of Paul Ray, the young boy kidnapped from Salisbury Cathedral School. I take it you know about this already from the news. I'm collecting dirt samples from several farms in the proximity of the school.'

She smiled and Jake saw that she only had a few teeth. 'Why?'

'I'm not at liberty to say exactly, but I'm assuming you would want to help us with our inquiries?'

'Of course,' Stella said.

Jake looked down at the young girl. 'How old is your granddaughter?'

'Daughter, Mr Pettman.'

Jake was taken aback by this. This couldn't be this woman's daughter, surely? However, she could be adopted, so he played it safe and didn't mention it; instead, he made a mental note to look into it later.

'Sorry, how old?'

'Twelve,' the girl said.

Stella tightened her grip on her daughter's hair causing her to wince.

'She should be in school.'

'She's sick.'

'My information says that your husband passed away?'

'Yes. It's just me and my daughter Martha now.'

'So who helps you with your farming?'

'Martha, of course.'

'But if she's at school—'

'She tends the pigs in the evening. We are not really a thriving farm any more since my husband died, we just keep the place ticking over.'

'That's okay, but I do want you to know that criminal charges can be brought against you if you keep your daughter from her schooling.'

'I know,' Stella said.

'Is it okay if I take a look around, and get that sample now?'

'Martha,' Stella said, now stroking, rather than pulling, her daughter's knotted hair.

'Yes, Mother?'

'Be a good girl and show the policeman around.'

'Okay,' Martha said, rising to her feet.

He'd seen it before. A beautiful, yet neglected young

girl, with a vacant expression in her eyes, left to only imagine a life that many others, elsewhere, were taking for granted.

'Let's start with the barn,' Jake said, pointing towards the wooden shack which was being immolated by the glaring sun.

WHEN THE PIGS became unsettled again, flashing their jagged teeth at one another, and pounding the floor until clouds of hay and shit billowed into the air, Joe knew with certainty that someone was coming over to the barn. Paul did too; his head trembled in his lap.

'We're in danger Dad.'

He stroked Paul's hair. 'No, we're safe.'

The pigs disagreed; they continued to barge and clamber over each other, scratching their thick hides against the wooden walls.

'I'll never go near another pig again,' Paul said.

Joe smiled and kissed him on the forehead. 'That's really going to annoy your mother when she makes you a bacon sandwich on Sunday.'

Paul managed a smile, but then his eyes filled with tears again.

Joe pulled his son tighter against him. 'I won't let anything happen to you, I promise.' And while rocking his terrified boy, Joe looked up at the roof and prayed for the police.

BENEATH THE BLANKET that kept her withered limbs warm, Stella checked the gun Lewis had given her was ready. Then, after Martha and the policeman had made their head start, she juddered down the ramp installed at the other side of the veranda.

The years and the disease had been unkind to her appearance, but she was experiencing a period of remission and her senses were sharp; she could see, even at this distance, the policeman bending down and scooping up some dirt. God knows what he hoped to achieve with that! Still, if the nosy copper wanted to go into the barn, that'd be a different matter and they'd have a big problem. If he made the request, she'd have no choice but to put a bullet in his back and empty his belligerent head into the swill for the pigs to eat.

She followed as fast as her wasted arms would allow – and they were stronger than they looked. She also enjoyed the energetic snow, which no longer seemed to spiral, but instead came in slanting skeins like falling guillotine blades.

THE SNOWFLAKES WERE COMING FASTER, creating confusion.

Can I trust my senses? Jake thought.

If he couldn't, then he was putting himself in danger.

He didn't expect to be ambushed here by a crabby old woman and her special daughter, but he had to be alert. After all, out here, with nothing for miles around, who would come to his aid if he did get into trouble?

No wonder they were struggling to get this boy back. In this emptiness, who notices anything out of the ordinary? Who phones in unusual occurrences?

No wonder the Ray disease had always prospered so well in isolation.

The barn ahead jutted out of the ground at an awkward angle, almost as if it had resisted being built there, and had squirmed under the builder's hands until it had become lopsided. The noise of pigs festering inside made Jake's stomach turn and he regretted his mouthfuls of processed ham the night before.

'They're certainly making a racket,' Jake said to Martha as they reached the door.

'They always do, they think it's their time. Mother says they're even more intelligent than me.'

'Well, you strike me as quite a bright young lady.'

Under her white, fleece-lined trapper's hat, which she put on before leading him out here, her pale face suddenly reddened.

There was a screech as a blast of ice-cold wind drove over the farmyard. Jake shivered and the pigs squealed louder.

'Poor bastards,' Jake said and then put his hand over his mouth. 'Sorry.'

'It's okay, Mother has a worse tongue.'

Jake headed over to the barn door and took hold of a rusty padlock hanging from it, 'The key?'

When Martha didn't reply, he turned around to see that the redness had gone from her cheeks.

'Why?' Martha said.

'So I can have a quick look inside.'

She took a step back. 'Mother says you should never disturb them unless necessary.'

'It is necessary.'

Jake could see Stella wheeling toward them.

Incredible, Jake thought, *the woman looks half-dead and here she is braving the elements.*

'Have you got the key Martha or shall I ask your mother?'

Martha looked like she was about to cry. 'I have the key.' She rustled in the pocket of her jacket and handed it over with a trembling hand. 'Be careful.'

But she said it so quietly that Jake could barely hear it over the frenzied sound of pigs and wind.

Joe watched the roof. Watched the dust motes swirl in the shafts of light spearing the barn and watched the cobwebs shimmer on the gables like filigree jewellery.

But nothing could distract him from what was coming. The padlock on the door rattled and in his belly, fear bubbled like boiling swill.

Moments later – moments which seemed to last forever – he heard the key in the padlock, and the clunk of it being unlocked.

The bubbles of fear exploded in his belly, and he held his son as hard as he could. He peppered Paul's tear-drenched face with kisses.

'What's he going to do to us, Dad?'

'Nothing,' Joe said, staring down at the mouse-grey, hay-strewn, cold-earthen floor, making sure his eyes and the lie in them were hidden from his son. 'Absolutely nothing.'

STELLA WATCHED Jake take the key from Martha, and thrust it into the padlock. She lifted the gun from beneath the blanket.

Readying the weapon several metres from her target, she smiled at her daughter, who turned away with tears in her eyes. She wanted to shout over to her, tell her how pathetic she was. But she had a better idea as she watched the copper open the door.

Seeing his guts might just harden her up some.

14

LOOKING AT THE Pettmans' terraced house from beside the bus shelter on the opposite side of the road, Yorke caught some snowflakes in the palm of his hand. *Definitely firmer than before.* He rubbed them away between his thumb and forefinger. *Icier too.*

He turned around and looked at the bus shelter where Lacey had been sitting and watching Sheila almost an hour ago.

What are you up to Lacey?

He crossed the road and met Willows, who was shielding her eyes with the back of her hand from the sun glaring over the rooftops behind him.

Behind her were two officers he recognised from the school. They were still talking to Sheila Pettman, who was safe. *Thank god.*

'Did Lacey approach the house?' Yorke said.

'Yes – she approached and stared in from behind the garden wall, before turning back and catching the bus.'

'To where?'

'Andover, but it stops in town.'

'Contact the bus company – get them to check cameras, find out which stop she got off at.'

'Will do.'

'How's Sheila?'

'Shook up, but not just because of the visit. Lacey Ray posted a memory stick too.'

'Go on.'

Willows took a deep breath. 'DS Pettman and Lacey were having ... relations on the video.'

'*Sex?*' His word shot out on a spear of icy air.

'Err ... yes, sir, but years ago, when they were much younger. Not now.'

'Still. Lacey's really stirring things up. Here we are trying to help her family as she tears another one apart! She's gone too far this time. Collette, we need to find her, and find her quick.'

IN A SMALL CONFERENCE room at the Salisbury Cathedral School, Yorke drank two cups of coffee while Phil Holmes was being brought to them by Laura Baines, the head teacher. He only drank this quickly when his instincts were fired up.

'It's boiling in here,' Gardner said.

'Schools,' Yorke said. 'My memories of them are based around excessively heated classrooms.'

'How are we doing this then?' Gardner said.

'We start with you interviewing him regarding the assault on Lacey, make him feel that this is his primary reason for us being here; if he doesn't give us any indication that he's connected to the case at this point, I'll move in, chip away, see if he's connected to the kidnapping.'

'You think we'll find anything?'

Yorke reached for a third cup of coffee.

The door opened and Laura led Phil in.

'Hello, Mr Holmes,' Yorke said.

He was dressed in a suit and his hair was tied back into a ponytail. As usual, he avoided eye-contact. Instead, he stared over them at a row of pictures of previous headmasters. 'I'm very busy.'

He peeled off his leather jacket; Yorke half expected steam to rise from the heavy-set man like a split jacket potato. He took a seat at the head of a circular table. Gardner and Yorke sat to one side of him.

'Can you talk us through what you did last night?' Gardner said, immediately taking the lead.

'Which part?'

'The part with Lacey Ray?'

Phil continued looking over them as he spoke. 'Nothing important. I went to her apartment. We spent some time together and then I left.'

'Can you define "time spent together?"'

'That's a silly question,' Phil said, bringing his gaze down from the parade of headmasters and making eye-contact with Gardner for the first time.

She leaned forward and opened a brown folder on the black, varnished table. 'Just after you left, she called the police and reported an assault.'

'An assault?'

'Yes - I thought you could help us with that.'

'I never touched her.'

'That's not what she claims.'

'She's lying,' he said, looking at Yorke for the first time.

'So, can you be more detailed as to what happened last night?' Yorke said.

'I arrived at ten-past eight, ordered a Chinese from Happy Wok, watched TV, slept with her and left.'

He sounded robotic; recalling facts like he was reading from a shopping list. *Where are your emotions?*

'And you never hit her?' Gardner said.

'No. Are you going to arrest me?'

'She's not pressing charges.'

Yorke looked for the look of relief on his face; he couldn't see any.

'Good, because I've not done anything.'

He felt it was time to move in. 'So why do you think she's done this. Made up this story and then refused to press charges?'

Phil shrugged and ran his fingers over a scratch on the table. 'I've no idea.'

'Do you like her?'

'Yes, but she likes to control.'

'In what way?'

'In every way.'

'Sexually?'

Phil didn't answer, content to continue fiddling with the scratch.

Yorke leaned over to make some notes. 'Has she mentioned her missing family to you?'

They locked eyes. A rare occurrence. Yorke searched for a reaction. He was usually good at doing that. *Usually, but not this time.*

'In passing.'

'Just in passing! Does that not strike you as strange?'

'It's none of my business.'

Yorke turned to Gardner and leaned over to whisper in her ear. He didn't actually say anything meaningful, just

'I'm going to up the tempo', but he did it to make Phil feel less comfortable.

'I would be happy with everything you've told me, Mr Holmes, but for one problem: if you didn't hurt her, who did?'

'That's your problem, not mine.' His eyes fell away again.

Am I boring you? 'What time did you leave her place?'

'Five-past eleven.'

'That's precise.'

Phil didn't respond.

'Tell me, what drew you to working at this school, Mr Holmes?'

'A good job.'

'How did you find it?'

'They advertised online. It was a long contract.'

'How long?'

'Twelve months.'

Yorke looked down at his notes. 'Of which you've completed six months.'

'Yes.'

'Is it well-paid?'

'Reasonably.'

'How much?'

'Fifty-five thousand for the year.'

'And how has the last six months been?'

'Hard work.'

'How so?'

'Setting up a VLE is time-consuming.'

'But you enjoy it?'

'Yes.'

'Did you ever meet Paul Ray?'

Phil locked eyes with Yorke again. 'I've been interviewed about that twice already.'

'I know. But you have to see it from our perspective, you work at the school where Paul was abducted, and then you are suddenly in a relationship with the child's aunt. In my experience, coincidences are always worth following up on.'

'I thought I'd explained myself well.'

Yorke glanced at Gardner. He wondered if she was holding back a laugh too.

'Up until now, Mr Holmes, you have been vague in interviews. Worryingly so.'

Phil fiddled with his watch. 'Social anxiety. Never been good in these situations.'

'Are you being treated?'

'I used to take tablets. They made my head cloudy.'

Yorke made some notes. He then opened his folder and slid a picture across the table. It was a still shot from outside the Sapphire restaurant. 'That's the man who took Paul Ray. Apart from the facial hair, he looks very similar to you; he even has the same long hair.'

'It's not me. I was in the school.'

Yorke stared. If the man was having any reaction to this, he was burying it deep.

'Look at the time,' Yorke said, tapping the digits in the corner of the photo. 'That was much later, after I'd left. The poor boy had been waiting in the van, hadn't he?'

'I don't know what you're talking about. I didn't know the boy.'

'Yes, so you keep saying. You have very little to do with the children. In a school! Do you not think that's odd?'

'Sometimes they see me with ICT problems, but there are many children, and I don't form personal relationships. At least, not easily.'

'Apart from with Lacey Ray?'

'She approached me.'

Yorke pretended to read his notes. 'That day I saw you, you had damp hair?'

'I'd been playing squash and had just showered.'

'Are you allowed to play squash during work hours?'

'There's no rule. I don't work standard hours. Some nights I stay late.'

'Who did you play with?'

'I played alone.'

'Played squash alone?'

'Practising my serve.'

'Did anyone see you?'

'I didn't speak to anyone.'

'It's just there was a lot of blood at the scene of the kidnapping. Whoever put it there may have had to wash.'

Phil shrugged and looked up. 'Ask the PE staff. Maybe, someone saw me?'

Yorke slid another photo over the table. This time it was the photo Harry had taken outside the barn.

Phil glanced at it.

'Would you say that was the same man on the other photo, the one that looks like you?' Yorke said.

'I don't know. It's not good quality.'

'Do you know where that is?'

'No.'

'Did you know Thomas Ray?'

'Heard of him. I know what he did. Saw that he was dead on the news today. I've never met him.'

'Where were you yesterday at two PM?'

'Here, working, of course.'

'Did anyone see you around that time?'

'Staff are always stopping in. I can check my computer

activity around that time, I'm sure I can find someone I was helping.'

Yorke looked at Gardner and gestured for her to go outside with him. 'Excuse us a moment, Mr Holmes.'

Outside, with the door closed behind them, Yorke said, 'What do you think?'

'There's clearly something wrong. We need to get this social anxiety confirmed.'

'We're lacking motivation though. Apart from his fling with Lacey, what is his connection to the Rays? I'm going to have his background thoroughly investigated. He's ambiguous with most of his answers, but most notably with his visit to the school sport's facilities. Head down to the sports hall and see if anyone saw him first period on the day of the kidnapping playing squash or having a shower. Then, could you find out if he was seen at the school between two and three PM yesterday during the time of Joe's abduction? I'm going to talk to Laura Baines again.'

'Have you seen the papers today?' The frosty, well-spoken head teacher said, staring up at him over her spectacles.

Yorke nodded, closing her office door behind him.

'They're dragging us through the mud.'

Accidental classroom injuries and minor complaints made by students against staff over recent years were being pulled to the surface.

'Yes.' *Bad for business*, Yorke thought. 'It'll blow over, it always does.'

'So, did you find out what you needed to know about Phil Holmes.'

Yorke pulled up a chair. 'What can you tell me about him?'

'Surely you don't suspect him.'

'We just want to rule him out, Mrs Baines.'

'Okay, what can I tell you ... he's quiet and reserved. He does not have anything to do with the other staff really, apart from when he's helping them with an IT issue. But he's effective, very efficient actually. He was the best candidate for the job, and his DBS check came back fine. He's been solid for six months. As I said, he's quiet, but I could say all this about some of my other teachers too.'

'He claims he has social anxiety. What do you think?'

'Well he isn't much of a conversationalist, and does have an annoying habit of avoiding eye contact, but I've come across many people like this. I just assumed he liked gadgets, and preferred to spend his time with them rather than people.'

'When I saw him at the school on the day of the abduction, his hair was damp and just now, he claimed to have used the squash court in the school sports hall during first period, rather than working. Is that acceptable to you as his employer?'

'Well, he doesn't teach, so it's not a massive problem, and he does stay very late some nights. But I will talk to him about this; he needs to be available during school hours in case any of the staff need him regarding an IT issue.'

'My partner is just talking to your PE department now, just to confirm he was there that day. Is this okay?'

'That's fine.'

Yorke looked at his notes. 'Can you confirm that he was in the school at two PM yesterday?'

'I didn't see him, but someone may have required his help.'

'He suggested an activity check on his computer.'

'I guess he'd be the one to do that, but I could ask someone in the business department with IT skills to look into that one for you.'

'Excellent. One more thing, do the students have much contact with Phil Holmes?'

'Yes, they do. He installed a new VLE, so they speak to him regarding this.'

'Yes, Phil mentioned the VLE to me while I was at the school. Allows students to access work on the internet and send it in for marking?'

'Among many other things, yes. Anyway, several students have been struggling to log-on in class and they have had to go to Phil to have passwords reset.'

'Can you find out which students have been to see him?'

'I guess so. I will have to ask the teachers which students have requested password resets during their lessons. It might take me a couple of hours to receive all the names back by e-mail, and the list won't be reliable, because they may have forgotten some of the requests. There will be a lot of them - Phil has been working here for six months.'

'Give it a go; I'm only interested in one name anyway.'

'Paul Ray, I'm guessing.'

'If his name shows up, phone me, immediately.'

15

THE NOISE OF pigs seemed to be coming from all directions. It was an illusion; the wind was surely messing with Jake's hearing. The squeals were only coming from within the barn, the door of which he was holding half-open.

His phone vibrated in his pocket. He reached for it and let the barn door clatter shut. Hopefully, it would be Yorke with news that they'd already found a match on the dirt, put him out of this misery.

While taking his mobile from his pocket, he rotated and then flinched when he saw the old woman only a couple of metres away from him; her tiny face, sucked of moisture, peered out from the old blanket.

'Are you creeping up on me?' he said.

She smiled, and Jake looked at his phone. He saw Sheila was calling and answered. 'Hello?'

'She came here.'

His blood ran cold. 'Who?'

'That crazy bitch.'

'Shit—'

'And she brought a movie with her.'

'*A movie?*'

'Yes. Of you and her.'

'I don't understand,' he said. Disturbed by the way the withered woman was staring at him so intently, he turned back around. Martha was replacing the padlock.

He was just about to tell Martha to stop when Sheila said, 'Of you and her fucking.'

Jake felt panic rising from the pit of his stomach. 'That's bullshit, I haven't touched her.'

'It's from when you were younger. A little souvenir of your time together.'

'Shit,' he said, remembering the time Lacey had filmed them together. 'Where are you now?'

'My mother's.'

'I'll be right there.'

'No—'

'We have to talk.'

'Not now.' The phone went dead.

He looked up at Martha and Stella who were both staring at him.

'An emergency, I have to go. Thanks for this,' he said, holding up the paper bag which contained the mud sample.

'No problem,' Stella said.

Jake turned and marched over the snowy ground towards his car. He heard Martha bid him farewell; then he heard the squealing pigs up their tempo.

They were probably glad to see the back of him.

JAKE WAS FURIOUS WITH LACEY. It was a struggle to keep his finger from the call button. But he had to. All contact had to stop immediately. Having her restrained, taken out of his life would now become a police matter.

Focus on Sheila, he thought, *make that right.*

After punching straight through the traffic from Devizes to Salisbury, Jake stood outside Sheila's mother's house. The lights were on.

Around his feet, mounds of snow rose from the concrete path. He rang the doorbell. No one bothered to answer. He tried the house phone, which he could hear ringing from where he was standing. Again, no one answered.

He rapped on the door until his knuckles burned, before heading along the side of the house and banging on the double glazing.

Eventually, his mother-in-law opened the front door, poked her head out, and stared at him through dyed black eyelashes.

'She doesn't want to see you Jake.'

He headed back to the front door. 'I know, just for a minute, to explain—'

She slammed the door. He took a step back, burst a mound of snow with his foot and began to shout.

AFTER HEARING from Willows that Lacey Ray had exited the bus in town and then disappeared into a shopping centre, Yorke received a call from a number that he didn't recognise. He took it outside the school beneath the bike shelter.

'Detective Chief Inspector Michael Yorke?' The voice sounded half-digested by tobacco.

'Yes, who is this please?'

'DCI John Hargreaves from Southampton – we met before at a conference not that long ago.'

'I remember,' Yorke said, recalling the bulbous man who was pinned to the buffet table for most of the evening. Yorke listened to the busy sounds of his department in the background.

Hargreaves said, 'Just this morning, we went to pick up Lacey Ray from her Southampton flat and found that she'd packed and left. We saw that you'd put out an APW for her. We need to get hold of her also.'

'What do you want her for?'

'One of the richest real-estate dealers in the city, Brian Lawrence, met a rather unsavoury end in a hotel room here several nights ago and, while investigating this, Lacey Ray has come onto our radar.'

There was a violent gurgle in Yorke's stomach. 'Are you sure?'

'We have CCTV footage of a woman arriving at his room before he did, wearing a scarf, hat and sunglasses like some kind of film star. It took a while to find someone in Lacey's *network* to recognise her behind the disguise, but after they did, we compared it to photos of her. The CCTV footage is not great, and any solicitor worth his salt would tear it to pieces, but we think it's her.'

'No one thought this disguise was peculiar when she checked into the hotel?'

'It's a love hotel for the great and the good apparently; everyone walks around in disguise and checks in under different names.' Hargreaves coughed; it was deep and chesty. The tobacco industry had taken his lungs too.

'What name did she check-in under?'

'Mrs Sylvia Seddon.'

'When you said "network" before, I assumed you mean those connected to the prostitution racket?'

'Yes.'

'Can you get confirmation from the agency that she was with this Brian Lawrence?'

'Tried that. Lawrence was being regularly serviced by four prostitutes; of which, Lacey was one. But she wasn't requested that night. Her day off apparently. It could have been an off-the-books arrangement perhaps?'

'Four prostitutes? Bloody hell! Have you interviewed the other three?'

'Of course. Shit, these girls cost thousands.'

'As the world around him slips deeper into the financial mire, he indulges in a thoroughly hedonistic lifestyle.'

'Real-estate agents, just like bankers, no conscience. Sociopaths.'

'Exactly like Lacey Ray,' Yorke said. 'She's causing all kinds of trouble around here. How was Lawrence killed?'

'Slowly and sadistically. She tied him to a chair before cutting off his fingers and stabbing him to death with a penknife.'

Thomas Ray was killed sadistically too, Yorke thought.

'Evidence?'

'A few fibres, no fingerprints or DNA. And the weak CCTV footage of her walking with her eyes on the floor. We were waiting on the confession really.'

'Off Lacey Ray? Not a chance. Do your research. She's a narcissist and prides herself on control. I suspect she wouldn't confess with a knife to her throat, and I imagine that she will have developed a real skill for lying.'

'Sounds like we best hurry up and find her,' Hargreaves said, coughing again. Yorke wondered if Hargreaves had left it too late to cut back on the cancer sticks.

'There's nothing I'd like more. She's taking a liking to a good friend of mine. This morning, she paid his wife a social call.'

'I saw it on the report.'

'I still have her mobile number, which I contacted her on earlier today. I've put a trace on the number, but I've tried it again recently and it's switched off. I wouldn't be surprised if she's ditched it by now. She was last sighted in town. I have officers trying to track her down. You'll be the first to know when we have her.'

'How's the search for the boy and his father going; it's all over the news here.'

'We're making progress.'

'Do you think Lacey has anything to do with it?'

'Let me find her first and I'll update you on that one.'

As soon as they said their farewells and finished the call, Yorke's mobile rang again. It was Tyler. He was flustered. 'DS Pettman is at his mother-in-law's house looking for Sheila. They're not letting him in, and he's refusing to leave. The neighbours are complaining about the commotion.'

'Okay, I'll be right there.'

ON THE WAY, Yorke tried Jake's mobile but was sent through to voicemail. He used his smart phone to put Topham, Gardner and Brookes on a conference call so he could update them with the information from DCI John Hargreaves.

'Bloody hell,' Gardner said.

'Shit, it's always the beautiful ones,' Topham said.

'What are you talking about Mark? This isn't French film noir,' Brookes said.

Irritated, Yorke's voice rose slightly. 'Anyway, we need everyone looking for her; Mark can you gather our troops?'

'Yep.'

'Also, thinking about the way Thomas Ray was tortured, we could do with a comparison, to see if his murder exhibits the same MO as the one used in the Lawrence case. Emma, if you could handle that.'

'Okay.'

'Iain, she was using the pseudo name, Sylvia Seddon, when she was suspected of going to work on Brian Lawrence. See if you can get any hits on that name.'

'What are you up to?' Gardner said.

'Following a lead,' Yorke said, turning into the road where Jake was apparently causing commotion. 'I'll let you know if it comes to anything.'

He parked outside the house; no-one was outside. When he knocked on the door, Sheila answered immediately. Her eyes were red from crying and she glared at Yorke as if he was the reason for her sadness.

'Yes?'

'Hi Sheila,' Yorke said. 'I know you've had a bad day, but I'm looking for Jake—'

'He was here. Shouting. Now, he's gone.'

'Do you know where?'

'Don't know, don't care. I suppose you've seen his Oscar-winning performance by now?'

'No, I haven't.'

A woman appeared behind Sheila. They looked dissimilar, but Yorke assumed it was her mother. She crossed her arms. 'I always told Sheila he was trouble.'

This really isn't something I want to get involved in, Yorke thought.

Sheila's mother continued, 'Jane next door was married to a copper. I remembered what it was like for her. She had severe IBS by the time she was fifty.'

'I'm sorry Sheila for what happened today,' he said. 'We're dealing with it and we'll let you know what happens.'

'Bye Mike,' Sheila said and closed the door.

Yorke took a deep breath. *Jake, you're going to be on that sofa bed a while longer I'm afraid.*

As he walked back to his car, he tried Jake's phone again. This time he got a response.

'Where are you?'

'Guess.'

Yorke sighed. 'You're joking.'

'Nope.'

'We're in the middle of trying to solve a double abduction and a murder.'

'I know.'

'And now we have a suspected murderer on the run.'

'And who is that?'

'Your turn to guess.'

'Shit.'

'I'm on my way to explain. Don't go anywhere.'

ABOVE THE DOOR, the picture of Dionysus, God of Wine — which always reminded Yorke of the fawn in The Lion, the Witch and the Wardrobe — seemed to be smiling, welcoming him to The Wyndham Arms, birthplace of the phenomenon, Hopback, the brewers of Summer Lightning. In the front parlour, he found Jake indulging in a seasonal special of Winter Lightning, which was spicier than its counterpart. Yorke looked at the bar, suddenly craving a pint of Gilbert's First Beer — the ale that first began the Hopback phenomenon. Knowing that alcohol in his bloodstream would do no good for his instincts right now, he resisted.

'Figured I might lose my job for drinking on duty. Sheila would most certainly approve of that one!' Jake said.

'Sheila would. I don't.'

'Sheila will be disappointed.'

Jake said, 'How about a random piss test; you never know, they gave me one a couple of years ago.'

Yorke saw that Jake had consumed half his pint already. 'Tell me that's your first.'

'Second.'

'It's your last then.'

'Tell me about Lacey being a suspected murderer.'

Yorke obliged.

'And she's stalking me and my wife. Great!'

'The next time you'll see her, she'll be in custody.'

'I was having enough problems; shit, Mike, I feel like my life is falling apart.'

Yorke squeezed his shoulder. 'I know, mate.'

'You're just about to tell me you've been there.'

'You know that more than anyone. We need a long hard talk once this case is over.'

A drunk local called Kenny swaggered by. Seventy plus and still going strong; by his own admission it was because he was 'fuelled by the Lightning'.

'Hello Michael,' he said, in a thick, Wiltshire slur. 'Not got yer pretty lady with yer today?'

He was, of course, referring to a girl Yorke had very briefly dated. Another one that had ended all too quickly when they'd realised he was still hung up on his first true love – Charlotte. Obviously, he'd never told Kenny that relationship was over, nor was he about to. He was the type of chap you drank a beer and laughed with. Stories of woe were not on the agenda. 'Not today, Kenny.'

'You naughty boy,' he said, wagging a finger, while spilling a mouthful of beer over his brown cords.

'I feel like killing her,' Jake said.

'Perfectly natural, I'm sure, but I'm pretty sure you won't do that.'

Jake smiled. 'Everyone can have their unpredictable moments.'

'True. But you don't have to do anything now. As I've just explained to you, the witch has already sentenced herself to a burning, we just have to hunt her down.'

Yorke took a mouthful of Jake's pint and then pushed it aside. 'That's enough.'

'Why?'

'Well, not only have you got to run in those dirt samples in the car, you're putting my reputation on the line.'

'How so?'

'I've been telling everyone that you're the best policeman I've ever had the misfortune of working with.'

'Misfortune?'

'No one likes to be argued with by someone who thinks they know better, especially when it turns out that they sometimes do!'

Jake smiled again. Yorke's phone beeped. A message to pick up from voicemail. He rang through. It was Laura Baines, the head teacher from the Salisbury Cathedral School. He felt his blood pressure rise as he listened to the message.

Afterwards, he jumped to his feet. 'I have to go.'

'Why?'

'I think I know who has Paul and Joe Ray.'

Jake started to rise to his feet too.

'No,' Yorke said. 'All you need to do right now is calm down, run those dirt samples in.'

'At least tell me who it is?'

'It's *not* Lacey Ray. But if she comes anywhere near you, you call me, okay?'

'Okay.'

Making his way to the exit, he heard Jake calling out from behind him. 'And I can't kill her?'

Above the door, the Hopback logo of Dionysus seemed to have lost its smile and appeared to frown instead; maybe, it wanted him to stay.

He had a feeling that things may just turn out a lot better if he did.

Lacey Ray threw the fake driver's licence she had used to check in with onto the hotel bed, followed by the bag containing her brand new passport. Then, she sat in front of the mirror, and removed her jet-black wig. She smiled. The male receptionist had said she was the spitting image of Uma Thurman in Pulp Fiction and had started to flirt with her. He wasn't bad looking, but he was barely out of his teens. *Not enough sin to pay for just yet*, she thought, smiling to herself.

Her muddy-brown hair flopped down around her shoulders. She scrubbed off the dark make-up with a baby wipe to reveal her purpling injuries.

The hotel room that Lacey Ray had just checked herself into at the *Mercure* under the pseudonym, Laura Bryce, was more of a citrus-green colour than her preferred blue. It didn't matter so much; following the beating, she'd already conducted the murder last night in the Blue Room. Tonight's eight o'clock rendezvous with Phil Holmes was a mere formality.

There were risks she knew. *But why fight it? It feels far too good, far too natural ...*

She hadn't been able to resist striking that blow to Jake's marriage, following his arrogant judgements and callous dismissal of her attention. The police would be hunting her now anyway, and it was only a matter of time before they linked her to Brian Lawrence in Southampton.

She'd be no worse off for killing Phil; she'd still be on the same plane tomorrow, in the same disguise, with the same new identity.

Then, she'd disappear into Nice with a new identity and she would be untouchable. She looked over at the bag which contained her new passport. *Lucy Evans, not long left until I bring you to life.*

She thought back to how she'd given the copper back at her flat the slip, disappearing out of the rear exit near the bins. At the end of all this, Salisbury's finest will be kicking themselves.

Above the bed was an artist's rendition of the cathedral in medieval times. Uneducated folk swarmed around it in rags. *How sweet they looked,* she thought, *uncorrupted by technology and ambition.* She paused to wonder if her motivations would have been different if she'd been born back then.

She went back over to the bed, opened her bag and took a quick inventory: a gag, rope, handcuffs, a penknife and a pair of secateurs.

Kyle Meadows, Alex Wright, Brian Lawrence and now,

Phil Holmes. Men who liked to control, men who had finally lost control.

She pushed her tools to one side, lay down and stretched out. Plenty of time to sleep. Keep her energy up.

She had a busy evening ahead.

16

THE FLICKERING BULB finally blew, leaving Sarah Ray's bare-box room to whatever sunlight the frugal winter offered through a tiny window. Lying back on the bed, she continued to be plagued by the same question that had been driving her insane all night:

Are my family dead?

She stood up and looked around. The safe house looked as if it would be a real nightmare to sanitise. Not that she could manage it right now anyway. Currently, she felt like a mummified corpse; dry, dusty and slowly decaying.

She walked over to the window and caught her reflection in the dirty glass.

Grey ...

Old ...

As a young woman, she'd wanted to be a model – she'd had a chance, or so those close to her had said. But she'd wasted her life on a husband who hadn't loved her and a son who pitied her. She *was* a mummified corpse. With mummified dreams.

She used a tissue to wipe dirt off the glass.

Why Paul?

Notoriety, violence and despair had followed the Rays throughout history. Was there a curse? A curse echoing throughout the generations?

It wasn't fair. Paul had been different; he was such a good boy, he'd had a chance ...

Until the curse which echoed in his blood had finally caught up with him.

Her phone beeped. It was a picture message and a tear sprang to her eye when she saw her handsome young boy looking exhausted, staring at her through a mop of greasy hair. She touched the picture of her son and then read the attached message:

"The car park of Lankton field in Woodford. One hour. Tell no one. Come alone and your family will live. Be punctual, if you are late, one of them will die."

They're still alive.

And may just stay that way if she followed the rules. But then she recalled the police's rule: if the kidnapper contacts, Bryan should be told immediately.

But hadn't they botched their last attempt at getting Paul back?

And she'd been so convinced that time that he was coming home. She couldn't go through that same disappointment again; it was her duty, as his mother, to go and get him.

She looked at her watch. It was half-past three. She had until half-past four.

She'd need a car.

Bryan's.

Twenty-five minutes after giving Bryan a coffee laced with a powerful hypnotic sleeping pill – and copious amounts of sweetener to mask the horrid taste – Sarah returned to the living room. The door was ajar, so she observed him through the narrow crack. He was sitting on a nauseating green and yellow sofa; a throwback from the seventies that the police department probably got gratis from the family of someone who had died. Because his feet were on an oak coffee table, the only object in the entire house that Sarah could stomach, that familiar irritability – a result of her OCD – swept over her. She fought with all her will.

Bryan was reading today's paper through wiry spectacles, stretched to breaking point by his chubby face. *Why was he not asleep yet? She'd have to leave and get the bus if she didn't get his keys, time was against* her. She pushed the door open fully, stepped into the room, winced at the smell of old smoke, and cleared her throat.

Over his wiry glasses, he looked up at her.

Unable to fight the irritability any longer, she gestured at the coffee table on which he rested his feet. *It doesn't matter how dirty the place is, there are no excuses for making it dirtier.*

'Sorry,' he said, and brought his feet down.

The relief was immediate.

'I'd like to go out for a walk, clear my head.'

'That's not a good idea,' he said, rising to his feet as if he was worried she might just run out. He pointed outside at the worsening snowfall. 'Besides, look at it out there.'

She noticed he was slurring his words.

She said, 'I'll go mad, if I stay in here much longer.'

'I'll go with you.' He took a step forward.

She realised she was sweating heavily despite the icy

draft reaching in through the single-glazed window. 'I'll be fine on my own.'

He stopped and put his hand to his forehead. While blinking rapidly, he staggered backward.

'Are you okay?'

'I must have stood up too quickly.'

'I'll get you a drink.'

'Yes, please.' Stumbling back, he fell into his chair.

Thank God, she thought, edging backwards to the kitchen. Grabbing a glass whitened with lime scale with one hand, she turned the tap on with her other. The pipes clunked.

After rushing the water back to him, he took a mouthful and spat it back in his glass. 'Tastes foul.'

The sleeping tablets were definitely kicking in; the metallic taste was the side-effect which always got her first too.

'Let me get you another.' She grabbed the glass from his hands. Five minutes later, when she came back in, his eyes were closed and he was snoring loudly.

As she rustled in the pockets of his jeans for the car keys, he didn't even stir.

Outside the safe house, the clouds were shifting and the sun was brightening. Sarah's eyes were drawn to the spiralling snowflakes – she likened them to the shavings from a glowing star. She raised her arms as she walked towards Bryan's black Audi and allowed the snowflakes to prickle the backs of her hands. After shining so gloriously in the air, she was disappointed when they turned to water and dripped off her skin.

After bashing snow from her boots, she climbed into the car and turned the engine on. There was a built in Satnav, so she punched in Lankton. It was less than ten miles away.

Thank god. The ETA sprang up - thirteen minutes. She reversed out of the drive.

THE AIR-CONDITIONING UNIT in the Salisbury Cathedral School reception churned out hot air. Yorke noticed that the Christmas tree beneath had expressed its discontent by shedding most of its needles while the presents around it, organised so neatly only two days ago, suddenly looked dishevelled. No carols hummed from the speakers today.

When he requested the head teacher, Laura Baines, the elderly receptionist picked up the phone and mumbled something into it from the side of her mouth. He couldn't understand a word that she had said, and assumed Laura Baines must have grown accustomed to her receptionist's slur.

The artificially-heated air was clinging to him like a hungry leech, so he peeled off his jacket and hooked it over his arm.

While waiting for Laura Baines, he checked in with Willows, and was disappointed to hear that there was still no sign of Lacey Ray, despite the sizeable chunk of manpower assigned to the task.

Baines was with him a minute later. She gripped his hand tightly and widened her bloodshot eyes.

Was she pleading with him to put an end to this whole infernal affair?

He almost spoke, but held back; he'd already made one promise too many since beginning this case.

'As I said on the message, Phil left the school after you finished interviewing him. I'll take you to his office,' Baines said.

249

Like last time, he matched her strong and purposeful stride and thought how unbelievable it was that it'd only been two days since he'd visited that toilet with its river of blood and sinister words scrawled on the wall. It felt like much longer.

There were children about, but not as many as you would have expected considering the school day had only just ended.

'Seems quiet,' Yorke said.

'Afterschool clubs are cancelled.' She sighed. 'We are having a hard time with our attendance figures. The parents are paranoid.'

A young boy held a door open for them. The new generation seemed far more polite than the tabloids would have you believe. He wondered if it was like this in other, less privileged areas – such as the one he was brought up in, twelve miles outside Salisbury. He hoped so.

'I heard your message,' Yorke said, 'but could you explain it to me again, just to make sure that I got the facts straight?'

'Lawrence Goodman and three other teachers have e-mailed me to say that Paul requested a password change in their classes.'

'Because he couldn't log on?'

'Well, Paul *claimed* to be unable to log on, and each of the four teachers allowed him to go to Phil Holmes for a password change. In fairness, the fact that he's had a password change doesn't become common knowledge, so none of the teachers knew about the other requests. To have to go four times in the past two weeks makes no sense.'

'Could there be any reason you can think of that the changes weren't working?'

'None. One change sufficed for every other student who went.'

'Why aren't the requests logged?'

'Well, I suppose they are, but Phil Holmes will be doing the logging. No one has ever had to follow up on it before. It's never been an issue.'

'Truanting from lessons is not an issue?'

'We don't have much of a problem with that here and as for Paul, he was an impeccable student, so I wouldn't have expected him to be doing that anyway.'

'Unless he had a good reason to, a reason you didn't know about.'

'This way, Detective Chief Inspector.'

He followed her and recognised this part of the school. He looked into Simon Rushton's classroom. Two days earlier Rushton's head had been in his hands, while Jessica Hart, the woman he was starting an affair with, comforted him.

She stopped by the door that had "IT OFFICE" written on it in bold letters, pushed it open and switched on the light.

Then, for ten minutes, Yorke haunted the IT office like a disorientated ghost.

Doctor Who, in various incarnations, and several Chelsea footballers stared down at him. There was a ghost of a smile on all of their faces; a suggestion, almost, that they knew something he didn't.

He stared at Frank Lampard the longest, recalling the date circled on Paul's calendar for his interview; a date Paul had been forced to miss.

'There's a lot of coincidence in this room,' Yorke said, turning to look at Baines. He pointed at several posters. 'Paul's favourite football team, favourite TV programme.'

He glanced around again, half-expecting to see a heavily-thumbed copy of Isaac Asimov's *"foundation"*; Paul's favourite book.

'They're popular interests,' Baines said.

'True,' Yorke said, looking over the poky little office, trying to find another clue hidden among the empty, coffee-stained mugs, disorganised piles of printed spreadsheets and unmarked CDs. 'But he could also have been using these popular interests to get close to Paul. Six months is enough time to do that.'

'Still, I cannot believe it, Phil is so reserved, he doesn't really socialise with anyone.'

'Paul came to this room four times in two weeks during lessons; additionally, his best friend, Nathan, told us that he had abandoned him to come into school very early recently – was it to spend more time with Phil? We *already* knew someone had been getting close to him inside this school; someone who had spiked him with a laxative and then had him wait outside the Sapphire restaurant in a hired van – it is very feasible that Phil could have convinced Paul to do this, if they were friends.'

'So, I employed the kidnapper?' The colour drained from Baines' face and she seemed to sag slightly.

'Sorry, just doing my job and thinking it through. I could still be wrong.'

But my gut says I'm not.

He phoned Topham and had an APW put out on Phil Holmes; he also made a request for a warrant so forensics could collect evidence from this office.

'He wants money, doesn't he?' Baines said, fighting off the shock, and straightening herself back up into a dominating posture. 'So, can't we give him it, and get the boy back?'

'It's not just about money.'

'What's it about then?'

He thought about the infernal message, "In the Blood," and said, 'I think it's something to do with his family.'

'Why would Phil Holmes be interested in Paul's family?'

'I don't know – but I'm willing to bet that the answer lies with his own family.'

SARAH SAW a squirrel in the road and despite Joe's constant ravings about her swerving around animals, she followed her instincts.

The force of the tyre hitting, and then mounting the raised ground alongside the concrete road, threw her back and forth, but fortunately, she managed to regain control of the car again and applied pressure to the brakes. With the left side of the car raised dangerously high, she tried to weave it back onto the road and away from the looming trees, but was met with a thump as her front-left tyre buried itself into a ditch; the front-right tyre followed quickly, and the car stalled.

Winded, she took a moment to compose herself. Then, with tears forming in her eyes, she restarted the car and tried the accelerator. The front tyres screeched.

'Shit!'

She punched the steering wheel and tried again. The car didn't budge. Knowing that she might be burying the tyres deeper into the snowy ground, she stopped and her eyes darted to the Sat Nav. Half a mile to the car park with five minutes to spare.

After clambering out of the car, she looked at the

damage; the left side was raised high by the sloped ground, and the front of the car pointed down into the ditch. She'd been lucky. If she'd not hit the brakes when she had, she'd have gone into that ditch with a dangerous amount of force. 'You stupid fucking woman.'

Snow-covered trees, seemingly piled on top of each other, suddenly appeared to be watching her, as if preparing to close in; this gave her the kick start she needed, and she started to run.

Despite the heavy snow, she didn't slip; the road had been gritted recently and she wore a good pair of trainers with a solid grip. The problem was the sinking sun and the lack of street lighting; she was as vulnerable as that squirrel had been only moments ago. Continuously brushing snow out of her eyes, she kept as close to the raised ground as she could without tripping.

Within minutes she was coughing and spluttering, but she was certain she was making good ground. She had to get there on time. She just had to. For Paul.

When she turned the corner, she was blinded by the sudden glare of headlights; shielding her eyes, she pressed herself to the raised ground, gasping when the driver hit the horn. Ultimately, she remained safe because the car was on the other side of the road; it might not end so well if one approached from behind.

When she first caught sight of the entrance to the car park ahead, she felt a burst of relief, but then the fatigue really kicked in. Her heart was smashing into her ribs with too much force, and a stitch threatened to bring her to her knees. She slowed, gasping for air and when she looked at her watch, she saw that she had only two minutes left and felt completely deflated.

The whiteness around her glowed, and another horn

caused her to jump out of her skin. A car *behind*. The lunatic screeched around her, missing by an inch.

Someone leaned out the passenger window and shouted. 'Stupid prick.'

She held her hand in the air. 'Please, stop!' She said, realising that she hadn't the energy to raise her voice loud enough. The speed freak disappeared into the growing darkness.

Down to a slow jog, she struggled to keep her tears back. 'I'm sorry, I'm sorry,' she said over and over again. Gritting her teeth, she willed herself onwards.

Her phone vibrated in her pocket. She glanced at her watch, and felt like the world was crumbling down around her.

Out of time.

She read the message. "Too late. I warned you."

Despite ice-cold fingers, she managed to text back. "Just not my son please not my son."

When she eventually reached the car park, she went to lean against a tree to catch her breath, but instead collapsed into floods of tears.

THE HOLMES' quaint townhouse was sitting in the cloudy shadow of a vast council estate; a stomach-turning hangover from the eighties. Yorke didn't like it around here; he found the memories it evoked from his own youth too distracting – old *Bros* songs buzzing from a transistor in a crumbling kitchen, a single mother labouring over a hot stove, and four siblings bouncing around a brick council house for ten years until it could barely stand any longer. He pushed the memories aside and parked on a patch of dead grass opposite the townhouse.

Outside his car, a hissing wind, sent from a cold place far beyond the clouds, tore into him. While zipping his jacket up, he quickened his pace. Tribal music, which would have been more fitting for a Jamaican beach rather than the snow-hit Salisbury Plains, poured from an open window.

I've never heard that remix of White Christmas before, Yorke thought, as the snow, which was several inches deep, soaked through to his feet. He got to the locked security gate in front of a Georgian-style door and rang the bell; despite Salisbury being a mild-mannered place, this particular patch always ended up high on the Wiltshire crime rate statistics. PCs whiled away many shifts here, dealing with sudden fractures in domestic bliss, and occasionally copping a black eye or two for their troubles.

The door opened before he rang the bell. A man in his late fifties, with a full head of black, gelled hair, unlocked the security gate and stood with his feet shoulder-width apart and his hands dangling loosely at his sides. He looked like a cowboy ready to draw; albeit an aging one like Clint Eastwood in the film, "Unforgiven". Yorke hoped he would look that confident when he reached fifty-plus.

'Mr Holmes?'

'Yes, I'm Roy Holmes, how can I help you?'

He flashed his warrant card. 'I'm DCI Michael Yorke; I'm sorry to disturb you—'

'*Police?* Are you sure you have the right house?'

'I believe so, sir. Is your son, Phil Holmes, here?'

Roy flinched. 'No, why?'

'It would be better if I could come in and talk.'

Roy's eyes narrowed.

'Please, sir, if it's not too much trouble, I really could do with talking to you.'

'Eileen, my wife, is ill.'

'I understand; I'll try and be quick.'

Several strands of shiny-black hair had fallen loosely over his forehead; he swept them back as he made space for Yorke to get in.

As he entered, a blast of hot air hit him and he heard the sizzle and pop of a log fire. Behind him, Roy closed the security gate.

The lounge he entered was small, but snug. Beside the fire was a plastic Christmas tree, and beside that, on the sofa, underneath a tapestry of a family toiling away in the fields, sat Eileen Holmes. It was clear she'd not aged as well as her husband; the greyness of her hair seemed to have spread to her skin. She knitted with quivering hands. She'd not stood up as Yorke came into the room and was yet to acknowledge his presence. Faced with a sick woman, the situation had grown more sensitive, so Yorke needed to be even more careful when discussing their son.

Roy sat down beside his wife on the sofa and put his hand on her lap. She continued knitting. Eileen looked weak and Yorke was surprised by how loud the knitting needles clicked. It was as if she was putting absolutely everything she had left into the blue and white scarf on her lap. *A parting gift for someone, perhaps?*

'Please sit down,' Roy said.

He perched on a wooden-backed chair opposite the sofa, which creaked, and wobbled, despite him not being particularly heavy.

'Hello, Mrs Holmes, I'm sorry to disturb you and your husband, but we believe your son, Phil, may be able to help us regarding a very serious matter. As you may already know, a young boy was kidnapped from the Salisbury Cathedral School two days ago.' Yorke looked at Eileen Holmes. She didn't lift her eyes, so instead he directed his stare back at Roy.

Roy nodded. 'Of course, our son has told us and we have read the papers. Have you tried Phil at work?'

Yorke nodded.

'Then we can't help you,' Roy said. 'We've no idea where he could be. He's been staying out a lot recently, so we assumed he had a new girlfriend, but he's always been very quiet about these matters.'

'But you must ask? After all, he's your son?'

'Yes, but he's so guarded, and it's never been wise to press these things.'

Yorke quickly surveyed the room. There were three graduation pictures of a younger Phil Holmes. He was more waif-like in his younger years, and had obviously spent some time in the gym, just like Jake had done.

The skinny boy complex really made for a big man.

'Manchester University,' Roy said, obviously noticing him looking at the pictures. 'And he had to work hard to get there too. Not like all his middle-class friends who headed off to University in their parents' Mercedes as soon as they turned eighteen.'

'Are you angry about something, Mr Holmes?'

'I'm not angry, I just want you to hurry up and get to the point of why you're here. Do you suspect our son?'

'We have evidence which suggests your son could be involved in the kidnapping of Paul Ray.'

'*Nonsense!* He'd never do that, and I know my son well enough.'

'Yet, if you knew your son well enough, you would

know where he is. Plus you've already suggested that he is quiet and guarded.'

'What evidence do you have?'

'I'll get to that in the moment. Has your son ever mentioned Lacey Ray to you?'

And then Eileen stopped knitting.

Yorke stared at her, but she didn't raise her eyes to meet his. He flicked his eyes back to Roy, whose cheeks had reddened.

'No,' Roy said.

The fire crackled. Yorke saw sap rising from a split log.

His phone rang and he saw that it was Topham.

'Excuse me,' Yorke said. 'May I use the kitchen?'

Roy nodded, but looked away with a scowl on his face.

In the kitchen, he answered the phone. 'Sir, bad news.'

'Go on, Mark.'

'Bryan Kelly fell asleep, and now Sarah Ray's gone too.'

'I don't believe it. How incompetent can one man be?'

'Bryan said he was drugged. Where are you at?'

Yorke told him and then said, 'Whatever you do, find Sarah Ray.'

He headed back into the lounge, his brain churning.

Three Rays missing; only one left, Lacey Ray.

And the reaction of this elderly couple when they'd heard that name had been like the plunging of pressure before the coming of a storm. He didn't bother sitting. 'Mr and Mrs Holmes, I need you to tell me what you know about the Rays.'

There was a moment of silence. Roy looked at Eileen, who continued to knit.'Lives depend on this, Mr Holmes; *three* lives.'

Roy scowled and said, 'Joe Ray owns the shop in town.

A ladies' man, so the rumours go. His wife is rarely seen out.'

'And Lacey Ray?'

'I don't know.' Roy looked away and Eileen stared at the scarf which hung loosely from her lap. Silence descended.

Yorke broke it, raising his voice slightly. 'I suspect that your son is involved in these abductions. If you don't start helping us, and this manhunt gets out of hand, your son could be in danger. Help us find him before it's too late. I want to help all concerned.'

Roy glared at Yorke. 'We really don't—'

'*Enough*,' Eileen said. Her voice was croaky, but she managed some volume.

Both Yorke and Roy stared at her, open-mouthed.

'This has gone on ... long enough.'

She rose to her feet, clutching her hip. She took a cane leaning against an old TV and hobbled around the corner. Roy shook his head. 'She's really sick and you had to go and dredge up the past.'

When she returned she was holding a small wooden box. She eased herself back down, wincing. After taking a deep breath, she opened the box and pulled out a photograph which she handed to Yorke. The photo was of a neglected young boy about two years old. His clothes were ragged and his thin face was almost as grey as the sick woman in front of him.

'Lewis Ray,' Eileen said.

Yorke shook his head. 'I've never heard of a Lewis—'

'You won't have done,' Roy said, running both his hands back over his gelled hair. 'Because the day after that photo was taken, he became Phillip Holmes, our son.'

SQUEALING swine startled Joe from his daze and he tightened his hold on Paul.

'Do you think the pigs are dangerous, Dad?'

Joe ran his fingers over his son's cracked lips. 'No, they're just pigs. And you're thirsty, young man.'

He watched Paul run his tongue over his dry lips, leaving slime, but no significant moisture. 'I'm okay.'

'I'm going to have another look round the barn for a way out.'

'We've both checked already, many times, we're stuck here.'

He knew his son was right, but tried to remain positive. 'We must have missed something. Most barns are like a small armoury. Spades, pitchforks, scythes—'

'I'm so scared, Dad.'

'I know,' Joe said, looking up at the air slits in the gables, wishing he could join the bright-eyed birds and bats up there with his only son.

Everything around him rustled. And not just chafing pigs either. Were there rats too perhaps? Something else to feast on their bones if the unthinkable happened?

I'm going to kill this bastard for what he's done to you, Paul.

'Do you love mum?'

Startled again, Joe looked down into his son's wide eyes. 'Of course I do! Why are you asking me that?'

'The other woman.'

He sighed. 'A mistake, son,' he said, thinking, *there have been too many mistakes.* 'I wish I could take it back.' *All of them.* There was a sting on his face; looking up, he could see snowflakes wafting in through the gaps.

The pigs squealed loudly and started to pound again.

His eyes widened, and when he looked at the front door it seemed to pulse like the heart of a vile animal.

'Dad—'

The door burst open. Cold air from outside rushed over his face. The sound of the terrified pigs faded into insignificance as the broad-shouldered man who had brought them here strolled into the barn with his sawn-off shotgun over one shoulder.

'Please Lewis,' Joe said. 'Anything you want, *anything*, I will get it for you.'

'You've changed your mind then,' Lewis said, stopping several metres in front of the pair.

'I don't understand, I tried to pay that ransom—'

'I'm not talking about that. I meant years ago, when I came to you, to your shop, for help, when I was desperate.'

'I don't know what—'

'I was dying then. At least I looked as if I was; skinnier, paler, thinning hair. I told you I was a Ray, told you that we were related.'

Joe gulped. His throat stung. He remembered. 'You asked for money.'

Lewis nodded and brought the shotgun down from his shoulder and aimed it at the pair huddled together on the floor. Paul tightened his grip on Joe. 'Dad ...'

'*Listen!*' Joe said, holding up the palm of one hand to try and pacify him. 'How was I to know if you were telling the truth? Anyone else would have had the same reaction!'

'You told me I was a drug addict. I was sick and confused. I expected you to listen. I told you I needed money for a psychiatrist, not heroin.'

'If you were sick, the doctors should have helped you. You wouldn't have needed money—'

'*Help?* The drugs made it worse. Six sessions with

someone who didn't understand. When I did see someone privately, someone who helped me, I ran out of money and I came to you. Do you not remember me telling you that I was so afraid to fall asleep, I had to burn myself to stay awake?' He rolled back a sleeve, but it was too dark for Joe to see the burn marks he was obviously trying to show him.

'Dad, is it true?'

'Yes, but I didn't know if he was being honest—'

'It was the same dream, the same fear. *Every single night.*' It was the first time Joe had heard Lewis raising his voice. He could feel his son shaking in his arms. His twelve-year-old boy. *How would it change him? How would he recover if they got out alive?*

'The cost of being a Ray,' Lewis said, calmness working its way back into his voice again.

'It's wrong to blame me,' Joe said. 'There was no proof.'

'For such a small amount of money,' Lewis said, kneeling before him, training the sawn-off shotgun at his head. 'And yet you've always had what you've wanted, haven't you?'

Paul said, 'You're a liar! You said you were my friend. You even let me call you by your middle name. You said only those closest to you were allowed to call you Lewis.'

'Yes, Paul, you're right, I lied. Lewis was my name, before I was given the name Phil.'

'Please, let us go, I'll do anything,' Joe said, still holding the palm of his hand out towards the shotgun.

'What could you possibly do? I realised, a long time ago, that me, you, *our* family are a problem. A massive problem.'

'You're not making sense,' Joe said. 'If you're family, let us help you, you don't have to suffer.'

'I don't need help. I know now that I was never really

sick. It was responsibility I felt. Towards a duty I am close to fulfilling.'

'Duty?'

'Stand up, Joe.'

'Why?'

'Just stand up.'

'And let you kill me?'

'If you don't stand up, I'll kill both of you.'

'No, Dad,' Paul said, tightening his grip on Joe.

Tears filled Joe's eyes. 'I can't—'

'Your decision,' Lewis said, readying the shotgun.

'*No, no, wait!* I'll stand up. Paul, let me go.'

'I can't Dad.'

'Let me go, *now.*'

Paul released him and Joe stood up.

'What's he going to do to you?' Paul said.

'Walk out the door,' Lewis said, taking a large step back, allowing Joe enough room to get past.

Tears were streaming down Paul's face. 'Please ...' he said, reaching out to grab his father, but he'd already moved out of reach. Pigs beat the sides of the barn as Lewis led Joe to the exit. When the burly man was less than a metre from the door, Paul sprang to his feet and ran out in front of them, 'Please, Lewis, I know you don't want to do this; it couldn't have all been lies—'

Lewis swung; Paul folded into a crumpled heap on the floor.

'*Paul!*' Joe turned back, but Lewis jammed the shotgun into his chest. 'Unless you want it to happen in front of him, get out the door.'

'Okay, okay.'

Outside, in the biting cold, Lewis threw the padlock on the floor in front of him. 'Lock it, and hand me the key. I will test it, Joe, and if you try and leave it open, Paul will hear you die.'

Crying, Joe padlocked the door and handed the key to Lewis.

'Please, you can do whatever you want to me, just don't hurt my son.'

He gestured to a barn in the distance with the shotgun. 'That's where we're going.'

'Why?'

'The talking stops now, Joe. I'm prepared to use this before we get there.'

———

AFTER FIVE MINUTES of trekking through the snow at gunpoint, Joe's wet feet started to burn. Around him was white emptiness; shouting would be futile, but running could be a possibility. But if he ran, and he wasn't gunned down, or caught, what would Lewis do then?

He thought of his son on the receiving end of this man's fury. Running was not an option. All he could do was fight.

At the door to a corrugated iron shed, Lewis said, 'Turn around and take this key.' Joe took the key, and after opening the padlock, he spun and launched it as hard as he could and charged. The padlock sailed over Lewis' shoulder. Growling, the towering man struck Joe across the head with his shotgun.

———

WHEN JOE WOKE, his throbbing head was pointing towards the ground, and his legs were being gripped tightly. Bobbing up and down, disorientated, it took him a moment to realise that the bastard had him over his shoulder.

'What are you doing?'

Lewis didn't answer. Joe continued to bob up and down like an empty backpack.

'You are going to rest. Like Thomas rests. Like we will all rest.'

'Not my son,' he said, bashing his fist off the small of Lewis' back, but he was too groggy to put enough force into it. He tried wriggling, but Lewis just tightened his grip on his legs.

They stopped at a concrete wall with a ladder running up it. He could hear pigs grunting again. But these sounded different than the ones in the other barn. Calmer, but more menacing.

'What's in there?'

'The end.'

He saw the ground beneath him move further away as Lewis climbed the ladder. 'If I'd known, if you'd shown me proof, I would have helped you, I really would—'

'Your rejection was for the best.'

He felt himself being flung and air rushing up around him. Then, there was a sickening crack, followed by agony across his chest.

Face down with his tongue pressed against cold concrete, he groaned.

'Getting a pig to eat a dead human is easy,' Lewis said from somewhere far above him. 'But getting them to eat a live one requires a certain species and a lot of training.'

Around him, Joe heard shuffling.

'I've had a lot of time to teach my European wild boars to appreciate their food.'

The shuffling became louder. He felt the side of his body being prodded and heard a panting sound in one ear.

With his eyes still closed, he rolled onto his back; agonising pain raced through his side and his mouth filled with fluid. There was panting at either side of him, and something moist and cold rubbed against his right cheek.

He gritted his teeth and used what remained of his energy to sit up. Then, he opened his eyes.

Half a metre away, a large boar stared at him. Knotted clumps of grey hair rose off its back like tumours. Its wet tusks glimmered.

Terrified, Joe bared his teeth and screamed in the boar's face.

It started to back off. 'That's it, get the fuck away.'

Behind him, he heard another animal shuffling around. The retreating boar stopped and continued its stare; its eyes were black and tiny.

'Go on, get away!'

Pain soared through his right bicep. He glanced to his side. The beast behind him had taken hold of his flesh and was tugging.

Displaying its twisted and broken teeth, the staring boar started to advance. Joe kicked out weakly, but the beast easily dodged to the side. It twisted its head and bit deep into his calf.

He glared up at Lewis. '*Please*, don't do—'

Jolted back by his bicep, Joe's head smacked the concrete. Above him, the creatures closed in.

'Help ...'

One of the boars bared its jagged teeth and darted for his face.

With a flurry of snow, the day finally disappeared into night. Sarah Ray had been standing in the car park for what seemed like ages.

There were few vehicles parked here, and there were no streetlights offering a friendly glow. She paced the car park, unsure of what to do in the darkness.

The lights of a parked Nissan pick-up truck flared into life. It reversed from its spot and turned to face in Sarah's direction with lights like burning eyes.

Unable to move, Sarah chewed at her bottom lip as the truck approached and its eyes flared.

Crossing her arms tightly against her chest, she stepped forward as the truck pulled up alongside her.

The passenger door opened. 'Paul?' she said.

No answer.

With her chewed lip stinging, she took the last few steps to the open door and climbed into the passenger side.

Staring at Sarah from the driver's seat was a young girl about the same age as her son; her chair was pulled forward so she could reach the pedals. Greasy and mousey hair draped around a face plastered with make-up. She looked like an excited child, who'd delved deep into her mother's cosmetic drawer for the very first time.

'Close the door,' someone said behind her. The words were growled rather than spoken and were difficult to understand.

Her hand shook as she gripped the handle and closed the door; the resulting clunk was loud, but not as loud as her racing heart.

'Turn around.'

Sarah turned and viewed a withered old woman under the inside light. If she hadn't already spoken, you'd have assumed she was dead.

'Where's my son?'

'Martha,' the old woman said, 'turn on the windscreen wipers, the snow is building.'

The wipers juddered as they did their work.

'Where's my son?'

'We're taking you to him,' Martha said. 'Paul is such a nice boy—'

'Martha! What did I say?'

'Sorry, Mother. I'm just so excited.'

The windscreen wipers squeaked as they drove over dry glass.

'Martha?' The old woman coughed and cleared her throat.

'Yes, Mother.'

'Switch off those fucking wipers.'

She obeyed and the squeaking stopped.

'Where is my son?' Sarah said again.

'Open the glove compartment.'

Sarah hesitated and the request was repeated. The compartment was heavy with clutter, and rushed open with a sudden thudding sound which made her flinch.

'Now, take out the bottle.'

She rustled around tapes, CDs and empty crisp packets before finding a plastic water bottle. She pulled it out and swished it around, barely a mouthful of a red liquid remained.

'Drink.'

'You can't expect me to—'

'If you want to see your son again, I suggest you do.'

'But what's in it?'

'Just something to help you relax.'

'Is my son okay?' she said as she unscrewed the bottle.

'He's been eating Mother's yummy, scrummy food, he'll be feeling better.'

'Martha!'

Sarah drank the contents of the bottle. It tasted of blackcurrant.

'What do you want from us?'

The old woman laughed. 'Martha, let's go.'

The car crunched over gravel. 'Please don't hurt my family anymore.'

'It's not me you should be asking,' the old woman said and this time her laugh grated so much that Sarah initially thought that the car was struggling to change gear.

270

17

'THOMAS RAY IS Phil's father?' Yorke said.

'*Birth* father,' Roy Holmes said. 'Let's get that right.'

Eileen Holmes stared at Yorke, and he wondered if the yellow tinge in the whites of her eyes could really be the glow from a fire which had suddenly ignited within her. 'I was a social worker most of my life, and we had a lot of dealings with Thomas Ray. I know that your police force has had their own set of experiences with this man too.'

'I didn't know he had a son.'

'It's not been made common knowledge. We adopted Lewis Ray at the age of two and we changed his name to Phillip Holmes.'

'I assume Phil knows?'

'Oh, he knows alright,' Roy said, staring at the floor, slowly shaking his head.

'When did you tell him?'

'When he was two of course. We told him that his real parents didn't know how to take care of him. That was sufficient until ...' He paused to look at the rising flame.

'Until?'

'Until the nightmares about what happened to him as a child began,' Eileen said. 'As you saw in the picture, Phil was suffering from extreme neglect. It was a neighbour who first reported it almost a year after Thomas' wife's death from cancer. But it wasn't the physiological neglect that really scared Phil ...' She paused for breath.

'It was the psychological,' Roy said. 'The bastard made him sleep in the barn with the pigs.'

Yorke widened his eyes and took a deep breath. 'Jesus, for how long?'

'Who knows?' Eileen said. 'Months, a year?'

Yorke stared at the fire; sap oozing from the split log looked like bubbling blood.

'How could anyone treat a child in that way?' Roy said.

'I wish I could answer that,' Yorke said. *But no matter how many times I see it, I'll never be able to.* 'What happened to him while he was in the barn with those pigs?'

'We're not one hundred percent sure, but Phil's dreams are a good indication,' Eileen said, looking down.

Roy said, 'You are referring to one of, if not the darkest hour in our lives, so I'll keep it short for you DCI Yorke and I hope you can understand why. Eileen is very unwell at the moment.'

Yorke nodded.

'At first, Phil bucked the trend; usually, following such extreme neglect, pathways in the brain struggle to form and the child usually experiences issues with cognition. This was never the case. As he grew, he developed into a happy, intelligent and quite carefree young man, quite contrary to what is often seen in these types of cases. This came to an end four years ago when Phil started to wake up screaming in the night. Despite knowing already about the adoption, it was only at this point, while asleep, that he started to remember and *experience* his childhood all over again. The screaming was unbelievable. Sometimes, I'd have to hold him down because it was so extreme and he'd start to thrash about ...'

Eileen cut in, 'It seemed to go on forever.'

'He was dreaming about being in the barn with those pigs. He must have been in the barn long enough for them to become confident enough to approach him, prod him, grunt at him. *Bully him.* He was on their territory I guess.'

'It was dehumanisation,' Eileen said. The bags under her eyes had started to glimmer with tears.

'And Thomas Ray never faced charges for this?' Yorke said, trying to keep the disgust out of his voice.

Eileen said, 'There was no real evidence. They took the boy into care due to neglect, and Thomas didn't really express an interest in trying to claim him back. It was one of the worst cases I've ever come across. Going into foster care was no good for this boy. He needed someone to care for him and love him, so we adopted him.'

'And so you eventually told Phil who his birth father was?'

'We didn't want to tell him, for obvious reasons, but after the nightmares started, we didn't really have a choice.'

'How did Phil react to the news that his birth dad was Thomas Ray?'

'Not well. His nightmares wouldn't stop, and eventually he developed chronic insomnia,' Roy said. 'He used to keep himself awake all night, often through self-harming. If he did fall asleep; he'd manage an hour or two before the dreams kicked in, and the screaming began, *again.*'

'He lost so much weight,' Eileen said. 'He went from

such a happy, carefree soul into someone weighted down by worry and anxiety.'

Roy said, 'The doctors put him on all sorts of drugs, but they seemed to make the situation worse. At one point they wanted him committed. He became more and more withdrawn.'

Eileen was crying more heavily now. Roy reached out and put his hand on her leg. She stroked his hand.

She said, 'It was an awful year. I couldn't see an end to it.'

'But then, there was,' Roy said. 'He seemed to come out of it. A different person than before; not quite as happy, and extroverted, but sensible, and often quite serious, but in a good way. A productive way. You know what I mean?'

Yorke nodded. 'And the sleeping?'

'He says it's fine now. He exercises regularly and has put on a lot of weight.'

'Most of it muscle,' Eileen said, gesturing to the pictures on the wall. 'Which I always find peculiar when I look back at the skinny boy that left us and went to university.' She smiled.

'He's got a good job, and he often talks about having a purpose – something he says he never used to have,' Roy said. We have our boy back and we never thought we would again – I can honestly tell you there's no malice in him.'

'But we have to look at the facts, Mr and Mrs Holmes. Thomas Ray is dead. And three of his relatives are missing...'

Roy sat up straight, '*Biological* relatives. He doesn't know them. They're not his *real* family.'

'Still. We cannot ignore this connection. We have circumstantial evidence that Phil befriended Paul Ray; we need to speak to your son, to rule him out as a suspect. You have to help me find him.'

Eileen was wheezing, and had turned a shade greyer than she was earlier. She leaned forward. Roy stood up and knelt down before his wife. He massaged her on the chest while looking her in the eyes. She sighed and nodded. He nodded back.

'We've told you everything,' Roy said, standing up and then turning to face him. 'We really have. If we hear from him, we will let you know. Eileen must get some rest now.'

Yorke stood up. 'Could you give me a list of possible friends, contacts, he might have?'

'Inspector, if you wish to continue talking, please can we do this at the door, away from my wife?'

Yorke nodded and they walked out of the room back to the security gate.

'I really don't know any of Phil's friends, but I will contact you if he comes back.'

'I'm going to station an officer at the door in case he returns.'

'You really think he's involved, don't you?'

Yorke reached out and touched Roy on his shoulder. 'Sir, I don't want to put you or your wife through any more stress than you've already been through, but you must let me follow procedure. Please contact me as soon as you hear from him.'

'She's dying you know.'

'I'm very sorry.'

'And this could shatter that last piece of her.'

Yorke removed his hand. 'I will do everything I can to avoid that. The officer?'

Roy sighed. 'Yes, of course.'

Outside in his car, Yorke made a conference call to

Topham, Gardner and Brookes. He told them everything. He suggested to Topham, that he get pictures of Lacey and Phil Holmes out to the press immediately.

He stared at Roy and Eileen's house.

Paul, Joe and Sarah had distanced themselves from the Ray family's notorious history while Phil Holmes had been completely removed from it. Yet here it was, catching up with them all again.

He considered the phrase, *Pray for the Rays,* which the long-suffering locals of Devizes had coined all those years ago.

Last month, Yorke would have scoffed at the thought of a cursed family.

Last month, but not now.

'BELIEVE ME SHEILA, I'm begging you, I did not make contact with Lacey. What happened with her nephew brought her back here and unfortunately, onto our radar,' Jake said into his phone, pacing around his office in the Salisbury station.

'And the seedy movie – you never thought of telling me about that?'

He bit his lip. If he lost control, he'd lose her again. It'd taken fifteen tries and the best part of an hour to get her on the phone. He took a deep breath.

'It was a long time ago.'

'Still, I've told you everything about my past.'

'But come on Sheila, would you really want to know about something juvenile I did when I was barely out of my teens? I'd rather not know.'

'It's irrelevant Jake. Bitch or no bitch. It's not like it's been going great recently anyway.'

'There've been problems, I admit, but every marriage has problems,' Jake said, desperate to keep her on the phone.

'You're married to the job. It's a cliché, but it doesn't make it false.'

'For better or for worse, remember?'

'There's been too much of the *worse*.'

'A career change then?'

They were the words she loved to hear. But, ultimately, words she would never believe. 'After you quit, you know where to find me.'

'That's not fair. I wouldn't lie to you, I'll do it, but I want to see you first. You can help me to decide what job I could do instead—'

'No.'

'*Jesus*, Sheila.'

'Jake, you losing your temper isn't going to solve anything.'

'It's frustration, I need you.'

'You've betrayed me once by keeping things about your past from me; how can I trust you to quit the job that you adore more than me?'

'*Nonsense*, I have not betrayed you and I love you more than anything. If I go back on this promise, I'll pay for the divorce.'

She sighed. 'Okay, you know where I am.'

'As much as your mother loves me, I'm pretty sure she doesn't want me in her house.'

'Well, what do you suggest then?'

'Meet me at home at half-past eight,' he said.

She paused. 'I'll think about it, but don't get your hopes up.'

'Thank you,' he said, but she'd already hung up.

THROUGH THE WINDOW, Lacey watched the cathedral spire pierce the sky. Bleeding white, it created the moon and, with a sudden spray of arterial blood, the stars.

At least, that was how Lacey imagined it.

Why not enjoy herself? She was coming to an end. As soon as tomorrow. *The greatest stars burn quick, but they also burn brightest.*

She reached out to her reflection, ran her fingers over the cold glass of the window and spoke out loud, 'Have you seen the time?'

Seven fifty-five.

She took a deep breath and blew out the words, 'Not long now.'

Turning and grimacing at the beige room, she thought, *it would be better if you were the colour of despondency.*

Just like the Blue Room.

On a bed made with satin sheets, opposite a formidable flat-screen TV, the props from the Blue Room were laid out: the Colt handgun inherited from her father; a gag; handcuffs; rope and a pair of secateurs she'd had to sharpen after working them really hard on Brain's stubby fingers. And finally, the pièce de résistance: a surgical scalpel with which to carve open Phil's throat.

She put the handgun in the bedside drawer, then wrapped the other instruments in a towel and placed them on a chair beside the bathroom door. Then, she stared in the bathroom where she planned to commit the deed, until her vision blurred, her eyes closed and she brought herself back to the Blue Room ...

Moments later, she opened her eyes, stared in at the beige, empty bathroom, and smiled. Soon, everything would be running red.

Chewing her bottom lip, she thought, *she was the greatest star! How bright she had burned!*

Then came the knock at the door.

———

PHIL HOLMES TUCKED the bouquet under one arm and knocked on the door a third time.

She was making him wait. A clear demonstration of her annoyance. But that was fine. Let her enjoy herself. It wouldn't alter the outcome.

His life had been about control and careful planning for so long now that losing his temper the previous evening seemed surreal to him. And not just surreal, but stupid. Responding to Lacey's taunts with violence had attracted the attention of that DCI. He'd done well to hold him off a few hours longer but, by now, he'd know about the adoption, know that he was born Lewis Ray. He wouldn't be able to go back to the school tomorrow; his plans had to be brought forward. Everything would have to end tonight. First, Lacey; then, back to the farm for Paul and Sarah. Finally, he would take out the last of the Rays.

Himself.

The door opened and he saw that she looked different. She'd restrained her elegant, yet wild hair with a clip. She wore no make-up.

Deliberate. To show me the damage I caused.

He presented the flowers to her, knowing already that

she would forgive him. He'd studied women long enough to know their weaknesses. And Lacey Ray was the same as all the rest.

He gave her an apologetic smile which he'd practised earlier in the mirror. 'I'm sorry.'

She turned her back to him and walked away.

He didn't mind the pretence. It delayed the inevitable. Delayed him having to touch her, another product of a diseased line, another pig. Just like him.

He followed her through the door. He said, 'I've never hit a woman before,' while thinking, *I've never killed a woman before either*.

But she should be thankful for what he planned to do. He was freeing her from the life of sin she'd been condemned to by their family tree.

She moved past the beige bed and stopped at the window that offered the best view of the cathedral spire. As he approached her from behind, he admired a picture of the same cathedral hung on the wall above the bed, rendered with long, patient strokes. He could, if he so wanted, sneak up behind her, and with a similar long and patient stroke, slide a meat hook between her two shoulder blades.

Slipping his arms around her waist, he lifted her shirt slightly, and let his wrists move against her toned stomach.

With eyes closed, he fought back revulsion and turned his mind to Sammie, an ex-girlfriend he'd had true feelings for before the nightmares had begun, before his life turned to mud, before he emerged, reawakened, with a purpose. With Sammie's beauty in mind, he took control of himself again.

The feeble woman, Lacey, welcomed his embrace. Easier than anticipated. She talked an angry game, but was biddable really.

In bed, Phil turned her on her front, making it easier for him to continue the illusion that it was Sammie and maintain an erection. As he penetrated her, he thought of his plan to eradicate all of the swine; and while he came, he thought of all the ways he could kill himself afterwards to complete the disinfection.

18

FROM THE RAFTERS, a pair of unblinking eyes reflected light from the dying lamp. Something else was living in here with him.

He turned onto his side, squeezing his sore eyes closed. Desperately trying to push the smells and sounds of these horrid creatures to the back of his mind, he imagined himself with his father, watching Chelsea FC.

But the howl of a wild dog reminded him of the awful shriek he'd heard earlier from his dad and his attempt to daydream was over. He curled into a ball. *I can't stand it anymore.*

Dad ... you have to get me out of here.

After uncurling, he pounded his fists and feet on the floor. The swine flared into life, and the creature with the glowing eyes – a bat perhaps – beat against the rafters.

Please come back.

Out of breath, he rolled onto his side and rubbed tears from his eyes.

The animals had only just started to calm down when a rattle from the barn door disturbed them again. Paul sat up.

Dad? The police, maybe?

'Help me,' he said, drawing the dying lamp nearer to him, 'Please.'

The swine relaxed. A good sign. It meant that it wasn't Lewis.

The young girl, Martha, came into his circle of light. He felt a wave of disappointment that it wasn't his father.

Well at least it wasn't him again.

'Paul, I brought you some food – I cooked it this time, Mother is feeling poorly.'

'I want my Dad. Where is he?'

'I think you'll like the food.'

'I'm not hungry, I just want to go home to my Mum. It's so horrible in here and Lewis is scary. . . what's he done to Dad? What will he do to me?'

She came nearer, and Paul saw that in one hand, she held the cattle prod while in the other, she held the familiar dog bowl—

Nothing's changed. Two days on and I'm still here.

'Where's my dad?'

She lowered herself to her knees a few metres in front of him and put the dog bowl down on the floor. She glanced behind her to check she was alone. 'I didn't want Lewis to hurt him, I really didn't, but he doesn't listen.'

'Where is he?'

'It wasn't me, I promise.'

'Tell me he's okay.'

'He says that you're all bad people. He says that when all the Rays are gone, he will go too.' She leaned in to whisper. 'I won't miss him, I hate him.'

Paul widened his eyes and sucked in enough air to shout. *'Where is he?'*

'Shush!' Martha leaned in, panic on her face. 'You'll wake Mother.'

The old woman in the wheelchair? So, she's in bed, leaving you with no one to back you up?

Martha looked down. 'Lewis gave him to them.'

'*Them?*'

'Simon and Colin.'

He felt dizzy. 'I don't understand—'

'Wild boars.'

He closed his eyes.

'I begged him not to.'

His whole body seemed to fold in on itself as he issued two loud sobs. He curled into a ball again, and when she tried to touch him, he shrank away. 'Get off me.'

He cried until he had little energy left, then he unfolded and lay limp, staring off into the darkness, feeling like he'd had everything scraped out of him.

'It wasn't me,' she said.

With tears and snot dribbling into his mouth, he turned back to look at her. 'Let me out of here. You have to.'

'It's not possible. My mother won't allow it.'

'Why is your mother helping him?'

'She loves him.'

'But he's evil!'

She stood up, leaving the cattle prod on the floor. His eyes widened. She took a step back, and despite feeling exhausted from despair and dehydration, he summoned up the energy to reach out. She didn't challenge him as he slipped his hand around it. Rising to his feet, slowly, he ignited the dancing spark. 'Are you going to let the boars eat me next?'

Martha took a step back with tears in her eyes. 'You're not next.'

'So someone is next – *who?*'

She was crying hard now as she continued to back off towards the door.

'Who?'

'I'm sorry, Paul. She's so pretty.' She turned, and buried her head in her hands.

'Who is?' He moved forward until he was only a metre behind her.

'She's in the house, I know, we took her there.'

'For the last time ... *who?*'

'Your mother.'

Paul's vision swelled, making the slats of the wooden barn appear as if they'd pried loose from the wall and were weaving in the air towards him like giant vines; he wielded the cattle prod as if it was a machete and hacked at them —

There was a sickening crunch and Martha crumpled to the ground. Then, he stepped over her limp form and charged through the open door, still holding the prod.

Outside, the sky was dark and silent, and snow emerged from this nothingness as if it was breaking through from another dimension. Everything seemed to be in constant motion, as if every pixel on a photograph was at war with one another, circling and striking. Ahead, he saw the two windows of the lit farmhouse glaring like the eyes of a wild animal.

He thought of the young girl he might have just killed lying on the floor of the barn and started to run.

He'd never wanted his mother so much in all of his life.

Yorke took a call from Dr Patricia Wileman.

'The fingerprint we just lifted from Phil Holmes' office

matches the one from the window of Joe Ray's house. *He was there.*'

'Thanks, Pat.'

'You don't sound too happy about it; I thought this would be good news?'

'It would be if we knew *where* he was.'

'You okay?'

'Yes, just worn out. Speak later.'

'I'd like that; I'd like a drink or two when all this is over.'

'Only one or two?'

After the call, Yorke joined Jake, Tyler and Willows in a small office at Salisbury police station; he informed them of what Patricia had just told him.

Yorke was still waiting on the records of adoption from the General Register Office so they could corroborate Roy and Eileen Holmes' claim. They did have medical records though and it confirmed what they'd been told. 'Chronic insomnia and extensive treatment with hypnotics; six sessions of CBT for self-harming; suspected schizophrenia, which he didn't attend the tests for; countless drug therapies for anxiety and depression. He went through an intense few years.'

Yorke wrote a list of all the doctors and psychiatrists that Phil had spoken to.

'How's the hunt for Lacey Ray?' Yorke asked Willows.

'We haven't found any more CCTV footage of her in town, but we have five officers on it – so, it's only a matter of time.'

'Can you get someone to handle these too?' Yorke said, sliding over the doctors' names to her. 'Find out what they thought of Phil Holmes, what he could be capable of. Anything. Places he could have gone ... liked to go. That kind of thing.'

'Okay, sir,' Willows said.

'Sean, if you could return to the parents. I have requested a warrant to search the property, but until that arrives, you could carry on digging. You need to be as forceful as you can, despite the fact that Eileen Holmes is dying.'

'No problem, sir,' Tyler said.

'And Jake, if you could have some officers check out all of Holmes' previous employers that would be great.' He slid another file over to Jake.

'I don't get it,' Jake said. 'He's a Ray. Treated badly by his real father, but ultimately, given a good life.'

Yorke said, 'A good upbringing does not necessarily undo damage—'

'Obviously,' Jake said. 'I don't mean that. I can understand why he may have motive for his father's murder, but why would he kidnap the other Rays? They didn't do anything to him.'

'Maybe, he thinks they owe him?' Willows said, 'that they had it lucky by inheriting that money?'

'I doubt it,' Yorke said. 'His effort to retrieve that ransom money was feeble and was unlikely to succeed. He doesn't care about the money and, if he has somehow lured Sarah in too, he's left no one to pay a ransom.'

'Lacey could pay?' Tyler said.

'No chance,' Yorke said. Jake nodded.

Yorke took a phone call from Topham.

'Bryan's car has been found run off the road less than half a mile from Lankton car park, stuck in a ditch.'

'Any sign of Sarah.'

'None.'

'CCTV footage?'

'Looking into it.'

'The fingerprint at the cottage was Phil Holmes.'

'I know, I just saw Pat.'

Yorke said, 'Finding this guy is our main priority. We need to saturate the media with Holmes' image. Have Emma liaise with Martin Price again.'

'Okay.'

Lankton, Yorke thought. 'Anybody got a map?'

Jake said, 'Ever heard of the internet?'

———

THE NIGHT MAY HAVE BEEN young, but the situation was getting stale.

Once the animal had closed its eyes, Lacey reached into the bedside drawer for the only worthwhile relic she'd inherited from her father: a Colt handgun.

From cheap-cotton sheets, an inconvenience after enjoying silk ones for so long, she emerged naked. She didn't mind the temperature. *Didn't they say that revenge was a dish best served cold?*

She walked over to her smartphone docking-station which she had positioned next to the TV, needing music to drown out any impending sounds of confrontation. Keeping the volume low to avoid waking him too soon, she selected a song by *Keane.* The keyboard introduction was gentle. After scooping up the remote control, she headed back to the bed, where she placed it so she could turn the volume up when it was time.

At the foot of the bed, she looked at the beast. Goosebumps rose on his thick arms like smallpox. His bulky, hairy chest, expanded then contracted like a sack of insect larvae. She pointed the gun at his head and a shiver of excitement fluttered down her spine.

I could make it quick ...

But that would spare you the pain you deserve.

It would also deny the Blue Room. And it could never be quick there. She owed that place so much. It had made her everything that she was today.

So, control your impatience Lacey.

She lowered the weapon, closed her eyes and imagined roots sprouting from the soles of her feet, worming their way into the ground, seeking nourishment. Vitality and clarity flowed through her. She imagined a silver rain, streaming down on her, washing away any lingering impatience. But within this meditative state, awash with clarity, patience and vitality, she found a realisation that concerned her:

What if Lucy Evans, the woman I am about to become, did not find truth and justice in the Blue Room?

Her eyes flicked open and she glanced at the bright and colourful bouquet lying in the corner of the room.

Could Lucy Evans be satisfied in a world with colour?

She looked down at her victim.

Would she be able to accept love?

When she cocked the old weapon, the clunk of the hammer was loud, but already the music was helping and Phil didn't stir.

Marriage? Even children?

The lead singer reached an operatic wail; she grabbed the remote control again and cranked up the volume. When she slung the controls back down, car headlights illuminated the room and Phil's eyes burst open.

Could Lucy Evans really leave all this behind?

Phil met her eyes; then his stare fell to the gun in her hand. Allowing time for his confusion to become awareness, she enjoyed another moment of realisation:-

Lucy Evans would appreciate where she came from.

289

How she was born. She would not, could not, turn her back on that.

The future was blue. Like the past, like the present.

Like always.

'Do as I say or I will kill you,' she said.

'What are you doing?' he said.

'What needs to be done. Get up.'

He turned his head slowly from side to side. 'No, you cannot tell me what to do.'

Lacey scooped up a pillow, placed it against his foot, and buried the muzzle of the Colt deep into the material. 'Yes I can.' She pulled the trigger. There was a thudding noise and a flurry of feathers.

He snapped his foot back.

'A warning. Next time, I'll make sure it takes your foot off.'

Holding his hands out in front of him, he sat up. 'Are you doing this because I hit you?'

'Come to the bathroom.'

'Why?' He climbed out of bed and stretched out his large-muscular frame; there was a break between songs, so she heard his joints cracking. He turned to look at her. 'What's in there?'

This is all wrong, I knew he was odd, but he seems almost ... unconcerned.

He turned and cocked his head from side to side as if to examine her. 'I asked you what happens in the bathroom.'

She took a step back. 'Follow me, and I'll show you.'

'And if I don't?'

She lowered her gun to point at his exposed genitalia.

As another *Keane* song kicked in with a cascade of keyboards and powerful vocals, she took another step backwards to ensure there was enough distance between them to prevent him pouncing. She raised the gun from his genitals to his wide chest; it would be hard to miss if he suddenly charged.

He said, 'I think it's time I told you something important.'

She snorted. 'Like what?'

'Who I am.'

'What the hell are you talking about? I know who you are!'

Phil took a step forward. 'No, who I *really* am.'

Lacey regarded him for a moment and then smiled. 'My, I knew you were odd, Phil, but you really are surprising me. Go on then, who are you? *Really?*'

'My name is Lewis Ray.'

Lacey creased her brow. 'Never heard of you.'

'I'm the son of that crazy man who killed the nurse, Thomas Ray. Our parents were cousins, which makes us second cousins.'

She laughed. 'Nonsense!'

'It's true. What's in my blood is in yours too, Lacey.'

She thought of the words on her brother's kitchen wall and her eyes widened.

He took another step forward and she tensed her hand on the gun.

'I was adopted when I was two.'

Another step.

'Stop moving, or I'll shoot.'

'But then you won't find out where your family are. You may be too late for Joe, but Sarah and Paul are still alive.'

Even if it's true, Lacey, she thought, lifting the gun slightly so it pointed at his head again, *it's irrelevant, stay in control, stick to the plan.* 'Have you not got it through your thick skull yet that I don't care about them?'

'But you must have some interest in *why* I have them.'

'Why would I have any interest in your primitive ways of making money?'

'Is that what you *really* think? There are easier ways to make money! We Rays have had everything our own way. We're greedy and cruel, and we've spent the last century, hurting people, using people, *killing* people. Ignorance is bliss, but it didn't last for me I'm afraid. But after a turbulent time, I am whole again, I have a purpose.'

'What's your purpose?'

'One that you, Lacey, are part of, but not able to stop.'

'That doesn't help.'

'So I have your interest now?'

'Not really. This makes no difference. Nothing changes. The outcome, *your outcome*, remains exactly the same—'

'I was thinking the same thing.'

Can you not see who is holding the gun? She thought and then started to laugh. And not the fake laugh she used to taunt prey, but rather a genuine laugh. In a way, looking at Phil Holmes was suddenly like looking in the mirror – the commitment, the drive, *the need*, staring right back at her. She couldn't believe she hadn't noticed it before.

'Why are you laughing? Do you really hate your family that much?'

She took a deep breath to bring her laugher under control. 'Yes and hearing the news that Joe is dead is actually quite exhilarating!'

He advanced.

Knowing that the bathroom door was just behind her and she was almost out of space, she tensed her finger on the trigger. 'Be careful.'

He stopped. 'How can you think that a woman's

vengeance is anywhere near as important as what I'm doing? Put your gun down.'

'You're giving yourself too much importance. You think this is just about you hitting me? You're not my first, Phil, and after the excitement of killing you fades, I'm sure there'll be someone else. Someone else who deserves it too.'

'You think you're a vigilante?'

'No - just the person who's going to cut off your fingers one by one.'

'Might be better to let you shoot me here then.'

'Might be. Up to you. But I'd prefer you in the bathroom.'

'You still haven't told me *why* I have to go in there.'

'To beg.'

'For what?'

'Death.'

She took several steps to the side to clear a pathway to the bathroom, keeping the Colt trained on him at all times. He started moving forward, but stopped when he reached the door. 'One last thing.' He clutched the frame of the door with one hand.

'*No!* Get in, Phil—'

'Fuck you, it's *Lewis!*' His hand moved suddenly. Something struck her hard on the temple, her head flipped back and her finger slipped from the trigger; then, he was crashing into her. Her body collapsed to the ground under his entire weight. She threw out an arm, but only succeeded in knocking the towel-wrapped instruments off the chair by the door.

Buried beneath him, she struggled to take in air. When her head flopped to the left, she saw that he'd surprised her with the docking-station remote which she'd left on the bed.

You stupid woman! The bastard must have swiped it as he was getting up.

She turned and looked up at the hideous man and spat as hard as she could, catching him underneath his chin. His fist came crashing down.

There was a wild moment of stars and confusion before she opened her eyes. He was smiling.

I've fucked up.

'Try not to blame yourself too much for what's about to happen,' he said, adjusting his position so he was kneeling on top of her chest. 'I came here to kill you anyway.'

THERE WASN'T a streetlight in sight. Around Paul, shadowy shapes swelled, and in every movement, he imagined crazy men vying for his life and the widening eyes of hungry animals. Crunching through the snow, with his face and feet stinging from the cold, willed on by thoughts of his mother, he ignored the exhaustion which came from lack of food and sleep, and made his way onward to the farmhouse.

In the light coming from the windows, he was able to see the ground he was walking on. He could also see the old rocking chair on the porch, and the spindles that resembled the prone fingers of a strange monster, ready to strike. As he climbed the stairs, he imagined the toothless hag rocking there while contemplating how best to skin her poor victims.

I should be finding the closest road and screaming at the top of my lungs until someone stops to help.

Cattle prod in hand, he tried the front door. It was unlocked. Inside, he could smell cooked meat. He closed the door carefully behind him, so as not to alert Stella, who, according to Martha, was now sleeping.

Yet what if Lewis was here? In one of the rooms?

But what choice did he have? He'd already lost one parent to this family, he couldn't lose another.

From outside, the light had looked bright, but inside, it seemed to be sucking the colour from everything around him. Ahead, were a set of stairs which disappeared into a pool of darkness.

Beside the steps were two doors. He slowly opened the second door and bright light stung his eyes. Squinting, he observed a kitchen which would be more at home in a busy restaurant than a farmhouse. Around a stainless-steel oven were white-tiled work surfaces and various pots, pans and utensils hanging from the walls. Despite an extractor fan humming in the corner, the smell of meat remained strong.

On his way towards a rack of knives, something clattered hard against the window and he stopped dead. He felt his heart thrashing in his chest, but remained rooted to the spot, despite wanting to run.

The second clatter was followed by a scraping sound which made him wince, but fortunately shook him from paralysis – he began to back off towards the door.

When it happened a third time, he stopped and breathed a sigh of relief. It was just the wind, forcing the talons of a monstrous tree over the glass.

Composing himself, he continued his journey to the rack beside the sink. *Chef's knives.* His parents had a similar set which they kept sharp. He hoped the owners of this set were just as proud. He ditched the cattle prod, drew the largest knife, turned from the rack, and grimaced at a sink half-filled with the insides of an animal, its eyes floating in the mess like large-mutated frogspawn.

There was a bang as the front door crashed open and a blast of cold air whistled through the house into the kitchen. The thrashing in his chest began again.

Did I not close the front door properly? Or has someone just come in?

He crept back to the entrance to the kitchen and pressed himself flat against the wall beside it, just in time to hear the front door banging shut.

It wasn't warm, but he sweated; with the back of his free hand, he smeared moisture across his brow. Scared, he glanced down at the knife in his hand for confidence.

There were two voices at the front door and he leaned closer to hear who they were and what was being said, but the noise of the outside wind made this impossible. Eventually, the talking stopped. The front door was opened again – he felt the blast of cold air on his face this time as well as hearing it – and then, it was shut. He looked at the back door.

Tempting ... but my mother is here.

He turned back and lunged out of the open kitchen door, holding the knife in front of him.

Stella's waxy head was slumped back and her wispy hair dripped over the support of her grey wheelchair. A wrinkled arm hung limply over one side, and the knuckles of a withered hand lay against one of the chair's three wheels.

He waited. She didn't move.

Could she be deaf?

He moved forward until he was a couple of metres behind her, readying the knife—

Her arm jolted into life and her hand clamped the wheel. The chair started to turn, creaking louder than the cursing wind outside. He kept the knife out in front of him.

Stella was dressed in white satin with a bright-sparkling jewel clamped around her neck; it reminded him of a film he'd seen in which the corpse of an old woman was dressed by a funeral home. Her toothless mouth spread wide into a smile.

His whole body was shaking, but he concentrated on making himself heard, loud and clear. 'Where's my Mum?'

'Is that why you're here?'

He stepped forward and held the tip of the blade inches from her face. 'I'll kill you, I swear. Just tell me where my mum is, I want to go home.'

She smiled. 'Like I always say to Martha, you can't always have what you want.'

'Where is she?' he said, moving the blade even closer to her face.

'Would you really hurt a harmless old woman?'

'You hurt my dad, and he meant no one any harm.'

'That wasn't me, but I can see you're serious, so ...' She coughed. Once her throat was clear, she pointed to the door. 'I'll take you to your mother.'

Before he'd had chance to reply, she'd turned the wheelchair, and was moving towards the front door. Despite her appearance, her hands were strong and steady on the wheels.

'Will you help a crippled lady through the door?' She allowed him space beside her.

He opened it and she wheeled herself out. Knowing that Lewis must be close, Paul moved close alongside her, so, if necessary, he could pin the knife to her throat.

She clattered over loose-wooden slats to the far side of the porch and trundled down a ramp.

'Where are we going?'

She didn't reply, and swooped right, taking him in a

different direction to the old barn where he'd spent the last few days. Wondering if she was concealing some kind of motor in her chair, he quickened his pace to keep up.

The snow was driving down fast and he had to keep his head tilted forward slightly to avoid being blinded. In the distance, he could hear dogs barking. On any other day they would have unnerved him, but he knew there were far worse things to fear right now.

When he sighted another large barn, he wondered if this was where his dad had been taken, and tears filled his eyes again. 'How could you let him do this to us?'

She stopped the wheelchair dead and turned to face him. He tightened his hold on the knife while she gripped the jewel tied around her neck.

'Listen, you little shit stain, when we met him, we were a mess.' Veins were sliding over the whites of her eyes like bloody worms. 'Why should I care about you and your family? No-one ever cared about me and Martha. Not until Lewis ... My husband and my daughter, Martha's real mother, dead. What gives you the right to judge me?' She pointed with a gnarled finger at the corrugated-iron barn, barely thirty metres ahead. 'We're almost there, that's where your mother is.'

They continued, and when they reached the barn door, it was pulled open from the inside by Martha – no doubt it had been her talking to Stella outside the kitchen earlier. Holding her hand to the back of her head, where Paul had hit her before, she stepped to one side and looked to the floor, ashamed.

'Your mother is inside,' Stella said.

'You'll lock me in.'

'Take Martha with you then.'

He approached Martha and lifted up the knife.

'You hurt my head,' Martha said.

'Take me to my mum.'

'I brought you food, I helped you—'

'Take me now.'

Martha led the way into the barn. It was bigger than the other one and there was a second separate section built towards the back which rose about eight feet off the floor and had a wooden door in the centre. He could hear shuffling sounds coming from the enclosure. Simon and Colin, the wild boars. This was where Lewis had brought his father. Sick rose from his stomach into his throat.

At the side of the barn, his mother was lying down. She was still, and facing the wall.

'Mum?' He ran towards her, dragging Martha by her arm. 'Mum?'

There was no reply.

'She's asleep,' Martha said.

'Stand over there!' He pointed at the corrugated wall. She obeyed.

He lowered himself to the floor and cradled his mother's head in his arms. She was limp and he put his hand to her chest to feel for her heart. 'Mum?'

Everything disappeared in an explosion of white light. He slumped forward and rolled onto his back. Through his swimming vision, he could see Stella looking down on him from her chair, holding a rock in her hand.

'Did you think I would let you get away with hitting my daughter?'

Desperate for the knife he'd dropped, he ran his fingers over the ground, but Stella swung the rock again. 'And that's for making everything harder than it had to be.'

His head felt like it was on fire.

'Martha, come on,' Stella said.

'But mother—'

'Remember when we met him? Remember when we were starving to death?'

Martha didn't reply.

'*Remember?*'

'Yes, Mother.'

Paul could feel the sick that had risen into his throat seep out the corner of his mouth.

He forced himself up into a sitting position. Martha, half-way to the exit, was looking back over her shoulder and caught his eyes. She stopped.

'*Now*, Martha,' Stella said.

'Coming Mother.' She broke eye contact and followed her mother out of the door.

Paul leaned over and touched his mother's face. *Still warm.* He heard the thud of the corrugated-iron door shut and then the clunk of the lock.

'Paul ...'

'Mum.' He pulled her up into his lap, where he'd also held Dad only hours ago. He leaned over and kissed her head, and tasted his own blood as it ran down from his head into his mouth.

The grunting sound started again. Deeper and louder than in the other barn. He wiped away the blood running into his eyes and turned to look at the enclosure.

The wooden door in the centre was shaking.

19

YORKE CONTACTED THE current officers in charge of collecting dirt samples and instructed them to narrow their search to the area immediately around Lankton carpark. He then took a phone call from Topham. 'Boss, I have the CCTV footage from the carpark. Digital this time, so I'll e-mail you a copy straight over.'

'Summary?'

'At four forty-one, Sarah Ray got into a white Nissan pick-up truck—'

'*Registration?*'

'Covered up.'

'Bloody hell.' He kicked a bin over by the desk he was pacing around.

'The van drove off. I'm sorry, boss. SOCOs are looking through Bryan's car, but they'll not find anything. The driver didn't get out of the van. We didn't get a look at them.'

He hung up and stormed out of the station. In the carpark, he lit his first cigarette in years. He took a long, greedy puff. Following the first initial rush, it felt like he'd never stopped.

Rule number one: never promise. Never fucking promise.

Not only had he failed to get their son back, but he'd failed to keep them safe too.

His gut feeling: they were all dead, murdered by an abused, possibly schizophrenic, bitter relative. The one that was cast aside like rubbish, forced to endure psychological torment, while the others prospered.

His conclusion: he, Mike Yorke, was on the verge of failure.

Headlights blinded him as he finished his cigarette.

Great, all I need.

Harry emerged from his car and came towards him.

'I've still got uniforms sitting on my house, and shadowing me.'

'I know.'

'So, I'm not in the clear yet?'

'No, but we are pursuing other angles.'

'And?'

'That's all I can say.'

'I know it's down to you that I haven't been charged. Thanks.'

'Harry, do not thank me. It wasn't a favour. It wasn't even the fact that I believed you, because I didn't. It's because I knew you weren't capable.'

Harry flinched.

'Try and take that as a compliment – it's a good thing not to be a killer.'

He looked down. 'Probably. Not that I haven't thought about it though.'

'I'm sure that's natural.'

Harry sighed. 'Can I have a cig?'

Yorke handed him one; he lit it and took a deep puff. 'There's not a night goes by I don't think about what I did. I'm sorry—'

'Not now.'

'I owe you more—'

Yorke widened his eyes and raised his voice. 'I said, *not now.*'

Yorke's phone rang. He turned his back to Harry, 'Emma?'

'Sir, a receptionist in the White Hart Hotel has recognised the image of Lacey Ray we sent out; she's convinced she checked-in over an hour ago.'

Yorke could feel his heart bashing against his ribs.

'I'm on my way,' Gardner continued, 'I already have some officers on the scene too—'

'I'll meet you there.'

GARDNER CRUISED into the White Hart hotel car park in a Mazda that had seen more owners than a paperback copy of the Da Vinci Code. As much as Yorke hated Mazda cars, it did suit her. Both gave a false impression. The Mazda looked expensive without being expensive; while Gardner looked bubbly, despite harbouring a cold ruthlessness that allowed her to do the job that she did.

For once, however, she didn't look bubbly as she strolled over to Yorke; she just looked cold. 'It's fucking freezing.'

He'd never heard her swear before and was taken aback. He locked the door of his car. 'Update me'

'Officers are in there now, identifying her. If it's Lacey, they'll arrest her.'

WES MARKIN

The front door of the hotel burst open. Yorke swung towards it, shielding his eyes and squinting. Someone was in the shadows, gasping for air. Together, they ran over, taking care not to slip on the ice and snow.

PC Tom Bridlington was stabilising himself against the wall. All the colour had drained from his face.

'You okay?' Yorke said.

Bridlington held up a hand to ask for more time and then lowered into a squat, taking deep breaths.

Yorke looked at Gardner, who glanced back at him and nodded.

It was clear that someone else was dead.

FOR HIS SECOND cigarette in as many years – and both within the last hour - Yorke found a tree under which to shelter, but with the building wind, he worked his way through half a box of matches to get it lit.

He finished the cigarette quickly; his addiction was flourishing again. As he stubbed it out, he wondered how he'd ever found the strength to give up in the first place.

Looking for a place, the Major Incident Vehicle circled the car park like a caged animal with cabin fever. Like spectators at the zoo, media reporters closed in, taking photographs, and thrusting microphones over the barrier of blue and white tape as if they were treats for the sick animal.

A bearded reporter smiled at Yorke and tried to wave him over. Yorke considered waving back at him with his index finger, but knew that wouldn't flatter him on the front page of the local paper tomorrow. Price, the Public

Relations Officer, would be here to deal with this vulture and his associates in due course.

He watched Gardner fend off a few reporters. He'd been in once, but he'd given the SOCOs some space to get settled. Now, it was time to go back in and take another look.

After crunching through the snow, he followed Gardner through the front door, and passed a vending machine which had been shaken too many times and now leaned far enough to one side to become a health and safety issue. He was led up some stairs, around a corner, nearly colliding with the taped line the investigators had strung out. One SOCO was laid on his side beside the open door at the end of the corridor while another dusted down a wall. He caught the eye of another SOCO, a fresh-faced girl straight out of university and nodded his approval. Securing a crime scene was a heavy task these days; over fifty unsettled people — most of them guests at a wedding held here earlier — had been evacuated from the hotel and were currently being found alternative sleeping arrangements by the staff.

Gardner handed him another bagged-up white suit – the one he was wearing was wet with snow. He took it off and checked the top button of his polo shirt was done up — an unbreakable habit he had developed at crime scenes to stop the cold getting to his neck.

After removing the white suit from the bag, he negotiated his way into it in the same way he did every time, without any grace. Gardner smiled. She'd already torn off her last one and put on her new one as easily as if it had been a pair of socks. They both slipped on latex gloves and disposable overshoes, and paced past the SOCOs into the room.

The windows were open, and the curtains billowed;

Yorke felt the cold bite. Wielding a camera, 'The Elf', Lance Reynolds, the Scientific Support Officer managing the SOCOS, darted round the scene, snapping shots from different angles. Yorke frowned when he danced to the foot of the bed, dropped to his knees, took three quick photos, before springing back to his feet like a gymnast. He'd heard Jake quipping once that the only cameramen that enjoyed their job as much as Lance Reynolds worked on porn sets.

Trying to avoid broken glass, but hearing the occasional piece crunch underfoot, Yorke edged further towards the end of the unmade bed, so that he could see the body properly. He stepped over a smashed picture of the famous stones at Avebury and a shattered bottle of perfume.

Through an open door, he saw a tall SOCO negotiating his wiry frame around the bathroom. The next burst of wind was shrill and made him flinch. He looked at Gardner beside him and noticed that she was shivering.

Divisional Surgeon Dr Patricia Wileman was hunched over the body. She looked up at him, but offered no readable facial expression; then, she looked back down at the corpse. After she shuffled to the side, Yorke saw Phil Holmes and his eyes widened. An earlobe, a left nostril and a cheek had been mauled. His neck was covered in bite marks.

Like a snake, Reynolds darted in. The camera flashed venomously.

The mauling wasn't the cause of Phil's death. A bullet hole sat in the centre of his forehead. The floor behind him was covered in blood and grey matter.

Patricia also pointed out a bloody stab wound on his left side. Yorke knelt down for a closer look and Patricia said, 'He's also had sex recently.'

'Lacey Ray, his second cousin,' Yorke said.

'Too soon to confirm that,' Patricia said.

'I wasn't asking.' He stood up, looked back at the open window, pointed and glanced at Gardner. 'Her escape route.'

'Probably. The hotel staff didn't see her leave,' Lance Reynolds said, coming up alongside him; his overused camera dangled down around his neck.

'Lacey Ray didn't strike me as someone who let things get out of control,' Yorke said, looking around at the smashed-up room, before looking down at Phil again. He'd been an imposing man.

He surveyed the scene again and saw a SOCO fiddling with a remote control, taking a sample from it, and bagging it.

How had Lacey pulled this off?

'She executed him,' Patricia said.

Topham came up alongside Yorke. 'The place is in too much of a mess for it to be a simple execution.'

'You got here quick,' Yorke said.

'Someone was kind enough to grit the roads.'

'I still think it's an execution,' Patricia said, pointing at the gunshot wound on his head, 'Point blank. She had complete control of him.'

'Unbelievable,' Reynolds said.

'Why's it unbelievable?' Gardner said. 'We women can be just as resourceful as you men.'

'I wouldn't compare us to Lacey Ray,' Patricia said, pointing at the crater on Phil's cheek. 'She's a wild animal.'

'Maybe she found out what he was up to with her family,' Gardner said. 'That could help explain why she was so savage.'

'I found this ditched in the clothes basket,' the wiry SOCO said, emerging from the bathroom with another officer who was holding up a plastic bag. 'Handcuffs, secateurs, rope, a gag, a surgical scalpel and a bloody penknife. All wiped clean of fingerprints.'

'She was into kinky stuff,' Topham said.

'Or torture,' Gardner said, flashing him a disapproving look.

'She planned all this. She was going to torture him first, but something went wrong. The state of the room shows a struggle. She was forced to change her MO, use the penknife and her teeth to get control of him, and shoot him before he could fight back, which in a way, still makes it an execution.' Yorke said, looking at Patricia.

'We have to find her, and quick, she may have found out where he was keeping her family,' Gardner said. 'She checked in under the alias Laura Bryce, so I'll contact Price and release that name to the press too. What do you think her next move could be?'

'Who knows? But if she's capable of this, we need to warn Jake immediately, just in case he bumps into her again,' Yorke said.

As they walked towards the exit, Topham turned to Yorke and said, 'Do you think Paul and his family are still alive?'

'I don't know, but we can't give up hope. Maybe he came here to kidnap Lacey, the last one; get them all together before he does whatever he's planning to do.' He turned around and looked at the body again, it looked helpless and pathetic. 'Only this time, he met his match.'

LACEY COULDN'T STOP FIDGETING in the back of the taxi, and had shuffled from window to window several times.

The driver hadn't seemed to notice and was happily engrossed in a medley of pop music.

Killing had never felt this good before. Nowhere near. So much risk and unpredictability. Phil had been her relative! And planning to kill her! She wasn't used to the absence of patterns, but she could get used to it. The adrenaline high was to die for.

She flicked the tip of her tongue over her top-front teeth, and tasted blood; the metallic taste of victory. Then, again with her tongue, she prodded at a tiny piece of his flesh which had wormed itself between two of her teeth; a souvenir that would last until she brushed and flossed.

So, why the fidgeting?

Maybe, because it was during times like this, one could get lonely. After all, she was heading to a hotel in Amesbury to hide out – no sharing of this experience with anyone, no opportunity to relive it, keep it fresh.

And tomorrow, she was busy with her new passport, a change of appearance, and a new identity; tonight's wonderful experiences would have to be pushed far to the back of her mind.

Unless I—

No, it was out of the question. Ridiculous. An unnecessary risk.

She looked down at the pay-as-you-go phone in her hand which she'd acquired in case of emergencies. Later, it would be relegated to the bin so no one could use it to trace her. So where was the harm? Could she use it to sustain excitement just a little bit longer, before retiring to the isolation of Amesbury?

She phoned Jake, but didn't speak immediately. Let the insolent worm figure out who was calling.

'Hello? ... hello? Sheila? I can't hear you. I'm at home already, waiting for you. I'll phone you back—'

'Hello, Jake.'

'Lacey?'

'Yes – you sound surprised. Why? We've been through a lot together recently, I felt it would be fitting for us to talk one last time.'

'Where are you?'

Lacey snorted. 'Come on Jake – give me *some* credit.'

'You're in danger—'

'I'm not an idiot.' She smiled. 'For someone who knows me, and knows me *intimately*, you are being rather dim.'

'Your funeral. The man you have been seeing, Phil Holmes, has taken all of your family, and he may come for you too.'

You know who it is then? But do you know he's dead? It doesn't sound like you do ...

'Don't pretend you care,' Lacey said. 'I tried to ruin your marriage earlier. Right now, I expect you'd love to see me dead.'

'Nonsense.'

You're doing very well to stay calm, Jakey, but then I guess that is your job. To try and guide me into the safe arms of the police.

'How is Sheila?'

'Fine.'

'You're meeting her now.'

'That's really none of your business.'

She felt a twinge of frustration – she had wanted the consequences of her earlier actions to be more hideous for him.

'If you tell me where you are, I will send someone to help you.'

'I'm leaving now, Jake.'

'Where to?'

'Your behaviour was despicable, you know. You brought it on yourself. Talking to me like dirt when you took me to the station.'

'I have no idea what you are talking—'

'You referred to me as someone without feelings, "emotionally stunted" I think you said. You treated me as if I didn't matter. Told me I degraded myself.' She paused to take a deep breath.

'Lacey—'

'Do you remember when we were young? When we used to hang out at that old churchyard together, where you slipped off that gravestone and cut your head ... where we experimented with each other?'

'Another time, another life, for me, and for you.'

'What I did to you today was merely a taste of what I could do, so no matter what happens, you will always know, who is really in control.'

'You made a hash of today. If anything, you've made our marriage stronger.'

She felt a rush of anger. 'Is that what you reckon? Sheila will remember what she saw on that movie for the rest of her life.'

'What, two young people having sex? She's mature enough to get over that pretty quickly.'

'It was more than two young people; it was intimate, passionate and it *burned*. She will know that those two people will always have something between them.'

'Do you describe your encounter with your tricks, the dregs of society, as intimate too?'

'Careful, Jake.' She felt sweat crawling out of her palm onto the phone.

'Of what Lacey? You're wanted by the police.'

'Why?'

'I'm sure you know already. Switch on the news, Lacey. You've chosen your life, I've chosen mine, and this really is where our paths divide.'

'I will decide when our paths divide.'

'You've lost. Accept it, and I'll see you at the station when we find you.'

The phone went dead.

She took a deep breath and slipped her phone back into her pocket. She then stared out over a desolate white field. Skeletal trees seemed to be reaching their arms up and around the distant cathedral spire.

Control yourself ...

She took another deep breath; tried to take herself somewhere far from here to find calmness—

There was a screech of brakes and she bounced forward then back. The driver shouted, 'Idiot'.

She gritted her teeth, leaned forward, tapped hard on the window and said, 'Turn around. *Now.*'

JAKE SHOULD HAVE BEEN A SALESMAN, he'd have made himself a fortune. During the last ten minutes, not only had he managed to convince Sheila to stop threatening to leave their house, but he'd even managed to keep her voice down to a civilised volume.

Admittedly, she still looked at him as if he was something on the butcher's floor rather than her husband, but there was no denying his progress.

Around him, the living room suddenly felt very alien to

him. As if someone else lived there, and he'd intruded. *Just nerves*, he thought. *Time to put everything right.*

His plan tonight had been simple. Keep staring. Don't look away. Not once. To do so would be to admit guilt. Tonight, was all about being assertive, and clear. He had never had any feelings for Lacey Ray, not when he was younger, not now and not ever.

She made eye contact with him; another small victory. 'My mother wants to talk to you.'

Jake's mouthful of tea went down awkwardly. Sheila's mother knew how to truly hurt a man; a traffic warden, a Sainsbury's queue dodger and a lecherous drunk in her local would all testify to that. 'You told her about the film?'

'What did you expect?'

'To see out the year,' he said, immediately regretting his sudden shift from remorsefulness to sarcasm.

'So who else am I supposed to talk to? We haven't slept together in over a month, we are falling out on a daily basis, and now an ex-girlfriend turns up with an X-rated video which could be all over the internet as far as I know.'

'It's not. And it means nothing. It was over ten years ago – I was very young.'

'It makes no difference to me when it was.'

Well, it clearly would do if it had been last week, Jake thought, biting his tongue.

His phone vibrated. It was Topham.

Sod him. He hit the button on the top of the phone to send him straight to voicemail.

'Add to the fact that you're a policeman and regularly putting yourself in danger,' Sheila said.

'We've been through this – Salisbury is not the Bronx.'

'But, it's not just the danger. It's the time. Ever since you became a sergeant—'

'I know, which is why we're here, isn't it? To discuss whether I should carry on.' He sighed as his phone vibrated again.

After sending Yorke to voicemail too, he noticed the living room curtains glow as someone pulled up directly outside their house.

***

STARING up at the flickering lightbulb which kept the barn lit, feeling as trapped as one of the hypnotised flies buzzing around it, Paul hugged his mother until his arms started to burn. She had started to sleep again; the drugs she had been given must have been powerful.

It had been a while since the doors of the enclosure had last shaken. He could still hear his trembling breath, and heavy heartbeat, but at least the sickening sense of panic had eased a little. Seizing this rare moment of calm, he slipped his sleeping mother off his lap, rose and moved quietly around the corrugated-metal barn, looking for an exit, or a weapon of some kind. Nothing. He tried the main door, but the padlock held firm.

No way out. His father was dead. Lewis had him and his mother. Desperate to disappear and wake up somewhere safe and warm with his family, he slipped to the floor and buried his head in his hands.

Minutes later, he wiped snot from his face, and stared at the enclosure again.

Be strong.

Fighting against nausea, and fear, he crawled towards the concrete enclosure. He touched its dusty side and poked his fingers in the tiny holes where a ladder must have been removed.

With his ear to the door of the enclosure, he listened to the bloodthirsty creatures' rasping breaths. There was something else too. He pressed his ear harder against the door ... ticking ... he bit into his fingers to stop himself gasping; then, with his heart threatening to burst from his chest, he scurried away back to his mother.

'Mum, I'm scared and ...' He stopped himself.

Not wanting to tell her there was a timer that he couldn't see and that he didn't know how long they had left, he instead cried into her hair.

BACK OUTSIDE IN THE CARPARK, after being circled and bated by journalists, Yorke managed to get in his car and try Jake for the fifth time; again, he was sent through to voicemail. He pounded his steering wheel.

Lacey Ray was rabid; you only had to take one look at the wounds on Phil Holmes' face to know that.

He tried Sheila on the off-chance that Jake was with her, but was met with another recorded response.

Jake, Sheila, answer your fucking phones!

Deciding to head to their house, he chucked the phone onto the passenger seat and started his engine. When his phone rang, he lunged for it.

'Shit!' The number was neither Jake's or Sheila's. 'Yep?'

'It's Louise, we've got a match on the mud.'

Yorke's hand was shaking so much, he could barely keep the phone to his ear.

'Animal droppings, seeds, pollen count all seem to confirm that the mud in the toilet came from the Morris pig farm, registered to Stella Morris—'

'The address?' Yorke said, driving for the exit.

Déjà vu.

On the way to another pig farm. And just like the last two times, he had no idea what he was going to find there. Last time, it'd ended with a dead man hanging from a hook; the time before, it'd ended with him pinning Harry to the floor metres from his dead wife.

He pushed the Lexus as hard as he could.

For some reason, he thought of his older sister, and remembered his promise to himself to find her killer.

Promises, promises ...

He took a corner hard. He took a deep breath.

I hope to God Paul and Sarah are still alive.

As he journeyed further north into Devizes, at a speed far too dangerous for current weather conditions, Yorke phoned Topham to let him know where he'd gone. He'd already tried twice, but reception kept dropping out on him.

'Shit, now you tell me?' Topham said.

'I was already driving and the reception was playing up.'

He gave Topham the address, but they were at least ten minutes behind him; the way he was driving, probably fifteen. The car bumped suddenly. If he hadn't been so used to these roads, he may have convinced himself it was a pothole; instead, he acknowledged that he had just scrambled another poor animal.

The Sat Nav refused to take Yorke all the way to the Morris Pig Farm. Maybe it knew something that he didn't. He pulled over to ask directions from a middle-aged farmer out walking his sheepdogs despite heavy snowfall.

'The Morris family,' the farmer said, leaning into Yorke's car window, exhibiting his heavily pockmarked skin. 'They stopped farming a few years back when the father and daughter both passed within months of each other. The wife and her granddaughter still live there. You know, the young one is simple, and Stella Morris, well, she has some kind of wasting disease. What do you want from them?'

'It's police business.'

With a creased forehead, the farmer pointed out the directions and then disappeared into the night with his dogs.

With his windscreen wipers going full blast, struggling against a snowfall that he imagined would take some victims this evening, he turned left off the main road, passed a sign that read "slow down, vehicles pulling out" and crunched down a country lane. The car didn't slip; someone must have taken the time to grit. But that's where his luck ended. The lights on the main road behind faded, and he was left with only his headlights.

The road seemed to spiral on forever, leaving him more and more to the mercy of the darkness. Over the screeching wipers, he could hear vicious-sounding dogs.

I was stupid to come here alone.

Eventually, he saw light. He passed a large wooden barn on his right and then a couple of hundred metres later, crunched to a halt beside the farmhouse. His headlights pointed out a second barn in the distance.

There was enough light coming from within the house to make the porch visible, but the gloom and its shadows made it a risky option. He turned his car, so his headlights shot straight into the house. The old porch looked like it belonged in Tennessee rather than Wiltshire. There was a figure hunched over in a chair. He waited a moment for the figure to move, to get up and welcome him in.

All remained still.

It would be sensible to wait the ten or fifteen minutes for Topham and company to arrive, but somewhere around here the Ray family needed him.

He killed the headlights and got out of the car.

SHEILA GLANCED BACK and saw Jake slightly hunched over in the doorway, waving. She waved back as she reached the end of the drive. That was all he was getting. Tonight, at least.

A taxi was parked outside their house. The headlights were on. After unsuccessfully trying to see who it was through dark windows, she started the short walk back to her mother's house, looking one last time at Jake.

Look at him with the weight of the world on his shoulders, what about me? What about the one who has to suffer all of this shit?

He closed the door.

I can't let him know he's forgiven – not until serious changes are made. Promises are not enough.

She thought of the packet of menthol cigarettes sitting in her bag, and realised she could murder one right now –

but it was something she'd have to resist, after what the doctors had told her a couple of days ago.

Turning down a dark-narrow path which acted as a short cut between the houses, she quickened her pace; not because of fear, but rather because of the smell of piss. A blast of icy-cold air convinced her to button up her wool-lined winter coat.

'I know what it's like,' someone said behind her.

She took a quick gulp of air, and turned with widening eyes. *Lacey Ray.*

'To not be the only one.'

Sheila snapped her head left and right looking for help. *Nobody. Alone.* 'What do you want?'

'Shush, if you shout, I'll have to kill you.'

Sheila felt pressure on her stomach. She looked down. Lacey had a long, kitchen knife pinned there.

'And do not think about sudden movements; I will be able to split your belly open very quickly.'

'I'm pregnant.'

'Congratulations.' Lacey smiled. 'So it really is in your best interests to make this easier for me.'

'What do you want?' Sheila said, feeling her lips tremble. She looked left and right again. Nothing but a solitary streetlamp at the end of the dark lane, spearing the darkness.

'What every girl wants.'

'My husband?'

'Come on Sheila, does every girl want your husband?'

'You obviously do, why else would you be doing this?'

She snorted. 'He probably told you I was in love with him. It's not love I'm after, Sheila. In fact, it's not love most girls are after, although they convince themselves that they are. It's respect. Simply, respect. Surely, right now, with

319

everything that has happened, you of all people can understand that?'

'My husband does respect me.'

'Really?' Lacey raised her eyebrows. 'Did you watch that movie? Did you see the things we did? Does he even respect himself?'

'It was years ago, and you probably convinced him to make it.'

'Is that what he told you? It's always our fault, isn't it? We make them bully us, hit us, rape us and kill us. Does he know he's going to be a father? Do you want me to tell him for you?'

Sheila saw a group of young people pass the entrance to the path. If she shouted now, they may hear her. Pressure increased on her stomach. 'Don't bother, Sheila.'

She looked down at the blade, when she looked back up, the group had passed.

'Good.'

'Couldn't you just leave us both alone?' Tears sprang up in the corners of her eyes.

Lacey reached out her empty hand to Sheila's face and brushed a tear away. 'He isn't worth your tears.'

'Are you going to kill me?'

'Shhh. Be calm, Sheila, this is all unplanned — for once — and I really want to enjoy the spontaneity of it all. It's already making me feel quite ... what's the word?' Lacey moved her empty hand down over Sheila's body. 'Perky?' The backs of her fingers brushed against her breasts.

Sheila took a sharp, deep breath and held it as Lacey's hand continued to trail down her body, until it came to rest on her thigh.

WEST, east and south faded into black and snow drove hard into the desolation as if it was deliberately trying to avoid the farmyard Yorke stood in. Before him, the old farmhouse appeared to be collapsing in on itself. The scent of boiled meat spilled through an open door while the old woman on the porch remained motionless.

As he stood at the foot of the steps leading up to the porch, her voice came at him like something that belonged hidden away in the woods, far from mankind. 'Who is it?' The stench of boiling flesh seemed to intensify as if it had come from inside her when she opened her mouth.

Yorke negotiated two creaking steps, expecting his foot to go through each one. 'Mrs Stella Morris?'

'Yes.'

'DCI Yorke, I'm here regarding a very serious matter.' He chanced another step. The old woman didn't move. *She was yet to move.*

'Really? And what is that?'

He remained cautious, ascending slowly. 'We have evidence which suggests that a missing boy and his parents may be on this property.'

He stopped when a young girl stepped out onto the porch and took hold of the handles of Stella's old-fashioned wheelchair. He recalled the reference the farmer had made to a "simple girl". The girl didn't look simple, just scruffy. Her hair hung in tangled knots and her face was dirty.

'My daughter,' Stella said.

Your granddaughter, you mean, Yorke thought, remembering the dog-walking farmer's words from earlier. He held back correcting Stella. If this young girl didn't know, this certainly wasn't the time to break the news to her.

He squinted, wanting to see the old woman more

clearly, but he couldn't even see her mouth moving. So he gambled on another step. 'Is it just you two here?'

'Would you believe me if I said yes?' This time, the words seemed hissed rather than spoken.

'Why wouldn't I? That's a strange question.'

'What evidence led you to believe that those missing people are here?'

Closer now, he saw her toothless mouth as black and desolate as the road had looked to him only moments ago. 'A sample of mud taken from the scene where a young boy went missing.'

'Ahhh, I remember the young policeman collecting samples.'

'Yes.'

'Martha, make our guest a cup of tea.'

'Yes, Mother. The leaf kind or the bag kind?'

'Inspector?' Stella said.

'I don't want a drink. Are you listening to what I'm saying here?'

'The leaf kind, can't you see our detective is a man of culture?'

The young girl, wearing a parka far too big for her, disappeared back into the farmhouse.

Stella freed an arm from beneath the blanket and pointed a bony finger at a familiar chair in the shadows. 'Please, take a seat'.

He took the remaining step to look closely at the chair. He recognised it instantly and shivered. 'Whose chair is that?'

'Thomas Ray's.'

For a moment, he didn't see the chair in the present moment, but rather in the past when he was pinning Harry to the ground metres from his dead wife; he remembered glancing up through an open front door at this hooped-shaped monstrosity rocking in the wind. 'How could you?'

'Because it's a Ray chair. Because they're very comfortable.'

He glared back at the old woman. 'What have you got yourselves mixed up in?'

'Please take a seat, Inspector. We have to wait for someone first.'

Of course, you don't know, do you? How could you? With a bullet, Lacey Ray has already ended your little game.

'Are you talking about Lewis Ray, Mrs Morris?'

She tensed in the chair.

'Or Phil Holmes?'

Her eyes darted from side to side. 'His name is Lewis.'

'Did you really think that the dirt was all we had to go on? Give us some credit Mrs Morris.'

He noticed she was dribbling. She dabbed at the corners of her mouth with the blanket, averting her eyes from Yorke's. 'No matter, Lewis won't care. He always wanted you to see his work when he was finished anyway.'

'He's dead, Mrs Morris.'

She paused, clearly stunned by what he'd said.

'I've just come from where it happened.'

She bolted upright in her chair, surprising him, and he took a quick step back. Her blanket fell away, revealing satin clothing. She gripped a sparkling jewel swinging from her neck. '*Lies.*'

'His second cousin, Lacey Ray shot him. They were having an affair. Did you know about her?'

'Of course I did, you stupid man,' she said with dribble bubbling at the corners of her mouth. 'He was bringing her here too.'

'I can assure you that neither of them are coming now,

which makes all this your problem, and yours alone. So, no more of this, save yourself a lot of trouble and take me to Paul and his family.'

'If you're telling me what to do, you really shouldn't have come alone.'

'Others are coming.'

'*Martha*, where is the damned tea?' She threw the blanket to the floor. 'You have no idea what that man did for us.'

Yorke noticed tears glistening on her wrinkled skin. He raised his voice. '*Tell me where they are!*'

'Martha!'

Her daughter appeared at the door, holding a sawn-off shotgun in his direction. Shock bolted through his insides. 'What are you doing?'

'I'm sorry, sir. I'm just doing what Mother tells me to do.'

'Martha, *shut up*,' Stella said.

'Lewis is dead and more officers are on their way. Do you really want to make this worse than it already is, for you and your mother?'

'Don't listen to him, and if I tell you to, shoot him,' Stella said.

Yorke held his hands out in disbelief. 'Come on, she's what ... twelve? You'd let her kill a policeman and ruin her life?' He watched the shotgun shake in the girl's hands. 'Can you even use that?'

'Lewis taught me. I don't like it though; it hurts my shoulders.'

'You heard her,' Stella said. 'She can do it, if I ask her to.'

'And have you ever killed anyone, young lady?'

'No—'

'And I'm sure you don't want to. And right now, I'm

worried about you using it accidently. Put the gun down, Martha, and tell me where Paul and his family are. This has gone on long enough already.'

Stella said, 'Keep the gun on him. But, you are right, Inspector, it has gone on long enough. I'll take you to them.'

FEELING MORE positive about the whole situation, Jake made himself a gin and tonic and collapsed onto the sofa.

He took a mouthful of the bitter drink and then smiled. By the end of their conversation, Sheila had been making continuous eye contact and had laughed two or three times. A promise had also been made that she'd at least consider coming back the next day. He was confident that a phone call in the morning could make that possibility a reality.

Channel-hopping brought him no possibility of entertainment, so he took his mobile out to surf the internet. Voicemail messages. He remembered the calls from Topham and Yorke that he'd not answered.

Without bothering to listen to the messages, he called back Yorke first, but after a minute or so was also sent through to voicemail.

'Hi, sir, returning your call from earlier. Been with Sheila. Went well—'

He could hear someone rustling about at his front door; then, he heard the clunk of the key being slipped in the lock.

'Someone at the door, she's either forgot something, or finally succumbed to the Pettman charm! Speak later.'

As he rose to his feet, he heard the front door opening and someone step into the hallway.

'Sheila?' he said, expecting her to burst through the hallway door.

No reply. The hallway door remained closed.

Funny, he thought, walking over to open it.

YORKE'S PHONE RANG. He plucked it out of his pocket. "Jake Pettman" glowed on the screen. Recalling the danger his friend could be in, he started to lift the phone to his ear.

'Don't answer it,' Stella said from behind him.

Yorke turned and looked at the young girl leading him along at gunpoint. Her hands trembled and he suspected Martha was more likely to discharge that gun accidently than follow her mother's orders and kill him in cold blood. 'This is already over, Lewis is dead, what's the point?'

'Maybe he's right, mother.'

Stella glared at her daughter. 'And think what will happen if he's lying and Lewis is still alive. What do you think he will do to us if we let this man go? If we let *them* go.'

Martha creased her brow as she thought about this for a moment. 'Please don't answer your phone, sir.'

Yorke lowered his mobile. With Topham minutes away, it wasn't worth the risk. Jake could wait. One of the others would have warned him about Lacey by now.

He held the phone out in front of him as a sign of submission, before sliding it gently back into his pocket. Then, he turned and trudged onward.

Closer to the corrugated-metal barn, he could hear hoarse grunting and flurries of movement coming from within. *Pigs...*

The thought of Phil Holmes wearing that horrendous

mask sent a shiver down his spine. At the door, a sudden banging sound from within made him flinch. 'What's going on in there?'

The old woman rolled up alongside him. The padlock was at just the right height for her to open, and she buried a key into it. He half-expected her spindly hand to break when she turned the key. But, in much the same way the speed and agility with which she moved did not match her waif-life appearance, neither did her strength.

The padlock fell to the ground with a thump, and she moved backwards to assume her position again beside her daughter, who was still looking dangerously under-confident with the gun.

'They're inside,' Stella said.

When he opened the door, there was a scuffle and another loud banging noise.

'Nothing to worry about,' Stella said. 'The pigs are just hungry. They always are.'

Hurry up, Mark, he thought.

Inside, the barn was lit by a solitary bulb hanging from the centre of the roof. His eyes were immediately drawn to two figures lying on the floor to the far right. 'Paul?'

'Yes!'

'Who's that with you?'

'My mum. Who are you?'

'I'm a policeman. Where's your Dad?' He jogged across the barn.

There was no reply. To his left was a large enclosure. The central door shook.

Paul sat up. Gaunt, dirty with tangled hair, he was barely recognisable from the photographs. His mother's head was in his lap; her eyes were half-closed.

'Is she okay?'

'They gave her the same thing they gave me. Makes you groggy. Are you here to get us out?'

'Yes. Your dad?'

Paul looked down, rubbed tears from his eyes, and then pointed to the enclosure. Yorke looked at it again and heard a loud, penetrating grunt that made the hairs on his arms stand on end.

Yorke watched Sarah sit herself upright. For a moment, her half-open glassy eyes moved back and forth over her visitors before finally settling on the girl with the sawn-off shotgun. 'So young,' she said in a weak voice.

Yorke turned back to see the peculiar pair of kidnappers directly behind him. He noticed that the child looked as malnourished as Paul, and sadness shone in her eyes. In the light, it was obvious that the gun was far too heavy for her; he hoped gravity might just come to their aid. He said, 'It's time for this to end. What's happening here is wrong.'

Martha opened her mouth to speak, but Stella got there first. 'Don't listen to him.'

The wooden door in the centre of the enclosure shook again.

'I don't know how long we have,' Paul said. 'I think that door is on a timer.'

Yorke glared at Stella. 'What's in there?'

'It doesn't matter. You're out of time.' She twirled her withered hand in the air. 'Martha, let's go.'

'Leaving without us?' he said, darting forward and grabbing her hand. 'I don't think so somehow!'

At first, she looked shocked, but then the expression on her withered face burst open like a salted slug. 'Shoot him!'

He looked at the broken girl, softening his expression. She looked as if she was about to collapse into tears. He attempted to offer her some kind of hope in his eyes. A promise of a way out.

'For God sake, Martha, shoot him, he's hurting me!'

After throwing a sideways glance at her mother, Martha looked back at him and her lips started to tremble.

'Are you fucking stupid, girl? *Do it!*' Stella said.

The boars charged again. Clattering around the enclosure, clashing with the door, calling out to their potential victims.

Still gripping Stella's hand, Yorke said, 'Paul, help your mother up.'

Yorke watched Martha's eyes widen as she observed Paul assisting his mother.

'Martha, do as you're damn well told!' Stella said.

The young girl continued to stare at Paul and Sarah. *Has their close bond caught her attention? Is there longing in her eyes? A desperation for something she doesn't have?*

Stella leaned forward as she shouted and bubbles of spit appeared at the corners of her mouth. 'You stupid fucking animal, Martha, I should have got rid of you years ago when my daughter died!'

Tears started to roll down the girl's face. She could barely hold the shotgun straight, and Yorke heard the fast, heavy beat of his heart as he considered what an accidental discharge would do to all of them. He said, 'Martha, I'm begging you, we're all innocent, *put the gun down.*'

She lowered the gun. He was careful that his sigh of relief wasn't audible and then he released the witch's hand.

'*Idiot.*' Stella reached out to Martha. 'Give me the fucking gun!'

Martha pulled it back out of her reach. '*No.* You lied, Mother. You said they were bad.'

'They are! Do you not listen to anything? Bad people are good at tricking folk.'

Yorke stepped forward. 'Okay Martha, give me the gun, then we can all leave, *safely*.'

One of the boars took the door head on. Startled, Martha dropped the shotgun.

Yorke turned to the Ray family. 'Go now, and take Martha with you.'

With his mother's arm hooked around his shoulder, Paul took Martha's hand as he passed her, and the three of them headed towards the door.

'Stupid little bitch. Your father will turn in his grave,' Stella said. There was a buzzing, followed by a thumping, as the door to the enclosure unlocked and came ajar. 'You're all too late anyway.'

Fear whipped through Yorke's belly. He shouted as loud as he could. '*Run.*'

He watched the three of them retreat while the old woman darted forward and smashed her footrest into his shins. Wincing, he stumbled forward into her, and the chair toppled. He hit the floor, knocking the bottom of his spine and squeezed his eyes shut against the pain. When he opened them again, he saw his aggressor lying a metre in front of him like a pile of dirty laundry.

The door of the enclosure creaked opened.

'Are you okay?' Paul called from near the exit.

'Get the hell out!' Yorke shouted back.

Desperately, he scanned the floor for the shotgun that Martha had dropped. Once he sighted it, he crawled towards it as the first wild boar, a sizeable grey beast with huge tusks, emerged from the enclosure. From the corner of his eye, Yorke watched it take several deep sniffs of the air and look around.

He heard Stella gasp beside him.

From the exit, the others continued to call to him, but he struggled to understand everything they were saying; he was breathing too quickly and his heart was beating too fast. He saw the boar take several lumbering steps towards both of them. His hand closed on the gun, but the creature already seemed too close for him to make any sudden movements.

Paul's shouts suddenly seemed like they were miles away. *'You have to get up and run!'*

The boar was barely a metre away from them. Its emotionless, black eyes seemed to regard Yorke for a moment, before swinging to Stella, and then back again.

Jesus! Was it choosing?

It began to sniff at Stella's feet. 'Help me.' She scrunched her eyes up, and tried to shuffle away.

Now or never. He held his breath and slowly rose to his feet.

Almost whispering, he said, 'Listen to me, Stella.'

She nodded while the boar continued to investigate her. 'When I tell you to, kick it!'

'I can't! Just shoot it, *please!*' The boar was dragging its twitching snout up her leg.

'It'll hit you too. You have to kick the thing away first.'

'I can't.'

'You really don't have a choice.'

Yorke heard the second wild boar emerge. He glanced over. 'Ah shit.'

This one was smaller, but far more energetic, and turned in circles while exiting, as if conducting a ritual dance. Clumps of mottled-grey hair rose from different parts of its body like weeds. It paused, clearly watching its companion sniffing at the crumpled-woman's stomach.

'*Now, Stella!*'

Stella kicked out. The stunned boar scampered back and Yorke fired. The force of the shot propelled him back a step and the bang reverberated off the corrugated-metal walls. Despite the sudden ringing in his ears, he could hear the boar squealing as it reeled in the air. For a second, he panicked that it might just have enough in it to charge back, before it slumped to its side.

'Shoot the other!' Stella said.

'There's only one shot.'

The second, more energetic, boar wasn't scared by the death of its companion; rather, it seemed incensed. It sprinted towards Stella and leapt. There was a sickening crunch as the beast closed its teeth on her face as if it was a piece of fruit.

The boar shook the screaming old woman; her arms and legs flapped about. Yorke charged forward, wielding the shotgun as a club, but the beast sensed him and started to back off toward the enclosure, dragging its catch along with it.

He followed, but the beast continued to back away, sizing him up with its mouth full.

She wasn't moving. A deep growling sound from its throat warned him that it would fight back. On his own, he had little chance. The creature was too savage.

'I'm sorry.' He ran for the door, trying to ignore the sounds of tearing and crunching behind him.

Outside, the barn was suddenly illuminated. Chewing the snowy field up with their vehicles, the troops advanced.

He waved his hands in the air, desperate for help, but knowing already it was too late.

Inside the barn, the boar was feasting.

EMERGENCY VEHICLES SPREAD like a rash and everything changed. Darkness and desolation were replaced with the beat of light and life. By the ambulance, Sarah had a motherly arm hooked around Martha. Paul had been given some glucose and looked a little better already.

The snowfall had also started to relent.

Yorke's phone buzzed in his pocket. He fished it out of his coat and looked. *Voicemail.* He recalled the phone call from Jake earlier which he'd almost answered.

He pressed the voicemail button on his phone, but when Paul walked over, he ended it before he'd heard the message.

'I thought we were going to die in there,' Paul said. 'Thanks.'

'Don't mention it. You were the brave one in all of this. Besides, it wasn't just me - there were many others involved,' Yorke said, thinking also of Jake who was worthy of some gratitude following the onerous task of collecting dirt samples. 'The care you took of your mother was incredible. She must be proud.'

'Is Lewis really dead?' Paul said.

'Yes. I'm sorry that he lied to you. It's never good when a friend turns out not to be a friend after all.' *And it won't be the last time you experience that either.*

'Was he really related to me?'

'It's not confirmed yet, but it looks that way.'

'Everything will be different now,' Paul said, turning around and looking at Martha and his mother.

'I'm sorry I couldn't help your father in time, Paul.'

Paul looked down at his feet. 'You did everything you could.'

'But not enough,' Yorke said, putting his hand on the boy's shoulder. 'You go and take care of your mother.'

Paul started to turn.

'One more thing,' Yorke said.

'Yes,' Paul said, turning back.

'Be nice to that girl, Martha. I don't think she has much experience of people being nice to her.'

'I will do, sir.'

Yorke watched Paul walk off to join his mother, who was still holding Martha tightly. He turned away and took his phone out. He hit the voicemail button again. 'You have one new message, received—'

He saw Gardner walking toward him from the van. She had a purposeful stride.

Now's the time to start relaxing, Emma!

He listened to the message from Jake. 'Hi, sir, returning your call from earlier. Been with Sheila. Went well ... someone at the door, she's either forgot something, or finally succumbed to the Pettman charm! Speak later.'

He hung up and called Jake. As the phone rang, Gardner reached him. 'We can't get through to Jake.'

'I'm trying now,' Yorke said. 'He tried to phone me, before.'

After he was put through to voicemail, he felt his blood run cold. 'He's not answering.'

'I'm sure it's nothing to worry about.'

'Yeah, you're probably right. Still ...'

He tried again. This time it seemed to ring for an eternity. And when he heard the click of the phone being answered, he assumed it was voicemail again, and his eyes widened from the sudden bolt of adrenaline.

'Hello?'

A woman's voice. A familiar voice ... 'Hello?'

'Thank god. Sheila, are you okay?'

'Yes, I'm fine ... well at least I am now.'

'Why? What happened?' He saw Gardner's eyes widen with concern.

'Lacey Ray ... again. Jake will explain. Here he is.'

'Sir?'

'Yes, what the hell happened?'

'Lacey threatened Sheila with a knife, outside, while she was walking home.'

'Jesus.'

Gardner moved in closer and mouthed, '*What*?'

Jake said. 'She didn't hurt her. Sheila ran straight back here, but she's no idea where Lacey went.'

Yorke looked at Gardner, sighed and mouthed, 'It's okay.'

'Sheila thinks that if she hadn't told her she was pregnant, she might have actually hurt her. Mike, I'm going to be a dad! Can you believe it?'

Yorke ran his hand through his hair. 'Congratulations, Jake. Now lock your fucking door and don't move until we get there.'

EPILOGUE

LUCY EVANS WAS enjoying her first day.

A night in the Holiday Inn, followed by a train journey from Salisbury to the airport had been and gone without incident.

There had been a few curious police officers at Waterloo station, but the dark-brown wig and the heavy make-up covering up her bruises had kept them off her scent.

At the airport, she stood in line for check-in. At the front of the queue an attractive BA check-in girl asked for her passport. A name badge read Jessica. She had a hole in her bottom lip where a stud belonged, and a Chinese letter tattooed behind one ear. Lucy smiled at her longer than she needed to. *If only I had time, we could have some fun,* she thought as she handed over her passport.

'Any bags for check-in?' Jessica said as she tapped on the keyboard.

'No.' *Of course not, I am new to the world, I have no possessions.*

She was handed her boarding pass, and then a

dangerous look of curiosity spread over Jessica's face. She kept hold of the boarding pass as Lucy tried to take it, locking it between them.

'Is something wrong?'

Had Jessica seen today's papers? Was she noticing the resemblance to Lacey Ray?

'No, Ms Evans,' Jessica said, smiling and releasing the boarding pass. 'I just thought we'd met before.'

'If you'd met me before, you wouldn't forget me,' Lucy said, winking. *You were just daydreaming about a night of passion, weren't you?*

Jessica blushed.

She headed toward the security gate, threw her passport, boarding pass, shoes, purse, phone, belt and some loose coins from her suit pocket into the plastic tray, and watched them disappear down the conveyer belt. A tired-looking man with a few remaining strands of hair glued down with gel waited for her on the other side of the security gate. She lifted her arms and he swept her with a metal detector. 'Looks like you've had a nasty accident,' he said.

No amount of make-up seemed to be covering up these bruises. Ah, Phil, you were such a bastard!

When she returned to the conveyer belt, a wiry man was holding the plastic tray and eyeing her up and down. 'Could you step over here, please Ms?' He nodded at a small area to his left.

'Why, what's wrong?'

'Please, Ms?'

She did as he said. 'Is there something in my purse?'

'No, it's not that.'

Lucy was yet to experience the thrill of killing. Of course, it came highly recommended from the now-departed Lacey. She wondered if it would be worth killing the security guard, before his colleagues arrived to arrest her. She didn't have any weapons on her, but she wondered if she could break his neck. He was thin and bony, and she did have strong upper body strength; Lacey had left her with a well-toned body.

She heard another security guard approaching her from behind.

It can't end now - I've not been given the chance to shine yet!

'John,' the wiry man said, 'is this really her?'

Lucy turned and looked at John; he was squat and well-built. It would be much more difficult to break his neck. He took another step toward her, looking her up and down.

'I can't believe it,' John said.

How unfair, what a waste! What a legacy I would have left, if I'd only got to France. Well, if I go down, you two are coming with me.

'Sorry, Ms,' John said. 'But I wondered if I could get your autograph?'

'Pardon?'

'My wife always watches your show.'

Lucy smiled. 'Really?

'Yes, she hangs off your every word!'

Lucy shook her head from side to side, smiling. *Unbelievable!* 'Who do you think I am exactly?'

'The presenter from that daily show, you know, the one after six, the name escapes me, as does yours sorry, but——'

Lucy laughed. She couldn't help herself. And it wasn't a giggle either; it was a full-on, teeth bared, chest-shaking laugh. It took a moment for her to collect herself, and when she had done, she noticed that John was red-faced.

'Her name's Lucy Evans,' the wiry man said behind her, looking through her passport. 'Ring a bell, John?'

John frowned. 'No, that's not the name. Sorry Ms, I could have sworn you were that lady.'

She turned back to the wiry security guard and collected her belongings. 'Never mind, I'll take it as a compliment!'

She walked off to find her boarding gate, still laughing. Her new life was proving to be a lot of fun already.

Later, during take-off, Lucy slipped Jake's business card out of her pocket.

She sighed and screwed it up.

You can't have everything.

She stared out of the window at the shrinking airport, chewing her bottom lip, thinking. Then, she looked back down at the ball of card in her hand and unscrewed it, smiling.

No, you can't have everything ... at least not in one go.

IT WAS a Saturday like any other for Michael Yorke.

Alone, worn out after a week of warming up cold cases, slightly hung over from six take-out beers from the Wyndham Arms the previous evening, desperate to go for a run despite the bad weather.

The letterbox flapped. He groaned and dragged himself from the sofa to retrieve a soft-brown package from the front door.

He read what was scrawled on the front of the package:

Eileen died yesterday.

She wanted you to give this to Paul.

Her way of saying sorry, I guess.

Roy Holmes.

Yorke tore off the brown paper and took a deep breath.

Holding it against his stomach, he let the blue and white scarf unravel like an umbilical cord.

He breathed out, put the scarf to his nose and smelled the smoke from the fire that had burned beside her.

He remembered the sound of her knitting needles. *Click-click. Click-click.*

He then thought about Charlotte. Not many days went by without his thoughts turning in her direction. He thought about his experience all those years ago. Thought about a time which, he believed, had truly defined him.

After slipping the scarf in his pocket, he opened the door and went out into the cold, suddenly determined to make this day different from all of the others.

WHO IS CHARLOTTE?

Find out in the FREE, EXCLUSIVE DCI Michael Yorke
quick read – *A Lesson in Crime*
https://dl.bookfunnel.com/77umhbozcf

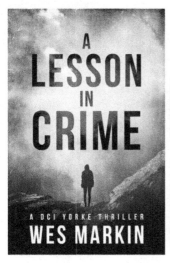

Scan the QR to
READ NOW!

CONTINUE YORKE'S JOURNEY WITH THE REPENTING SERPENT

A vicious serial killer slithers from the darkness, determined to resurrect the ways of a long-dead civilisation.

When the ex-wife of one of DCI Michael Yorke's closest allies is left mutilated and murdered, Yorke and his team embark on their greatest test yet. A deeply personal case that will push them to their very limits.

And as Yorke's team are pulled further into the dark, the killer circles, preparing to strike again.

Scan the QR to
READ NOW!

The Repenting Serpent is a true edge-of-the-seat, nail-biting page turner.

START THE JAKE PETTMAN SERIES
TODAY WITH THE KILLING PIT

A broken ex-detective. A corrupt chief of police. A merciless drug lord.

And a missing child.

Running from a world which wants him dead, ex-detective Sergeant Jake Pettman journeys to the isolated town of Blue Falls, Maine, home of his infamous murderous ancestors.

But Jake struggles to hide from who he is, and when a child disappears, he finds himself drawn into an investigation that shares no parallels to anything he has ever seen before.

Held back by a chief of police plagued and tormented by his own secrets, Jake fights for the truth. All the way to the door of Jotham MacLeoid. An insidious megalomaniac who feeds his victims to a Killing Pit.

And the terrifying secrets that lie within.

Scan the QR to
READ NOW!

JOIN DCI EMMA GARDNER AS SHE
RELOCATES TO KNARESBOROUGH,
HARROGATE IN THE NORTH
YORKSHIRE MURDERS ...

Still grieving from the tragic death of her colleague, DCI Emma Gardner continues to blame herself and is struggling to focus. So, when she is seconded to the wilds of Yorkshire, Emma hopes she'll be able to get her mind back on the job, doing what she does best - putting killers behind bars.

But when she is immediately thrown into another violent murder, Emma has no time to rest. Desperate to get answers and find the killer, Emma needs all the help she can. But her new partner, DI Paul Riddick, has demons and issues of his own.

And when this new murder reveals links to an old case Riddick was involved with, Emma fears that history might be about to repeat itself...

Don't miss the brand-new gripping crime series by bestselling British crime author Wes Markin!

What people are saying about Wes Markin...

'Cracking start to an exciting new series. Twist and turns, thrills and kills. I loved it.'

Bestselling author **Ross Greenwood**

'Markin stuns with his latest offering... Mind-bendingly dark and deep, you know it's not for the faint hearted from page one. Intricate plotting, devious twists and excellent characterisation take this tale to a whole new level. Any serious crime fan will love it!'

Bestselling author **Owen Mullen**

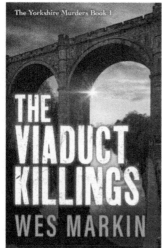

Scan the QR to
READ NOW!

ACKNOWLEDGEMENTS

Massive thanks must go to both Jake for his encouragement, enthusiasm and know-how – without him, this book would surely still be just an ambition; to Cherie Foxley for her relentless pursuit of a good front cover.

Thank you to all of you who took the time to read early drafts and offer valuable feedback, especially my wife, Jo, my father, Peter, and fellow author and editor, Eve Seymour. Please know that every recommendation to a friend, share on social media or kind message, means so much to me.

Lastly, thank you to every reader who has taken the time to read my work and listen to my stories, and to the amazing bloggers who have done so much to help me along this journey.